Praise for *Lie or Die: Blood Moon*

'Clack raises the stakes in *Lie or Die: Blood Moon* with plenty of plot twists racing towards a gripping ending – a thrilling sequel.' Ravena Guron, author of *This Book Kills*

'A high-octane thriller packed full of twists, trials and betrayals – I couldn't turn the pages fast enough! A fantastic sequel to *Lie or Die*, this will leave readers absolutely shell-shocked.' Kat Ellis, author of *The Devouring Light*

'Twists, turns and tension from the first page, the story flies at breakneck speed towards the adrenaline-fuelled climax. *Blood Moon* is fun, terrifying, emotional and a fantastic read!' Tess James-Mackey, author of *You Wouldn't Catch Me Dead*

'I flew through this fantastic thriller in one sitting. *Blood Moon* is an impeccable follow-up to the brilliant *Lie or Die*, with even more twists, turns and edge-of-your-seat moments. *Traitors* meets *Squid Game* meets Werewolf, with an atmospheric castle setting and an intriguing cast of characters – YA readers are in for a treat!' Jan Dunning, award-winning author of *The Last Thing You'll Hear*

'*The Traitors* meets *Squid Game* this is reality TV at its deadliest. An adrenaline-fuelled, dark and twisty race for survival where everyone is out for themselves and even those you trust will throw you under the bus. I couldn't put it down.' C.L. Miller, author of *The Antique Hunters Guide To Murder*

'A cleverly plotted heart-racing ride, packed with unpredictable twists and turns and culminating in a shocking climax which will leave you reeling and desperate for more…' Sue Cunningham, author of *Totally Deceased*

'This book kept me on my toes from start to finish… But when they say trust no one, TRUST NO ONE!' Zeena Gosrani, author of *This Dark Heart*

'Another heart-pounding thriller from A.J. Clack, this sequel takes the gore and twists to a whole new level, and I loved every minute of it!' Amy McCaw, author of *They Own the Night* and the *Mina and the Undead* series

'A thrilling follow up to Kass' story in *Lie or Die: Blood Moon* is like if *The Hunger Games* met *The Traitors*: bloody, brutal and brilliant. The tension and pacing are impeccable and like in all good games of Werewolf, you're never sure who to trust. I'll be thinking about this series for a long time to come.' Elle Machray, author of *Remember, Remember*

'I thoroughly enjoyed *Lie or Die: Blood Moon*. It's exactly the kind of propulsive puzzle I've come to expect from Clack, and it's equally delightful and terrifying to be back with familiar faces and brand new players in an even more unpredictable game. An adrenaline-fuelled new round of thrills and heart-pounding twists!' Jess Popplewell, author of *The Dark Within Us*

LIE OR DIE
BLOOD MOON

A.J. CLACK

Firefly

First published in 2025
by Firefly Press
Britannia House, Van Road, Caerphilly, CF83 3GG
www.fireflypress.co.uk

© Alison J. Clack 2025

The author asserts her moral right to be identified as author in
accordance with the Copyright, Designs and Patent Act, 1988.

All rights reserved.
This book is sold subject to the condition that it shall not, by way of
trade or otherwise, be lent, re-sold, hired out or otherwise circulated
without the publisher's prior consent in any form, binding or cover other
than that in which it is published and without a similar condition
including this condition being imposed on the subsequent purchaser.

All characters in this publication are fictitious and any resemblance to
real persons, living or dead, is purely coincidental.

A CIP catalogue record of this book is available from
the British Library.

print ISBN 978-1-917718-06-6

This book has been published with the support of
the Welsh Books Council.

Typeset by Elaine Sharples

Printed and bound by CPI Group UK

For Imi, my partner in crime.

More things I've learned about reality TV

Big viewing figures mean there's always a sequel.

*Drones. Outside broadcast trucks.
Bigger budget, better location.*

*At no point did anyone mention that when you're
on top there's nowhere to go but down.*

Or that murder was just the beginning…

LIE OR DIE: *BLOOD MOON*

Rules of play

Castle Dwellers: All contestants (Peasant or Werewolf) are referred to as Castle Dwellers.

Werewolves: Werewolves must masquerade as Peasants and remain undetected. Each night phase during the blood moon they must murder a Peasant by placing the name of their intended victim in the campfire.

The Alpha: A Werewolf with special powers. He/she has the ability to turn Peasants into Werewolves. How many the Alpha may turn is determined during the gameplay by the audience. When and who they turn is up to the Alpha.

Peasants: Peasants must uncover the identities of the Werewolves at the Castle Council and avoid being murdered.

Castle Council: Held each day. The Castle Council will nominate a suspected Werewolf. Each nomination must be seconded. Two nominations must be made in each council.

The Gauntlet: If found guilty by the Council, the Castle Dweller must run the Gauntlet. If completed, they may leave the game. Players leaving by the Gauntlet will not win the prize money.

Character Cards: Various character cards are hidden within the game. These cards allow the holder special powers. These powers can only be used once.

Action Cards: Hidden within the game, these cards give the bearer a specific action or ability. This action can only be used once.

Shields: Hidden throughout the game are a series of immunity shields. These grant the bearer immunity from Castle Council nomination. They may only be used once.

The faction with the majority remaining at the final Castle Council will win the prize money and the title of Ultimate Champions. Production reserves the right to add or take away character cards and action cards and to change any status without warning or explanation.

Status of players will be revealed after an eviction via the Gauntlet and not from murder or death by gameplay.

LIEORDIE:BLOODMOON©**Skyegreenproductions**

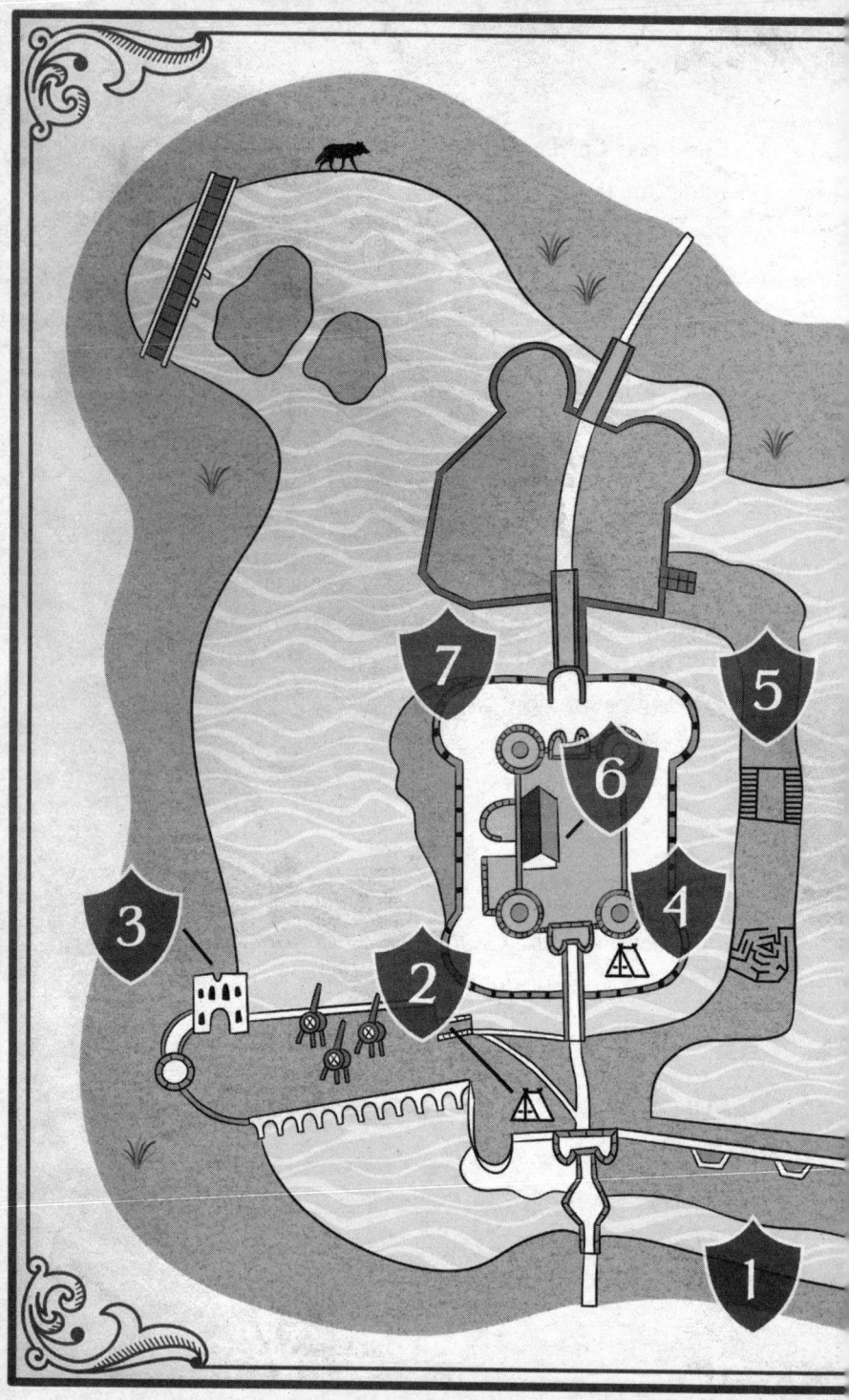

Lewis

My knees grind into solid ground, the weight of the world sitting heavily on my shoulders. My fingers claw at the icy soil, splitting nails as the nature beneath my palms fights back. I want to bury myself in the earth but its frozen surface refuses to let me in, as cold and heartless as the castle that spat me out but devoured my friends in one gigantic gulp.

My eyes squeeze shut. *You don't get to feel bad. You just get to breathe… One … two … three.* My heart's pounding so fast it's gonna break my chest… *Four … five.*

Footsteps hurry towards me. A thick blanket covers my shaking shoulders. Hands under elbows pull me vertical in one easy move that makes me cry out in anguish and tremble with fright.

'Can you tell us your name?' Police surround me, as hungry as the *Blood Moon* wolves.

My words stick in my throat as I struggle to speak. I need to tell them. They need to know what I did.

I chose life. And my choice will forever kill me.

Dragging my eyes away from the castle, I focus on the first face I see.

'My name is…' I force myself on, stumbling quickly through my confession. 'My name is Lewis Ellis, and I killed Kass Kennedy.'

1

Five days earlier

Kass

'What the actual?' Lewis is staring into my bedroom mirror, hands flapping in the air like helicopter propellers, the hair-dye box squashed beneath his feet. 'It said copper not bloody tangerine!'

I count to five, forcing my lips straight, and wait.

He pirouettes like a pro, his eyes never leaving his reflection. 'Actually, it's pretty cool. I look like Helios, the sun Titan.'

'More like a titanic pumpkin.' I giggle as the light reflects off the colour making a haloed ring around his head, sun-like and just as godly. 'We won't lose you in a crowd, that's for sure.'

'Kass Kennedy, you are *so* funny,' he says smacking his lips together. 'I am goo-ood. You should try it; it's liberating. Makes you feel alive…' His eyes flood with pain.

My stomach plummets to its now normal low and I scramble to lift the mood back up.

'Maybe,' I say gently. 'It's better than a *Lavender Haze*.'

He smiles, but his eyes tell a different story as unwelcome memories gatecrash my bedroom. He doesn't do Swiftisms anymore, not since… And I miss it. I miss before-TV-show Lewis.

He shrugs it off, his shoulders a little more slumped than before, and runs his hands through his bright new hair.

I check my phone, a common enough move I know, but ever since *her* message it's become an obsession. Despite a huge police investigation and our own dedicated DC Brown, Skye Greenhill's still out there. We may be free of Central Studios and the *Lie or Die* reality-TV show, but she still has us trapped within an imaginary house, forever looking over our shoulders, trusting no one.

And I hate her.

At first we were just happy to be alive, left to grieve the friends we left behind. But then came the attention and the relentless harassment by the media, the followers and the conspiracy theorists who reimagined our story and rewrote our lives.

No one cares about the truth. No one wants to face the facts. Everyone believes the lie. It's like the world's gone mad.

And I'm trying to make sense of it all.

And I'm beyond sad.

And I'm angry.

And guilty. I survived while they died. Why? For what? A reality-TV show ambushed by a fame-hungry wannabee and a psychopath.

My phone pings. I grab it, my heart dancing.

'And what does the tattooed sexy stud want?' Lewis says. 'Come on spill, you only get that look when he texts.'

'What look?' I push my phone into my pocket. It's not Rhodri anyway, some number I don't recognise, prob spam.

'You *lurve* him.'

'Do not,' I protest as my cheeks flush warm. Arrogant, stubborn and the token bad boy, I so didn't like him in the game. But Rhodri proved himself to be the strongest and bravest of us all, going into the game to provide his mum and his little sister, Carys, with a better life. He was the one good that came from all the bad. Six months later and I still can't believe that he's into me.

'Oh please, you so do. He's the only one that can make you smile these days. You're proper blushing.' Lewis flops onto my bed. 'So? How is love in Tonypandy?'

'Porthcawl.' I correct him.

'And what's Welsh for I'm totally lusting over your bones?'

'*Cau dy geg,*' I say.

'Sorry, what?' Lewis chokes.

'Shut up. It means shut up.' I giggle. 'Not sure that's how you pronounce it, but it's how I remember it.'

Lewis lies back on the pillows. 'Ahh, how very sexy.'

I pull a face.

Lewis' eye-lined eyes sparkle with laughter. 'You've got it bad.'

I throw a cushion at him. 'Stop.' Lewis and I have been friends since forever. With Thea we form a tight friendship that's lasted since Reception. Since the game we're unshakeable.

There's a knock at the door.

'This just came for you,' Mum says handing me a parcel. 'Hi Lewis, nice colour.'

'Thanks, Mrs K, felt like a change.' Lewis pushes his hair back from his eyes. 'It's the Helios look.'

Mum's smile is wonky, betraying her confusion but she goes with it. 'Wasn't he the one who got too close to the sun?'

'That was Icarus,' I say. My fingers drum on the cardboard, waiting for her to go.

'Helios *is* the sun,' says Lewis.

'Of course he is.' Mum closes the door behind her.

The box is light in my hands. Lewis passes me the scissors.

'What you been buying?' he asks.

'Nothing.' I run the scissors down the centre and peel back the flaps. My hands hover over the delicate white paper covering the contents. A weird bubbling sound escapes my throat as I read the small shiny sticker holding it together.

My phone pings again… I ignore it.

'Kass?' Lewis scooches towards me, reading over my shoulder. 'Skygreen Productions.' He whistles. 'Shiiiit.'

Every part of me is screaming not to open it but my hands move robotically, independent of my brain. The tissue paper crinkles as I fold it back. Beneath is a handwritten note.

> **You are cordially invited to:**
>
> # LIE OR DIE: *BLOOD MOON*
>
> Following the success of series one, we're looking for more confident & competitive contestants to take part in this **ULTIMATE** reality-TV survival show.
>
> And we want **YOU!**
>
> Further instructions to follow.

I can't breathe. I'm back on the *Lie or Die* set, the theme tune thumping in my head. It's been months since Skye sent us all the text inviting us to play the game Werewolf. One short text just weeks after the show, then nothing but a claustrophobic silence. We thought she was messing with us, letting us know that she got away, outsmarting and outmanoeuvring us in the game and beyond. As the weeks turned into months we allowed ourselves to hope it was over. All that was left was for the police to do their job and catch her.

Lewis takes the box from me. Ripping it open, he unfolds a white piece of cloth. He recoils with a high-pitched yelp, throwing it onto the bed, eyes wide and terrified.

I force myself to look. It's a T-shirt, loose with age

and grubby with wear. On the front is a worn Storm Trooper. Smeared across the picture is a bloody handprint.

My heart is pounding in my ears. I know this T. It belongs to one of the survivors of the game, a geeky Mafia super fan, the most 'real' contestant. And if I know the wearer, then the blood soaked across the front like a calling card must also be his.

It's Max's.

And he's in trouble.

2

I want to scream. I want to shout to my mum downstairs, to Dad, to DC Brown, to anyone who'll listen. I want to yell until my lungs burn, but the words on the back of the invitation compel me silent.

> **This invite is confidential and intended for the addressee only.**
>
> **Any attempts to inform a third party will be met with the most extreme consequences.**

Lewis fumbles with his phone, filling the silence with an expectant ring. No answer. No crazy voicemail message with some weird music that I always say is *Star Wars* instead of *The Mandalorian*, which makes Max really, really mad.

'He's not picking up,' Lewis squeaks.

'She has him,' I whisper over the monotonous ring. 'I know it.'

The ringing stops.

Lewis stares at his phone. 'Doesn't mean anything. He's probably gaming. He got a new game. If he's wearing headphones he won't hear his phone.' His palm hits his forehead. 'What was it called?'

'Lewis.' I try to tell him what he already knows but he's not listening.

'He'll be playing. It's all a setup. Skye's screwing with us.' He slumps onto my bed.

I wish I could hide in Lewis' denial but the words on the invitation burn my eyes. I perch next to him, Max's beloved *Star Wars* T in a poisonous heap on the floor.

I know Skye.

I know how she plays.

My phone buzzes. Max is video calling.

'What the hell, Max? So not funny.' Nothing but silence. 'Max?'

Max presses his face right up to the camera, tears streaming down his cheeks. He looks awful, his lovely dark eyes puffy and bloodshot. His left eye's bruised and swollen and dried blood cakes the corners of his mouth. The camera pans out to reveal him sat on a chair, hands tied behind his back. There's a sign hanging around his neck – a snarling wolf's head, the words *Blood Moon* in bold black. His head keeps dropping to his chest, like it's too heavy to hold up, his dishevelled jet-black curls flopping over his face.

He lifts his eyes back to the camera, wild and terrified. 'Help me.'

The phone goes blank.

We don't move, frozen to the spot, my horror mirrored on Lewis' face.

Lewis' phone pings. Reluctantly he holds it out:

52.08393°N, 1.43325°E
BLOOD MOON
23/01-22.00
Don't be late. I'm dying to play.

'What does it mean?' Lewis whispers.

My eyes scan the numbers, they look familiar in a haven't-got-a-clue sort of way.

Lewis is pacing, shaking his hands out in front of him. 'She wants to play Werewolf. Okay, we can do that. Or not. We can go, but we don't need to play, just grab Max and get out before she can do anything.' He stops. 'We beat her once; we can do it again.'

I nod, unconvinced by his kamikaze plan, my brain transporting me back to the last game. Skye's ability to manipulate us at every turn had us all running in circles. It won't be easy to beat her at her own game; she's way too clever for that. Maybe there is something in getting in quickly and getting out. I reread Lewis' message over and over. There's something recognisable about the numbers: *52.08393°N, 1.43325°E*.

Lewis is still pacing. 'If she hurts Max—'

'Coordinates,' I say in a welcome eureka moment. 'They're coordinates.'

'So, it's like a code?' He watches me punch the numbers into Google Maps.

'Yeah, like what3words without the words,' I say. 'Look. It's a location. Rendlesham Forest. It's not far.'

'Perfect.' Lewis strikes a pose, his face one big sneer. 'Let's run off to a forest with a serial killer because she asked so nicely.'

'Not you,' I say. 'The invitation is just for me.'

'Uhhh, I got the text.' Lewis' sneer morphs into an indignant frown. 'Like I'm gonna let you walk back into the mouth of hell alone.'

'But you hated Mafia, even before…' I stop. Lewis wasn't in the game; he got trapped in the studio but locked out of the set, forced to witness the murder of contestants while being helpless to stop it. Would he survive a game of Skye's Werewolf? Can I risk it? 'You hate Werewolf even more; you don't even know how to play.'

'Hel-lo?' Lewis counts on his fingers. 'One, I've watched you and Thea play Mafia enough to be a mastermind in the subject. Two, I was there with you all the way in *Lie or Die*; I saw everything. And Three, how hard can Werewolf be? It's Mafia but with Werewolves and Villagers instead and some other weird characters designed to make the game even easier. I can do this.'

He's right. But ever since she sent that first text I've been obsessing about the game Werewolf. It's just a different version of Mafia, the principle's the same. Find the Werewolves hidden in the group before they kill you. Lewis was there; he understands what's at stake. Sceptical and petrified must be plastered all over my face because he changes tack, cocooning me inside a safe Lewis hug.

'We knew this was coming.' His voice is surprisingly

wobble-free. 'We do this together. We find Max before the game even starts and get out smelling of heroes.' His words fill the room with strength, but the shake of his arms betrays him.

I love him for trying.

'I don't want to be a hero,' I mumble into his shoulder. When I think of a hero, Tayo Asagu leaps into my head, the rugby-playing model and super brain from *Lie or Die* who had the strength and courage to stand up to our attackers in a move that got him murdered.

'Well tough shit, girl, you already are.' Lewis interrupts my thoughts.

I wrinkle my nose. 'What does a hero smell of anyway?'

Lewis squeezes me tighter. 'Hugo ICED, freshly ground coffee and swimming pool changing rooms.' He pauses. 'No judgement. Now call your sexy boyfriend; we need a shit-hot plan.'

'No.' It comes out as a yelp, reaction rather than thought. 'If we tell him he'll come.'

'That was a big part of the shit-hot plan.'

'We don't even know if he got an invitation.'

'Why wouldn't he? He got the first text, we all did. Skye's after everyone who survived, right? She'll need us all. And some. I wonder who else she'll get to play, maybe some D-list celebrities trying to revive their careers?'

'The only thing we know is that we don't know anything,' I say trying to stay on track. 'And if we can keep Rhodri safe, then that's good right?'

'Uh hello? Welsh boy won't want to miss an opportunity to show us all what a hero he is.' Lewis presses his lips into a hard line. 'Wow, that was channelling major catty.' His mouth relaxes. 'Soz.'

I let it go. Lewis and Rhodri's relationship is beyond complicated, and I don't have time to play a round of *who do I like more?* There's only one cohesive thought in my head right now and that's to keep Rhodri out of it. Angry Rhodri is dangerous Rhodri. There's no telling what he might do if Skye starts pushing his buttons.

'What about Thea?' As soon as he says our best friend's name his head starts to shake in time with mine. 'No way.'

'Agreed,' I say. Although Thea's injuries healed on the outside, she's struggling big time on the inside. When the real footage came out and the lies and conspiracy theories filled the socials it was too much for her. She got so much hate for just being her. Those people who cast judgement from snippets they saw in a manufactured reality became her judge and jury and sentenced her to a lifetime of misery. They don't know her; they've no idea how much their words tore her apart. Then came Skye's sick message about playing Werewolf and she was totally triggered. Her dad's taken her somewhere quiet, somewhere social-media free. 'We need to keep her out of this, she's been through enough already.'

'But what if she gets an invite?' Lewis says.

'She won't see it; she has no phone.'

The true extent of Thea's mental health revealed in one small sentence. Thea without a phone is like Tom without Jerry, Rick without Morty; you'd never have believed it – until the game. *Lie or Die* was supposed to change her life, not ruin it. It should have been her big break. Instead, it broke her big time.

'We need to tell the police.' My mind's whirring so fast I can't keep up. 'DC Brown said to tell him if we heard anything.' I have his personal number on speed dial. 'We should call him. It's the—'

'No!' Lewis shouts and I stop, my finger hovering over the number. He waves the invitation in my face. 'If we tell ANYONE, Max will die.'

'You don't know that,' I say.

'Really?' Lewis points to the T-shirt, his finger making frenzied circles over the blood. 'You don't think this is a seismic warning for us to keep our mouth shut? You saw Max, you don't think she'll kill him the instant we tell our friendly and little-bit-sexy detective or any-bloody-one else?' He collapses on the bed. 'We have no choice. We are proper screwed.'

I slump to the floor, gripping the soft carpet between my fingers. A part of me wants to bail, to bury under the duvet and refuse to come out.

'We could ignore it?' I mumble. 'Don't look at me like that.'

'Like what?'

'All judgy.'

'Am not.'

'You totally are.' I don't look up. 'I'm just saying what if we didn't go. What's the worst thing that could happen?'

'Max would die?' Lewis says.

'She could be bluffing?'

'Sorry hun, that bitch don't bluff.'

'So much for being the hero,' I say. 'Now you hate me.'

'I don't hate you,' he says. 'And I'm not judging; I thought the exact same thing. But I don't think I could live with myself if he…'

His words hang in the air. Max gatecrashes my thoughts. He went into the first game not for fame or fortune but just to prove that he was the best – the best reality fan and the best Mafia gamer. He wasn't prepared for what came next and survived by keeping his head down and staying under the radar. He's not strong like Rhodri or savvy like Lewis. To be held prisoner by Skye will be killing him, even if she doesn't intend to carry out her threat. And if we did nothing? How do you go on living knowing that someone died because of you?

My thoughts return to Lewis. 'Let me do this by myself. It's me she wants.'

'Not happening, no way are you leaving me behind to tell Welsh that I let you go alone.' He waves his hands to stop me interrupting. 'We're in this together, Kennedy. Thank god I did my hair this colour.' He flips his fringe. 'Nothing says screw you Skye Green more than tangerine.'

'Skye Greenhill.' I correct him.

'Whatever,' he says, his eyes wandering back to his phone. 'I think under the circumstances I can afford a little artistic licence with my rhyming.'

I watch my best friend, his new orange fringe tumbling over his face as he scrutinises the message, and I've never loved him more.

'Uhh.' His hand flies into the air. 'If those first two numbers are coordinates then I'm thinking the last numbers are a date? Twenty-three, zero one.' He looks at me, eyes like saucers. 'That's today. And 2200 a time?' His voice rises. 'We've less than four hours to get sorted and get to Rendlesham piggin' Forest.'

He rummages through my messy desk, his movements jerky and uncoordinated.

'She said we couldn't tell anyone but she didn't say we couldn't leave our phones behind with all the information on, did she?' Lewis drops a pencil, bending quickly to pick it up while gesturing impatiently for my phone. 'What's your password?'

'password1#,' I mumble, handing it over. 'All lower case.'

Lewis chuckles nervously. 'Wouldn't take a detective to figure that out.' He takes a picture of the invitation.

I frown. 'But they won't see it, they won't come in here until it's time to wake up tomorrow.'

'That's what I'm counting on.' He sticks my password on a Post-it and attaches it to the screen.

'We're sticking to the rule; we're not telling anyone,

but if they accidently find your phone when your alarm goes off in the morning, then that's not on us.'

'But they—'

Lewis holds up his finger in a shush. 'Alexa set an alarm for 7.30 a.m. tomorrow.'

Alexa responds.

'Technically we're not *telling* them anything,' Lewis says. 'And by the time Skye finds out it will be too late; we'll either be gone or in the game.'

I pull a *not-convinced* face but unable to come up with a better idea I stay quiet.

'It's lame but what can you do? The parents are going to kill us when they find out we've done this. We just have to hold on until help comes.'

My flight reaction ramps into overdrive.

'Kass?' Lewis is shaking me. 'Kass?'

All I can see are the faces of the dead, the ones who didn't make it out of the last game.

'Kass?' Lewis holds my shoulders with both hands, his face right up in mine. 'Plan now. Panic later. And we have one. It's dangerous and very stupid and probably not going to work but at least it's a plan.'

He's right, there's no time for panic. She's timed this perfectly. We've no time to think, to do anything but exactly what she wants. Anger replaces fear as I pull myself back into the room. I'm so sick of feeling scared. I want this to be over and if that means facing her again then so be it. I force my mouth into what I hope is a convincing smile. 'I'll drive.'

Taking a step back he splutters. 'I don't think so. I don't want to die before we get there.'

I play along, pulling a *haha* face while feeling empty inside. We've got the convincing faux bravery down to a T. I try not to shudder every time he says the D-word. I'd never really given it much thought before the show, but now death's my new normal.

Skye's victims live inside my head. How can I move on when Tayo Asaju's last words replay nightly in my ears, as he names his murderer over and over and begs me to understand? Death and I are close friends now and, thanks to Skye Greenhill, I barely think of anything else.

3

It's quiet on the roads; the January dark makes the evening dusk feel like midnight. Venitiwa, Lewis' beloved Vauxhall, is working overtime to defrost our bones. Fear is so present that the car's bursting with its mighty weight. I clutch my small rucksack to my chest, letting my heart bang freely against its cold surface. My feet fidget, a blade of cold steel hidden in my boot – insurance, Lewis called it. I'm taking no chances with Skye.

Guilt taps a rat-a-tat-tat on my temples when I imagine Mum and Dad finding my phone tomorrow with Max's bloody T and discovering me gone. I'd promised to talk to them more, be secret-free after the show. And when I think of Thea my lungs tighten so much that I doubt I'll ever be able to breathe again. But they'll all understand, they have to. It's not like we had a choice.

We drive in silence, lost in dark thoughts – each one more terrifying than the last. This plan sucks. How can I save Max? I couldn't save Thea. I had no clue about Skye. I trusted her, shared a bed with her, wiped away her phoney tears and practically led her out of the door to freedom. And I'm meant to be the one with the talent for reading people; the joke's not lost on me.

Soon the road's enclosed by trees, line after uniform line stretch out in all directions. There's a sign. It's black with a white wolf's head, teeth bared, underneath the words:

FOLLOW THE WOLF

'I guess we follow the wolf,' I say.

Venitiwa groans and rattles along the bumpy path. Seconds later there's another sign, then another. We follow obediently until the trees surround us and the dirt track disappears.

'Venitiwa's done,' Lewis says as the wheels strain in the mud. He turns off the engine, leaning forward to stare at the track, illuminated by two unbroken paths of headlight yellow that stretch forlornly away from us, fizzling out into the all-consuming night.

Lewis turns to me. 'I need you to do something for me.'

'Anything,' I whisper.

'Don't die.' Looking up he dabs his fingers under his eyes impatiently. 'We get through this, no matter what. We get Max and get out. Leave Skye for the police. No hero stuff. We survive. 'Cause I sure as hell don't want to live in this world without you.'

There's a lump in my throat blocking my voice. I press my tongue up to the roof of my mouth willing the tears away. Lewis sniffs loudly.

'Bollocks.' He checks himself in the mirror. 'Let's shake it out. Don't want crazy-face Skye seeing us in a mess.' He checks the time. 'Nine thirty.' He bites his fingernails, a tell I've not seen since primary.

It's freezing. My breath's one big steam cloud.

Climbing out of the car Lewis fumbles under the back wheel.

'I'm leaving the keys there,' he says. 'Think escape route. If you can get away, then you go.'

'I'm not leaving you,' I say.

Lewis holds my shoulders. 'If we get separated and you get the chance, run.' He stops me with his hand. 'If we can't find Max, get back here and get help. Non-negotiable, Kennedy. I need to know you'll do this. Take Venitiwa, I'll be fine.'

No way am I leaving him but I mumble under my breath. It's enough to satisfy him. I move first. The winter mist swirls amongst the foliage, framing the dark with wispy-white. Lewis follows, his wheelie yellow suitcase sticking to the forest floor. He pulls a face when he picks it up. He's still refusing to admit he's overpacked: '*Hoping for the best but planning for the worst.* Lie or Die *took four days and nights. If I'm gonna die on TV, I'm going out in style. If we're forced to play, I'll be looking fabulous. No four-day-old boxers for me...*'

The moon's playing peek-a-boo between the trees refusing to light our way.

'Up there.' I point to a small path that slithers along the damp ground.

A noise stops us dead.

'What *is* that?' Lewis drops his suitcase.

Hovering under a branch is a drone. Its round, bulbous camera moves with a familiar whirr as it locks onto us, the red light pinging awake. Four metal arms stick out, little fans whirring busily in each corner. It lurches from the tree to hover over our path like a gigantic mosquito, loud and just as unwanted.

'At least we know we're in the right place.' I push my hands deep into my pockets and my face further into my scarf, refusing to look at the camera.

Then I hear the growling.

4

'That's a dog, right?' Lewis whispers.

I remember the game. 'If it's on brand it's a wolf.'

'That's a joke?' Lewis' voice is unnaturally high. 'Please tell me you're joking. Let's stick with dog please. A cutesy miniature sausage dog or a tiny handbag Chihuahua.'

'I'm happy with that,' I say.

The growling continues. It's coming from the trees. Lewis pulls me towards the flickering lights, his pace way more enthusiastic than before.

The growls intensify, our pace quickens to an almost run. We reach a makeshift high gateway spanning the path, the sort you'd make in ARK from wood not metal, primitive but totally fitting for the location. A banner's draped across the top illuminated by the wooden torches flickering either side.

BLOOD MOON CONTESTANTS WELCOME!

There's a picture of a wolf's head, mouth open in a vicious snarl. Behind us the growls have stopped, vanished into the dark of the forest like some spooky Halloween trick. Ahead the darkness opens into a clearing illuminated by more flaring torches. In the middle is a huge campfire. Around the edges sits a camp of canvas bell tents.

'They better not be expecting us to sleep in them,' Lewis says as we hurry to the safety of the fire.

A figure appears. Dressed head to toe in black, their face completely covered by a mask.

'Oh, they're really leaning into the whole Werewolf theme,' Lewis whispers.

The black mask is a perfect wolf's head. A wide forehead sits above diamond-shaped eyes, shining blood red as they stare at us. Angular cheekbones slide into a strong jaw and a long, blunt muzzle. Ears, slightly rounded at the tips point upwards from the top. The glossy smooth surface catches the light from the campfire, making it shine menacingly in the dark.

The masked figure holds up a gloved hand.

'Welcome.' A low robotic AI voice speaks, as impersonal as the mask itself. 'Follow me.'

The guard leads us to a tent. There's a circular logo on their sleeve, red against the black. They pull open the flap before I get a proper look, gesturing us inside.

'Contestants to meet at the campfire at twenty-two thirty hours,' they growl. 'Do not leave camp unattended. Welcome to *Blood Moon*.'

The flap is closed behind us and zipped up from the outside. The space is surprisingly big. Like a mini circus tent, a pole rises in the middle and the canvas drops down from it. Apart from two beds, it's empty save a small stool at either side of the doorway and a camping light hanging from the central pole. On the bed is a card: Rules of camp.

'*Do not leave camp.*' I turn the card in my hand. 'That's it? No game instructions?'

'They'll give us rules, right?' Lewis drops his suitcase on the bed. 'I lied before. I've no clue how to play.' He starts to pace. 'I'm not like you or Thea. I'm not good at games. I hate Mafia and I'm crap at it. What do I do if I get a Werewolf card? Oh my god. I'll be caught first round.' He shakes his hands out. 'This is not going to end well.'

I grab his hands between mine. 'Hey.' I force him to look at me. 'Chances are you won't be a Werewolf and if you are, then find the other Werewolves and you won't be alone. If you're not sure, do nothing and follow their lead.' I lower my voice. 'Besides, we're not planning to play the game, remember? Find Max and get out, right?'

Lewis bounces nervously on the spot. 'Right.' He takes a deep breath. 'Sorry, shat myself for a minute. All good now.'

Sitting on the bed my eyes search for cameras, but we're clear. I lift my finger to my mouth. He makes a locking lips motion with his fingers. Best to be extra paranoid than have Skye one step ahead of our every move. Not knowing what to say, and too scared to say anything meaningful, we sit on our beds … and wait.

A scratching outside the tent makes us jump up. A voice whispers through the canvas. My heart leaps and falls at the exact same time.

'Kass mun, you in there?' The Welsh accent is clear over the oh-so-loud whisper.

I freeze, rabbit in the headlights, like I've been caught doing something I shouldn't. The zip opens and he's there, coat zipped up tight, scarf wrapped securely round his neck, cheeks blushed pink from the cold.

My emotions are tumbling like a washing machine on spin cycle. I'm happy to see him and terrified at the same time. I want to hug him and scream at him to get the hell out of here, glad he's here and so angry that he's put himself in danger.

'Let me in then before I freeze.' He ducks to get inside, zipping the tent up behind him. 'Alri, Lewis?' Rhodri nods at Lewis then gestures outside. 'What's with those creepy dog masks?'

'Werewolf?' Lewis says.

'Talk about lame,' Rhodri says. He turns to me. 'Hey.'

'Hey.' I mumble back but neither of us move. Suddenly self-conscious and no clue what to do I start to pick at my bottom lip with my teeth. Lewis' eyes dart from me to Rhodri and back again.

'How's Carys?' I say, desperate to fill the yawning silence.

'Good,' he says.

'Great.' I smile while cringing on the inside. Why would I think that now would be a good time to bring up his little sister? I shuffle on my spot, trying to tame the kaleidoscope of emotions whirring around my stomach.

'Do I get a cwtch then?' he says, his smoky green eyes

dark, a smile dancing on his lips. The spell's broken and I can move. His coat is cold against my cheek. He envelopes me in his strong embrace and I'm safe.

'Why didn't you tell me?' he whispers gently, and my eyes fill with unwanted tears. I pull away.

'I wanted to keep you safe.' I rub the back of my hand across my face in a not very sexy gesture. 'I didn't want you to come and...'

'Die?' He finishes unhelpfully. 'The only one who's dying today is Skye. And I don't give a rat's arse who hears it. Calling us here in the middle of the night is insane.'

'Technically it's not the middle of—'

One look from Rhodri is enough to shut Lewis up. 'I'm not playing her fucked-up games.' Rhodri carries on ranting. 'We finish this. Tonight.'

'Wow. Calm down, Welsh,' Lewis says.

Rhodri's eyes blaze. 'Why is he here?'

I roll my eyes. Lewis and Rhodri tolerate each other because of me but that's about as far as it goes.

'Brilliant. Thanks so much,' Lewis says sarcastically. 'Actually, I was invited. I got a text.'

'Thea?' Rhodri says, ignoring Lewis.

'She's away, no phone,' I say.

'Thank god.' He paces about in the small tent. 'And Max? Anyone seen him yet?'

I catch Lewis' eye. 'You don't know?'

'Know what?'

Shit, he has no clue about Max.

Lewis crosses his arms over his chest. 'How did you know to come?'

Rhodri looks confused. 'I got a text, some coordinates and the time. I called you loads but it went to answer phone.'

'Left my phone at home,' I say. 'My parents will…' I can't say more in case they're listening, so I just stare at him and hope he gets it. 'Why did you come?' The overwhelming emotions make the question come out way harsher than intended.

'And how come you got here so quickly?' Lewis doesn't bother to hide the suspicion in his voice. 'We're a long way from the Severn Bridge.'

'He was in London.' I glare at Lewis. 'I told you.'

'Doesn't tell us why he came though does it?' Lewis says his arms folded tight over his chest, his chin raised stubbornly.

Rhodri's eyes flash angrily. 'I got a sodding text from a psychopath and I figured I didn't have a fucking choice.'

He's lying. I know Rhodri's tics so well by now and he always gets aggressive and sweary when he's on the defensive. I stare back fiercely refusing to let his temper intimidate me.

'Sorry,' he says rubbing his buzz cut, another tell-tale tic. He's hiding something. 'Can't say I wasn't expecting something like this.' Rhodri stares back for an unblinking moment. 'It's what we've been waiting for, a chance to find her and make her pay. Figured we'd all got them.' He looks at me. 'We did all get them, right?'

My eyes flit from Rhodri to Lewis and back again.

'What?' Rhodri says, puffing his chest out like he's gonna get all angry again.

'Skye has Max,' I say.

His expression's guarded but I'm close enough to hear the small whimper that leaves his throat. 'No way,' he says. 'Not possible.'

'When did you last talk to him?' Lewis says.

'Few days ago, four maybe?' His tone's tense, his words clipped. 'He was fine.'

'We saw him, tonight,' I say. 'Over video message. He was all beat up. He looked really bad. And terrified.' I hate the way my words are hurting Rhodri but still I carry on. 'If we don't play, I think she'll kill him.'

The expletives that leave Rhodri's mouth are unreal as he explodes with anger and frustration. We watch in silence, waiting for him to calm down. He and Max were close in the game, the bad boy and the geek, two opposites who gelled instantly and just vibed off one another. Like Thea, Max became the scapegoat, an easy target to troll and terrorise. His trademark 'Whoopsie' went viral for all the wrong reasons, seen as a weakness, proof of his cowardice. Rhodri's been keeping a special eye on him, worried that, like Thea, the experience was way too much for him to handle.

Soon, the ranting slows and the redness in Rhodri's

cheeks fades. He takes a jagged breath. 'It's just us then?'

Lewis hasn't taken his eyes off him the entire time. 'Looks that way.'

Rhodri begins to pace again. 'Nice hair, very … bright.'

'Ta.'

A super-sized howl sounds outside.

'I guess that's our cue,' I say.

'What's the plan?' Rhodri looks at me.

I open my mouth and close it like a goldfish, open … closed … open.

'Get Max. Kill Skye. Don't Die,' Lewis says.

I step in quickly. 'Uh no, we said leave Skye for the—'

'I can work with that,' Rhodri interrupts, turning to Lewis. They grab each other's arm and hug, slapping each other on the backs in a show of testosterone.

'Seriously?' I stammer. How is this a bonding moment? 'No more death. We find Max and get out.'

Rhodri's face is dangerously cold. 'I have a different plan.'

'No.' I can't believe I'm saying this. 'We're not hurting anyone.' My lip quivers as I cling onto my conviction. 'Don't let her turn us into monsters. If she does, she wins…'

Rhodri's arms are around me, his cold cheek nuzzled against mine, instantly calming the freakage. 'Chill, there's only one monster here and it's not us.'

Opening the tent flap he steps out into the cold night

with Lewis. I've no choice but to follow. Outside I stop. Something's way off.

'What is this?' I say unable to believe the scene in front of me. Bodies are milling around the campfire, moving silhouettes surround the blaze. The smoky aroma of BBQ hits my nose. The feel is relaxed, festival-like. And there are too many people. *Lie or Die* had ten contestants. My eyes count the mingling masses. So much for a small game of Werewolf, this is *Lie or Die* season two on an epic scale.

Rhodri and Lewis are talking but I can't hear them through the chattering hum. The world moves in slow-mo when I catch sight of a figure in the crowd. He's standing by the campfire, the amber light catching his profile, his silhouette a tower of strength against the night sky. I blink, waiting for the picture to change as my brain catches up with my eyes, like it always does when I see my dead friends.

Only this time he doesn't disappear like a ghostly will-o'-the-wisp.

This time the face turns in my direction and with a startled cry I find myself looking into the beautiful face of Tayo Asagu.

5

My hand clamps over my mouth to stop the scream and I force my eyes back towards the campfire. Tayo's gone, disappeared once more into my memory vault, a figment of my grieving imagination. I tell myself to get a grip and firmly lock him away with the others, a coping mechanism I've adopted since the show which usually works unless I'm alone or wasted or … now apparently.

Lewis is talking to Rhodri, both oblivious to my minor meltdown. 'Big fan of Werewolf then?'

Rhodri shrugs. 'Mafia's the better game. Werewolf's got too many characters. Max always argues that Werewolf is better, but I told him…' He stops abruptly. 'We need to find him and quickly. He can't cope with anymore…'

'Kass?'

I do a comedy double take that's not remotely funny and just manage to hold onto my heart as it jumps out of my mouth. He's standing right in front of me, his deep dark eyes fixed on mine.

Tayo.

Only it's not. I calm my racing breath and turn my open mouth into a smile. The boy in front of me is so like my friend that my heart and brain can't cope. He's tall like Tayo and just as beautiful. Full lips are turned upwards in a hauntingly familiar smile. The tilt of his chin is different. His face is thinner, more angular, his afro buzzed short.

But his eyes are all Tayo, staring at me with the same reassuring gaze, deep, dark, soulful eyes that make you instantly feel calm. Eyes you can trust.

'Sorry,' he says, his voice gently concerned. 'Didn't mean to startle you.'

'Demi mun, what the hell are you doing here?' Rhodri takes his hand, thumping him on the back in a genuinely warm embrace, followed by a heartfelt greeting from Lewis, giving my brain time to catch up with my eyes.

Ademide, Demi. Tayo's brother. The realisation makes me feel ridiculous. On second glance the raw sadness in his eyes is obvious and his smile is layered with a recognisable grief.

'It's Demi,' he says to me. 'We met at my brother's fu—'

'Of course,' I interrupt. 'I wasn't expecting to see you here, it threw me.'

'I get it,' he says.

'You shouldn't be here. This is not a good place,' I say. What reason would make Tayo's brother come? 'Why are you?'

'Same reason as you,' Demi says. 'I jumped at the chance to play.'

'We didn't jump,' I say.

'For Max?' Lewis whispers.

Confusion flickers in Demi's eyes. 'Max? No, I'm here for Skye. She needs to pay for what she's done.' His jaw is set as determined as his stance. His eyes burrow into me with a disquieting intensity that makes me squirm. 'Look around you. She's gonna keep on doing this until she's caught. She needs to be stopped. And I'm not the only one who thinks so. Cali's sister is here. And Amara's dad.'

A small guy turns our way. Demi signals and he shuffles over. 'You must be Kass,' he says, like it's no surprise to see me. 'I'm Ravi.'

I mutter a hello and quickly introduce Rhodri and Lewis. A familiar guilt is spreading through my veins. We've never met. Amara's funeral was closed, family only. All the guilt and anger that I've tried to bury bubbles up to the surface. I've no clue what to say to her grieving father.

The boys must feel the same; they just stare at the ground.

'Nice to meet you.' Ravi finally speaks again. We all smile like he's just told a joke. This is too painful. He's old, like parent old. Streaks of grey pepper his jet-black hair and straggly beard. But the stoop of his shoulders and the misery reflected in his eyes ages him more, like grief has sucked all the energy from him. My dad has a similar look. He blames himself for letting me play the first game and guilt haunts him relentlessly now. I don't think either of my parents would recover if I didn't come back from this.

Please someone speak.

Ravi offers no conversation. Amara was in your face full of life and so loud. Ravi's the polar opposite; his is an instantly forgettable energy.

Demi finally breaks the stalemate. 'We want justice. For Amara and for my brother.'

'And for Cali.' A small girl pushes her way into our circle, her highlighter-yellow hair so bright it makes Lewis' tangerine-Titan colour fade into a pastel blush.

'Kass, right?' Her sharp gaze falls on me. 'I'm Mai. Cali's sister.'

'Your look is fierce. Love the yellow.' Lewis runs a hand through his hair. 'I am so on trend.'

Lewis is right; Mai's make-up *is* fierce. Her eyes are made up to look like electricity bolts, yellow zigzags lined with white. Her hair's swept up, yellow streaks over black pinned off her face with huge silver hairpins. She has a real '90s, Y2K aura – an Asian Sporty Spice with all the Scary and Ginger attitude.

'I want revenge for what Skye did to my sister,' Mai spits, hatred on the tip of her tongue. 'I ain't stopping till I have her head on a spike.'

My heart sinks. It's one thing to be here to save another life, but a revenge quest is insane. It's way too dangerous. Skye is *waay* to dangerous. Is that why she invited them, to see just how far they would go for revenge? That's beyond twisted, even for Skye. And to set all this up in just six months tells me she's had help. We've no idea what we're playing with. I pray that Rhodri doesn't get carried away with this rhetoric, but he's already leaning in to hear more.

'Guys,' I say, my eyes searching for cameras. 'This is crazy. You have no idea what she's capable of.'

The conversation stops.

'Why?' Demi's eyes flash with a rage I never saw in Tayo. 'Because we didn't play the first game, we don't have a right to be here?' His underlying grief is way too raw, and I remind myself that it's his pain talking. 'Tayo's dead because of Skye. And no one stopped her.'

'We tried. I…' I stutter. 'I really did.'

Mai's eyes narrow. 'You sent my sister to her death with that Necromancer card.'

Guilt punches me right in the guts. She's right. I did kill Cali to save Noah. And Tayo tried to tell me about Skye, but I couldn't read the signs. 'I didn't know… I swear… I…' I stammer. I had the chance to stop Skye, and I blew it. I was too trusting, too gullible, too stupid to not see her coming. They're all staring at me, eyes hard. 'I'm so sorry… I…'

'Steady,' Rhodri growls a low warning. 'They were our friends too. Put the blame where it belongs and leave Kass be.'

Mai and Rhodri remain in a standoff for what feels like forever.

Mai breaks away first. 'Catch you later, *friends*.' Turning away she heads back to the fire.

'Sorry about that,' Demi says. Anger gone, he just looks broken.

'Look, we need to work together,' Ravi says. I'd almost forgotten he was there. 'We—'

Demi interrupts. 'What's happened to Max?'

'Skye has him. She's using him to blackmail us,' Lewis says. 'We think he's here somewhere.'

I move closer to Demi. 'Our plan is to get him and get out before the game starts,' I whisper. 'Help is coming, just go with it. Leave Skye to the police. If you don't you—'

'Don't worry about me.' Demi's smile turns cold. 'I've made my peace. I'm prepared for any outcome.'

What's that supposed to mean?

'Kass Kennedy?'

A wolf-masked guard is standing at my elbow. 'Come with me.'

'No.' The cry that leaves my lips is instinctual.

Rhodri and Lewis surround me.

'Where are you taking her?' Rhodri growls.

The guard doesn't answer.

Standing behind the boys my once active girl-power streak ripples angrily under my skin. I was never the girl who needed protecting. I was always perfectly capable of doing my own saving. But since *Lie or Die*, there's a huge hole in my once unbreakable convictions. It was slow at first, things I used to do easily I suddenly felt unable to do on my own, and so insidious that I didn't even realise it was happening. After-TV-show me is more than happy to hide behind the boys in a quivering pathetic mess and let them take the lead.

Another wolf guard gestures for Rhodri to follow.

'I'm not going anywhere with you,' he snarls.

'Where are you taking us?' My voice is nothing more than a whisper.

My guard speaks. 'There's nothing to fear.'

Although the mechanical voice is completely devoid of emotion the slight tilt of the head and the gentle way their arm is gesturing to follow suggests they're telling the truth. Leaving Lewis behind with Demi, I force my legs to move, channelling one small act of bravery as my insides turn to mush, praying that Rhodri complies, terrified of what will happen if he doesn't.

6

I'm led away from the hubbub of the fire and out of the camp. Flaming torches light the way as I tread the mud path through the trees. Rhodri's behind me, his angry energy burning into my back. His presence gives me the strength to keep moving forward.

Soon the path opens into a clearing. Three large trailers fill the space, their grey rectangular shapes highlighted against the dense black of the forest.

The guard bangs on the door of the nearest trailer and gestures me inside. Rhodri's face is easy to read. *Don't do anything rash, Kennedy.* I throw him a quick, *back at ya* as I step inside.

The brightly lit space makes my stomach lurch with unwanted *déjà vu* as my mind recalls a TV studio with a stool in the middle of a lime-green cloth.

Before I can sit, I'm ushered into a cubicle.

'Change.' The door closes behind me.

A pile of clothes are folded on a bench under a mirror. I dress quickly, squeezing my knife down the side of the boot where it sits against my calf, a sharp reminder of why we're here and a small comfort that I'm not completely helpless.

The clothes are warm against my skin. Thick tight leggings tuck into chunky knee-high boots. A long-sleeve top falls below my bum covered by a chainmail tunic that hangs heavily over the top. A belt sits above my hips. Gloves complete the all-black outfit making sure every part of me is hidden, except my face. The girl staring out from the mirror is miles away from the shiny reality star of series one. She's wearing a cynical frown, tired eyes creased into a frightened gaze. I mourn the Girl Next Door with her innocent smile. She died in that TV studio along with the others.

A bang on the door signals my time's up. I shake off the pity-party. There's no point in grieving – that girl's gone.

The crew are safe behind their uniformity, unrecognisable under their masks. They're all wearing the logo sewn onto their right arm. On closer inspection it looks like a red dragon in a circle eating its tail.

I walk to the stool in the middle of the green cloth and sit.

'You're familiar with MIVs?' The wolf-masked cameraperson says in the same robotic voice.

Of course I know what MIVs are: master interviews, pieces to camera to introduce the contestant to the audience, little snippets of the contestant's personality. What sick game is Skye playing? Does she expect me to simply perform for the camera like I actually *want* to be here?

Think, Kennedy, use this to your advantage. If this is going to be shown to the world then send the world a message, or at least those who'll know where to look. The friendly face of DC Brown pops into my head and I catch a hopeful breath. I can help him; I just need to be smart. I sit up straight, staring past the camera, waiting for the small red recording light to appear, just like last time. Screw Skye. I'll play her sick games, but I don't have to follow her rules.

A guard places a large card on a stand to the side of the camera. 'Read this,' they say in a tone that needs no translating. If I don't there will be consequences.

The recording light pings red in the corner of my vision. I blink rapidly; my rebellion immediately squashed. Max's face sits in my head and refuses to leave. I daren't go off script, the stakes are too high. Staring at the card through watery eyes I swallow down my fear and do as I'm told.

MIV done, I'm led back to camp. Shaking with frustration and anger, I scour the forest for any signs of Max. If I was Skye, I'd keep him near, a horrifying reminder of why we're here and a weighty insurance to make us play her game.

The guard leaves me on the edge of the clearing. Other guards pass, leading players up the hill to the trailers and their MIVS. Some catch my eye, excitement flickering over their faces.

People are mingling around the campfire, gravitating towards the heat. My mind can't marry the laughter and excitement with the knowledge that we're here to play a game that's sure to have deadly consequences.

Do these people even know how much is at risk?

A hand brushes my elbow making me jump.

'*Cariad*.' Just one word in that low Welsh accent calms me. I have no idea what it means but it doesn't matter. The hand moves down my elbow and finding my fist unclenches it gently, taking it in a gloved palm and squeezing.

'Come with me,' Rhodri whispers. He's wearing the same black costume as me. 'I've found Max.'

7

Rhodri pulls me back into the trees, his voice low and steady. 'We need to check the trailers. There were three in that clearing and they're only using two. I'll put money on Max being in the third.'

'But Lewis.' I pull back.

'He's been taken for his MIV. I saw him walk past,' Rhodri says, squeezing my hand. I let him lead me back up the hill towards the trailers. My eyes default up towards the trees, watching for any sign of drones, my ears straining for the growling Lewis and I heard before.

'Thought that bloody camera run would be the last time we'd be doing this,' Rhodri whispers, his jaw tight with tension. 'Demi's right. She won't get away with it, not again. If she hurts Max, I'll…'

A noise behind us makes me pull Rhodri into the trees. We stay hidden, pressed against a tree trunk. I'm thankful for the all-black camo costume that lets the night swallow us whole. Rhodri's body presses tight against mine. The frantic rhythm of his heart bangs against my breast. My palm presses against his chest to calm him. His arm curls around my waist, his quick breath fans my face. A guard walks past with Ravi.

Hidden in the trees, held close by Rhodri, I feel safer than I have all night. When he pulls away the feeling of terror pulses back over my skin and I long to hide in the refuge of his arms. We follow behind, alert and cautious. Reaching the clearing, we circle round to the third trailer.

'I don't get it,' Rhodri whispers as we crouch in the withered bracken. 'Where are the guards and the cameras?'

The clearing's empty. There are no guards, no drones. In fact, I've only seen two cameras since we got here. Rhodri's right: if we're about to be filmed 24/7 where are the cameras and the crew?

We crouch in the undergrowth and wait.

Ravi appears from the middle trailer dressed in black. Lewis comes out of the furthest trailer. Unlike Rhodri the tunic-style costume does nothing for his gangly frame. They're led down the hill and out of sight.

'I don't get it,' I whisper. 'We look like crappy medieval knights in this get up. It's stupid.'

Rhodri shuffles uncomfortably. 'Totally out of place.' He shrugs. 'Unless they're going for a bad Robin Hood vibe?'

The forest falls into an oppressive quiet.

'Wait here.' Rhodri moves towards the third trailer. I immediately follow. He stops and turns to me, *wtf?* plastered over his face.

'Not gonna happen,' I mutter. He frowns but carries on. To our surprise the door to the trailer opens easily.

'Max,' Rhodri whispers into the room. 'Max?' There's nothing inside but darkness. Rhodri slips inside.

I'm about to follow when a noise stops me. I turn towards the dark forest, my skin prickling in warning.

A padding, rhythmical and strong, is quickening through the trees, like a galloping army stampeding through the undergrowth, puncturing the quiet with its relentless beat.

'Rhodri,' I whisper-hiss into the trailer. The sound's getting louder. The charge is peppered with a chorus of canine song. Howling mixes with yelping and excited barks.

'What the hell is that?' Rhodri's at the door, his head cocked as he listens.

Feeling exposed we dive into the dark refuge of the trees. My eyes search the darkness but it's impossible to see into the black folds of the forest. Is Skye just messing with us?

A scream pierces the air, loud and shrill and unquestionably human, followed by a gasping cry and the sound of running. Rhodri's wide eyes lock onto mine, no words necessary as we both share the same conclusion. Someone's being chased.

And they're moving closer.

I press my body against the tree as dark shadows move towards us. My gloved hands cover my ears when the chorus of howls reaches a terrifying crescendo.

Screaming, barking, howling, tearing, ripping.

I squeeze my eyes shut. Rhodri's arms are around me, holding me tight, his face buried into my shoulder. We try to shut out the horror and make our bodies disappear.

Another scream, lung filled and final, cut off by a silence more terrifying than anything that went before.

'We need to go.' Rhodri grabs my hand. His begging eyes flash wildly. His finger presses against his mouth and he signals for us to creep further into the forest. We half crawl, half stumble through the darkness, my senses on high alert, praying that whatever is out there is far away and that we're moving in the opposite direction.

8

We put a forest between us and the trailers, stopping only because our bodies demand rest and our lungs threaten to burst.

'Whatever that was, it wasn't real,' I pant. 'Skye's playing with us.' I'm drowning in denial. My eyes frantically scan the trees for movement while my brain tries to process what it heard. 'Mind games. Just a trick, played into the forest to scare us. It wasn't a real person. It sounded like dogs or wolves, but it couldn't be. There's no way—'

Rhodri stops me with a kiss. His lips crash down on mine, hard and desperate as though words have no meaning, obliterating my terrified thoughts in a heartbeat as my body melts to liquid. I kiss him back; the only comfort is to kiss away the bad with something good and normal and safe. And it works. I forget about everything. Here in this forest, in the middle of the night, kissing Rhodri, nothing else matters.

The moment's over too soon. Rhodri moves his hands down my arms, leaning his forehead on mine. He's shaking as much as me. 'It was real, *cariad*. And I think they were wolves. The game's called Werewolf. Only Skye would see the value in real wolves and if she's had anything to do with it there'll be nothing normal about them.' My eyes fill with questions I'm too scared to voice but Rhodri answers. 'They won't be nervous of humans like natural wolves are. I'll bet my life they'll be big and wild and raised to kill.' I swallow down the cry of despair. 'We need to get back. No clue which way though.'

I follow his gaze. In our panic we've lost all sense of direction. We're surrounded by dense woodland. The forest remains eerily quiet. A shiver crackles down my back to my boots as I turn in every direction. There's no sign of the camp or the torches that lead us to it. The moon's just visible hanging over the forest canopy. Not quite full, it's trying to map our way, but we've no clue how to read it.

'Which way?' Rhodri scans the trees.

Taking his hand, I push down the fear and step forward randomly. 'This way.'

Our eyes scour the darkness, our ears straining hard against the stifling quiet, punctuated only by our ragged breaths. I freeze at every snapping twig, waiting for the sound of paws to thunder through the undergrowth, or fevered howling to signal our pursuit. I can't shake the feeling of being watched. Is it real or just my paranoia working overtime? My brain's imagining the scene of a wolf hunt and the bloody picture of what happens when they catch their prey. This is way more than I bargained for. This is a whole other level of extreme.

And the game hasn't even started yet.

The trees thin, allowing the moon to scatter light onto the trail, casting a silver sparkle on the ground. I recognise the path, remembering how Lewis dragged his yellow suitcase over the forest floor. One way leads to camp and the other to Lewis' car.

'Venitiwa,' I whisper.

Rhodri's chuckle is raw. 'I hope you don't think that's Welsh cos you're way off.'

I run down the track. 'Lewis' car is around here somewhere.' It's all he needs to follow. We soon find it, still parked at the edge of the track, waiting.

I lean on the bonnet, catching my breath before reaching under the back wheel.

Rhodri shuffles through the undergrowth. Picking up a rock he marches over to the driver's window.

'Rhodri, no!' I shout, holding up the key.

'Yesss, Lewis,' he says climbing into the driver seat. Leaning over he opens the passenger door from the inside. 'Get in.'

At least in here it's marginally warmer.

For a brief second, I imagine us driving back down the road and out to safety. My heart beats double time with relief as my need to get away from here overrides all my senses. What the hell was I thinking? I grossly underestimated Skye. Rhodri feels it too; his hands fumble with the keys in a desperate attempt to flee. Escape is all we can think of. Terror has turned us into quivering cowards, our flight reaction kicking in big time as our minds scream *run*. But as we contemplate escape, Lewis and Max creep into my head.

'Stop.'

Rhodri turns, key poised in the ignition. 'This is a chance to get out. This is bigger than us. We need to get help.'

He's right but that doesn't change anything. 'We can't.' I can't control the wobble in my voice.

'Lewis and I spoke,' Rhodri says. 'We agreed that if we could, we'd get you to safety.'

'And you go into the game without me? No way.' Lewis and Rhodri have never agreed on anything, until now. Irritation races through me at the thought of them deciding my fate without me.

'Kass, please. You heard what's out there. We've no idea if that was for real. One thing we do know is that Skye's not playing. Whatever she has planned is a hundred times worse than anything we could have imagined. I'm—'

'Not gonna happen.'

'He said you'd agree.'

'He was wrong.' I move to open the door.

'Wait.' Rhodri stops me with one word. His eyes shine deep emerald, filled with such tenderness my heart almost breaks. 'I hear you; I do, but let me try. I need to at least try. Please, it's our one chance to get help.' His hand gestures towards the dark outside. 'And if that was real, if *they* were real, we need it.'

I get it. Anything we can do to stop the feeling of

hopelessness right now is a bonus. And I get that he wants to make it safe for me, but no way am I abandoning my friends to save myself no matter how terrified I am or how overwhelming my instinct to run.

Rhodri turns the key. Nothing happens. He tries again. Venitiwa refuses to start.

'FUCK.' He jumps out of the car.

A wolf howls through the darkness.

He lifts the bonnet, blocking my view.

'Fuck.' He's back in the car, slamming the driver's door. The sound reverberates around the forest, dissipating into the cold night air. 'Battery's gone. Like fucking taken.' He thumps the steering wheel in frustration. 'Bastards.'

Shit. Even if I wanted to, without the battery, Venitiwa's going nowhere.

More howls.

Rhodri locks the doors.

'They're not real,' I mumble. 'Not real.'

Frenzied barks slice through the air.

We freeze, our rapid breath steaming up the windows.

My hand finds Rhodri's and his fingers entwine with mine.

'You're bleeding,' Rhodri says.

Puzzled, I look at my hand. There's a hole ripped in the back of the glove exposing my skin beneath. Rhodri gently pulls it off. Jagged marks zigzag the back of my hand, blood oozing from the thin lines.

'It's nothing. It doesn't even hurt,' I say as he grabs a

napkin from an old MacDonald's bag scattered across the back seat and gently wipes away the blood. 'Must have caught it on a tree.'

Pulling off his gloves, his fingers slowly trace the line of the wound. His touch sends electric shivers down my back. '*Cariad.*' That word again, softly spoken, makes my heart stutter. 'I'm sorry.'

'What for?'

Rhodri frowns. 'Making you come look for Max.'

'I didn't exactly need much persuading,' I say. I know Rhodri, if I let him, he'll get angry and blame himself.

'I didn't think.' His eyes darken to a deep seaweed green. 'Should've known she'd be one step ahead of us.'

'I think we all underestimated Skye,' I say. 'Besides, being out here with you … way better than trapped in a camp full of delusional wannabes.'

He chuckles; the angry line of his jaw softens. 'True,' he says. 'Been there, done that.' He pulls me closer. 'I'd much rather be lost with you, surrounded by blood-thirsty devil wolves.'

'You big romantic,' I say.

'What ya gonna do?'

Without thinking I reach up and kiss him. His lips feel soft and comforting. I run my hand up his chest, the chainmail of his costume rough against my fingers. I want to banish the terror, even for a moment. This car and this boy have become my safe space. Rhodri must feel it too; his eyes blaze with pain. His hand weaves though my hair, his other curling tightly around my back. We pull each other close, trying to expel the space between us, desire chasing away the fear. Our lips crash together, moving in perfect sync. In this moment there's only him. The terrifying reality outside disappears. In the here and now, we control our destiny.

His hand tugs at the bottom of my tunic, tucking inside the thick woollen top. His palm is freezing against my back and makes me gasp. He stops, staring into my eyes, desire replaced with concern. Undoing the belt tied tight around my waist, I pull the mesh tunic over my head, then the black top beneath, giggling an 'ouch' as my elbow hits the window and my hands bang against the car ceiling. I'm stuck in a tangle of arms and clothes. He's laughing too. The sound fills the small car, sharp and strange. Ignoring what's outside in the darkness, we focus only on each other.

An empowering sense of freedom washes over me, that somehow this small action is defying Skye and her terrifying game. It feels good to take control. And why not? We've nothing to lose. Rhodri kisses my elbow making me shiver. He helps untangle me, teasing my top gently over my head, then my bra. It's his turn. I undo the belt, my impatient fingers struggling with the buckle as he shunts the thick leggings down. We stop, half naked, no longer giggling, our bodies shivering in the dark. My skin's alive with anticipation not prickling with dread. For the first time in forever I'm not scared. I pull him to me. I want to escape, to hide. I want his skin on my skin, his breath on my body, his kisses burning on my lips. I want to forget everything but him.

My hand slips down the side of the seat to the lever I know is there and my chair drops back. Rhodri's on top of me, balancing his weight on his elbow. I pull him to me, enjoying the feeling of his abs against my fingertips. I trace the line of his tattooed sleeve, dropping kisses along the inky patterns. He shudders.

'Kass,' he whispers. 'We don't have to—'

My finger covers his lips. 'I want to.' It's the truth. I've never done this before. I've done bits – *we've* messed around a load – but never sex and I want to. Suddenly it's the right thing to do. If we're going to live this unspeakable nightmare one more time, then I want something to remember. I need to feel something wonderful. And I sure as hell don't want to die a virgin.

'Are you sure?' he says.

I've never been more sure of anything.

'Shit, we can't.' Rhodri sits up so quickly his head hits the car ceiling. 'I don't have anything.' He falls back into his seat. 'Wasn't exactly expecting this to happen tonight.'

I smile a secret smile. Leaning forward to the glove compartment I rummage through Lewis' crap, ignoring the pens and wrappers and rubbish that fall onto the floor until I find his condoms.

Rhodri's face breaks into a smile. 'Bloody love that boy.' He falls back into my arms, kissing down my neck to my chest. My hand slips inside his boxers, his bare skin warm against my palms. His eyes widen in response. His hand cups my breast as his hot kisses move lower. Everything else fades away. It's only us in this tiny car, hitting our arms and legs against the walls, butting heads on the soft ceiling, dodging the gear stick and laughing and kissing and shagging.

And it's perfect.

9

The moon's watching us lazily through the car window. We lie in a happy mess, squeezed onto the seat, entangled in each other's arms. The windows are all fogged up, shutting out the forest and the fear and I stubbornly refuse to let them back in.

Snuggled and safe in the crook of his arm, my hand traces the outline of his latest tattoo – a lightning bolt – in memory, he said, of those we lost and a reminder to live the shit out of life. I shiver as the ghosts of our lost friends dance though my mind. Rhodri grabs my top, mistaking the shiver for cold.

'*Cariad,*' he says.

'What is that?' I groan, reluctant for this moment to end.

'*Cariad?*' He kisses my cheeks. 'It's Welsh.' He kisses my lips. 'For love.'

How is it even possible to feel this happy right now? Rhodri shuffles. Reaching down to the floor, he picks up a Sharpie. Rummaging through the rubbish that fell out of the glove compartment, he finds an old KitKat wrapper. Opening it out and smoothing it down he writes on the inside, the black ink popping against the shiny silver. Finishing, he drops a kiss on it and hands it to me.

I take it in my hands. 'It's in Welsh.'

'It says, *Fy merch Saesneg hynod*. We call the English

Saesneg, so it translates roughly as: My extraordinary English girl.' He turns his face to the window but not before I see him blush. 'It's stupid. I thought you could keep it with you, tuck it into your bra or something, in case I—'

'I love it,' I say before he finishes that sentence. 'And I will.' I giggle looking around the car. 'Just as soon as I find it.'

As I search for my underwear, guilt forces its way back into my head. We need to get back to Lewis. Sensing my mood, Rhodri grabs his clothes. We dress in silence, neither wanting words to bring us back to the now. Folding Rhodri's message into a small tight lump I kiss it and tuck it into my bra.

'At least she won't find it there. No cameras watching right now,' I say.

Rhodri almost chokes. 'I hope not. That would be a completely different kind of show.'

We stop laughing at the same time. 'It's weird there aren't more cameras,' I say. 'No Max, no cameras. It's almost like this isn't—'

'The location?' Rhodri finishes my thought. 'You think she's going to move us?'

'It's possible. She must have realised we'd leave clues behind, bring weapons.' I point to our costumes. 'If I was her, I'd strip us of all our outside gear and take us to somewhere secret, somewhere we can't tell anyone.'

'That's one hell of an operation. You think she has help?'

I shrug. 'Maybe.' It totally makes sense. Leaning into the back I grab the MacDonald's bag and take the pen.

'Kass?'

'I left the coordinates at home. DC Brown will come, I'm sure of it.'

'But we may not be here?' Rhodri sounds confused. 'What is that?'

I look down at my drawing of the symbol of a dragon eating its tail, the badge on all the guard's arms. 'Maybe this means something. We may not be here, but Venitiwa will. We can leave a clue.' I tap my rough drawing. 'Maybe DC Brown can trace this symbol and find us through it.'

'It's a long shot.' Rhodri's hand brushes my arm. 'But he is a detective, not a mind reader. Might be an idea to write a description underneath?'

His eyes are teasing and the smile on his lips is almost convincing as we realise the implications of our theory. If this isn't the location of the game, then we're screwed.

Rhodri's smile cracks. 'Kass, please, I'm begging you. Run, while you still can.'

'And how far do you think I'll get before Skye's new pets hunt me down?'

Pain covers Rhodri's face. I take his gloved hands in mine. 'We're gonna find Max and get out of here,' I say, thankful my voice sounds strong in the dark. 'Wherever here maybe.'

Rhodri starts to argue. 'This is my choice.' I place my

hand over my chest where the wrapper is hidden in my bra, feeling anything but extraordinary.

He kisses me. I wonder whether it will be the last time he does. The sadness in his eyes tells me he's thinking the same. Leaving the car, I place my sketch on the driver's seat with the hastily written description underneath. A desperate plea for help and a small insurance in case our instincts about Skye are proven right.

Hot tears tickle my cheeks as we trudge back in the direction of the camp. It takes every ounce of strength to walk back towards the danger. Rhodri's message is scratchy against my breast, a little piece of magic that we made despite the nightmare. Even Skye can't take that away from us.

'Shit,' Rhodri mumbles, looking up.

A drone hovers in the trees, its small propellers whirring excitedly. We quicken our pace. It follows.

A menacing growl stops us dead. A huge wolf blocks our path. His grey fur is peppered with silver, matted and darkened red with blood. Grey ears stand erect, one ripped, a scar visible over his left eye and jowl. His stance is as aggressive as the sound coming from the bared teeth and exposed gums that drip saliva onto the forest floor. A heavy chain choker hangs around his neck, the fur worn away exposing red raw skin beneath. Ribs poke out from under patchy fur. Rhodri was right, this wolf has been bred with cruelty and fear to create a powerful and terrifying killing machine. The chain's wrapped around a tree, holding him a prisoner as much as us. He lunges towards us in a frenzied fit of barks and growls. The chain stretches taught, holding the creature back with a reassuring clunk. He's only inches from where we stand, so close his breath moves the air in front of my face. He snarls and growls and paws the ground looking at us with half-crazed, ravenous eyes.

A wolf-masked guard prods the beast with an electric baton making him yelp and fall back against the tree, shocking him quiet but no less angry. The chain rattles when the wolf shakes his furry head. We try to put space between us, but more guards block the path behind. We're surrounded.

Rhodri pulls me close, his arm stretched out in a futile attempt to protect me. We turn one way, then the other, searching for an escape. The guards close in, one impenetrable circle of uniformed black. The wolf snarls. A new guard appears with an all-silver mask.

The circle opens to let them through.

'Kass. Rhodri. Welcome to *Blood Moon*. I'm so glad you could make it.' Rhodri's arm tightens around my waist.

It's Skye, hundred per cent. She's made no effort to mask her voice, she wants us to know it's her. I grit my teeth. 'What have you done with Max?'

'Max is safe,' she says. 'For now. You know you really must pay more attention to the rules. There was only one and it was very clear. Stay. In. The. Camp. It's almost as if you want Max to be punished.'

Rhodri lunges at her but is held by two guards. 'I swear to god if you hurt one hair on his head…'

The guards push Rhodri back. He lunges again. They each take out a baton with an efficient click, extending it with a menacing twitch of their hands.

'Stand down, Welsh boy,' Skye chides. 'You're going to have to control that temper if you're going to win.'

Rhodri is poised to attack. The guards stay still, weapons in hand, heads tilted, waiting for instructions. The wolf remains quiet, wild amber eyes burning into us.

Skye speaks again. 'I think it's time to get you into the game. You're going on a little trip.'

I knew it.

Skye's dainty giggle sounds so out of place. 'You didn't think I'd be stupid enough to have the game here? Shame on you, I thought we knew each other better than that.'

'Where are you taking us?' I can't keep the wobble out of my voice.

'You'll know soon enough,' Skye says. 'Everyone else has a much more comfortable ride but we've a special trip planned for you two.'

The guards take a step towards us, their batons raised. I shrink behind Rhodri.

'We can do this the nice way or… Who am I kidding?

You broke the rules. *Duh*. There is no nice way.' She claps her hands.

We're grabbed from behind. Rhodri fights like a wild animal. The batons come down on him over and over, heavy thumps again and again. He falls to his knees. They grab him, keeping him kneeling, holding his arms out straight. A guard appears holding a long needle.

I struggle and scream but the guards hold me firm and the forest swallows my cries. Rhodri thrashes against his captors as they hold him down. His head is yanked back, but still he struggles. An arm squeezes round his neck, forcing him still. One sleeve's pushed up to his elbow revealing his tattoos. The needle is plunged into his arm. He struggles again, gasping for air as they hold him tight. His shoulders slump. The guard releases their grip and he falls forward onto the forest floor.

'Rhodri.' I'm screaming. I can't stop. I kick and bite and shout, but it's no use. A hand is on my chin, forcing it up so I'm looking at the silver mask.

'See you in the game, friend.'

I don't feel the needle slide deep into my arm, just an ice-cold sensation rippling through my veins. My knees buckle beneath me. A whooshing fills my ears, louder and louder. My head's heavy. My chin drops to my chest and I fall to the floor. Damp leaves cling to my cheek. Rhodri's still body lies in front of me. My head is cotton-wool thick. A deep darkness dances in front of my eyes until the forest disappears and the world goes black.

10

I open my eyes to darkness. For a cruel minute I'm transported home to the safety of my bed before the cold seeps through to my bones. My fingers fan out touching hard and smooth. Reality comes rushing back. I'm jolted into awareness as my final thoughts tumble from my head.

Rhodri.

Fear yanks me to my feet. I stop, dizzy in the dark.

The lights snap on. The sharp brightness stings and I cover my eyes with my hand.

I'm in a small room. The floor is bare beneath my boots. It's empty save for the guard standing in the corner. My hands run over my body, searching, checking, feeling their way over the chainmail tunic. Something jogs my foggy memory; my hand paws my bra feeling for the wrapper. It's still there, scratchy against my chest. My heart double beats as Rhodri's words fill my head. Is he okay? As I pat down my legs an involuntary cry escapes my mouth.

There's a space in my boot where my knife used to be.

My eyes sweep the room. I've got nothing; everything and everyone is gone. Something pricks my hip from my trouser pocket. Reaching inside, my hand folds over metal. It feels like a key, but to what?

And who the hell put it in my pocket?

'Where am I?' My dry voice croaks as I demand answers from the guard. 'Where's Rhodri?'

The guard doesn't answer. Something thuds on the floor before me. I pick it up. It's a black hood. The guard gestures for me to put it on.

I'm wrong – it's not a hood but a balaclava. My whole face is covered, the thick wool scratches at my cheeks and tickles my mouth. Only my eyes are free.

Another thud.

I pick up a new pair of black gloves, pulling them over my shaking hands.

The guard opens the door. I shrink back, reluctant to face whatever's out there. Their hand grips the baton resting at their hip. With a deep intake of dizzy breath, I step forward.

A cold wind slaps me around the face, stinging my eyes. I'm thankful for the balaclava's warm protection. The forest's vanished. The canopy of trees has been replaced by a cloudless sky and a busy hum of activity. The moon's still visible, sitting low in the sky. The morning sun is battling for position, making the light a grubby winter dawn. *How long was I out?* A fine drizzle coats my eyelashes as I take in my surroundings.

Large trailers fill my view, the *Blood Moon* logo on the side, the snarling wolf's head staring out at me. My heart sinks, I was right; Skye's moved us during the night to who knows where. The dragon circle is painted in the corner of each truck, teasing me: our last hope of rescue now a badly drawn logo on a MacDonald's bag in an abandoned car in the middle of a forest.

Behind the trucks are buildings. My heart leaps into my mouth. There's a town out there. Every part of me wants to bolt for civilisation. I want to scream and shout, to wake up the oblivious townspeople. It's so close. I can almost reach out and touch freedom.

But I don't.

I daren't.

Max's bruised and frightened face is cemented in my head keeping my feet still and my voice silent. And she has Rhodri and Lewis too. If I try to escape, Skye will hurt them.

With a heavy heart I turn my back on the sleeping town.

Guards and people scatter everywhere, busy as ants. There's a buzz in the air. Black-costumed contestants follow wolf-masked guards in flock formation. A rumble of low conversation dances on the wind. Excited, nervous energy sizzles around us like static electricity.

My eyes search for Rhodri and Lewis but find only an unrecognisable mass. Heads are covered, features disguised by balaclavas. *Shit*. I can't recognise anyone in the mob.

I walk forward, reluctant to follow lemming-like over the cliff, but unable to stop myself. Behind the trucks and the crowd is a scene I could only imagine in a nightmare.

Rising out of the winter morning dew is a castle.

And it's huge.

I'm jostled and pushed along by the crowd, all heading towards the edge of the embankment in front of the towering castle walls.

The medieval turrets sparkle seductively. Ancient grey stone reaches up towards the wakening sun, teasing us with its dark majesty. Icy wind whistles around my face, slapping my cheeks and whispering, *Run Kass…* with its frosty breath, *Run away and hide.*

My brain responds in kind. *You can't do this on your own. You are not brave.*

I shrink back, terrified of the scene in front of me. But the crowd is indifferent to my internal turmoil. Shoulders jar against mine, bodies push me forward and I'm swept along, unable to swim against the rolling tide.

A moat sweeps around the castle like a giant serpent, it's blackened surface rippling as it dares us to cross. The drawbridge is shut tight like a monster's mouth waiting to pounce and swallow us whole. Flaming torches bob and dance along the perimeter walls casting shadows in the morning half-light. The scent of burning wood mixes with the sour perfume of fear-tipped anticipation. We huddle in the cold, faces hidden, eyes flashing, wide eyed and breathtakingly terrified.

Or maybe that's just me.

I can't find my friends. I twist and turn in the sardine cram but we're all identical. And I don't get it. There're too many of us; I count at least fifty heads facing forward, way too many to play. I swallow down panic, the sense of overwhelming danger pinching my skin.

A loud buzzing interrupts the silence. A mechanical swarm of drones rises high above the crowd to hover over the moat, small red lights bouncing playfully in the air. Two guards with cameras strapped to their chests on a kind of mechanical cradle move side to side, recording the mass of bodies waiting on the bank. Squinting, my eyes focus on the top of the gatehouse. Two more guards point cameras down at us. My stomach flips with a familiar sickening sensation. I stick out my chin and stare defiantly back, willing them to sod right off. Indifferent to my solo revolution they stay poised, each small recording light blinking red in the early dawn.

I stand alone, surrounded by a swarm of faceless strangers, listening to my breath as it staggers in and out, slicing at my throat with each icy gasp, waiting for the familiar theme tune to hit my ears while the credits roll and the game starts all over again.

There's movement down the line. A tall figure is making their way along the row, examining each person as they pass. My heart thumps a happy rhythm when our eyes lock. I'd recognise those fierce green eyes anywhere. No one can look at me with such anger and love mixed into one. Rhodri pushes towards me elbowing bodies out the way like skittles. He reaches me and my finger flies to my lips in a *shhh*. Instinctively I know to keep our identities hidden. Isn't that what the stupid balaclavas are for, to prevent us from identifying allies? His eyes mirror my relief. His hand grazes mine and the jolt that rockets through my body is superpowered. The urge to reach out is intense; the need to feel safe, overwhelming. Sensing my anxiety, he turns to face the castle shuffling towards me, so close we're almost touching.

The drones buzz energetically over the water like a swarm of happy bees in a wildflower meadow. The camera guards move up and down the bank. The cameras don't bother me. I stare at them with nothing more than contempt. Who is watching this? And why? It can't be streamed on regular sites; it would be shut down. It's like some archaic game. Only I'm no Roman gladiator and that castle is no Colosseum.

A figure appears on the bank opposite, facing us across the moat. Hands raised for silence – an unnecessary gesture as fear and excitement has stolen every voice.

'Okay, people.' The voice is disguised by the same AI voice as the guards but the way they move and the motion of their hands as they speak is so familiar. And I recognise the silver wolf mask.

Skye.

I can hear her perfectly despite the wind buffeting across my ears. She's mic'd up, obviously. It's strange that we're not.

'We're about to start. Don't worry, we're not going live. This opening sequence is a little complicated so we want to edit out any bad bits.'

That Skye feels the need to use a prerecord or a delay between the live action and the broadcast raises so many red flags. What exactly does she mean by *edit out any bad bits*?

I watch her across the bank. She's dressed in a sharp black suit, silver trim around the lapels and the cuffs. A long metallic cloak flows out behind her, which she's working fully as she moves. The silver wolf mask hides her face. Gloves cover her hands; a tight hood conceals her neck and head so every piece of flesh is hidden.

'We may be prerecording this opening sequence but there will be no do-overs, no reruns,' she says. 'You only have one chance to conquer the trial ahead of you.'

The floodlights snap off, leaving the torch flame and the dawning light to illuminate the castle walls. The *Blood Moon* logo appears on the middle of the drawbridge, the wolf's head staring menacingly down at us. I remember the wolf from the forest, his face a snarling blur in my mind. Was that real or part of some drug-induced dream caused by whatever Skye pumped into my veins? I firmly evict the image from my head, opting for denial over clarity. The number ten appears in bright blood red and starts to countdown.

9

8

7

6

There's a collective hush.

5, 4, 3, 2…

The wolf's mouth opens to reveal a set of sharp white teeth and a salivating pink tongue as it turns towards the sky and howls.

The standing torches flare; long flames shoot into the morning sky signalling the start of the game. The theme tune pumps into the air, recognisable but different, adapted for the new location while staying fully on brand.

Skye's voice booms over the water.

'Welcome to *Blood Moon*.' She's talking directly into the drone buzzing in front of her face. 'I am the Host for this, the most deadly, devious game of murder and deceit ever to be streamed. For those of you who've yet to play' – she opens her arms out – 'where have you been?'

Everyone is facing forward, mesmerised by the Host. I scan the lines searching for Lewis, but it's impossible in the sea of chainmailed costumes and balaclava-covered heads.

The Host, Skye, turns to the bank. 'You have all fought to be here today, either by being the best, paying the most, or by realising that you'd simply die if you stayed away.'

The ripple of laughter from the huddle makes my skin crawl. Who are these people? I can't believe they're finding this funny.

'We're going to play the game a little differently this time. As you know there's a sizable cash prize for the winner, or winners.' The Host pauses. The drones buzz overhead, repositioning lower over the water, facing us. I guess to record our reactions, which is stupid as we're all completely covered up. They hover over the moat like an AI army.

'We've raised the stakes and raised the reward. This season's prize fund will see the Ultimate Champions walking free with a share of TEN MILLION POUNDS.'

A cheer erupts from the crowd but there's no surprise in the applause. These people knew exactly how much they were playing for. A few don't pick up on the wave of enthusiastic clapping. Rhodri's body tenses beside me. I know we're having the same thought. This is the number. When you're asked *that* question: how much would you be willing to put your life at risk for? The answer for most of this crowd is clearly ten million pounds. I want to run up the line screaming at them, to make them listen. This isn't a game; this is literally the amount they could end up dying for.

Again, I don't move, silenced by fear. Is Max imprisoned somewhere inside this formidable castle? He's alive, I'm sure of it. Skye won't hurt him as long as we do as she says. He's her insurance, her guarantee that we'll play the game.

The Host speaks again. 'This series is about survival. Of the fittest, the cleverest, the most devious and the most calculating. This is extreme reality television like you've never seen before. To win, you must survive by any means. Only the most ruthless will make it to the end. You need to ask yourself right now: Do you have what it takes to be the Ultimate Champion?' She pauses as if waiting for contestants to change their minds and leave – they don't. 'The same rule applies – trust no one. Those closest to you are likely to stab you in the back. Within these walls anything goes.'

A shudder runs down my spine as I remember *Lie or Die*.

'But the game of *Blood Moon* has not yet begun.' There's a murmur of confusion from the crowd. 'First, you must prove yourself worthy. This is the North Dam Platform.' She gestures to the wall of stone behind her. 'Only those with the fortitude and strength to scale these walls will win a place in the game.'

Rhodri whistles. 'No way are we getting over them. They must be at least eight metres tall.'

'We have to.' My eyes run up the castle walls. 'For Max.'

'When the wolf howls,' the Host continues, 'you must cross the moat. We have provided you with the materials to scale the wall. But we're not in the game of spoon feeding, there is no health and safety here. The first fourteen to scale the wall and grab a flag will win a place in the game.'

On the top of the walls a row of small blue flags dance on the morning wind. We have to be in that first fourteen if we're gonna get to Max. Not the best swimmer, but not the worst. I could swim it if I was in a swimming pool and I wasn't wearing this pseudo-medieval get up, not to mention that it's January. The moat sparkles anything but invitingly. Some have taken a step back, others push forward eager to get a head start. Arguments break out down the line as contestants push and fight for the first-row advantage. Piles of wood are stacked against the castle walls. Nothing looks long enough to reach the top. Maybe that's it, maybe we have to make a ladder somehow?

And we have to be quick.

I search the huddle of costumes for Lewis. I think about moving down the rows to find him but there's something comforting about being in the middle of the line and the coward in me can't persuade my feet otherwise.

'Lewis,' I loud whisper. Most of the masked heads turn away, ignoring my plea, but someone catches it and throws it down the line. I wait for any sign of my friend.

A flurry of activity behind me makes me turn and a body pushes forward.

'Lewis?' I whisper through the balaclava gag. Is it him? I can't tell. The gangly body takes the place at my side. Gentle, perfectly-lined eyes stare down at me. 'Lewis?' I repeat, hope and relief surfing on that one word.

The eyes blink and the head nods. I exhale panic and breathe in hope. With Rhodri on one side and Lewis on the other my legs cease their uncontrollable wobbling as their strength seeps under my skin.

We can do this.

I face front, staring over the murky water. The Host opens her arms wide. 'There are no rules here, only progress. Those that don't gain flags…' She shrugs. 'Well, that, as they say, will be the end of your journey.'

I'd happily be a loser if it meant I could go home. But Skye's already winning, and I hate it.

'If we don't get over the wall we lose, and if we do…' I stop, silenced by fear.

'Small steps, concentrate on one challenge at a time.' Rhodri nudges me. 'We've got this. Let's show this bitch.'

'When the wolf howls, you go,' the Host says. 'But beware, once the moon bleeds no one is safe, for the blood moon belongs to the Werewolves.'

The wolf's head reappears on the drawbridge staring out at us with a disinterested gaze. I take a deep breath and get ready to run.

'Good luck, contestants.' With a sweep of her arms the Host steps back, disappearing from sight.

The wolf gazes up towards the sky and lets out one almighty howl.

11

The icy cold hits me like a sucker punch, knocking the breath from my lungs. I don't stop, forcing my body forward, fighting as the freezing water tries to swallow me up.

The bank falls away until there's nothing beneath my feet. I fix on Rhodri swimming like a boss ahead of me. The water's winning, the weight of my sodden boots is pulling me down beneath the icy surface and I fight to keep my chin above the water. It's not pretty but it's working. I'm already halfway across.

The air is heavy with the frantic sound of splashing. A panicked swimmer grabs for another pulling him under in his struggle. Heads disappear beneath the black. I force my eyes front and will myself faster refusing to let the bitter cold and Skye Greenhill beat me at the first hurdle.

'Kass,' Rhodri shouts from the bank, his arm beckoning in urgent circles. Surging forward I grab his hand, thankful for his strong grip when he pulls me unceremoniously onto the side. I face plant the mud, trying to calm my staccato breaths.

With an exhausted cry, Lewis flops next to me. I grab his hand, our gloves squelching as our fingers squeeze together. Rhodri's already working on the ladder. His urgent cries force us to our feet. The bank's filling with a dangerous chaos. Shouting replaces splashing as players scream instructions at one another. Tenuous alliances are made, more from necessity than friendship, as we all compete to be the first ones to scale the castle walls and reach the flags.

Wood and rope are strewn across the grassy bank; short ladders lean against the stones. Contestants are tying ladders together and attempting to scale the walls, but they're not tall enough. The ladders buckle and break under their weight. A consistent thudding enters the circus of sound as bodies fall from varying heights. Most get straight back up. Across the bank, the sound of shouting and fighting obliterates the morning quiet.

'Kass!'

My name carries on the wind. I turn in circles trying to find its origin. Nothing.

'Kass!' It sounds like Lewis but he's right here. I look again but there's only a sea of panicked black. I banish the call and concentrate on the task.

Rhodri's fighting for a piece of wood, screaming like a Viking warrior when he tears it from a stranger's hand. I stand frozen in the middle of the madness. It's not working. The ladder's too short. There's not enough time.

Lewis grabs my elbow pulling me along the wall and away from the crowd.

'Forget the ladders, come with me.' He's shouting to be heard, his voice distorted by horror and fear.

'Rhodri,' I shout. He pushes his opponent to the floor, dropping the wood and follows.

Lewis leads us to a less crowded area. The castle wall runs the entire length of the moat, along which four gatehouses stick out onto the embankment, each in varying states of disrepair, all impossibly high.

The fourth tower marks the end.

'This way.' Lewis points towards the line of guards barring the way.

I stop, hesitant. Rhodri almost powers into me.

'Quickly.' Lewis' voice is urgent as he pushes us towards the guards.

Cheers explode behind us when a ladder touches the top of the castle wall. They start to climb but are pulled down by a huge beast of a man. He scales the wall quickly. Reaching the top, he turns, kicking his boot at the contestant behind. They plummet to the ground, dislodging another as they go. The beast of a man scrambles onto the parapet and holds a flag up high, his victory scream slicing through the cold air.

'Come on.' Lewis' voice sounds strange under the balaclava, nerves making it wobble into an unrecognisable whine. We follow him towards the line of guards.

As we get nearer, a space reveals itself behind the long wall defences, hidden from sight. We run towards it. There's a derelict gatehouse hidden on the north corner. Squeezing into the space a tall iron gate blocks our way. Behind it a steep path climbs upwards to the very top of the wall where blue flags wave tantalisingly, mocking us through the iron bars.

A triumphant cry echoes over the ramparts as a second flag is claimed.

Rhodri and Lewis struggle with the gate. It's locked. Rhodri throws himself at the iron bars and tries to pull himself up and over but it's too high. Exhausted, freezing and all out of ideas, I crouch down, burying my head in my cold hands.

Something sharp sticks into my hip.

Delving into my pocket I pull out the key I'd forgotten about in the chaos. It's old, totally the type of key that could open an ancient iron gate. I push it into the keyhole and turn. There's no time to question it as the gate swings open. Lewis pushes ahead, rushing up the steep slope.

'Nice,' Rhodri grunts. We follow, the gate crashing to a close behind us.

The top is a narrow walkway with a low parapet wall either side. The flags are positioned across it. Grabbing the nearest flag Lewis waves it manically.

Contestants swarm the ramparts like cockroaches, fighting for flags. Victors hold their flags high, celebrating and congratulating each other, brutally guarding their prize. I count three unclaimed flags. I run towards them and others do the same. I grab one and hold it tight.

Someone claims another. One flag remains.

Rhodri pushes past me with such force that I have to steady my balance to stop myself falling over the parapet and plunging to the ground below. He dives for the last flag at the exact same time as another. They both fall on the flag. The contestant punches Rhodri hard in the stomach. Gasping, Rhodri tips backwards.

My screams are smothered by the wet balaclava clinging to my mouth but Rhodri manages to right himself. The other contestant pounces on the flag but Rhodri tackles him to the ground, climbing over him he grabs it, holding it high.

The last flag is claimed.

A wolf howls out across the walls.

Trial over.

Rhodri doesn't see the contestant lunge towards him.

'Look out.' My warning scream makes him turn. He sidesteps quickly and the contestant, too committed to the move, lurches towards the wall. Rhodri tries to grab him, but it's too late. Unable to stop, the contestant vanishes over the edge.

Contestants run to the wall, the euphoria of the win quietened by the sight of the lifeless body below.

The wolf howls again.

The contestants still climbing ladders stop. Realising it's over, they climb down. Those who never made it up the wall rush towards the fallen body, screaming for help.

Guards push the crowd out of the way, placing a barrier around him, hiding him from view. Drones fly over the wall, avoiding the scene.

'I didn't... I couldn't...' Rhodri's shoulders rise with ragged breaths. He stands on the castle wall staring down, gripping tightly onto a blue flag.

I squeeze his arm, gently pulling him away from the edge.

Skye's voice bellows over the parapet. 'Congratulations. Fourteen contestants have made it to the next stage of the game. You may now enter the castle.'

The shocked silence is punctuated by a jarring cheer when the beast of a man from earlier bangs his chest in a disturbing show of masculinity. Others follow in full-on celebration, the fallen contestant forgotten.

I didn't even know their name.

12

We're standing in a huge gatehouse, herded like sheep into a pen, a fine mist of steam rising from our moat-soaked costumes. It's dark in here, as though the morning light has been refused entry by the powers that be. I stay near Rhodri, his presence reassuring in the anonymous squash despite the tension pouring from him. Lewis stands quietly beside me, his chest rising rapidly underneath the chainmail tunic.

'I'm piss wet through,' a voice moans next to Rhodri and is met by a chorus of 'shhh'.

'You're not wrong,' says Rhodri. I can tell by his voice that he's scowling right now. 'Fuck this.' He starts to peel off his balaclava.

My hand reaches out to stop him. His eyes flame with anger. 'What they gonna do? Kill me?'

A ripple of nervous giggles erupts from around us. I push my finger to my lips.

Rhodri's eyes crease into a frown. 'You don't need to *shhh* me. No microphones on account of all the pissing water.'

'Guess we'll get them when the game starts,' says the voice beside Rhodri. He's only recognisable by a thick pair of glasses which he's busy trying to dry with a soaking wet glove.

'Don't you get it?' Rhodri snorts. 'Game's already

started; we've been playing since we walked into that forest. There's no going back now.' He stares down at Glasses Guy, waiting for him to reply. He doesn't.

I'm so cold. The wet costume clings to my frozen skin sending chills through my body. I can't feel my fingers. I wiggle them inside my soggy gloves. Lights glare into our eyes and drones buzz above us. I long to reach up and swat them like the flies they are.

Behind us an aged portcullis has been lowered barring our escape, its thick patterned bars more sinister than any prison cell. In front of us, huge arched doors furnished with iron studs are open signalling our path into the castle, blocked by a line of guards.

Behind them lies the castle. Imposing towers stand tall casting long shadows on the narrow castle green. Flagpoles stretch up to the clouds. Large, colourful flags dance on the wind with the *Blood Moon* logo – a wolf's head open mouthed, sharp fangs bared with the blood moon behind, bleeding red against the blue sky.

It can't be long now. Mum and Dad will have found my phone and got help. DC Brown will have reached the forest, I'm sure of it. He'll be looking for us; we just have to hold on. Hiring a landmark like this would surely leave a paper trail. And someone will be posting this on their socials. It's hard to hide a castle and a whole gaggle of OB trucks. That symbol's everywhere and I pray DC Brown and his team fit the pieces of the puzzle together in time.

A trumpet sounds, its shrill call shattering the impatient

silence. The guards march out of the gatehouse back towards the moat behind. That they've left us unattended worries me more than their presence; if they don't need to guard us, there must be no way out. I pull my wet balaclava further down my face hiding as much of me as possible from whoever is watching.

'Contestants, by completing the first trial you have earned entry into this magnificent castle.' Skye's voice booms above me, silencing my noisy thoughts. 'And a place in the most extreme reality show ever to be streamed.'

A nervous cheer ripples through the air. A camera-person sweeps past my row. I stare right into the lens, willing whoever is at the other end to really see me. Okay, so they can only see my eyes, but I concentrate every bit of my energy into my gaze. Let them be under no doubt that I've zero desire to play this game.

'Contestants, the time has come to enter the South Dam Platform. Let the game begin and the blood moon bleed.'

We surge forward. The camera people walk backwards focused on us. Someone pushes into me forcing me faster. We spill out into a grassy area that spans the length of the castle walls, my feet squelching in my sodden boots.

This place is huge. Another moat ripples in front of us as uninviting as the last and as big as a lake. In the middle is an island enclosed by a stone wall, joined to this long grassy bank by a guarded wooden bridge. Beyond the bridge the colossal towers of yet another gatehouse loom above us, studded with arrow loops and murder holes. The very heart of the castle lies within those circular walls, surrounded by more stone battlements cornered by imposing towers. One tower betrays its age, leaning heavily, stone broken away from the wall as gravity takes its toll.

My heart sinks as I realise the impossibility of our task. The castle protects itself with layers within layers of thick impenetrable stone. Max could be hidden anywhere inside that medieval labyrinth of rock. Behind us, the castle walls surround the entire area blocking any means of escape. Walls behind and water in front. We're completely trapped.

To our left is a camp with three bell tents, flags bobbing from their tops – one red, one blue and one green, matching coloured bunting hanging from their doors, cheerful and very medieval. Suddenly our costumes don't seem so out of place. The only difference to the forest tents is that these have completely see-through sides.

In the middle of the camp a huge campfire blazes. Further along the green strip of grass are two wooden structures. They look like giant catapults. Trebuchet, I think they're called, used to hurl shit and burning stuff at the enemy. My heart lodges itself firmly in my throat as my mind flips through all the possible 'games' Skye could make us play with these medieval killing machines. Rhodri nudges me when we walk past a set of wooden stocks set up to entertain a modern-day crowd. Surely not intended for us?

We spill over the green, exploring the area. There's movement above. Guards are spreading out along the top of the ramparts. Camera lights wink from the turrets. The sight of them watching us, like prisoners in a camp, is terrifying. I keep my head down and walk towards the fire.

Groups are forming already, bonds made from working together to get over the wall and into the game. The guy with the glasses has gravitated towards a woman with bright purple hair. They seem pretty tight, huddled together by the fire watching everyone with wary eyes. Stood between Lewis and Rhodri, I cast an inquisitive eye around the others. Most are too busy to take any notice of me, but one contestant on the opposite side of the fire stands out. Tall and gangly, there's something desperately familiar about him.

I look away before he catches me staring, doubt snaking through my veins. Lewis is right next to me, warming his hands by the fire. I turn to the balaclava-covered figure. This is Lewis, *right?*

'I half expected Skye to have *Who's Afraid of Little Old Me?* plastered all over the walls,' I say.

Lewis doesn't react. I try again, keeping my voice light, my spider senses tingling a warning. 'Or *Don't Blame Me?* The girl's delusional after all.'

Lewis nods half-heartedly, not looking up from the fire.

Is that it? Is that all the reaction I'm gonna get? That he doesn't get it, makes warning bells ring. I mean, since when has Lewis ever had no reaction to anything, especially a Swiftism? I study his body language more closely, looking for other 'Lewis' clues in his posture: the way he rubs his hands against the flames and the way his head tilts slightly to the side. He folds his arms as he catches me staring, puffing out his chest in a pseudo-macho move that would totally suit Rhodri but is completely out of place on my best friend.

Did I get it wrong back at the start? My stomach rolls. Did he *actually* say he was Lewis? It all happened so quickly. There was the shouting and the screaming and the whole terrifying swim for our lives. Did I totally misread the signs? Is the person I helped get into the game an imposter? *Shit*, paranoia has set in, big time. Am I only seeing what I want? Is Lewis even here? A thought hits me right in the gut. Maybe he didn't make it over the wall?

The gangly guy's moving around the fire. There's something so familiar in his movement and stance, the way his hands are planted firmly on his tilted hips like he's pissed off.

But if that's Lewis, then who the hell am I standing next to?

13

I step back, all the air expelling from my lungs. Rhodri turns to me, eyes flashing with concern. At least I think it's Rhodri. It sounds like Rhodri but fear is filling my head with doubt and making me question everything. Shouldn't I be able to tell the people I love just by their eyes? Isn't that the basis for a million love stories; when you know you know?

'Rhodri?' I whisper.

'Uh-huh?' Green eyes narrow.

'It's really you?' I whisper.

'Of course it's me! Who you expecting? Timothée fucking Chalamet?'

It's Rhodri, hundred per cent.

I turn to the boy I thought was Lewis.

An ominous rumbling thunders across the sky. Drones gather above. Cameras on the walls turn in our direction. Am I imagining the shake I think I feel beneath my feet?

Everyone's attention is focused on the wall as something huge approaches.

Skye's voice booms over the grassy area. 'Contestants, it is with great excitement that I introduce to you Cohin 2.0, bigger and even better than our series one narrator-bot.'

The rumbling intensifies, small bits of grass and dirt spit into the air.

Skye's on top of the wall, arms raised high like a reality-TV show announcer, loving her role as the Host. 'Using the very latest in holographic technology and state of the art 3D Realtime LED effects, may I introduce our *Blood Moon* narrator – Draigodân.'

Fire spews up from the grassy corners sending bright orange fountains into the air. Giant sparklers erupt between the flames, gold glitter shimmers in the sky as sparkle rain floats down on us. The heat warms my face. An awed hush fills the space when a mighty dragon hologram appears on the wall, its majestic red wings beating slowly as it hovers over the virtual rock that's magically appeared beneath. Its muscled body glistens with red pearlescent scales that glimmer in the January sun like precious jewels. Its scaly legs bend when it sits upon the rock. Taloned claws spread out holding the beast firmly in place. Strong muscles hold up beautifully opaque, bat-like wings as he fills the entire wall with his majesty.

The holographic dragon puffs out its armoured chest and lifts its head, stretching up to the top of the castle wall. It's terrifying and beautiful. Huge jaws bare to show hundreds of shark-sharp teeth. Nostrils flare as it takes in its surroundings through beady blood-red eyes, its face a mixture of scales and spikes which extend from head to neck to make a Jurassic-type mane. A tail sways behind, the arrow-pointed tip sharp and virtually deadly.

He's magnificent.

'Draigodân, welcome to *Blood Moon*,' Skye says.

Draigodân bows low in one graceful move. 'I am honoured to be here.' His voice is deep and melodic.

The Host bows back, holding the position for a moment before straightening and turning to us. 'Remember, there's only one rule in this game: trust no one.'

She disappears in a flourish of smoke, and we're left with the virtual dragon.

Draigodân turns to us, eyes gleaming. The crowd gasps as his entire head and neck appear to come right off the castle wall and into the air between us stopping only feet away from Glasses Guy, who takes a hurried step back.

'Fuck me.' Rhodri's breathless voice is at my shoulder. I say nothing – that kinda said it all. I check myself. This 'thing' may look magnificent, but I've no doubt that Draigodân will be as deadly as his predecessor.

It's not real. I repeat to myself over and over. It may look and sound stupidly real but it's a hologram just like Cohin was, some kind of state-of-the-art 3D hologram. *Cohin* – the thought of the narrator-bot from season one makes my skin crawl and my flight response kick in. Real or not, he still haunts my sleep and turns my dreams into nightmares.

'I am Draigodân. I am your guide and narrator throughout your journey into this resplendent castle.' His nostrils flare. There must be speakers on the back wall because I can *hear* his mighty breath and the force of his wings appear to shake the air around him.

He straightens, towering so high we have to crane our necks to look at him.

'Your game starts here on the South Dam Platform. To win you must gain entry into each part of the castle by completing a series of trials over the next four days and three nights.' His virtual gaze peruses the crowd. 'First a bit of housekeeping. Contestants are required to wear microphones during active hours. Microphones should be removed for sleeping and placed on the chargers by the side of the beds in each camp. Failure to wear your microphone while awake will constitute a rule break. Any attempt to hinder or cover cameras or drones will not be tolerated, and any interference will be considered a rule break.'

An involuntary shiver fills my bones, his meaning crystal clear.

Draigodân continues. 'It's time to discover who will be innocent Peasants and who will become deadly Werewolves.' His voice is surprisingly calming, maybe it's just me but the whole dragon thing is very cool. I almost forget where I am – almost. 'But first, contestants, you may remove your balaclavas and throw them in the fire.'

We all rip off the material that clings to our skin, shaking our hair and rubbing our cold faces with our gloved hands. I throw the soaked mask into the fire where it hisses for an instant, refusing to burn. I immediately turn to the boy by my side. The high-pitched shriek that leaves my lips surprises me as much as him. 'I knew it.'

It's not Lewis. He's tall and gangly just like my friend but that's where the resemblance ends.

'Who the hell are you?' I squeak.

He raises his hands in a surrender pose. 'Now wait, I never said, I never...' he stammers. 'You just assumed. I went along with it. You've played before.'

'How did you know who I was?' I say.

'You called me Lewis?' he says. 'On the bank. Everyone saw you two together back at the bonfire. Didn't take a genius to work it out. Figured it was a good way to get in. There's no harm in that.'

'A good way to get in?' I repeat like some zombie parrot. 'Why?'

Now he's looking at me as if I'm the one whose missing brain cells. He speaks slowly. 'Ten million pounds?'

All the fear I've tried so hard to bury is projected directly at this intruder. 'Idiot,' I spit. 'Do you have any idea how dangerous this game is? You know your chances of making it out of here are probably one in ten million?'

'You don't know that.' He shuffles awkwardly. 'And you don't know me. There're fourteen of us and more than one can win. That's pretty good odds. The winners get to walk out mega rich. When else am I gonna get this chance?'

'Are you for real?' I can't help the scorn that layers my words. 'You're totally gambling with your life.'

'I'm taking a chance.' He turns away. 'That's my choice. Besides I don't believe everything I see on social media. All that stuff about murder?' he says, raising his chin to look me straight in the eye. 'Why would you even be here if it was true. If it was so dangerous, why play again? Desperate for another hit of fame?'

'What's that supposed to mean?' Heat is rising in my cheeks.

The hand on my arm grips me tight. 'Steady,' Rhodri says. 'No harm done. Now is not the time for making enemies.'

I scowl. This cuckoo can sod right off out of my nest. Werewolf or not, he's definitely on my radar.

Lewis taps me on the shoulder. I literally jump into his arms, bear-hugging him tight as the imposter slinks into the crowd.

'Eww, you're all soggy.' He peels me off him, holding me at arm's length, checking me for damage.

I beam at him, Fake Lewis forgotten in a heartbeat. 'Why didn't you look for me,' I say punching him on the arm.

'He-llo, needle in a haystack,' he says, his tone a little colder than usual. 'And ow, you didn't exactly send out a search party for me either.' Before I can explain, a boy slides up to him. 'This is Billy. We came over the wall together.'

'Talk about a meet-cute,' Billy says.

'Totally,' Lewis says. Something tells me that the flush in his cheeks is not just from the cold. The way Billy's beaming back, the feeling's mutual. Lewis tilts his head to one side. 'Although technically we met back in forest camp.'

'Oh yeah,' Billy says as they giggle conspiratorially.

'We... We thought you were with us,' I stammer.

Lewis waves a dismissive hand. 'It's fine. Billy and I made a pact to stick together no matter what.'

Is that a dig? There's an ever so slight edge to his words like he's cross with me. And what the actual? He's known Billy for less than a day and they're besties?

'Alri?' Rhodri says to Billy. Billy smiles back. He's the opposite of Lewis, smaller and stockier. Messy straw-coloured hair flops over slate-grey eyes, high cheekbones sit on his very cute face.

'Why are you here, Billy?' I can't help myself. I just don't get why anyone would choose to play this game and I'm desperate for a better answer than Fake Lewis gave.

'Didn't have anything else to do,' he says, grinning.

'I'm serious,' I say, ignoring the dark look on Lewis' face. 'This is dangerous and stupid and you could get hurt. Or worse. There are plenty of other games you could go on if you wanted fame and fortune.'

'I don't care about fame,' Billy says.

'So it's the money then?' I say, barely concealing the scorn. 'What could you possibly need it for so badly that you would risk your life?'

Billy stands his ground, his shoulders tense as his face takes on a haunted expression.

'You don't have to answer that,' Lewis says leaning in and catching his elbow, a subtle move that I wasn't prepared for. 'It's none of her business.'

Nice. Lewis' reaction knocks the air out of me. I'm not prepared for the hostile look he's now giving me. I pull a *what?* face. He only frowns more.

'Reckon it's all our business if people start dying,' Rhodri says impatiently. 'You think you can beat this, beat Skye? You're having a bloody laugh. If I was you, I'd get out now.'

Billy stares right at Rhodri. 'But you're not me. You've no idea. So keep your opinions to yourself and stop with the judging. We all have our reasons. What's yours?' He holds Rhodri's gaze until Rhodri looks away but not before I catch the pain that flashes across his face. Billy's definitely hit a nerve and I'm not convinced it's just Max. Rhodri's hiding something. I note that Lewis' hand is still curled comfortably around Billy's elbow.

Draigodân speaks. 'Marcus, please go to the Outer Main Gatehouse.'

Everyone looks around. Fake Lewis steps out, saluting me cheekily, making my anger bubble all over again.

Draigodân nods in the direction of the huge gatehouse we started in, his mane of spikes rippling. Marcus jogs in that direction, disappearing through a small dark doorway.

Draigodân calls another name.

'Artemis?' I snort. 'Is that even a name?' A huge hulk of a body steps forward, bedraggled hair dangles like seaweed to his shoulders reminding me of a rain-soaked Hercules.

'Rhodri, please go to the Outer Main Gatehouse.'

There's a sudden space by my side when Rhodri follows the others across the green, disappearing through the dark doorway. I ignore the panic stampeding through my veins. *Get a bloody grip*, my inner Amazon warrior snarls. *You don't need him or any boy to protect you.*

Draigodân calls another name, his voice like softly rumbling thunder.

'Ravi.'

The old guy, Amara's dad, obediently follows Artemis and Rhodri. I risk a small smile as he passes, glad to see he made it over the wall. Demi and Mai are here too, hunkered by the fire, heads together deep in conversation. My emotions are confusing the hell out of me right now. I'm glad to see familiar faces but terrified for each and every one of them. They're all putting their lives in danger out of some crazy sense of revenge and duty and it doesn't sit right with me. Is this what Amara or Cali or Tayo would have wanted: revenge at all costs? I really, really doubt it.

One by one contestants are called and they trudge towards the Outer Main Gatehouse. As we mill around waiting, the rock under Draigodân turns into a huge screen which he perches majestically on top of.

Meet the *Blood Moon* Contestants

The words appear on the screen with the *Lie or Die* theme tune pumping into the area.

Name – Artemis, aka Arti

The name appears first followed by the head and shoulders of the hulking giant who just disappeared into the gatehouse. His back's turned to camera spinning slowly round to reveal his face. Statistics appear by the side while he stares confidently into the camera.

Age – 19
Occupation – Computer Analyst Student
Hobbies – Body Building

The image speaks: *'I'm not looking to be a hero. I'm here to win and I won't stop until I do. Money first, hero later. It's amazing how generous you can be when you're not skint.'*

A nervous giggle erupts from my lips. He looks nothing like a nerdy computer analyst. The orange hue of his obviously fake-tanned skin gleams against the bright green of his top. With the hair and the tight, tight vest and the air of confidence worn like a halo, I'm seeing Saturday night *Gladiators*. I can almost smell the Lycra.

'Shit, his neck is the size of my thigh. And those arms?' Lewis pulls a face. 'Popping veins give me the ick.'

'Now that's a Titan,' Billy says nudging Lewis. 'But there's only one sun god in this castle.'

'Too right.' Lewis flicks his hair dramatically. 'There's more to a god than huge pecs.'

I smile despite being a little on the back foot from

their banter. They like each other, that's obvious, but the vibe I'm getting is way strong. How have they bonded so much in such a short space of time? Something's scurrying across my skin which I refuse to acknowledge as jealousy.

A new caption appears under Artemis' pic.

Gamer and 2 x TEMO UK
Body Building Champion

I lean into Lewis. 'This guy is huge *and* a champion *and* a gamer. We've got no chance. There's more testosterone in him than the rest of us put together.'

Lewis shrugs. 'He may have muscles bigger than a demi-god but he's a meat head. This game isn't about strength. And he may be a gamer but he's no Max. Relax, we got this.'

I wish I shared his optimism. Artemis is a million miles away from the self-confessed Werewolf geek we're here to save. Another contestant flashes up on the screen.

Name – Marcus

Up on the wall, Marcus aka Fake Lewis looks nothing like real Lewis. That I could ever get them mixed up seems ridiculous. If Lewis is spring, then Marcus is winter. Long platinum hair hangs over his perfectly lined eyes, hiding a steely ice-blue stare. Sharp cheekbones ping out from the thin, super-pale face. He's pretty, rather than handsome, full cherry-red lips pouting a little tartly towards the camera suggest that Marcus is more cunning and resourceful than he looks.

His statistics read:

Age – 18
Occupation – Sixth Form Student
Hobbies – Clubbing, Dancing and Werewolf

Marcus speaks: 'Carpe diem, *seize the day. I'm not waiting for the game to come to me. I'm taking the game on, headfirst.*' He talks to someone off camera. *'Did that sound lame? It did, didn't it? Can I go again?'* He turns back, angling himself, full pout straight to camera, hand posed on chest. *'Look, inflation's a bitch right now and this boy has needs. I'm ready to cash in.'*

I humph at his peacocking; it's so obviously a play. The boy's deluded if he thinks he has a fair chance of winning. If Skye's in charge nothing in this game will be fair.

A flash of yellow in the crowd catches my attention. Mai. She's wearing the same as the rest of us but has tucked the heavy chainmail tunic into the belt which hangs loosely around her waist, managing to layer the top and the tunic into a stylish-looking outfit. Her tight leggings are rolled up to make the most of the military-style boots. Even in the identical black she stands out.

Draigodân continues to call names out. I keep one eye on the doorway that swallowed up Rhodri.

Demi jogs over. Mai follows.

'You made it,' he says with genuine relief.

Mai claps her arms around her chest, warming herself. 'And Ravi too. We all made it over.'

'Love your look,' Billy says to Mai.

'Loud and proud, that's me,' she says. 'And I don't conform for no one.'

'You look like a ninja warrior,' Billy says, a friendly grin stapled onto his face.

Mai turns on him. 'I must be a ninja is that what you're saying?'

Billy stutters an apology. 'No, no.'

'Cause fyi ninjas are Japanese, and I'm half gen Chinese.'

'No... I didn't mean... I... So sorry.'

'Use your words, Billy.' She's totally intimidating him. Her eyes shine as brightly as the lightning bolts painted above them. 'Chill, I'm messing with you. I'm small. I overcompensate by being mouthy. All good.'

Billy crumples in relief. Mai may be small, but she's fierce.

'Lewis, please go to the Outer Main Gatehouse,' Draigodân interrupts.

Lewis' face drains of colour. 'Here we go,' he says. 'Be nice to Billy.' He stops me with a look. 'For me?'

I nod sulkily, resenting his new friend getting in our way.

'Love you.' His voice wobbles.

'Love you more.' I put Billy firmly to the back of my mind and squeeze his hands in mine. 'You've got this.'

'Totally.' He takes a deep breath. 'I don't do dogs. Or wolves. Let's hope she got the memo.' With a defiant salute he spins on his heel and sashays all the way to the gatehouse. Spinning one more time, he blows a kiss into the camera before disappearing into the dark.

Noisy thoughts whip around my head as sharp as the icy breeze. I hadn't thought about Lewis in the game. How will he cope if he's given Werewolf status? Can he lie? And if he does, will he lie to me like Thea did? I kick myself for not coming up with some kind of game strategy. I should have planned more. I should have prepared him.

Rhodri appears carrying a wooden chest under his arm. There's a subtle difference in his step as he walks across the green. He looks older, like the minutes spent in that dark tower have aged him. Is he a Werewolf? Am I reading the weight of the game as it sits firmly upon his shoulders? Skye would be that scheming, to pit one of us against the other for some cheap thrill.

Draigodân calls my name.

Rhodri smiles as we pass but his face gives nothing away. I hurry to the door. Inside there are two more doors. A guard opens one and directs me inside. The door slams behind me, making me jump. Rhodri was right, the game has definitely begun.

14

The room is dark. There are no windows. The only light is from torches attached to the walls and a bright wash of yellow from a hot head in the corner. A scaffold bar hangs from the ceiling, a camera hanging down from the middle along with a pencil-thin stick microphone. I walk to a white X marked on the floor. In front there's a large camera draped in black cloth. As I approach it moves, adjusting its height to mine. A figure appears from behind the drape, uniformed and masked just like all the others.

I stare into the wolf mask as they place a cable loop around my neck. The small lapel mic hangs loosely between my boobs. I raise my arms so they can attach the battery pack around my waist where it sits snug in the hollow of my back, cold and hard and terrifyingly familiar. They bend to check the pack.

'Help us. Please,' I whisper.

They don't react, clipping the battery pack into the mic cable with an efficient click. They return to the camera, pulling the drape over them. Anger simmers beneath my fear.

In the middle of the room is a large rock-like formation with three holes carved into the stone one above the other, dark and uninviting. It's creeping me out.

'Hello, Kass.' Skye's voice fills the room. 'How are you?'

She's not even trying to hide. I recognise the sweet smugness. I don't answer, staring at my feet in one small act of defiance.

'Kass?'

I lift my eyes and glare down the lens. 'Where's Max, Skye?'

The red recording lights flick off in unison. Whatever she has to say she doesn't want the world to hear. The pause that follows is epic.

'Where is he?' I shout into the lens.

'He's deep inside the castle. Play the game and you'll reach him.' I can hear the smile on Skye's lips. 'You see, last time you were fighting to get out. In this game you fight to get in. It's brilliant don't you think?'

I ignore her laughter but it's like picking at a scab; we both know it's only a question of time before I bleed.

'It's like the knights of old besieging the castle to rescue their precious princess from the clutches of the evil dragon. It's perfect. And you're the knights in shining armour, Kass; you and your little posse of miscreants and sad little Swifties.'

'Why are you doing this?' I snarl into the camera.

'Oh, come on, Kass. It's fun! These people are hardcore. They'll do anything for money, even the threat of danger and possible harm doesn't hinder them. Everyone has a price that they're willing to risk everything for; you just have to find it. Don't you think that's fascinating?'

'You gave us no choice,' I say, my jaw clenched in anger.

'I'm not talking about you. Of course *you* needed an incentive. You're so good and Girl Next Door that money and fame doesn't interest you. But friendship does, and love.' She pauses. 'But you're a cheat.'

What?

'I watched the footage back, all your clever little actions. Fake. You got everything wrong. You tell the world you beat me, but you're wrong. You and your stupid friends broke the rules. You cheated. No one beat me. You didn't win.'

Her words hit upon the survivor's guilt that's been lodged in my gut since the first show. 'Nobody won, Skye.'

'I was there, remember? I saw everything. At least Thea had the balls to speak her truth. Unlike you with all your' – she mimics my voice – *'I'm the Girl Next Door and I'm so sweet and I can read minds. It's my superpower.'*

I squeeze my hands over my ears. 'Get out of my head.'

'You think you can cheat me and get away with it? You and that Welsh boy with a chip on his tattooed shoulder.' She laughs. 'I want the world to know how fake you are. Play the game, lie or die – I don't care which. Rescue your friends if you can but you'll never outsmart me.'

'Please don't do this,' I say.

'*Blood Moon* is taking reality TV to the next level,' she says. 'And it's going to be a wild ride.'

'This is between me and you.' I know I can't reason with her but that doesn't stop me trying. 'Let Max go.'

Silence. Has Skye got bored and left me here to rot in this dungeon?

'Kass.' The voice returns, as stony cold as the walls around me. 'Our audience is expecting TV-friendly contestants and has paid a fortune to watch you. They will not be disappointed.'

'I don't have to play,' I say. 'I could get voted out first round.'

'Any failure or reluctance to play the game will be seen as insubordination and will be punished.'

I square my shoulders and stare straight down the lens. 'Do your worst, Skye. I don't care. You forced me here with your threats, but you can't make me play.'

The room falls into an expectant silence. My heart thumps against my chest.

A wolf-masked guard appears in front of me and places a small box on the rock.

They hold up a tablet and tap it. The screen bursts to life.

It takes a minute for my eyes to connect with my brain. A figure is slouched in a chair, head down, hair hiding their face. A sign hangs around their neck with *Blood Moon* in black letters and a snarling wolf's head. Just like Max.

Only it's not Max.

The hairs on my skin rise in warning way before my brain recognises the face.

'Thea.' My desperate cry fills the room.

Thea's head jolts up, her face streaked with tears, make-up smudged, her eyes terrified and disorientated.

'Kass, help me.' She screams into the camera, her words obscured by jagged sobs. 'Play the game. It's the only way.'

'Thea?' My brain is whirring so fast it's making me dizzy. Questions thump at my temples. Skye has Thea? How is this possible? She was safe. There's no way.

My eyes flash from tablet to camera, refusing to believe what my mind is telling me.

'It's not true. This is some kind of deepfake trick,' I spit down the camera, anger flaming my denial.

'Open the box, Kass.' Skye's voice is calm.

I reach for the box. Clicking it open, I look inside. It's a silver ring, a Celtic weave that I recognise immediately.

My fingers shake as I turn it in my palm, fear coursing through my veins as I read the words I already know are on the inside.

'Please read out the inscription.' Skye's voice is cold and cruel.

'*Strong*—'

'Louder,' Skye interrupts.

I raise my shaking voice. '*Strong like steel.*' It's Thea's, hundred per cent. I have one the same and so does Lewis, only our inscriptions are a little different, all three make up our childhood saying. There's no way Skye would know this. We had them made after the first show. I stare into the camera with a heart full of loathing. 'If you hurt her—'

'Whether Thea gets hurt is up to you,' Skye says matter-of-factly. 'For every act of rebellion or failure to commit fully to the gameplay, your friend Thea will lose a digit. We will start with her fingers and then move onto her toes.'

'Skye, no…' My hatred turns to panic. 'Please… How could you?'

'Help me.' Thea's voice fills the room. 'Kass, please.'

'Thea?' I shout.

Thea's scream is ear-shatteringly painful.

'I want to make sure you're getting it, so I'll be clear.' There's a dangerous edge to Skye's words. 'Play the game or Max and Thea get hurt. Refuse and they die. Try to run and Rhodri and Lewis will join them. Do we understand one another?'

I nod at the camera, willing the tears to stop.

'Excellent.' Skye's voice returns to eerily cheerful. Like nails on a chalkboard, every word scrapes against my skin. 'Now, happy face please. As long as you play the game, Thea will be safe. You win; she wins. You lose… Well, let's not focus on the negatives. Now wipe your eyes and smile.'

I do as Skye demands. The recording lights snap back on.

'Welcome to *Blood Moon*, Kass. As one of the winners of *Lie or Die* we're so excited to have you here.'

Since when did not dying become the benchmark of a winner?

'Please remove your gloves.'

I do as I'm told.

'For this task the audience have been voting to give you a reward. All you have to do to gain this reward is put your hand inside the bottom hole and take out the token.'

I kneel in front of the rock, my hand hovering over the lowest hole, while I imagine the horrors inside. Ignoring every instinct I have, I hold my breath and plunge my hand in.

The hole devours my arm up to my elbow. My fingers touch something cold and I jerk away. I push my clenched fist back down into the writhing sea. *Think of Thea, just think of Thea.* I force my fist open. Small, slime-filled bodies coil around my fingers, squirming against my bare skin.

Slugs. My arm is elbow deep in my biggest fear. My fingers move quickly, pushing the heaving bodies aside. The taste of bile burns at my throat. I can't feel anything but slugs. I dig deeper.

My fingers hit something hard. Gripping it tight I pull out my arm shaking wildly to dislodge the greasy bodies, trying to keep the disgust from my face as the camera records every detail.

'Place the token on top of the rock.'

The dragon-shaped token slots into the space on top of the rock.

'Now for the second task. You have one minute to retrieve the token from the middle hole. If you successfully complete this task you will be rewarded with a game advantage.'

I can do this. Nothing can be worse than the slugs. The loud ticking of a clock fills the room, making the hairs on my neck stand to attention. I'm catapulted into that TV studio with a ticking time bomb counting down and no time to save my friend. I freeze, paralysed with fear, my mind and body refusing to comply.

'Your time has started.' Skye's voice oozes glee. I can't move.

And the clock counts down.

And my best friend Thea died.

I force my racing thoughts quiet. No, she didn't die. She didn't die. She's here and she needs my help. I need to get it together.

The ticking rolls around the stone wall like a marble, clear and sharp, slicing through my memory like a hot blade.

Somewhere deep inside my anger takes control. *Skye's winning. Move your damn hand or Thea will lose hers.*

It takes all my concentration to override the stop signal triggered in my mind and move my hand into the hole. I don't react to the ants that scatter up my arm, angry at being disturbed. They bite, sending hundreds of razor-sharp pinpricks across my skin but I hardly feel them. The ticking of the clock thunders in my ears. My fingers find the token. I tug it, but it doesn't move. I've watched enough of these shows to know what to do so I twist it, clockwise, and it moves.

The token falls from my fingers.

The ticking stops.

'Time's up,' Skye says. 'You have failed.'

Suddenly aware of the relentless stinging of the ants I pull my arm out, brushing them off. Skye did that on purpose. She knew that sound would trigger me.

'The last task will determine your status.' The camera repositions. 'Place your arm in the top hole. If you are bitten, you have received the mark of the Werewolf. If you feel nothing, you are a Peasant.'

The torch lights flicker dramatically. Something tells me that this will be more than an ant bite.

I plunge my arm into the hole.

'Bite me,' I spit into the camera.

Nothing. I wait until my lungs burn and burst.

'You may remove your hand and put your gloves back on,' Skye says.

My hand remains free of any Werewolf mark.

'You have undertaken three tasks. The first was to retrieve a token from the bottom level. You were successful. Therefore, you have won a reward voted for by the audience.

Unless it's a free ticket out of here, I hardly think I'm gonna love it.

'For the second task you were unsuccessful in retrieving the token in the allotted time. You failed to win a game advantage. The final task determined your game status. I can confirm that you are an innocent

Peasant.' The room falls quiet. 'You may take the chest and return to camp.'

There's a wooden chest in the corner of the room. It's heavy. The need to get out of the stifling room and away from Skye is as overwhelming as the crushing sense of despair.

'Kass?' Skye stops me at the door. 'Let's leave our conversation to ourselves, shall we? No need to upset your friends.' I open my mouth, but she interrupts. 'Don't worry, they have their own personal incentives to play their very best game.'

I turn to leave. She has us exactly where she wants us. I've no choice. I have to play; she's made it crystal clear. I can only pray that it's enough to get us all out alive.

Heading back across the green I stop to calm my erratic breathing. The image on the castle wall is me, taken from the Portakabin in the forest. I look defiant – only those that know me would recognise the terror behind my eyes. My statistics appear:

Name – Kass
Age – 17
Occupation – Sixth Form Student
Hobbies – Social Deduction Games,
'Lie or Die' Winner 2024

I'm here to make amends. I didn't win the first game fairly. I'm here to win on my own merits and prove I'm the ultimate Lie or Die *champion.'*

The words they forced into my mouth make total sense now. Skye must be loving this. And I hate her even more.

As I head towards Rhodri and Lewis my path is barred by two equally bouncy girls.

'Oh. My. God. It *is* her,' one says to the other.

'Told you.' The other claps her hands. 'It is you, isn't it?'

Not sure how to answer such a stupid question. 'I guess?'

They scream in unison, jumping up and down, arms clapping, hair bobbing, grinning in delight, their icy-white veneers dazzling in the sunlight. It's more like they've bumped into their favourite artist at a festival, not standing in hell's own game.

'Oh my god, oh my god,' the one squeals, she's talking to me but looking over my shoulder at the drone hovering behind us.

'Sorry,' says the other. 'It's just we love you so much. What you did in *Lie or Die*...' Jazz hands flutter around her face.

I smile and try to pass. They're about my age. Dark hair immaculately frames their faces and their cute noses wrinkle in laughter. My eyes move from one to the other. They're exactly alike, identical in every way. Except their hair, one has thick long locks that fall gracefully down her back while the other is sporting a shoulder-length bob. 'Are you…?'

'Twins,' they say, and the excited bouncing starts again, more for the camera than for me, I'm sure. They're way too over the top for my limited patience. The costume looks different on them. The unflattering tunic is tapered in at the waist, like it's been fitted perfectly to their figures. And they're squeaky clean. I'm carrying half the moat on my mud-caked boots and costume. Their hair and make-up is flawless. How the hell did they get over the wall and remain so Barbie-doll perfect?

The twin with the bob taps her chest. 'I'm Portia. I'm the eldest.'

The second twin elbows her in the ribs. 'By fourteen minutes. I'm Ophelia. We're playing as one,' she adds as though I asked a question. I frown, these girls are annoying, but harmless. She smiles a honey-sweet smile and flips her hair from her shoulder. 'We cut our hair so you could tell us apart.' They look at each other then back to me. 'You're welcome.'

'I wish I had my phone. The *todiefor* group would just love this,' Portia says.

'You have a *todiefor* group?' I say trying to keep the mocking tone to a minimum.

'U-huh, big fans,' Ophelia says her arms outstretched. 'HUGE. I can't believe they voted for you as *one of the most deceitful*.' She places her hand over her heart. 'I would never.'

'Thanks.' Not knowing what else to do I chew my lip.

They giggle in unison; it's massively irritating. I walk backwards towards camp, faux giggling and nodding as the twins fangirl me the whole way to the fire.

15

'I see you've met the Shakespeare Sisters.' Rhodri takes my reward chest and places it by the fire.

'Nice name,' I say. He's studying my face, checking for any tale-tale signs of freakage. I force a casual smile as Skye's warning thunders in my ears and silences my voice.

'Lewis named them,' he says.

'Lewis did what?' Lewis strides over. Billy follows. My mood worsens as I realise that Billy's shoehorned himself into our trio and doesn't appear to be leaving any time soon. I get that Lewis has found someone to cling onto for dear life; I'm on the same page. I'd just expected that person to be me.

'Shakespeare Sisters,' I say, 'Funny. Good job they have different hair, or I'd have no clue.'

'Portia's more of a game player,' Billy says. 'The one with the short hair. She's the one to watch.'

I bite back a snarky comment and smile through gritted teeth. Like I asked him anyway. Both Rhodri and Lewis are watching me with concern. I wonder what sick blackmail Skye used on them, swearing them to secrecy too. Needing to divert, I wave a finger at Lewis' smudge-free eyes. 'How the hell did you manage to find a mirror in here?'

'Billy helped,' he says.

Course he did. I have to admit Lewis is surprisingly

calm given the circumstances and I've a hunch a lot of that is to do with his new friend.

'Open the box,' Rhodri says, noticing me shiver. After the harsh bitchiness of Skye, his gentle Welsh lilt is beyond reassuring. I unbuckle the latch. The chest is full of dry clothes – the same black costume – and a sleeping bag. I look for somewhere to change.

'Come with me,' Rhodri says.

I pull Lewis towards me. 'Be careful.' My eyes default to Billy. 'Trust no one.'

He nods and I ignore the frown that creases his brow as I walk away.

Rhodri leads me past the trebuchets to a ruined gatehouse at the very end of the green. Either side of a battered arched opening are two rooms. The right is barred with a tall iron gate. We step down into the left room. It's dark and damp and in the middle stands a Portakabin, hidden from the cameras. Inside, the Portakabin is small, just a sink and a loo but it gives a minimum amount of privacy. We check for cameras. Nothing. With no drones following us we're clear.

I'm suddenly shy which is ridiculous considering what we did in the woods. Thankfully, Rhodri gets the message without the need for actual words, a glimmer of amusement dancing in his eyes before he turns his back to me. I change. Smothering the small microphone within the folds of the chainmail top, I quickly fill him in on Skye's twisted justification of her actions, trying to keep the angry tears firmly on the inside and the details to a minimum, her warning still ringing in my ears. Even with his back turned, his frustration is palpable. As I finish dressing, he turns and takes my arms.

'You are not to blame for any of it, understand? That bitch is gaga.'

It's the first time we've been alone since the car and I long to pull him closer. But something about his body language stops me moving further into his embrace. He feels a million miles away. The tears I've tried so hard to hold back explode down my cheeks. He gently brushes them away.

'She's going to pay for everything.' The cold edge to his words terrifies me.

'Don't,' I beg. I press my hand to his chest, my palm covering his mic. 'Please. We need to play the game. I need you to play the game.'

His body tenses even more. 'Oh, I'll play her twisted game. Promise.'

'Just until we find Max and...' I quickly swallow down Thea's name before I get us both in trouble. 'Help will come.' I can't hold the sob in any longer. 'It's like Fort Knox in here and he could be anywhere. He could be de—'

'Don't say it.' Rhodri's hands squeeze my shoulders

tight. 'Not gonna happen. We need to keep our heads. For Max's sake. We need to stay strong.'

He stares expectantly into my eyes, waiting for a word of encouragement, a glimmer of strength, a plan, just like last time, but I'm not that girl anymore. Post TV-show me is nothing more than a blubbering mess. Right on cue my bottom lip begins to tremble.

I take a breath. 'They must be keeping him in that main bit on the island. There's only one way in across the bridge and that's guarded.'

He nods. 'The only way in is through the game.'

I blink quickly to stop the tears from falling.

'*Cari...*' He stops, swallowing the endearment in a hurried gulp. He drops my arms. 'We should go back,' he says, struggling with the door in his sudden need to get away from me.

The question bursts from my mouth. 'Are you a Werewolf?'

He pauses for the longest time. 'I'm a Peasant.'

'Me too,' I say unable to hide my relief.

Awkwardness fills the silence. I know he's not telling me everything and it's making me nervous. How can I trust him when he's just promised to play the game? Memories of another game and another promise come flooding back. 'You're really not a Werewolf?'

'I would never lie to you, Kass.'

I don't miss the huge dollop of hurt in his voice or the disappointment in his eyes. Game or not I should trust him, but we haven't talked since the car, and everything feels different since we…

'We need to go.' Pulling open the door he disappears. Rhodri's not good at hiding his emotions. He's way more insecure than he shows behind his tough-boy crap. Something's different; is it me or just my paranoia? He's mentioned nothing about his time in the task room. Time he spent alone with Skye. Who knows what hell she's putting him through. All I'm getting from him are guilt and anger, both coming off him in one tsunami-style wave.

And I have no idea why.

I dump my wet clothes in a heap outside the Portakabin and head back to camp. Rhodri's talking to Demi. He looks over as I approach but doesn't smile. I leave it, but his abrupt change of mood worries me. Is it game related or did I do something to piss him off?

'Gloves,' a voice from behind startles me. I turn to find a man leaning on the wall.

'What?' I say. I remember him from the race for the flags. I'm pretty sure he was the beast whose boot met that contestant's face on the wall ladder.

'Forgot to put your gloves on,' he says pointing to my bare hands.

Shit. I stuffed them in my pocket and forgot about them. I put them on quickly, careful not to knock the scab on the back of my hand, a small reminder of the forest and the wolves. He's still watching me, his expression guarded.

'Thanks,' I say trying to keep my shudder on the inside. I can't help it; this guy creeps me out.

Everyone's collected a reward chest and thanks to the audience we're all dressed in warm dry clothes. It's a little reassuring to know the viewers are on our side, at least for now. I'm glad everyone succeeded in the first task. I wonder how many successfully completed the second part and won a reward. No one is giving anything away; their poker faces are as effective as the balaclavas we burnt.

'Drai… Dri…' Billy says. 'What's the dragon's name again?'

Rhodri looks over. '*Dry* as in *not wet*, *go* as in *fuck off* and *dan*…' He shrugs. 'You get it.'

'Dry-go-dan.' Billy smiles, his eyes flit around the circle. 'So, are we all Peasants or does somebody have something to confess?'

I snort impatiently. Lewis throws me an unimpressed look. 'Chill babes,' he says to Billy. 'Not like anyone's going to admit it.'

Billy flushes an embarrassed pink but stays quiet, playing with the loop of his microphone. He reminds me of my aunt's golden retriever – handsome and cute but really over-the-top excited by every single thing. As if to prove my point he jumps up. 'Maybe I should boil some water for rice. We'll be getting hungry soon.'

Lewis beams. 'Starving already.'

My eyes linger on Rhodri and Demi. If Billy is a golden retriever these two are a pair of Dobermans, cautious and guarded. They're talking too quietly to hear. Their bodies are taut, shoulders tense and their eyes flit around the campsite as if trying to keep every single player in their sight. I'm worried they might do something reckless. In this game, one wrong move could have serious consequences, however well intentioned.

And I can't lose Rhodri.

16

We may be huddled around the same campfire but there are definite factions emerging. One group has formed on the opposite side of the fire, full of all the idiots so far to the left of rational they make The Joker look stable – those who have come on here for fame or money or both and don't care how high the price. The huge guy from the wall trial, the Beast, is lording over them. Glasses Guy is by his side, so obviously sucking up to him that it's too painful to watch. The purple-haired woman is there too, hanging off the Beast's every word while the twins' shrieks of excitement grate against my nerves.

Either side of the campfire are two stands with columns of wooden plaques hanging down on hooks. There are seven on each side, and each plaque has a contestant's name carved onto it. Ophelia and Portia's names are on the same plaque.

The castle wall lights up as another status appears, projected onto the grey stone like an open-air cinema.

Head and shoulders fill the wall, muscled and tattooed. Thin lips press together under his goatee as the Beast stares arrogantly down the lens. A cheer goes up from his group.

Name – King John
Age – 28

Occupation – Special Forces
Hobbies – Winning

'Special forces? Is he bollocks. He's totally nicked that from *Who dares Wins*,' Lewis whispers.

'They call me King John because I'm on a crusade to slay.' He smiles an ugly smile into the camera. *'I'll conquer this game and defeat my enemies – no one strikes harder than me.'*

'Oh yeah.' King John raises his fists in celebration.

Marcus walks up to the fire. 'Is he for real?'

Lewis holds his hands up in an *I told you so*.

'King John?' Demi snorts. 'What a wanker.'

'Well, he puts the dick in dictator. Should we bow?' Mai says loudly. ''Cause I don't curtsy to no one.' Everyone laughs, except me. He may be playing the villain, but underneath all that reality bluster there's a real dangerous edge. He isn't playing. He's here to win. He proved that in the race for the flags. He faces us, a challenge spread all over his face.

The ground starts to rumble.

Billy covers his ears. 'How are they doing that? It's freaking me out.'

Draigodân appears, landing gracefully on the virtual rock. The 3D wings look like they're about to hit us. Billy ducks. I step back, accidently bumping into Ravi.

'Sorry,' I say, totally didn't see him there. He smiles and I turn back to the dragon.

The hologram looks so real. His paws pad along the

rocks, and I swear I can hear the talons clipping on the stony surface.

Rhodri's standing protectively by my shoulder. His actions are confusing me more than the game right now.

A dark-haired girl slides up next to him, a flirty smile on her lips. I risk a sneaky sideways glance. Her hair is pulled back into a thick braid that hangs seductively down her back. Dark eyes lined Cleopatra-style and olive skin are complimented by an athletic body which looks good even in this stupid castle garb. There's something familiar about her. She's giving off medieval Lara Croft energy and it hasn't gone unnoticed. Rhodri's smiling down at those big brown eyes with a look usually reserved for me. Suddenly I'm feeling like a gate crasher at a private party.

'Castle Dwellers, you have all received your game status. You are one of two factions: a Peasant, innocent and vulnerable with only your guile and daring to keep you alive; or Werewolf, hidden amongst the Peasants disguised in human form ready to kill as soon as the blood moon rises above the Outer Main Gatehouse.' Every time Draigodân says the word Werewolf he rolls the *rrrr*, making it sound like a growling beast.

The dragon pauses while everyone surveys the crowd, looking for any tell-tale signs of trickery. We all look guilty and innocent in equal measure. No one can be underestimated.

'Peasants remember, once the blood moon rises high

above the castle towers the Werewolves will hunt, looking to satisfy their carnivorous appetite. Decide now that it won't be you on their menu.'

Draigodân pauses dramatically, his tail flicking from side to side, his scaly head turning back and forth. His razor-sharp teeth catch the light making a shudder sprint down my back. *It's not real,* I chant to myself. *It's not real.*

'Among the Werewolves is the Alpha – one more powerful than the others. The Alpha controls the pack. They have the ability to turn Peasants into Werewolves. But these abilities must be earnt and how much power will depend on the audience.'

An awed rumble ripples through the crowd. Catching the Werewolves is going to be almost impossible if the Alpha's not caught quickly. The longer he or she remains in the game the more Werewolves they'll create and the harder it will be for the Peasants to gain a majority win.

'Werewolves you must find your leader and your pack before the moon bleeds. How many Werewolves roam among you will remain unknown to the Peasants. To kill a Peasant you must take the name plaque of the contestant you wish to murder and throw it in the fire. You must do this undetected and before the sun rises. The Peasant selected by the Werewolves will be immediately removed from the game.'

'If they burn the name how will they know who's been killed?' Glasses Guy says.

King John snorts scornfully. 'Uh fifty million cameras, four eyes. Big Brother is always watching.'

Glasses Guy drops his head and shuffles on the spot as King John's 'team' all sneer and laugh. I look away, embarrassed for him, and catch the girl next to Rhodri staring right at me.

I don't flinch. I'm no Werewolf; I've nothing to hide. She smiles, friendly enough, making me feel bad. I need to keep the paranoia in check. Unless she's playing with me and is a Werewolf? Maybe she thinks Rhodri's the Alpha and is planning to get rid of the competition in the first round. The hair on my skin rises like hackles; she can jog right on if she thinks she can play that game.

'Castle Dwellers, you will be called to a daily Castle Council where you must make two accusations each meeting. You will then vote. Those found guilty will face the Gauntlet.' Draigodân puffs out his chest. 'Now this is where it gets interesting. In this game time is your friend. The audience will award life-saving seconds to their favourite players. The more seconds you win, the bigger the advantage and the easier it will be to beat the Gauntlet. So, remember players, all actions, good, bad or just plain ugly will be judged.'

'I don't get it,' Lewis says, his face screwed into a panicked frown.

Billy squeezes his arm. 'The audience are watching. They'll vote for their favourites. The more they like you, the more advantages you'll get.'

'It's a popularity contest,' says Rhodri. 'I'm screwed.'

'What's the Gauntlet?' Marcus asks, his eyes searching the sea of blank faces. No one answers.

I gulp down the fear. That's a major change from the first game.

'I am so not liking the sound of this,' Lewis says, dragging his hands through his hair.

'Chill,' Billy says, his voice calm and I notice the way his hand remains on Lewis' arm.

'Whichever faction, Werewolf or Peasant, left in the majority at the final Castle Council will win the Champion's crown and a share in the prize money.' Draigodân beats his wings. 'Remember, Castle Dwellers, there is only one rule.' He cranes his neck to the sky and booms, 'Trust no one.'

Fountains of orange flame spurt into the air as he disappears.

'Okay.' Mai steps forwards. 'The Werewolves have to throw names into the fire at night, right? It's easy. I say we guard the shit out of the fire. All night. If we're watching them, they can't burn anything.'

'How many Werewolves do you think there are?' the girl next to Rhodri says.

'Three, maybe four?' Arti says. 'The ratio is usually one to three, so one Werewolf to three Peasants.' We all stare at the big guy over the fire. He grins. 'I play a lot.'

King John steps forward. 'I say we find the Alpha and burn him.'

'Uh hello?' The twins speak as one, turning to each other they shout. 'Twin jinx.' High fiving the air as if they've won some great prize, checking their positions in relation to the drones in calculated unison. These two are way more interested in the cameras than the game and their complete lack of nerves baffles me. Don't they realise what's at risk?

The one with the bob turns to King John; I think it's Portia. 'Who said the Alpha is a guy?'

'And ewww,' says Ophelia, screwing up her dainty nose in disgust. 'Bad taste.'

'Hello?' I say, unable to hold my tongue. 'You know someone has already been badly hurt, maybe worse?' They stare at me, clueless. 'The guy on the wall?'

Ophelia's eyes are so wide they've disappeared under her fringe. 'I know, right?' she pouts a faux-sad face towards the drone. 'I hope he's okay.'

King John snorts. 'What did you expect?' He talks slowly. 'Ultimate … survival … show… You think they're going to hand over ten million smackers for nothing? Come on, people.'

Everyone stares at the floor, the fire, anywhere but him.

King John shouts. 'This isn't a cosy little game on terrestrial telly where we all get to hug one another and sing *Kumbaya*. This is hardcore survival shit. Fuck up, you get hurt. Or worse.'

Ophelia screws up her nose. 'No need to swear. Besides

I'm not doing any of the dangerous stunt bits. They can edit me in later.'

'Get real, princess. There are no reruns or edits in post-production. Play hard or go home. Didn't you watch the first show?' King John says. 'That guy on the wall was careless, and it cost him the game. But hey, one less between me and the win.'

The twins giggle nervously.

Werewolf or not, I don't like this guy. I open my mouth to argue more but Mai has moved closer and nudges me.

'Don't rock the boat,' she whispers. She's right. We have bigger worries right now. She nods at King John. 'He shouldn't even be in here; he's way old.'

'So's Ravi,' I say. 'And that woman with the purple hair.'

Mai shrugs. 'No clue what her story is but Ravi's a relative of the dead, great backstory, good for sympathy ratings, the audience will find him relatable.'

'Is it you?' King John gets right up in Portia's face, his attitude bordering on aggressive. 'Are you a supernatural devil dog?'

'No,' Portia says with a huge dollop of sass. 'And rude.'

'You?' he turns to Ophelia.

'No?' she says, not in the least bit intimidated. She points at Portia. 'Playing as one, remember?'

'Chill dude,' Arti says, stepping between them. 'You've made you're point. That's not the way to make friends.'

'Not here to make friends.' King John turns back to

the fire. A handful of players group around him. He's intimidating enough to be a Werewolf or is he just too obvious? We all return to our small huddles, conversing in hushed whispers as suspicions become facts and we all attempt to identify the enemy among us.

Lewis is sitting by the fire, super pale, his orange hair accentuating the terror in his eyes.

'Babes, I'm fine.' He catches me looking. 'Be more ostrich, that's my new motto; stick my head in the sand and refuse to acknowledge the truth. This is my game plan and I'm sticking to it.'

'Good plan,' I say squeezing his hands until they stop shaking. 'Be more ostrich.'

Rhodri snorts. We ignore him.

'Where even are we anyway?' Demi says.

'Wales,' Billy says. 'This looks like—'

'Caerphilly Castle,' Rhodri says.

Billy stutters. 'Yes… I… I…'

'Rhodri's from Wales,' Lewis says, colour returning to his cheeks. 'We call him Welsh on account of his irrational love of all things Welsh.'

'You call him Welsh,' I say. 'The rest of us call him Rhodri.'

'Fun fact,' Billy says. 'Do you know that blood moon in Italian is *luna rossa*?'

'Are you Italian?' Rhodri asks.

'No.'

'Then shut the fuck up.'

Billy retreats to the other side of Lewis.

'Who's the girl?' I ask, trying to sound casual and Peasant-like. Rhodri doesn't answer. 'The one you were whispering to when Draigodân was talking?'

'No clue, some delusional wannabee like the rest of the idiots in here.' Rhodri frowns. 'It's one hell of a price to pay for five minutes of fame.'

'Not even that,' Demi says. 'This is fame on the dark web, whatever that is.'

'Fame is fame,' I say. 'I don't think anyone here is fussy.'

There's a whirring.

'You hear that?' Demi asks, his face turned skyward.

'There.' Billy points. A small drone is flying towards us, bobbing in the air as it weaves towards the campfire. It's a different shape from the camera drones and bright red.

'It's a dragon,' I say.

Lewis bounds over, following under its path. 'It's so cute,' he sings. He's trying too hard. I know exactly what he's doing, embracing the ostrich and compartmentalising the bad. He may project fun and sunshine, but he'll be dying on the inside. I get it. If I'm going to get through this, I need to do the same. '*Bore da,* little dragon.' He looks smugly at Rhodri. 'See? Not the only one who can speak the old native tongue.'

We all laugh. It's hollow and fake but it helps with the dealing.

'*Prynhawn da*,' Rhodri says.

'Sorry now?' Lewis says cupping his hand around his ear.

'You said good morning,' Rhodri says. 'It's afternoon.'

'Potatoes, potato or should I say' – he puts on a clumsy Welsh accent – 'pot-aytoes, pot-harto.'

'Look,' I say, breaking up the conversation before they start bickering more.

The drone's stopped, hovering over the grass beside the campfire.

'There's something underneath it,' Portia says making no attempt to get it.

Mai leaps into the air and grabs the drone, yanking a scroll away. Job done, the drone lifts itself high and flies back towards the Main Gatehouse. Unrolling the scroll Mai reads, '*Castle Dwellers. The audience have been voting.*'

Arti makes a whistling noise. Nervous glances fill the circle.

'Hey,' Demi says calmy. 'It's cool. They were good to us last time. We all got the welcome chests.'

Frantic glances are replaced with relieved nods as we remember the dry clothes courtesy of the viewers' vote.

Mai continues. '*Two Castle Dwellers have been chosen for a special castle challenge. Should they be successful, the camp will be rewarded with an advantage.*'

We all cheer. Any advantage would be good right now.

'The two Castle Dwellers chosen are…' Mai unfolds the rest of the scroll. 'Rhodri and Faith.'

Who the hell is Faith?

My medieval nemesis walks out from behind the fire and my heart nose dives. She strides over to Rhodri with a confidence I lack and smiles. 'Let's go.'

Rhodri stares at her.

'Does she look familiar to you,' I whisper to Lewis.

Lewis whispers back, 'Yeah, I'm getting total Lara Croft vibes.' I elbow him in the ribs.

'Ow,' he says. 'You asked.'

I frown. I don't need Lewis' truths right now as I'm watching the girl who made Rhodri speechless. Maybe he's right and that's why she looks so familiar. She's like a levelled-up version of me, if I looked anything like Lara Croft, which … I wish.

Rhodri finally comes to his senses. 'What now?'

'It says to go to the Outer Main Gatehouse,' Mai says.

Before I can wish him luck, he strides away with Faith.

'Bye then,' I say unable to keep the sarcasm out of my voice.

'She may be hot,' Lewis whispers, reading my mind. 'But you're the OG. Girl's got nothing on you.'

'That obvious?' I say.

'About as obvious as those twins,' he says. 'Besides, this game? Guaranteed boner buster. The boy ain't thinking with his dick right now.'

I try to smile. He's not wrong. Rhodri's got so many other things on his mind and, as he disappears through the gatehouse with Faith, I can't ignore the niggling feeling that not one of them is me.

17

The scream is as shrill as the icy wind, grabbing our attention in a shattering heartbeat. Bodies jump up from the fire in a flurry of nervous activity. Marcus dives out of the tent, beyond panicked, running up and down, looking frantically for the source. Ophelia bursts from the ruined gatehouse at the end of the green, Portia at her shoulder – her actions mirroring her sister's.

'Oh my god. Come see,' they scream excitedly. 'Come see.'

'I think they want to show us something,' Demi says.

'Really?' Mai has disgust firmly plastered over her face. 'Bet the bog's not bougie enough.'

'Play for the cameras, love, play for the cameras,' Marcus says. 'S'pose we should go see.'

We follow Marcus across the green to the gatehouse with the Portakabin loos.

'Murder,' Ophelia screams like she's auditioning for some am-dram Agatha Christie play. 'Mur-der.'

Portia's face is blushed an excited pink. 'Werewolves,' she pants making her hands into claws. 'First victim.' She points to the gatehouse and into the dark room opposite the Portakabin loos. 'We were just using the facilities which are' – dramatic gag – 'so gross. We found him, her,' – shakes her head – 'whoever.'

135

Both girls scream, an ear-splitting, high-pitched noise for maximum attention.

Bodies cram into the small doorway.

'It's a prop, right?' Glasses Guy pulls off his glasses and cleans them manically.

'Obvs.' Ophelia turns to Portia. 'Aww cute.' They squeal with laughter.

Ignoring them I push forward. Behind the iron gate, hanging from the ceiling in the middle of the room is a cage. Slumped inside, illuminated by a single light, is a body, dressed the same as us.

'Is it?' Billy loud whispers.

King John pushes his way to the front and peers through the gate. 'Dead as a dodo. Look at the hand.' An arm hangs from the cage bars, limp and lifeless. There's a mark on the back of the gloveless hand – three red lines like a deep gash. 'I call Werewolf.' He rubs his hands together. 'Here we go.'

'So, the first victim is in play.' Glasses Guy is rubbing his chin with his gloved hand like a super-geeky Sherlock Holmes. 'Interesting. The first kill is always outside the group – a means to get the ball rolling and the accusations flowing. We haven't had a night phase yet, so the Werewolves haven't had time to throw a name in the fire. This is an opportunity for us Peasants to get one step ahead.' He gestures to all of us. 'Look for clues, however small, anything that could be construed as suspicious behaviour.' The woman with the purple hair nods enthusiastically.

'Oooh.' Ophelia claps her hands, her hair swooshing cutely around her shoulders. 'It could be any one of us.'

'Well, it's not me.' Portia giggles.

'Me neither,' Ophelia says as they both stare up at the drones. 'Pinky swear.'

Glasses Guy humphs impatiently. He looks straight at me. 'Didn't I see you over here with the tall fella?'

'Yeah?' I say immediately defensive. 'Changing my clothes not murdering. Since when did wanting privacy become a suspicious activity?'

'The minute you walked through that gatehouse.' He squints at me through his glasses.

'Thought we were supposed to be looking for guilty ass Werewolves not stalking each other while we're changing?' Lewis says.

'Playing the game, son. Why not get on board?' King John grins a slimy grin at Lewis. 'Any suspicious activity should be noted.'

'Well you're barking up the wrong tree there.' I edge closer to Lewis.

'Nice punning,' Lewis says, his tone light but his face pale. 'That dummy in there remind you of anyone?'

'Dougie.' I shudder recalling the dummy from series one. Okay, so it's not hanging from a tree like Dougie was but it's giving off the same vibes and it's creeping me out more than I want to admit. I lean in and whisper, 'It's not real?'

Lewis shakes his head. 'No, I'm pretty sure it's a

dummy. It's really dark in there. Besides, Action Man "I'm an SAS soldier" would know if that was real.'

That doesn't help. Dougie wasn't real, until he was. I turn away, not wanting to see as the others push into the small space, desperate to catch a glimpse and look for clues that could help them identify the Werewolves.

Ravi's hanging back, his presence so understated that nobody notices him. He catches me watching him and smiles. I smile back. It's weird having the old guy in here. He's so out of place in this setting and I hate Skye even more for using his grief as a means of entertainment.

The Dougie-like dummy is triggering way too many ghosts, so I make my way back to the red tent and curl up on one of the beds. From the central pole hangs a small camera and a stick microphone. By each bed is a hook.

'It's for your microphone,' Demi says. I hadn't realised he'd followed me back. 'I guess we don't need them at night. The screaming will be loud enough.' He coughs, embarrassed. 'Sorry, bad joke.'

'It was funny,' I say.

Demi sits. His grief-fuelled energy is angrier than Tayo's but I still find his presence in here calming. Ravi shuffles in, potters about the tent then shuffles back out without saying a word. Demi's face is an open book.

'We should protect him,' I say.

Demi nods awkwardly but it's obvious we're on the same page. Amara's ghost joins us in the see-through tent as we share a moment of grief.

Lewis bursts in with Billy, his overly cheery voice cutting through the moment. 'It's so weird we can totally see you from out there. It's like you're in a giant condom.' He slumps down next to me.

Mai follows them in, rolling her eyes

Billy flops on the bed opposite nodding through the wall towards King John. 'He's got some serious small-dick energy going on.'

Lewis and Billy disintegrate into nervous giggles, and my now familiar Billy irritation begins to bubble.

'Hey, Billy?' Mai says. 'All these beds are taken.'

Billy jumps up, his cheeks flushing red, giggling immediately silenced. 'Shit, sorry. I didn't know.'

'Easy mistake, bro.' Demi is calm to Mai's fire and pats Billy on the back like an old friend. He points to the tent next door. 'Think you're in that one.'

Lewis bites his lip, a tell-tale awkward sign. I wait for him to argue but he holds his tongue, smiling an apology at Billy. Billy walks into the other tent and, finding a bed next to Arti, he waves through the glass-like plastic.

Lewis turns to me. 'We so need a catch up.'

Mai and Demi excuse themselves, giving us a few minutes of privacy. As soon as they leave, Lewis' face falls. 'This is next level. I keep pinching myself, waiting to wake up but it's not happening. Oh my god, in the forest? When you didn't come back, I figured you were dead.' He flicks his hair in a move to hide the tears threatening his eyes. 'That's when I found Billy, or rather he found me.

Totally has my back. Plus, he gets how this outfit is such a sucky disappointment. I mean, what the actual?'

'Lewis…'

He holds his microphone up to his mouth. 'I had so many fabulous outfits in my suitcase. Probably never see them again—'

'Lewis,' I interrupt. 'You can't—'

'Trust him?' Lewis lets his mic hang back around his neck. 'I know. But I like him. Figure I should take the win while I can. He was there and you weren't.' He shuffles up the bed, whispering, 'Where were you anyway? How did you even get here?'

I want to answer but with the mics picking up everything, I daren't breathe a word. I'm desperate to overshare about Rhodri but I've no desire to broadcast my loss of virginity to the world or the niggling sense of regret I'm starting to feel for doing what we did in Venitiwa. I need best-friend perspective. My stomach flips are making me queasy. I open my mouth to tell him about Thea, but the words won't come out. He's watching me expectantly; I need to give him something.

'The guards found us in the forest. It's all really blurry. They gave me something, knocked me out. When I came round, I was here.'

'And Rhodri?'

'Same,' I say leaving out the screaming and the yelling and the being forced to the ground while they stuck needles in him.

'Shiiit.' Lewis whistles. 'They put us all on a coach, blacked-out windows, all very secret service. Slept the whole way. Come to think of it, that's weird, right? Do you think they gave us something, too? Can they even do that? Is it even allowed?'

'I think we're way past what's allowed,' I say.

Lewis mimics King John. 'Ultimate survival.' He pauses. 'I'm so piggin' scared. And that dragon?' He shudders. 'Promise me you won't do anything stupid. I can't bear the thought of someone hurting you. I can't...'

I pull him to me. He's shaking in my arms. I close my mouth and swallow Thea's name. There's no way I can tell him, even if I could without Skye hearing. I'm scared he may not be able to come back from it and I need him strong.

He pulls out of my embrace and wipes his eyes. 'I'm fine.' He sniffs. 'All good. Someone'll find us. They have to. It's hard to hide a six-metre tall, fire-breathing dragon.'

'It breathes fire?' I say, eyebrows raised.

'You can bloody bet my life it does.'

'Not funny.'

'Not laughing.'

'Just need to hold on a bit longer,' I mouth, squeezing his hands in mine, begging him to understand. The hope that floods his eyes tells me he does.

We sit in silence trying to turn our words into bravery. 'I had to climb that humongous wall.' Lewis slaps his hands on his knees. 'How the hell did *I* climb that wall? I looked for you and shouted but I couldn't find you in all the bodies.'

I remember my name on the wind as I crossed the moat. 'I'm so sorry,' I say. 'That guy, Marcus, I thought you were him and...' The words trail off. 'Well done for getting over by the way.'

Lewis raises an eyebrow. 'I know, right? Go me. To be fair, Billy helped massively and that big guy with the neck.'

'Artemis?' My eyes widen in surprise.

'He likes to be called Arti. You would know if you weren't totally distracted by lover boy.'

'Am not.' I resent the accusation.

'Arti's nice. Once you get past the fake tan, he's all right,' he says. 'Yes, I know, we can't trust anyone, but I think he's one of us is what I'm saying. First impressions. Urghh, this place is gonna kill us.'

'Don't say that,' I snap. 'Don't even joke.' I nod to the camera above us, its beady little eye watching our every move.

Lewis looks straight into the lens and sticks his tongue out.

We can't talk in here. I pull Lewis out and towards the fire. Crouching in front of the crackling flames I push my mic underneath the neck of my top, bunching the fabric around it. Lewis does the same.

'Billy reckons...' He stops as I roll my eyes. 'Seriously?'

'Sorry,' I say, one eye on the circling drones. They don't

stop, their attention's focused on the twins and Marcus. 'Carry on.'

'He said this castle is concentric in its formation. He's like a proper medieval history buff.' I wait. 'Yeah, so circles. This one, the South Dam, is the biggest and it goes into the smallest on that island where all the towers are. That's where I think Max is.'

'Agreed,' I say, glad we're on the same page. I'd bet my life Thea is in there too.

'We just have to get in and get him out,' he says.

Easy.

'It's a game,' Lewis continues. 'We have to play. Werewolf, *Blood Moon* or whatever. So, we play. And we,' he mouths, '*wait for DC Brown*. We get inside the island bit and get Max. The only thing we have to make sure is that we—'

'Don't die?'

'I was gonna say, *don't get accused* but that works too.'

We fall into silence staring across the lake to the castle on the island.

'Are you…?' I ask.

'Peasant,' Lewis says without taking a beat. 'You?'

'Same.' Neither of us push it, what's the point? It really doesn't matter who is what.

'You think Rhodri is?'

'No clue.' I frown. Is my paranoia being made worse by a dollop full of jealousy? 'Do you think he's acting weird?'

Lewis shrugs. 'Could be, but to be fair he's always a bit of a prick.'

I nudge him, grateful that he can still make me smile.

'Help will come,' I whisper, giving as much as I can to calm the worry and fear that's creeping back over his face. I can't risk telling him about the note left for DC Brown in Venitiwa. As much as I want too, there's too much at stake.

'What you not telling me, Kennedy?' Lewis watches me suspiciously, his ability to read my mind on track as usual.

'Nothing.' I pray my cheeks don't heat up. I hate the way my lies are piling up, but I don't have a choice.

Mai and Demi appear.

'S'up?' Mai says. We shuffle guiltily which is stupid; it's not like we've been talking about them. If she notices she doesn't show it. 'Water's boiling; thought we'd get the rice on.'

'I'm happy to do it,' Ravi says. 'Some are getting hangry.' He chuckles like he's told a joke. He potters about collecting up the rice, lifting the huge pan onto the fire without complaint. He's a quiet man, so unlike Amara. In all the time we've been here I've yet to hear him speak her name.

'It's getting dark,' Demi says.

I hadn't even noticed that the castle was filling with dark shadows. My stomach does an urgent flip. The Werewolves?

Demi puts a reassuring hand on my shoulder. 'It's still early. Draigo-whatever said when the moon is over that tower the Werewolves can put names in the fire.' He points above the huge gatehouse that we started in. 'We're talking midnight I reckon.'

My eyes keep drifting to the doors, but there's no sign of Rhodri or the girl, Faith. I need to stop obsessing.

A dragon drone bobs its way to the circle.

'It's a message,' Portia says. Spurred into action by the sight of the drone and the cameras that follow, both twins try to reach the small scroll underneath its belly. Honestly, they have more energy than a Duracell Bunny. The drone hovers tantalisingly out of reach. Arti steps forward, his giant form overshadowing both of them. Reaching up he grabs the scroll, handing it to Ophelia with a friendly smile.

Facing the drone, Ophelia reads the message.

'*Castle Dwellers, the day's almost done but there is still work to do. It is time for your first Castle Council. Justice is needed for the brutal murder of Seth Gooder. Gather at the meeting place to decide who is a Werewolf hiding in Peasant's clothing.*'

Ophelia gasps into the camera. 'Seth Gooder.' Portia grabs the scroll and carries on reading.

'*All Castle Dwellers must make their way to the meeting area. The council will commence soon.*' Pulling an excited face, Portia lowers the scroll.

I wish for one second they would take this seriously.

Castle Council means eviction and, if this game is anything like the first, that doesn't end well.

'Can't we eat first?' Arti moans rubbing his stomach. 'I'm very sorry for dummy Seth and all, but we haven't eaten since early this morning and I'm likely to vote someone out just because I'm friggin' starving.' The face he pulls is comical and I note the way he says friggin'. This guy may be big and powerful but I'm beginning to think there's a gentle giant under all that fake tan. My instinct is Peasant; he's acting way too genuine to be Werewolf.

'Where's Welsh and the other one?' Lewis says. 'They need to be back for this.'

My stomach is full of knots as I look for them in the fire light. I don't know what's scaring me more, that they're not back or that we're about to vote. The only thing I know for sure is that none of us are safe.

18

The thought of Castle Council and the impending nominations makes me dizzy. I bend over, resting my hands on my knees.

Demi's by my side. 'Breathe,' he says. I concentrate on the gentle melody of his voice. And it helps, my racing pulse slows and the headrush fades.

'Thanks,' I say.

'No problem.'

Lewis jogs over. 'They're back.'

Rhodri and Faith are walking through the Main Gatehouse doors. I hang back as everyone rushes to meet them, trying to gauge their reactions. The slump of their shoulders and the shake of their heads tells me they failed whatever challenge they were set, confirmed by the chorus of reassuring *it's okays* and *it doesn't matters*.

But I know Rhodri too well and a fail will devastate him. They stay close to each other, hands almost touching. The furtive glances that pass between them show they've bonded over that shared experience, however bad.

I'm suddenly feeling the chill a little more.

Rhodri's eyes find mine in the crowd. I recognise the tiredness and despair.

He raises his hand in a wave.

I wave back but make no move to close the gap between us. The girl, Faith, stands close to Rhodri, watching me with a look I can't read. I wish I could tell her to sod the hell off. Instead, she comes closer. Rhodri follows.

'I'm Faith,' she says.

'Didn't ask,' I blurt snarkily.

'Ouch,' Billy says, clocking my less than friendly reaction. I glare at him. Rhodri says nothing.

Faith smiles and I feel guilty. A strand of dark hair's escaped the braid and curls around the nape of her swan-like neck.

We shuffle on our spots waiting for someone to speak while a drone buzzes overhead recording our frosty introduction for all to see.

'We have to go,' Mai says.

Rhodri finally springs back to life. 'Where?'

'Castle Council,' Lewis says.

Faith leans up to whisper in Rhodri's ear in a move that suggests a comfortableness between them I wasn't prepared for. What the hell is up with my friends? They're bonding with total strangers in a millisecond, leaving me shivering out in the cold. Finishing whatever was so important, Faith gives me a quick nod and jogs to catch up with Arti and Marcus, an alliance clearly formed.

'Seth Gooder has been found hanging in a cage down there.' Lewis points to the ruined tower. 'Dead, obvs.'

'Who?' Rhodri looks startled.

'Not real,' Lewis says quickly. 'Playing the game is all. Werewolf attack. So now we have to accuse and then vote.'

Rhodri's cheeks turn red. His mouth vomits expletives all over the grass.

Lewis nods. 'Yep, that's about the gist of it. Anyone got a plan?'

'This is a game of numbers,' Demi says. 'We need to stick together. Go for someone we don't know. It's easier, in case they—'

'Die?' Mai says. 'Got no patience for these idiots; they know what they signed up for.'

'I'm not sure they do. Nobody signed up to die,' I say. 'Shouldn't we warn them?'

Mai snorts. 'Look, we don't know how this is going to play out or what Skye's plan is. Maybe this is just an extreme game of Werewolf, and we'll all live to tell the tale. Either way, it's them or us. My focus is Skye. If they want to risk their lives in this then that's their problem. I ain't got time for idiots.'

Ravi nods. 'I agree,' he says. We all turn to listen, having heard so very little from him all day. 'They knew the risks. I'm taking no chances.'

Demi's face is one big grimace. 'Look, Mai's right. All we know is we can't second guess Skye.'

'We have to play the game.' Lewis' eyes are moon sized.

'Until we can stop her,' Mai says.

'That's not what we're here for.' I look to Rhodri for help. He just shrugs. 'We're here for Max.' I spell it out to him before he goes rogue. 'Get Max and get out.'

'But we have to play the game to get to Max.' Rhodri's eyes darken.

'Right then,' Lewis says reverting to his faux-happy tone. 'Glad we got that sorted. Try not to die, or kill anyone, play the game, find Max and get the hell out.' He links arms with me. 'Come on. Time to—'

'Hey, watch it,' I shout as Marcus bashes into me and almost sends me flying.

'Woah,' Lewis shouts as he keeps me upright.

'So sorry,' Marcus shouts back over his shoulder not even bothering to turn around.

'Wanker,' Lewis mutters. 'Dick moves like that? Not good at this point of the game.'

'So true,' I mutter.

We grab torches and light them in the fire, walk past the visitors' centre, dark and closed, and through a small gate, glad of the torchlight in the early winter night.

A whole new area opens up before us revealing another huge lake stretching out into the darkness. On the far bank more stone walls block our escape to the town beyond and freedom. My heart sinks as I realise the enormity of our task. Even if we do find Max and Thea, how the hell are we going to get out?

'One step at a time,' Lewis whispers, reading my mind and pushing his torch into the stand. 'We've gotten out of worse.'

We filter into a circular space. Round wooden stumps

are set around another blazing campfire. A giant hourglass sits on a podium. Walls rise on three sides, their grey stone glistening with silver damp. Wooden torches are set between the seats illuminating the space with their bobbing flames. Two sets of wooden stocks face us.

We sit staring at one another. How am I supposed to vote one of them out? I literally have no clue who's a Werewolf let alone the Alpha. My eyes fall on King John as he swaggers into the circle and plonks himself in the middle of his team, one leg extended in front of him deliberately in the way of others trying to pass. He looks around with cold eyes. What's that saying Mum always uses, *If it looks like a duck and quacks like a duck…*

Lewis sits next to me. Rhodri's on my other side, close but distant.

Billy, Mai, Demi and Ravi all sit nearby. Arti and Marcus are opposite with Faith. The Shakespeare Sisters fidget with nervous excitement, reminding anyone in earshot that they're playing as one.

Camera people are positioned on the ramparts.

Draigodân appears, his talons digging into the virtual rock. His huge head bends towards us. 'Welcome to the Castle Council. Tonight, one of you will be leaving the game for good.'

Gazing at the others, I'm not sure they all realise the danger concealed in the dragon's words.

'Lewis,' Draigodân says and my attention's firmly back on the dragon. 'Please come to the podium.'

'Oh shit, shit, shit,' Lewis mutters standing on the podium.

'Please turn the sand timer over.'

Using both hands Lewis flips it over.

'Castle Dwellers, you have been gathered here tonight to exact justice. Seth Gooder's mutilated body was found earlier today, savaged by vicious Werewolves.' I cringe. Across the fire the twins are lapping it up, their eyes wide and horrified in the firelight. 'It is up to you to find the beasts that terrorise this castle and stop them before they attack again. Who's been acting suspiciously today? Who do you not quite trust? Who are the killers hiding amongst you? You have until the sand runs out to make two accusations. Each accusation must be seconded.'

Draigodân disappears.

The crackle of burning wood is the only noise in the quiet evening. You can almost hear our noisy thoughts as we all try to find a reason to nominate.

And the sand in the timer continues to flow.

'Those stocks are creeping me out,' Ophelia says with a pretty shudder.

'Oh, they're pillories,' Billy says. 'Common mistake. Stocks were used to hold the feet. The pillory was used for arms and head.'

Ophelia stares at Billy open mouthed.

'Fun fact,' Billy mutters as his eyes hit the floor.

'I nominate Kass.' King John's voice is loud and clear as it cuts across the silence. My heart stops.

Everyone starts speaking at once. Mai and Demi are talking fast. Lewis is shouting. Angry words blur together in one chaotic noise.

Rhodri jumps up. 'You can't just nominate like that.'

King John leans back, his smile cruel. 'Think I just did, mate. That's the game. I think she's a Werewolf.' He talks to the rest of his group. 'She played the first series and won. She was a Player. What are the chances of her being innocent second time round? He's right.' He gestures to Glasses Guy. 'She was seen in the area, very suspicious. Probably checking it out.'

Rumblings of agreement ripple across his team. I open my mouth, but my denial is stuck in my throat.

'This is bollocks,' Rhodri says.

'Why not let the girl speak for herself?' King John is smug, his eyes challenging. 'If she's innocent, prove it. Show us your hands.'

I have no choice; he's totally stitched me up. Everyone's staring. Whatever I do I'll look guilty in their eyes. 'Fine.' I pull off my gloves and show the scab on the back of my hand. Everyone gasps.

King John seizes the moment. 'We all put our hands in the hole and we all waited for the bite to define our status.' He points dramatically at my hand. 'And there it is, the mark of the Werewolf.'

'It's not what it looks like.' I wave my hand at them. 'It's a scab. It happened in the forest.'

'She's right. I was with her. It's nothing,' Rhodri says.

Glasses Guy jumps up. 'How do we know you're not a Werewolf protecting her?'

'Because I'm not?' Rhodri impatiently pulls off his gloves to show them the back of his mark-free hands. 'See?'

'What about you?' Mai jumps in pulling off her gloves, too.

'What about me?' King John shows his bare hands. 'I've nothing to hide, no mark of the Werewolf. In fact, let's all show our hands.' One by one everyone pulls off their gloves. No one has a Werewolf mark.

Except me.

King John shouts triumphantly across the fire. 'I rest my case. She's the only one with the mark of the wolf. She must be the Alpha. If we get her out, we're halfway to winning.'

'Or the Werewolves are marked in a different way,' Rhodri says. 'No one knows except the Werewolves, that's the whole point. Shall we all strip naked so you can check?'

Ophelia and Portia fall into a fit of giggles.

'Then why are we all wearing gloves?' Faith says.

'To keep our hands warm?' Arti shrugs. 'Maybe don't overthink?'

'It's madness trying to come up with plausible theories. It's the first round. We need to stay calm and talk things through.' Demi's voice is full of reason, but no one's listening.

Mai jabs a finger at Marcus. 'I saw you...' She shouts to be heard. 'I *saw* you.' Everyone stops and listens. 'After the status task, you were rubbing your hands like you'd been bitten, like you were a Werewolf.'

'I was cold,' Marcus says raising the back of his hands for all to see.

But you lied to me about your identity right at the start, I want to say but alarm has shut my mouth tighter than any gag.

Lewis speaks up and I love him for it. 'There's no way it's Kass, no way.' He falters in fear, but the stumble makes him look indecisive. Still I don't speak.

King John opens his arms, a satisfied grin on his smug face. 'She's the biggest threat and the most obvious choice. Take her out now. Who'll second me?'

'I will.' A voice from behind him seals my fate. The thin-faced woman with purple-dyed hair smirks and folds her arms across her chest. I haven't spoken one word to her since we've been here; I don't even know her name. Her obvious alliance with King John has definitely put me off approaching her. Glasses Guy looks pissed he didn't get in there first. Satisfied, King John puts his gloves back on and everyone follows.

'Thank you, Sandra.' King John bows to her.

'I nominate him.' Rhodri points to King John spitting out the *him* like a sour taste.

'Seconded,' Demi shouts beating Lewis by a second.

'You have to give a reason,' purple-haired Sandra, says.

'Because he's an arsehole,' Rhodri says. 'Anyone who decides that quickly can't be trusted. He's a Werewolf, hundred per cent.'

'And we thought it was 'cause you were shagging her.' Sandra mocks to a loud rippling of laughter.

Rhodri's eyes blaze with anger.

'Don't,' I beg him. 'It won't help.'

A drone dips down in front of me. I stare right into the camera. 'I'm innocent.'

The last sand in the timer flows into the bottom. Our time has run out. My chest tightens and I struggle to breathe as my reality becomes crystal clear. My game is very close to being over.

For good.

19

My head and hands are trapped inside the wooden holes of the pillory. I'm bent over, awkward and uncomfortable and have to crane my head upwards to see. They've taken off my mic. The only thing keeping me upright is knowing King John is in the pillory next to me. One of us is about to be eliminated and my chances of survival don't look good. Previous winners are targeted first. It's what always happens in all-star games.

Thoughts and questions thump against my temples in double time. What will happen to Thea if I'm evicted? Surely Skye won't punish her?

Now would be a really good time for DC Brown to find us.

Draigodân speaks. 'Castle Dwellers, you have accused two of lycanthropy and of the brutal murder of Seth Gooder. This is your chance to remove one threat from the game before the moon bleeds tonight.'

The castle is silent.

'The accused will now defend themselves. You will vote by placing a black stone at the feet of the guilty.'

Everyone gets to see how you voted? If I wasn't fighting for my life right now, I could use that information to my advantage.

'The audience will also be contributing to your fate. They have the power to decide how you fare on the Gauntlet.'

Every part of me is screaming for help. I need to think of something quick.

'King John, you have thirty seconds in which to defend yourself.'

There's shuffling beside me. 'I came here to win. I've made no secret of that and that's why I'm standing in front of you now. I'm no Werewolf but I am a danger.' He sounds too cocky, too confident, like he knows something I don't. 'Kass,' he spits my name out like a bad taste, 'has the Werewolf mark on her hand. We all saw it. AND she was seen at the murder scene. She may not have put any names in the fire yet, but she is guilty. She's a Werewolf, possibly the Alpha and that's why she's the only one marked. We must eliminate her now.'

The ripple of agreement makes panic surge through my body. He's already won their vote. How can I argue with that?

I raise my head awkwardly.

'I'm a Peasant,' I say. 'It's the perfect double bluff to play me as an innocent again but I swear I'm telling the truth.' I sound so guilty as I profess my innocence and try to keep the desperate begging out of my voice. 'And this' – I wiggle my gloved hand from the secured hole – 'this is a scratch from the forest. Only Seth had a mark on his hand and he was murdered, maybe it's how the Werewolves mark their victims? It's coincidence, not proof. It doesn't mean I'm a Werewolf, or the Alpha, it doesn't mean anything. Please don't waste the vote.' My mind is screaming attack, but I hardly know the guy standing beside me. 'Look, just because King John says something doesn't make it true. You may think he has all the answers, but he doesn't care about you. He's in this to win. He'll throw you all to the wolves to save himself.'

Draigodân interrupts my pathetic pleas. 'It's time to vote.'

One by one the players come forward and place a black stone at our feet.

Seven stones to five in my favour. It's close but our alliance is holding up.

'The Castle Council has spoken. With seven votes, King John is the first to be eliminated.'

Relief is making me drunk as the world sways in front of my eyes. A cheer from the fire makes me smile. Definitely Lewis.

'Wait.' King John interrupts the celebration. 'I have a shield.'

What?

The circle disintegrates into shouting. I recognise Rhodri and Lewis in the noisy protests. How the hell did he pull that off?

'You have a shield?' Draigodân's unsurprised, which of course he would be as he can see and hear everything that happens in here.

'In my pocket,' King John says. 'Someone help me.'

I strain my head to see the action next to me, my skin rubbing against the smooth wood. Purple-haired Sandra's next to him. Reaching into his pocket, she pulls out a small dragon shield, holding it up triumphantly.

Panic surges through me. I try to free myself from the pillory. It doesn't work. I'm stuck waiting to hear my fate from a red dragon hologram in a medieval castle somewhere in Wales.

A drone buzzes in front of my face.

Draigodân lifts his head. 'King John has played a shield. All votes for King John are now voided. The accused—'

'Wait.' A shout interrupts Draigodân. The voice is familiar but I can't place it. 'She has an action card. In her pocket.'

What? There's nothing in my pocket.

'Somebody check.' The voice is urgent.

Rhodri's by my side. 'Which pocket?'

'I don't know,' I sob.

His hand dives into my trouser pocket. 'There's nothing there.' He's swearing under his breath.

'Try the other,' Lewis says his voice cracking as he hovers beside me.

Rhodri's holding something. 'I've got it.' His relief is tangible. 'I've got it. It's an action card.'

Lewis kisses the top of my head. 'Well played,' he whispers. 'Did you pick it out of the middle hole?' There's an imperceptible change in his tone. 'Why did you tell Marcus?'

Marcus? My mind is in overdrive. What the hell is

happening? I didn't have anything in my pocket. I didn't tell Marcus anything.

Draigodân speaks. 'The accused has played the Dungeon card.' His hologrammed image glitches in the dark. 'The Dungeon card is an action card.'

The sigh that floods the air is so palpable I can taste it. I lean against the wooden struts to keep me vertical. How did Marcus know I had an action card in my pocket and how the hell did it get there? I failed the task. I got nothing from the middle hole. My mind is screaming questions while my heart thumps double time.

A huge pause fills the space as Draigodân freezes, silent and still as though this whole Dungeon card has taken him by surprise too. His magnificent head judders then moves freely. 'Whoever plays the Dungeon card will be removed from play for one night phase and placed in the dungeons.'

Wait, what? Panic surfaces again.

'Both accused are free.'

A loud cheer erupts. Guards appear and unlock us from the pillories. As my hands and neck are released my legs give up and I crumple to the floor. Strong arms curl under my elbows holding me up. I look up expecting Rhodri but find myself staring into a pair of trusting, brown eyes.

'We've got you,' Demi whispers, helping me stand.

King John's stretching. He salutes me. 'Till next time.' He walks towards his 'team'. Glasses Guy and Sandra whoop and pat him on the back like he's just won an Olympic gold.

I guess, in a way, we have.

I move towards Lewis. I want to tell him that I didn't *not* tell him but the guards bar my way.

'Come with us,' the robotic AI voice demands.

A hood is thrown over my head. There's struggling and shouting behind me and I'm dragged away from my friends.

'Kass.' Lewis' frightened voice rings out of the scramble. 'Kass.'

My heart beats a panicked rhythm once again. Night's about to fall and the Werewolves are preparing to hunt. Tonight the moon will bleed and one of us will be murdered.

20

Unsympathetic fingers curl around my shoulder, guiding me. There's nothing but black behind the hood. My pulse races like it's turbo charged. I concentrate on calming my breathing and trying not to trip on the stupidly steep steps. Hands pull me to a stop. Pulling off the hood they push me into a room. The door slams behind me and I'm left alone.

The room is circular, lit by torches hung onto the walls. Arrow-slitted windows create shafts of moonlight, too high and too thin to give away my location. Wooden boards creak underfoot.

'Kass?' My name echoes against the cold stone walls. Hidden in the shadows, huddled under blankets is a body. The form shuffles up, tripping on the blanket.

'Whoopsie.'

'Max!' I dive forward almost knocking him over.

'Ow.' His voice is muffled against my shoulder. 'Hurting now,' he says as I squeeze him a little too tight.

I release him. I haven't seen Max in real life for ages and the months haven't been kind. I'm used to the dark bags under his eyes from nightly hours of gaming, but the haunted look is new, as is the anxious way his eyes flit around the room. The trembling in his hands and his body flinching at every small noise tell the story of his current confinement way better than words.

'Kass?' His eyes are puffy and bloodshot. Tear lines streak his dirty face. His bruises look worse close up. As well as a black eye, his face is swollen down one side and a blue-black bruise hugs his jawline, spreading up to his cheek. Dried blood mixes with dirt to darken his cheeks and chin, and the skin underneath is sallow and stretched. He looks like he's been here for months not days.

'You came.' He clings to me.

'We're here, Lewis and Rhodri too. We've come to get you out.'

My eyes scan the room looking for blinking red lights or microphones.

Max pulls away, wiping his nose with the back of his hand. 'There're no cameras. We're safe.'

I cringe at the irony of his words. Trapped inside a room in a castle held hostage by a psychopath, we're anything but safe. My hand feels for the mic hanging around my neck. It's gone. I check the battery pack around my waist before remembering they removed it when they put me in the pillory.

Max shuffles back to his corner. 'Thea's here too. She—'

'Where?' I interrupt. 'Have you talked to her?'

'She told me she was here.' He puts his hands over his ears and crouches into a ball, making himself small.

'Thea?' He's not making sense. 'Thea told you? You've seen her?'

He shakes his head. 'Skye. She comes to see me; she likes to talk. She tells me things.' He lifts his head and shouts, 'Hold onto your fingers, Thea.' He holds his arms out, showing me his grubby hands. 'I'm holding onto mine.' He pauses. 'Sometimes I hear her crying.'

He's rambling, it's hard to understand. 'Max.' I take his trembling hands in mine. 'It's okay.'

Tears roll down his cheeks. 'She hates you, you and Rhodri. She wants you to pay for what you did. She wants us all to pay. It's all our fault … my fault.'

My heart breaks to see him so broken. I whisper gently, 'How long have you been here?'

'Seems like forever,' he says. 'Days I think?' He rubs his head and leans back against the wall. 'She'll never let us go. She thinks you cheated her.'

'How could we? That's insane,' I say.

'You outsmarted her. She hates that. She can't accept the truth, so she's changed it.' He shrugs. 'She's changed the narrative so the only possible way you could have escaped *Lie or Die* was by cheating.'

'We didn't cheat; we survived.'

'But you didn't earn it. You don't deserve it.' He laughs, a sharp bitter sound that shatters like glass. Turning his attention to the wall he scratches at the surface with his broken nails. 'Not me apparently. More stupid than stupid, the one who piggy-backed on the heroes to save his own skin. What did they say?' He lifts his chin as if quoting from a book. '*Max trampled over the dead bodies with a simpering whine. He should have died in that house and let the more worthy live.*'

Those cruel words slice into me. I remember every spiteful comment the trolls fired out at us, every hurtful line they typed so righteously while hiding like cowards behind their screens.

'I think I deserve it.' His voice trembles. 'All the hate. That's why Skye chose me: the pathetic one, the victim, the one who always needs rescuing. I don't deserve to be here when—'

'Stop,' I say before he names the dead. If *Lie or Die* broke him then those trolls smashed him into tiny pieces. Just like Thea. They wanted someone to blame, someone to hate and they turned on them. Skye has picked at those barely healed scabs until they've burst and bled, and the small amount of healing has been wiped away in a guilty heartbeat leaving nothing but shame and guilt and an overwhelming sense of blame.

Max takes a shuddering breath. 'I think it makes her feel like she's winning, you know? Like she has all the power. She likes to talk about how she's in control. I want to tell her how much I hate her. I want to make her pay, I really do, but I just can't.' He sobs. 'She's right. I'm just a spineless loser.'

Skye's unbelievably cruel. 'What else do you know?' It's hard to project strong and brave when I'm dying inside. 'Please.'

He squeezes my hands. 'I listen to the guards outside the door. It's easy. Those masks don't make for indoor voices.'

'What do they say?' I whisper.

'That she's not doing this alone.'

I knew it.

The more Max talks, the calmer he gets. 'She has a backer, some zillionaire-guy and that's no exaggeration. He's minted, like on another level super rich. He's funding all this like it's pocket money. And the audience? Skye boasts how she's ripping off the fat cats and the rich elite, making them pay shitloads to watch. They're all part of his world and he's totally using them for profit. It's dark web shit, really dark.'

The thought of someone more powerful than Skye makes me tremble.

'Tell me about him,' I say.

'Skye's nothing compared to him; he's like Ganondorf to her Bowser.'

I'm not getting his references, but I get the idea. If this guy – this boss – is worse than Skye, then we're in way more trouble than I imagined.

'We did this.' Max interrupts my thoughts. 'I've had a lot of time to think in here. We gave them *Lie or Die* and all the power that came from Henry's video of horrors. We showed them how to level up. By exposing reality TV, we forced it underground, made it bigger and stronger than ever before. We showed them what was possible. They hide in the cloud of anonymity, safe in a cocoon of riches and wealth. They believe what they want to believe, the truth is obsolete.'

'We need to get out of here.' I run to the door, pushing against the solid wood. 'Now.'

'The only way out is to play the game,' Max says.

My fists pound on the door. 'There must be another way.'

'Stop.' Max is behind me. 'Please, if they hear you, they'll get angry.' I let him lead me back to the blankets. 'Tell me. What are you? Peasant?'

I nod.

There's movement on the other side of the door and we press ourselves into the damp walls. Guards step into the room, long batons gripped menacingly in their hands. Another walks between them placing a tray on the floor. The door shuts behind them with a heavy groan.

Max runs to the tray, carrying it back to the corner. On the tray are two bowls of steaming food. He sits and grabs one, not waiting for me.

My brain's whirring fast. 'There're two of us. We can overwhelm them and escape.'

Max shrugs. 'And go where? Out there is just more castle. We'll end up running around in a circle until they catch us. This place is totally secure. The only way out is through the gates or over the walls.'

'Then we jump,' I say. Any plan, however insane, is better than no plan.

'Too high, and even if we did manage to find a bit where we fell in the water and not break our necks on the bank the guards will get us. I'm serious, Kass. I may be the biggest coward going but I've thought about it. Shit, I even tried it and got this for my effort.' He points to the shiner surrounding his eye. 'There is no way out.'

I believe him.

'Eat,' Max says.

'Is it safe?' I ask remembering the drugged water Skye used in series one to keep us all asleep.

'It won't kill you. You're Skye's star player, her Maximus Decimus Meridius.'

I don't react.

'*Gladiator*? Russell Crowe?' Max looks so disappointed. 'If we ever get out of here, you are going to have to get some proper pop culture.'

'I have culture,' I mumble.

'Rhodri would know.' He carries on with a sigh. 'The audience have paid a lot of money to watch you and they want their money's worth. She won't waste your death off camera.'

'Why don't the audience help us? Don't they know what they're watching?'

'They know but they don't care. That's the thrill. To know they are part of an exclusive club that has the power to do anything. We're not real to them; they watch us from their screens and don't give us a second thought. They've completely dehumanised us.'

We fall into silence. Max wraps layers of blankets around him and gestures to the food. Reluctantly I take the steaming bowl. It's soup and it's warm. I'm so hungry I hardly taste it.

'Help is coming,' I say. 'We just need to hang on.'

Startled, Max looks up. 'Help? How?'

'It's a long shot,' I explain, wanting to give him some small breadcrumb of hope. 'I left a note in Lewis' car, a clue. DC Brown will find it, I'm sure. He'll figure it out and find us.'

Max's reaction is not what I expect. He buries his head in his hands, his dark black curls tumbling through his dirty fingers. 'What have you done?'

I squeeze his arm in reassurance.

'It's all going to be okay,' I say in my best grown-up voice. 'He'll come.'

Max raises his head and looks at me, his bloodshot eyes swimming with tears. 'That's what I'm afraid of.'

21

When I wake, Max is gone. The room's empty. I almost believe it was a dream, then my eyes rest on the two empty bowls and I know my nightmare's real and my dream's the safe place.

The January castle cold has seeped to the very marrow of my bones. It's dark, still night. But where have they taken Max?

I stand, shaking out my limbs to exorcise the damp and search the corners of the room. It's stupid; I know he's gone but I need to do something to fight the panic. I stop at the door.

It's ajar.

I hesitate. My brain fights against the idea of freedom. Is it a test? A trap? I push through the panic. There are no cameras, no microphones. I'm not being watched. Why would Skye set a trap for me here when there's no one to witness it?

My fingers curl around the door and pull it open, my ears straining for sounds. There's nothing but cold silence.

I step outside, closing the door behind me.

I'm on a spiral staircase. Torches hang on the walls illuminating the space. Up or down? I've no idea. The staircase is so steep I can't see anything either way but the worn-down stone steps. Choosing down, my hand clings onto the metal handrail, my shoulder against the wall, my hand clutching the centre column as I descend in a swirl. As I reach another door I stop, stepping onto a small platform. There are voices below. I strain to listen but it's hard to hear over the banging of my heart.

The exchange is hurried and urgent. The whispered conversation carries up the spiral and I recognise Skye's voice.

She sounds impatient. 'I told you, they're safe, but I'm not liable for their own stupid actions, that's on you.'

The second voice, male and authoritative, talks over her. 'Portia has a more level head than her sister. They'll be fine, just keep them safe.'

Portia? Why would Skye and this man care about the twins' safety?

'They're being closely monitored, and they're fine.'

'Just make sure they are.' The male voice carries weight. My heart jumps into my throat. Could this be the big boss Max talked about? What do they mean 'being monitored' and why?

Footsteps echo on the stone steps. *Shit.* Someone's coming.

I step back, leaning on the wooden door behind. It moves under my weight. I dart into the room. Closing the door softly I press my body against it, the side of my face glued to the wood, straining to hear. The steps get louder. They pause outside the door. I don't breathe.

The footsteps continue up the stairs. I wait, half expecting them to notice the door to Max's room is unlocked, but the heavy tread doesn't falter, soon fading into nothing. I take a long breath out. Why did they both sound so invested in the twins? Maybe they're the most popular, the favourites to win?

I step back so focused on the door I don't see the obstacle that gets right under my feet, tripping me up so completely that I find myself falling backwards into the dark room.

What the...? I land on my bum in one almighty bump, knocking the wind right out of me. Pain rockets through me. I struggle to catch my breath as my eyes search the dark.

There's something on the floor, a silhouetted bulk. No wonder I went arse over tit. I tut, impatient with myself for being so clumsy. My hands reach out and touch it.

A sliver of moonlight catches in the window and the room is afforded a small ration of light, just enough for me to make out details. My body jolts backwards while my eyes lock onto the dead eyes staring back at me from a face I know.

The face I've been waiting for.

The face of DC Brown.

22

I stare at the body of DC Brown. How is he here inside the castle?

I press my body against the wall, desperate to make space between me and him, but that doesn't stop the horror or the sense of overwhelming despair as our one chance of rescue lies dead on the floor.

He's lying face up, head tilted towards me, eyes glazed and staring. Blood has oozed over his denim-coloured shirt and dried like a giant inkblot. There's a deep gash in his side. A knife wound. I hate that I know how he died. I hate that I'm not surprised.

Reluctantly, I force myself to search the body. His right arm falls towards me, something clutched in his hand. Inhaling a huge dollop of courage through gritted teeth, I pull the paper from his cold fingers.

It's my message, my dragon logo picture. It worked. He found a way to track us here. Or did Skye kill him at the car and bring his body here just to torture me? Either way, it's my fault. I led him to his death and destroyed our only chance of escape.

My pulse races. How could I have been so stupid? Skye's been playing me from the minute she sent that invitation. She knew exactly what I'd do. Did she put that Dungeon card in place so I'd be brought here? Did she leave the door open so I'd escape and find him? She wants me to know I can't beat her, that she's too clever for me.

I dart into the corner as my stomach heaves. My legs buckle and my last hope vomits over the wooden floor.

Wiping my mouth, I gulp in the blood-tinged air and pull myself to standing. I can't stay here. Dawn is creeping through the window casting a yellowed glow over his corpse. The guards will be coming for me soon.

A sound makes my heart stop.

Sobbing.

I look around the empty room trying to find where it's coming from. Max's room's above so it must be coming from below.

Crouching on all fours I press my ear to the dusty floorboards. The sobs seep up through the wood.

Gently, I knock on the floor. The crying stops.

'Max? Thea?' I loud whisper. A muffled cry confirms my suspicions.

I scramble up and head down the stairs, twisting round the worn stones until I reach another door. I squeeze my body into the small platform space next to it.

'Max?' The whisper sounds so loud in the quiet stairwell. 'Thea?'

There's the sound of sobbing inside.

'Kass?'

One word that makes my heart sing. Thea. I've found her.

'Kass?' The voice sounds urgent and terrified.

'I'm here,' I say. 'And Lewis and Rhodri, and we're going to get you out.'

'Help me.'

'Is Max with you?' I ask but receive nothing but sobs in reply. The sound makes my heart break. I fumble with the door and the latch. It's locked. I thump the wood in frustration and Thea cries out again.

'Thea, listen to me, I'm so sorry. We will get you out.' Thea goes quiet. I press my face into the door. 'I promise.' Taking a small chunk of my sleeve between my teeth I bite down hard and pull until a piece rips away. I push the black material into a small hole in the stone wall outside the door. Heavy footsteps signal someone's coming. 'I'll be back, I promise. Help is coming.'

'No ... don't leave me. Kass?'

Footsteps are getting closer; I need to go. I quickly climb back up the stairs, past the room with DC Brown's body and up into the room I shared with Max. Closing the door I crumple into a ball, my body shaking with uncontrollable despair as the magnitude of my situation takes hold.

I just lied to my best friend. There is no way out.

And no help is coming.

23

The guards walk into the room, batons thudding in their palms, the sharp thwack, thwack, enough to intimidate me into silence. I don't fight as they hang the microphone back around my neck and throw the black hood over my head. I let them lead me out and away from Max and Thea. Skye's playing with me – dangling Thea like a carrot to make me jump through her twisted hoops.

DC Brown is dead. No help is coming. We're completely on our own. It's up to us to stop Skye, but right now she's got us so deep into the game I can't see any way out. Anger raps around my despair and keeps me standing. I won't let her get away with this, not again. My hatred for Skye and all she's done rages like a forest fire, the desire for justice and revenge fanning the flames.

A sharp push from behind keeps me walking. The push was slight, but I adopt my best football dive and fall, feeling the ground with my hands, trying to paint a picture of where I am. There's smooth stone beneath me – cobbles? I'm dragged back to my feet. Frosty grass crunches under my boots then the hollow sound of wooden boards before more slippery grass. After what seems like forever, I'm pulled to a stop and the mask is removed.

I'm back in camp. Demi's sat with Billy and Arti, huddled around the heat of the campfire. Lewis has his back to me, his tangerine hair a little more faded than last night. Mai's next to him, her hands moving quickly as she talks. Ravi's facing my way, his exhausted face haggard as he stares into the flames.

I can't see Rhodri. A quick sweep of the campfire tells me he's not there. I frown, ignoring the suspicion that's scratching at my skin and making me ridiculously needy.

'She's back.' Ravi jumps up.

There's an ear-shattering squeal from the Shakespeare Sisters. King John storms into his tent, Glasses Guy following. Arti fist pumps the air looking genuinely relieved to see me, and Marcus nods gravely. Lewis races towards me, Mai and Demi close behind.

Lewis picks me up in a twirling embrace, his head buried in my shoulder. 'Don't you ever leave us again,' he sobs. 'Don't you bloody dare.'

'We knew you'd be fine,' Mai says thumping my arm. 'Just knew it.'

'I found them,' I whisper into Lewis' ear. He immediately pulls back, so many emotions flying across his face.

'Where?' He frowns. 'Wait, them?'

Shit, I forgot I hadn't told him about Thea. Pulling him to one side, I turn my shoulder to shield us from the watching drone and smother my microphone with my top. 'Skye has Thea; she's in the castle with Max,' I whisper. 'I wanted to tell you before, but she said—'

'You knew and you're telling me this now?' Lewis' cheeks flush a strange shade of beetroot.

'Dude, where's your microphone?' Demi taps Billy on the chest.

Flustered Billy turns white as his hands claw at his tunic. 'Shit … I forgot.'

'Well go get it. That's a rule break,' says Mai as they shoo him away from us and into the tent.

Lewis turns back to me, the hurt and anger easy to read.

'I didn't want to freak you out,' I say guiltily.

'Well colour me freakin',' Lewis shouts. Calming himself he whispers, 'Tell me everything.'

'She's here. I found her but I couldn't get her out.'

'And they're okay? She's okay?' Seeing me nod, Lewis clutches his chest, the shock and relief so great it's almost flooring him.

'You should have told me,' he says.

I stumble over my words in my guilty rush. 'I know but there was the whole Marcus imposter thing, and I couldn't…' I hate the way he's looking at me. 'I didn't want to make it any worse.'

'Is that everything?' His eyes bore into mine. 'Don't lie to me, Kass. I'm a big boy. I can handle it.'

I want to tell him about DC Brown, but I hesitate. Would it help?

'That's all.' I struggle to maintain convincing eye contact as I swallow down the truth. I can't take away the last trace of hope. Why is the lie so much easier? 'I'm sorry.'

'You said that already.' Lewis turns and strides away.

I start to follow but Faith bursts around the corner, Rhodri right behind. I pretend not to see the guilt or the way Faith dives into the tent the moment she sees me. The relief that fills Rhodri's face when his eyes catch mine leaves me wondering if I imagined it. I hesitate, unsure. Moving towards me, he takes me in his arms and holds me close.

And I'm safe.

'Time for the told you sos,' Demi teases, coming out of the tent. 'He was about to start a riot assault on the inner keep to get you back.'

Rhodri stiffens at Demi's words and pulls away. His palm wipes his face, leaving behind a scowl. 'Was not,' he says so vehemently everyone stops to look at him. 'What?'

Faith calls him through the glassy wall of the tent. Rhodri tenses. He mumbles something I can't understand and ducks into the tent and right back to Faith.

What just happened?

Lewis takes my elbow and leads me to the other side of the campfire. His anger's cooled; the fire in his eyes has burnt itself out. Billy joins us, microphone secured around his neck.

The air is charged with tension so palpable I could reach out and grab it. 'What the hell happened last night?' I whisper.

'Last night was—' He can't find the words which for Lewis is rare.

'Intense,' Billy finishes his sentence.

Looking at the faces surrounding the fire it's clear whatever happened last night was bad. Everyone is way jumpier than yesterday. Apart from the twins. Sitting, munching on a bowl of breakfast rice they're as chatty and starry-eyed as when we first came in. Marcus is hovering by the tent flap, watching them. He catches my eye. His cheeks flare a guilty red and he ducks inside the tent.

I turn back to the campfire. No one will look me in the eye.

'What are you not telling me?' I say.

Billy puts a comforting hand on Lewis' arm, and I notice the way Lewis' hand covers it with a tender squeeze.

'Sandra is...' Lewis stops.

'Sandra is...?' I say remembering the purple-haired woman who seconded my nomination. Rhodri and Faith are huddled together in the tent and it's making me want to scream.

'It's like Dougie,' he whispers.

My eyes run across the names hanging by the fire. Sandra's is missing.

'Show me.' I jump up eager to put space between me and the green tent. 'Where is she?'

Lewis leads the way back to the Portakabin in the tower, Billy following behind. He stops outside the room with the caged dummy. The iron gate bars our way, the black space inside as uninviting and eerie as a house of horrors. Billy hangs back, gesturing for me to go first, hiding his eyes behind his hand. A crow caws ominously from a castle turret. A low buzz fills the quiet when a camera drone catches us up and hovers in the entrance, watching.

I step closer, my fingers curling round the iron bars and I peer inside. It takes a minute to adjust to the dark of the dungeon-like room.

The body in the cage is Sandra. I recognise the purple hair. Her dead eyes are open. Three sharp lines are carved into her cheek. The mark of the Werewolf. Blood meanders down her chin and drips from the metal cage, pooling on the floor beneath.

Lewis is tugging at my elbow, his free hand covering his mouth. I ignore him, searching for any clue that might tell us how she got into this cage and who put her here. She's curled up, her face set at an unnatural angle. Pressed against the metal bars she's staring out at us. Someone wanted us to see her hair and the mark, they wanted us to recognise her from the doorway.

'King John says her neck's broken,' Lewis says. 'He knows these things apparently.'

Waves of nausea roll through my stomach. 'What happened?'

'There was howling,' Lewis says. 'Like when we arrived in the forest. Some of the guys wanted to go take a look. We told them not to, but they were being all pseudo-tough and Big Balls was showing off.'

No need to ask who Big Balls is; he's obviously talking about King John.

'They left the fire; they thought it was all part of the game. The howling got louder, like there was a whole pack and then...' Billy shudders, his eyes flitting to Lewis.

'Then what?'

'Nothing,' Lewis says. 'It got really quiet. Demi and Rhodri wanted to go after them.'

'But the Werewolves have to put a name in the fire for there to be a murder,' I say. 'Someone stayed at the fire, yes?' Lewis and Billy stare at the ground. 'Please tell me someone stayed at the fire.'

'You weren't here,' Lewis says defensively. 'Everyone was freaking out. No one was thinking straight. It was just for a minute.'

'Giving the Werewolves time to double back to the unattended fire,' I say. 'Shit, Lewis, that got her murdered.'

'You think I don't know that?' Lewis slams his hands on his hips. 'Do I look like I need your judgement right now?'

'We couldn't have known it meant actual murder. We were just playing the game,' Billy says. We glare at each other and guilt races through my veins. Truth? I doubt I'd have acted any differently. I'd have been scared shitless just like everyone else and Sandra would still be dead.

Billy gestures back into the room, his voice shaking. 'I proper don't trust anyone who calls themselves King. He could have lured us away, hidden until we all left the fire, then doubled back. No one will suspect you if you murder one of your own. It's textbook gameplay.' He grimaces. 'I don't mean King John actually killed her. He's a prick not a murderer, even if he did know how her neck was...' he trails off.

'King John didn't do this,' I say. 'Skye did. It's all part of her game.'

'And the game just got real,' Lewis says.

Billy's eyes flit between us. 'I didn't sign up for this... I never thought...' He turns to Lewis. 'I wish I'd listened to you, back at the forest camp. I don't want to die.'

'Then don't get caught,' I say, my words sounding way more harsh than intended. Lewis glares at me but my mouth keeps on going. 'The only way out is to survive the game. *That's* the reality.' I know I should be more patient but I've got my own problems. I can't babysit those stupid enough to sign up to play. I'll leave that to Lewis. 'Why are you here, Billy?' The question tumbles out of my mouth once more. 'Why *are* you playing?'

He takes a while to answer. 'Because what's out there waiting for me is way worse.' He looks at me, his eyes heavy with regret. 'At least in here I have a chance, or so I thought.'

'What did you—'

'Thirteen left.' Lewis cuts me off. 'With the twins playing as one. And the general consensus is the number will be culled in the trial today.'

'We could leave. Escape.' Billy's eyes flit eagerly from me to Lewis. He points to the lake in front of us and the bank on the far side. 'We could swim it. It's do-able. We could get the hell out. There's a few in camp who'd do the same.'

'The twins?' Even they couldn't brush this murder off as some TV trickery.

Billy pulls a face. 'Actually no, I don't think they think it's real. They were laughing at the body. They thought it was a Sandra dummy.' He gestures to the room. 'You can't blame them; we can't get close enough to really see.'

'You've got to be kidding me!' The last remnants of my patience explode all over the castle green. I point through the bars. 'How is that not clear?' How could they not realise the danger they're in? It's one thing to think you're playing a game with serious consequences but another thing entirely to be so completely oblivious to the danger that you ignore a dead body that's literally staring you in the face. Angrily, I point up to the guards on the wall. 'See them?' I say. 'You think they're just going to let us walk away?'

Billy's eyes narrow suspiciously. 'You don't know.'

'Yes, I do. Because I know Skye and I've played this game before.'

Lewis grabs his hands. 'She's right, hun; playing the game's our only chance. And not everyone is going to make it.'

Billy pulls his hands away and steps back. 'You don't know that. You don't know.' Spinning on his heel he runs back towards camp.

Lewis scowls at me and heads after Billy. I follow.

This place is ridiculous. It's bad enough having the drones and the cameras and the mic hanging round my neck making proper conversation impossible, but now both my best friend and my boyfriend seem tighter with delusional people they've only just met than with me. I can feel them both slipping away and I've no clue if it's me or the game.

I bite back a sob as paranoia and self-doubt threaten to hijack the last threads of common sense.

I reach the campfire and I stare across the moat to the inner island. That must be where they're keeping them. The wooden planks I felt beneath my boots must have been the connecting bridge. If I can get in I can find my way back to Thea. I need to keep my head in this crazy messed-up game and remember exactly why we're here.

I try to breathe out all the weak but the soul-crushing fear that moved in after *Lie or Die* has burrowed so deep into my bones I've no clue where post-game Kass starts and before-TV-show Kass ends.

'Kass?' Rhodri's walking towards me. I smile, he doesn't. I'm desperate to talk to him, to come up with a plan to take down Skye, just like last time, but the set of his jaw and the way his fists are clenched so tightly by his sides makes me pause.

'We need to talk.' Without waiting for my answer, he strides past me back towards the tower and Sandra.

I follow, increasing my step to catch up. Faith's

watching me from the tent, her arms folded across her chest. I ignore her but the sense of dread rising in my stomach is harder to overlook. Whatever he's about to say, I'll bet my life it isn't good.

Rhodri leads me to the furthest part of the green, well out of earshot of the camp. He hovers against the castle wall, hands in pockets, head down staring at the grass.

A camera drone settles above us.

'I'm sorry,' he says.

'What for?' My voice sounds squeaky. 'Just say it before one of us is dead.'

'That's not funny.' His eyes flash angrily as they flit from me to the drone.

I shrug. I'm not the one who should be apologising.

'I can't do this.'

I brace myself. 'Do what?'

'You and me. Here. The game.' He kicks the ground, hands in pockets, eyes firmly stuck staring at the grass. 'It's too much. There's too much at risk.'

I say nothing, concentrating on keeping my face set like rock. I'm listening to his lame excuses, but his words fall on my ears in fractured snippets while my insides scream in agony.

'It's putting both of us in more danger… It's for the best … bad timing … can't do this right now.'

'What exactly are you saying?' If he's dumping me in here, in front of the world, he can damn well say it.

His face is blushed red. Still he refuses to look at me. 'It's over.'

My throat makes a weird noise. 'You know there's a dead body in there, right?'

'That's exactly my point,' Rhodri says. 'I can't do it. I can't play the game if I'm worrying about you.'

'I'm not asking you to,' I say. His argument's not making any sense. Less than twenty-four hours ago he was calling me *cariad* and begging me to run away in Venitiwa.

He stares at the camera. 'I can't keep saving you.'

I swallow down the disbelief. No way, I'm not buying it; I know him too well. This has Skye all over it. Whatever is happening here I can bet my life it's being stage managed by her, just like the way she's controlling me with Thea. 'Rhodri, please, whatever this is we can—'

'You two look very suspicious all the way down here by yourselves.' Faith appears and cements herself firmly to Rhodri's side. 'Whatever could you be talking about?'

'Could you leave us for a minute?' I say, immediately thrown by her presence.

'Stay,' Rhodri says.

Faith's eyes move from one of us to the other and I don't miss the stab of glee that flickers across her face.

'You said you would never lie to me.' Ignoring her, I push my shoulders back and stare at him, challenging him to look at me.

'I'm not lying,' he cries. The intensity of his words catches me off guard.

I shake my head in disbelief. 'I don't believe you.' He stares up to the sky, a sign I take as frustration. I step closer, my voice one pathetic beg. 'You don't mean this. Please, let's talk…'

Rhodri's eyes flash icy cold. His arm reaches for Faith. His hand curls behind her neck and pulls her towards him until their lips meet.

Nothing could prepare me for the sight of them kissing. Betrayal detonates through me, eviscerating Skye and this game in one horrified heartbeat. It's real, I'm sure of it. No one could fake it that well. And I just stand there, unable to tear my eyes away as my heart shatters into a million pieces.

Finally, Rhodri pulls away from her, his head snapping towards mine. The disdain burning in his eyes is like a fist punch straight to my guts.

I take a small step back willing my legs not to crumble beneath me. 'You're right.' It takes all my strength to look impassively into those cold eyes. 'It's for the best.'

Pulling his note from my bra, I throw it on the floor where it lays in a screwed-up mess. Childish maybe, but it's all I have, and I *need* to do something. I turn and walk back to the camp. He doesn't stop me.

The only thing that follows me is the camera.

24

The cold breakfast rice sticks in my throat, making me gag. I blink rapidly to stop the uninvited tears from cascading down my cheeks. I'm trying to pull myself together, to act like nothing's happened but I'm not sure I'm pulling it off. Rhodri's left me alone since my big dumping on camera and public humiliation. He's hanging around with Faith now, obviously. She's walking around with a look of barely concealed smugness on her stupid Lara Croft face, and I hate her almost as much as I hate Skye. I hope Skye's happy. I bet we delivered good ratings for that storyline.

I was gone for a night and while I was away the whole universe shifted. Everything I thought I knew has been turned upside down and dumped on its head and I've no idea how to process it.

'Everything okay? You look weird.' Lewis scans my face in concern. I rub my eyes quickly. I want to talk to him so badly but I'm scared if I start, this not-so-brave face I've cemented on will crumble and crack. I won't give Skye the satisfaction of seeing me broken. Or Rhodri and *her*. So, I'm trying to push it down, turn it to stone like Medusa and hold onto the one thought that's keeping me going – getting back to Thea and Max and getting out.

I plaster a false smile onto my lips and pray he doesn't see the shake. If Lewis can pretend to be fine, then so can

I. 'I'm good,' I say. 'As good as I can be trapped in a castle with a psychopathic serial killer.'

'Same page, babes,' he says with an equally false grin. 'Same page.'

'I'm sorry about before, with Billy,' I say, trying to make peace before all my bridges burn.

Lewis holds up his hands. 'Don't worry about it. He's a good guy, just made some bad choices. Go easy on him.'

'You like him.' I nudge him, glad of a conversation we can actually have in front of the cameras.

Lewis grins. 'Yeah, I do.' Grin turns to a frown. 'I'm not stupid, Kass. I know what I'm doing.'

I put my hands up. 'No judgement. Just be careful.'

He nods. 'King John's not to be trusted. And unpopular opinion but I don't trust Ravi.'

'Amara's dad? He's harmless enough.'

Lewis pulls a face. 'I'm not so sure. There's something about him that makes me—'

Draigodân appears, his voice show-host cheerful. 'Good morning, Castle Dwellers. I trust you slept well.'

Rumblings of dissatisfaction fill the air. The haunted expressions on everyone's faces prove the opposite. We gather around the fire, freaked out and super scared. Maybe now everyone's realised what kind of game we're playing. All except King John who's smiling at the dragon like he's actually enjoying himself. Rhodri's stood with Faith. I pretend not to notice.

'Under the pull of the blood moon, the Werewolves

have claimed their second victim. Goodbye, Sandra, so sad to see you go.' Draigodân sounds sincere until a small chuckle escapes his mouth. 'But I did warn you not to let the dogs out.' His huge mouth forms what can only be described as a smile. 'Somebody thought Sandra was a risk. Somebody thought Sandra was a danger to their game. Or was Sandra simply in the wrong place at the wrong time, her despicable murder designed to keep you all off the scent?'

No one dares challenge the dragon. Draigodân moves making those closest to him jump back. 'It is now time to progress to the next stage. Castle Dwellers will compete in a trial.' Draigodân turns to look across the moat.

Three coloured rafts are pushed up onto the grass. The two trebuchets have been moved to the edge of the bank facing towards the island in the middle. Next to each medieval machine is a fire basket, burning brightly and a large mound covered by a tarpaulin.

'Castle Dwellers must race across the South Lake in three teams. The first ten contestants to reach the island and enter the middle ward will win the trial. Remaining contestants will be eliminated from the game. Hidden in the South Lake are chests containing immunity shields. You may choose to delay your journey to retrieve them, but this will waste valuable time. The choice is yours. You must now get into three teams: one of five and two of four.'

Draigodân disappears. Dotted across the lake are red

buoys with dragon flags waving in the air. It's tempting, a shield would give immunity and protection. They don't look too far away, and the lake is very crossable. My confidence rises. With the right team we've totally got this.

'The numbers don't make sense,' Mai says counting on her fingers.

'The twins,' Arti says. 'Playing as one. What the dragon should have said is two fives and one four.'

Mai throws up her hands. 'Why didn't he just say that?'

Arti smiles and ambles over to the blue raft with Demi. The twins are making a B-line for me.

'Quick.' Lewis grabs my arm. 'Rhodri?'

Rhodri strides over, nodding his agreement which surprises me. I bite back the snarky comment on the tip of my tongue. Maybe his head is thinking stick with who you know even if his heart's gone rogue.

'You've room for more,' Portia says, bounding over. 'We're with you. You've only got three.'

Marcus is hovering behind them. 'Mai and Demi want you on their raft,' he says to Billy.

'He's on here, so we're a four,' Lewis says.

'But Arti wants you with him,' Marcus says folding his arms.

Billy pulls a face. 'What's it to you?' he says. 'I'm staying here.'

Marcus unfolds his arms, for a minute it looks like

he's going to beg. Looking up at the drones he beckons to the twins. 'Ophelia, Portia. Come with me.'

Ophelia pouts. 'I want to go with Kass and Rhodri.' She leans her head on Rhodri's shoulder in a cutesy move. 'Two for one? We're terrific at rowing. We did it at school.'

Rhodri pushes her away roughly. 'I bet you did. I bet you raced at Henley before lunching in your private yachts.' Ophelia's cheeks blush red. 'We're full.'

Portia's eyes narrow as thin as her pursed lips, her privilege radiating from her like a beacon. 'That's not fair. We got here first.'

'Don't give a flying fuck. We don't need a couple of vacuous airheads wasting our time and getting us killed,' Rhodri says so harshly I cringe. Say no, fine, but don't make enemies, not in here. 'Go on, get lost.'

'No need to be so rude.' Portia's voice is stone. I doubt anyone has ever said no to her in her entire life. Tucking her arm into Ophelia's she turns on her heel. 'You're not all that, y'know. Just wait and see how this plays out. Come on, Fee, let's go somewhere we're wanted.' The look Portia is giving him is full-on toxic. She walks towards Marcus. Ophelia pouts and follows her sister.

Rhodri's already turned his back on them.

What is up with him? He can be moody but he's never usually downright mean. That was harsh. No matter how ridiculous they are, we're all in this together. I'm about to argue we're only four and we could fit one more even if it is Miss Precious or Miss Privileged when Faith ambles over to Rhodri's side and takes his hand. He doesn't pull away. Faith stares right at me, a triumphant challenge cemented across her face.

'My brother was a rower,' she says with a mocking grin. 'He could have gone pro but he had other plans.'

'Really?' Lewis' indignation speaks for me.

'You've got him,' Rhodri nods to Billy.

Lewis looks flustered. 'Yes, but—'

'We're done here.' Rhodri walks to the green raft pulling Faith with him. If she's feeling awkward, she's good at hiding it.

'That was rash,' Lewis whispers to me. 'Speak to him. He shouldn't be making enemies in here.'

'Won't do any good,' I whisper back. 'He's listening to someone else these days.' I cringe at the sympathy flooding Lewis' eyes. 'I hate her,' I hiss. All my insecurities and desperation mix with a simmering anger.

'Steady, remember you're being watched,' Lewis whispers. 'Focus on the game, hun. Let karma do its thing.'

As we reach the green raft Rhodri turns on us, eyes blazing. 'Forget top ten, I plan on being first. Anyone not willing to give one hundred per cent go join another raft. I don't have time for losers.'

'All right, King Welsh.' Lewis spits the words out.

'I don't have time for weak sidekicks,' Rhodri growls. 'I won't risk her for anyone who can't pull their weight.'

'Oh, I can pull my weight.' Lewis' hand dances in front of Rhodri's face. 'So wind your neck in.'

I'm used to Rhodri's mood swings, but this is different. I'm pretty sure the *her* he's referring to isn't me. I'm not even sure it's Faith. Whatever Skye's holding over him has him well and truly spooked.

Billy squeezes my arm. Brilliant, now strangers are sympathising with my relationship.

Eventually three teams stand on the bank. Mai, Arti, Demi and Ravi take the blue boat while King John, Marcus, Glasses Guy and the twins are in the red. The South Lake stretches out in front of us.

'See you on the other side, losers,' King John shouts across from the red raft. 'For those of you who don't make it, I'll see you all in hell!'

His raft jeers noisily.

'Ignore them,' I say. 'He's trying to get in our heads.'

I wait for Rhodri to retaliate but he just stares straight ahead, a small muscle on his temple pulsing with tension. Faith's by his side; Billy is with Lewis. Suddenly I'm feeling like the odd one out.

From the top of the castle wall a trumpet sounds. We grab the wooden raft as Rhodri barks instructions. It takes all of us to get it to the lake. The icy water hits our skin and steals our voices. It claws at our heavy clothes and infiltrates our boots making them drag against our racing steps. We drop the raft, jumping on quickly as much to be out of the cold as to be in the race. Lewis mistimes his jump and belly flops into the water. Hands lean over, dragging him in, losing valuable time. He nods an *I'm ok*, but I'm not convinced. His pale-to-the-point-of-snow-white face tells a different story. He's already shivering. If we don't all sink to a watery grave the threat of hypothermia is very real.

Water crashes against wood while we try to get into optimum position – if any of us had a clue what that was. Standing is impossible as the water beneath us dances every time we move, causing the raft to bob and tilt and throw us off balance.

'Row,' Rhodri screams. 'Row.'

The South Lake stretches out ahead, dark and intimidating. As I plunge my oar into the icy water I add to his fervent command: *Row like your lives depend on it because in this game, they really do.*

25

Rhodri's balanced perfectly at the front of the raft, plunging his oar into the water on one side while Faith mimics him on the other. To be fair she's nailing this whole rowing thing. I stand behind them, opposite Billy as we all try to row in unison. The raft leaps forward.

I'm terrified of falling off; climbing back onto this slippery surface would be almost impossible and could capsize the whole thing.

'Might be better if we kneel?' Billy says.

We drop to our knees and the raft calms. Lewis crouches in the middle making noises of encouragement which, not gonna lie, are more irritating than helpful.

'Row,' Rhodri bellows.

The red raft is in front, Portia screaming instructions. The blue raft's spinning in circles behind us. Mai's voice travels across the water, strong and focused as she tries to pull her team together. I push my oar into the water, concentrating on the rhythm of the team, trying to unify my stroke with theirs.

King John's jeering at us, flicking the finger from the red raft's pole position.

'Faster,' screams Rhodri, his oar hits the water so hard each stroke splashes me with freezing moat water that stings my eyes and trickles down my cheeks. I don't stop, my eyes set on the bank ahead.

It takes forever to drag the raft through the water. My arms ache and my knees scream but fear of sliding off the deck keeps me from moving a muscle.

King John and the red raft suddenly veer to the left and into the centre of the lake.

'They're going for the chest,' Faith shouts, her voice strong, which pisses me off even more. I'm knackered and we're not even halfway.

'Ignore them,' says Billy. 'Just keep going.'

The red raft's heading straight towards one of the buoys. They're so far ahead they'll probably get the shield and still win. King John leaps from the raft to the buoy. Grabbing on with both hands he navigates around the metal shape. It bobs wildly under his weight like a bull in a rodeo. He clings on, his arm outstretched grabbing for the chain that holds the chest below. A triumphant cry tells us he's found it.

Sweat trickles between my shoulder blades.

Lewis is using his oar like a rudder, half submerged in the water he's steering us towards the bank.

'Could be worse,' he shouts. 'At least there're no man-eating sharks.'

As the words leave his mouth a huge splash to our left almost topples the raft.

'I was joking,' Lewis screams.

Looking over my shoulder, my heart stops. The trebuchet's long arm is swinging into action. A whistling bursts through the sky followed by a thunderous splash when a missile falls into the water behind the blue raft.

Screams hit my ears.

There's no need for Rhodri to bark commands. We row with an increased determination, desperate to reach the shore before the trebuchets hit their targets and capsize our raft.

'Look.' Lewis points towards one of the towers on the middle ward. I strain to see, water blurring my eyes. On top of the tower stands a figure. The silver wolf mask sparkles in the morning sun. Skye's watching.

Anger and hatred fuel my tired arms. The raft jumps forward with our combined strength, invigorated by the sight of our enemy.

Missiles rain down, hitting the water like a deadly hailstorm. The raft bobs in the swell and we're forced to stop rowing and grip the slippery wooden surface as the once glass-like water stirs in rage. Faith loses her oar; Lewis hurriedly hands her his.

The red raft has been knocked away from the buoy. King John struggles to balance as the buoy rocks dangerously. Ophelia and Portia scream commands in a manic attempt to get back to him.

'Personally, I'd leave him there, one less to worry about,' Faith says.

I agree. Werewolf or not, this game would be easier and safer without him.

Every missile whizzing through the air brings a new fear of capsizing and every face full of freezing water tells us that so far, they've missed. The red raft loses an oar.

Panicking they spin around in circles, going nowhere. The blue raft passes them. We row like crazy, finally in sync until the island is so close I can smell the damp soil.

Rhodri and Faith leap onto the bank. Spinning around they grab the end of an oar and pull us to safety. Exhaustion mixes with relief, but the trial's not over yet. We still have to make it inside the middle ward.

At the top of the bank, large gates bar our way. Rhodri rattles the metal, but it's locked.

'That's the middle ward.' Billy pants pointing to the huge stone wall looming before us. 'This curtain wall surrounds the whole area.'

'Who *are* you?' Rhodri rams his shoulder into the iron gate but it refuses to move.

'Guys?' Faith's further up the bank staring at three gold buttons set on individual plinths each engraved with a scarlet dragon.

We run to her, the drones following like pets on a lead.

Above the plinths is a riddle. I read it aloud:

A key in the wrong lock is as useful as an ice-cream hammer and as dangerous as a starving wolf:

Which came first, the Blood Moon or the Werewolf?

Rhodri's face is one frustrated frown. 'Who said anything about a fucking riddle.' He kicks the grass, his boots sending up a shower of icy mud.

'Wait,' says Lewis. 'I know this. Look.' On each plinth is a card, each one with a different saying. He reads them out. *'Safe and Sound, Carolina* and *Jump then Fall.'* His face lights up in a smile of recognition. 'They're all Swifty titles.'

'What do they have to do with Werewolves?' Rhodri bangs his head in frustration. 'And ice cream?'

'I knew I should have mugged up on Swiftisms before,' Faith says. I cringe at her intrusion into our lives.

Billy and Lewis are talking quietly, trying to decipher Skye's puzzle. 'The song titles are the key to unlocking the gate,' Billy says. 'We just have to find the right one to answer the riddle.'

'Well hurry the fuck up,' Rhodri shouts.

Behind us the blue raft has reached the bank. Demi and Mai head towards us. Arti stays with Ravi while he catches his breath, helping him up the slope. They join us in front of the plinths. Nine of us stand on the bank.

King John is back on the red raft. Two missiles fire simultaneously. One misses. The red team lay flat on the boards as the raft veers up and down. Seconds later the second missile finds its target and splits the raft into pieces. Portia, Ophelia, Marcus, Glasses Guy and King John are thrown into the icy water. Distorted sounds of yelling and screaming reach the bank as they struggle to swim to shore.

'Just pick one already,' Rhodri shouts. His eyes are dead set on the five swimmers and the frantic tension pulsing from him fills me with dread.

No one makes any attempt to help the swimmers, despite their desperate cries. If they reach us before we open the gate then who knows what we'll have to do to be in the first ten – or how far some of us will go to survive.

'We think they're all connected,' Billy says his voice tinged with a fearful excitement. 'They're all songs from films: *Hunger Games, Where the Crawdads Sing* and *Valentine's Day*.'

'So?' Rhodri says.

An idea is forming in my head. '*Which came first? The Blood Moon or the Werewolf?* Is it sequential? Does it mean which order do the songs come in? Or the films?'

'So? Which one is it?' Rhodri cries.

'Quick,' Mai shouts.

'*Crawdads* was last,' Billy says.

'Sure?' Rhodri says.

'Hundred per cent.' Lewis nods emphatically. 'She totally fangirled the book and wrote the song just for the movie.'

King John and the twins have almost reached the shore, if they figure this out before us then it's all over.

'Which one came first?' Lewis says. '*Valentine's Day* or *Hunger Games*?'

'I don't know. I only remember Taylor Lautner,' Billy wails. '*Hunger Games*?'

Lewis takes a deep breath. '*Hunger Games*, so that's *Safe and Sound* right?'

'You sure?' Faith says. 'We need to be sure or…'

'Seventy-five per cent.' Lewis squirms.

Rhodri moves to the plinth with the *Safe and Sound* card.

'No,' Lewis shouts. 'It's *Jump then Fall*. *Valentine's Day* came first.'

Rhodri rubs his head. 'Shit man, don't do this to me.'

Lewis' face is set firm. '*Jump then Fall.*'

Rhodri's hand hovers over it forever. 'I can't…' His words come out as a sob. I get it, it's too intense. Who knows what will happen if we hit the wrong button.

Ravi pushes forward and slams his palm over the button on the *Carolina* plinth. It all happens in slow motion. Lewis and Billy scream 'No' in unison.

It's done.

'Why the hell did you do that?' Rhodri shouts in Ravi's face.

'Someone had to make the decision,' Ravi stammers, his face is as shocked as ours, like his actions surprised even himself. 'I did it so you wouldn't have to.'

'Was it right?' Demi says. Arti runs to the gate. It's still locked.

Shit.

Demi holds his palm up, calling for silence. 'What's that smell?'

A new stench is wafting through the air, thick, strong and familiar.

From the top of the castle turret a fanfare sounds. The drones that were glued to our faces two seconds ago are circling and flying back in the direction of the lake. Back to where the others are still swimming.

'Fuuuck,' Rhodri breathes.

'Look,' Mai says, pointing to the far bank where the trebuchets are on fire. No, not the trebuchets, the missiles.

The whizzing sounds the same as they launch into the sky but the missiles burn like falling comets.

'Petrol,' Faith shouts. 'They've flooded the lake with petrol.'

Shit. King John is close. He turns in the water, recognising the strong smell. Cold and exhausted Portia's struggling to reach the shore. Ophelia's a long way behind her. Marcus is clinging to a piece of the red raft. Glasses Guy's splashing around in the water, screaming for us to help.

Arti's the first to react. Running to the lake, he wades towards the swimmers shouting for them to hurry. The first wave of missiles hits the water, and the moat erupts into flames. Screams mix with splashing. Demi drags Arti back onto the bank.

The heat from the water slams into our faces.

'Holy fuck,' Rhodri shouts. Arti's leg, covered in the petrol-filled water is on fire. Ripping off his chainmail and his tunic Rhodri smothers the flames with the wet fabric, holding it firm until the flames die and all that remains is the stench of burning flesh.

And still the missiles come.

The lake is consumed with orange flame. Agonising screams from those still in the water bombard our ears, each more harrowing than the last.

'We have to help them,' Mai screams. 'We have to help.'

But the wall of fire holds us back.

'There's nothing we can do.' Demi stands helpless on the bank, flames licking at his feet.

The fire rages across the surface of the lake. Black smoke fills my lungs, making me choke. The stench of burning flesh triggers a terror I've felt too many times before. I hook my wet top over my nose and breathe in short, punctured breaths burying my head in Demi's chest to hide from the horror playing out in front of us. The twins' faces flash before my eyes, Marcus, Glasses Guy and King John.

Time stands still while we wait for the fire to die out. The screams subside with the flames until only ghostly silence remains. Pockets of water reveal themselves and so does the damage. The lake fills with a disquieting stillness. A body floats towards us, blackened and burnt. I swallow down the horror as my eyes sweep the flame-ravaged face of Marcus.

Mai is visibly shaking, her breathing loud and ragged in the smoke-filled air. Faith is sobbing into Rhodri's chest. Billy and Lewis cling to each other tightly. Ravi's fallen to his knees; his eyes glued to the lake. Arti crouches at the water's edge with Demi, clutching his leg.

A body bursts up out of the water, noisily gulping down air. King John pulls himself onto the bank dragging a body beside him.

'Quick!' Demi drops next to him.

The body lies face down on the ground, unmoving. King John turns it over to reveal one of the twins. The short dark hair clinging to her unresponsive face tells me it's Portia. With Demi's help, King John begins to resuscitate her.

We huddle around Portia, willing her to breathe.

'Give them space,' Mai cries.

There is nothing but the sound of the melodic thwack, thwack, thwack of King John's palm on Portia's chest as he massages her heart with his fist.

'Come on.' King John's voice is urgent.

The incessant whirring of the drones has stopped. The sky is clear. The walls above, once filled with guards and cameras, are now empty.

The cameras have stopped recording.

King John works on Portia's lifeless body for what seems like forever until she coughs and splutters and vomits the lake right out of her lungs. I've never been so relieved to see someone puke their guts up.

Demi and Rhodri are pacing by the lake, their faces turned to the black folds of water. A small motorboat zigzags across the lake.

We do nothing. There's no anger, no rage, no horror. We all watch as the bodies are recovered, one by one.

The bodies.

And still we don't react. Is this shock?

Something taps against my boots. A pair of glasses float in the water, bobbing against the bank. I choke back a sob and push down the revulsion and the hopelessness until my body is completely numb.

Lewis is at the puzzle agonising over the answer to Skye's riddle. His shaking hand hovers over *Jump then Fall* the song from *Valentine's Day*.

This game is payback, designed as our karma for outsmarting her with our Swiftisms in *Lie or Die*.

'It's right. It's *Jump then Fall*. It's the song that came from the first movie. That's what the riddle means,' Billy whispers but Lewis doesn't move, paralysed by shock and fear.

Doesn't really matter now, the damage is done. Three are dead from Ravi's rash decision.

I search for the man responsible. He's crouching in a ball, arms hugging legs, head bent to the ground, sobbing uncontrollably. It's hard to be angry when he's so obviously broken but I can't bring myself to comfort him, not even for Amara.

He must have known there would be consequences for pressing the wrong button. Did he know people would die? I quickly banish the ugly thoughts from my head. I must stay focused. Skye's the villain; we're just her pawns. She wants us fighting amongst ourselves. But even though my head's telling me it's not his fault, my heart's screaming for vengeance.

An agonising high-pitched wail turns my attention to

Portia. Demi and King John are struggling to hold her back as she fights and keens and tries to dive into the lake. Her brutal outpouring of grief is as unbearable as watching the guards lift Ophelia's body from the water. I turn away, unable to watch.

Guards appear on the bank behind her, heads bowed respectfully, waiting. In that moment we all share a moment for the dead.

We're playing as one, Ophelia's ghost haunts my ears. I guess it's Portia's time to leave. Slowly the guards help her to her feet with a deference I've not seen before. They almost carry her towards the iron gate, their bodies blocking our way, preventing us from getting close.

As she passes Rhodri, her grief turns to rage. 'You did this,' she hurls the accusation at him. 'If we'd been on your raft, she'd be safe. She's dead because of you.'

Rhodri steps back. 'I … I…'

'You killed my sister,' she screams in his face. 'You will pay, I promise you. You will pay for this.'

The iron gate closes behind her and she disappears behind the castle wall.

We remain on the island bank. There's nowhere else to go. Rhodri stands alone, his breathing ragged, shivering uncontrollably without his top, which is still wrapped around Arti's burnt leg. A single crow circles our heads, its rough cawing slicing through the silence like a bad omen.

I move to comfort Rhodri, but Faith pushes past me, steering him into a corner and away from me.

Demi speaks first, wiping his eyes with his gloved hand. 'We can't stay here. It's Baltic.'

Mai's small body shivers in quick spasms. She folds her arms around her chest and tries to convince us that she's 'absolutely fine' through chattering teeth. This can't be good. We need warmth before the cold claims another victim.

Lewis is still hovering over the buttons. I curl my arm around his waist.

'Can't do it,' he says. 'My hand won't move.'

My fingers curl over his. '*Strong like mountains…*'

His intake of breath sounds like a loud whistle. '*Strong like steel.*'

Together we push down on the golden button.

There's a clunk and a groan and the iron gate opens.

The jagged cheers stop abruptly, sounding so wrong in the grief-filled silence. Panicked eyes flit from one of us to another.

'Ten,' Demi says, his eyes filled with pain. 'We're only ten.'

Mai pushes back her shoulders and with a ragged war cry storms through the door. 'Day two,' she shouts up to the tower where Skye stood and watched. 'Chin up, chest out, I am ready. And we're coming for you, bitch.'

26

We enter a new space, leaving the fallen in our wake. We've no choice. The lake trial proved beyond any doubt that moving forward is the only way out.

'Where are we?' I ask. More walls surround us in another layer of never-ending castle prison.

'The middle ward.' Billy's voice shakes. 'It's an island. The inner ward, or main castle area is in there.' He points over the high wall. 'This' – his arm follows the castle wall as it snakes around the island – 'forms the second line of defence, it's a relatively low curtain wall considering.'

I wish I'd never asked. The only thing I need to know is we're one step closer to Thea and Max, but I get that talking history is an easy escape from reality. The old bouncy Billy's gone, drowned in that lake with the others.

A dragon drone leads us to the next camp. We follow like a swarm of zombies. We pass a gatehouse even more imposing than the last, its huge doors shut tight. Up there on its battlements Skye stood watching us burn. I crane my neck; the battlements are empty.

Everyone's stopped to stare down into a large pit. In it are two dragons.

'These are the Cadw Dragons,' Billy's saying. 'There's a whole Welsh legend about the white and the red dragon—'

Rhodri interrupts. 'Are they virtual holographic talking monsters?'

Billy stutters. 'N-n-no they're animatronics, a tourist attraction.'

'Unless they're about to breathe fire, I couldn't give a shit.' Rhodri turns to Arti. 'That dude annoys the hell out of me.'

Lewis gives Billy a sympathetic pat on the shoulder.

The camp's set up in the far corner. Two see-through bell tents with coloured flags bobbing on the tops next to a blazing fire. Ruins poke out from the grass like jagged giants' teeth, remnants of a once mighty tower. Behind, the lake stretches out to the northside, a constant reminder that escape is futile.

The tents provide dry costumes, but the warm clothes do nothing to thaw the chill of this morning's trial. There's a haunted look tattooed on every face. Cooking smells emanate from a cauldron set over the burning fire helping to mask the stench of petrol and death that's followed us from the bank and clings to our skin. Nobody's talking about the huge elephant in the room or the dead in the lake. It's like talking will make it real, and how the hell do we deal with that?

By the time we've changed, the sun's sat low in the sky and the winter dusk's closing in, robbing us of the last few daylight hours. We surround the fire. I ignore the names hanging either side, a clear reminder of the next impending blood moon when the Werewolves will claim another victim. The screaming in my head is playing on repeat. Images dance in front of my eyes. I'm shivering, unable to feel the fire's warmth. Stepping closer my hands reach towards the flames.

I lean in more, just a little closer.

'Careful.' Demi pulls me back, jolting me out of my head.

'Thanks,' I say.

He moves away, distracted. The flames have singed the fingers of my gloves making them crunchy to the touch. King John helps himself to a large bowl of soup, moving to sit alone on a piece of levelled ruin. All his 'team' have gone. I wonder how he feels to be the last one standing. The thick clouds filling the sky only add to the claustrophobic feel, making the air itself unbearably oppressive.

Arti ladles out some soup.

'Are we not going to talk about what just happened?' I say, my words booming in the strained silence. Terrified eyes flit my way and then fall back to the ground.

Arti offers me a bowl. I refuse.

'You should eat. It will warm you.' Arti has kind eyes.

I cup the bowl in my hands, but don't eat. My stomach's not ready for food.

'How's your leg?' I nod to his boot, the laces tied loosely around the blistered and burnt skin.

He dismisses it with a hand gesture. 'All good.'

It doesn't look good. Bits of wet costume are stuck to blistered skin, angry red and painful.

I smile back, complicit in his lie. 'You know Artemis is a girl's name? She was the daughter of Zeus and twin sister of Apollo.' I don't know why I said it, I don't even know where the knowledge came from. It's just good to fill the silence.

Arti chuckles, a comforting sound and a welcome distraction. 'Yeah, my wife pointed that out. She's also the goddess of chastity and childbirth. Not my wife, Artemis,' he adds quickly. 'Real name's Craig. I needed a stage name, and it sounded pretty neat. Besides, being the goddess of childbirth's kinda awesome.'

Wife? But he's our age? Suddenly that feels so very grown-up and mature. I can't even hold onto a boyfriend. And *Craig*? The distraction's doing the trick; the images fade a little. It's obviously doing the same for him as he embraces the conversation eagerly.

'And yes, I know I'm way too young to be married, but we met at school and when you know, you know.'

Wow, totally unrelatable. I've no idea what to say to that. 'Arti's cool. I get why you changed it.'

'Right?' he says.

'Your wife sounds nice,' I say for no other reason but to keep the conversation on topic and steer my mind away from the lake.

'She's awesome.' His face floods with pain. 'She's

dying. Brain tumour, very rare.' A small drone hovers in his direction. 'That's why we got married. Why wait? When you don't have much time, you realise what's important. There's a cure but the treatment costs millions. It's in Baltimore, Maryland. That's in America. There's a specialist there, Dr Galanis. He can help. So, the money from this could be a life saver.' Pain strikes through his eyes like lightning. 'I have to save her. And yes, I'm aware of the odds but they're a hell of a lot better than doing nothing. Or so I thought. I guess I underestimated the game.'

I open my mouth to say how sorry I am because I really am, but the words stick in my throat. I've so many questions and conflicting emotions I'm not even sure where to start.

A slow clapping sounds from the shadows.

'Well done, mate.' King John's still clapping. 'Everybody loves a sad tale and that's one hell of a backstory.'

The pain on Arti's face is hidden in a flash. 'Whatever.'

I give King John my very best *screw you* look. I'm so confused about my feelings for him. He's a dick, hundred per cent, but his quick thinking saved Portia's life. If he hadn't pulled her under the water she'd have shared her sister's fate. His one lifesaving act has thrown me; I don't know where to put him anymore.

Arti follows my gaze. 'Don't trust him as far as I could throw him.'

Lewis squeezes in beside me, refusing a bowl of soup.

I'm worried about him. He may look fine but inside there's a whole lot of freakage. Billy appears with a blanket and wraps it around his shoulders.

Lewis directs his anger at Ravi. 'Why did you do it? You had no idea; you just raced in.'

'I'm sorry,' Ravi sobs. 'I didn't know.'

'Well duh,' Billy says snidely. 'They'd still be alive if it wasn't for you.'

A chorus of agreement erupts; the silence replaced by a collective anger.

'Have you seen Mai?' Demi asks Billy.

Billy shrugs. 'Tent?'

Demi moves towards the tents.

'Why did you?' Faith says stepping closer to Ravi.

Billy stands next to Faith. 'We deserve an explanation.'

We all crowd around Ravi releasing all manner of hell as we look for someone to blame.

'Dick move, mun,' Rhodri says, his cheeks an angry shade of beetroot. 'Fucking stupid.'

Ravi turns from one of us to the other. 'I… I had no idea… I didn't know.'

If I wasn't so angry I'd be worried we were ganging up on him, but right now I don't care.

'This is all your fault,' Faith spits the words at him. 'You pushed that button and you killed them.'

Ravi buries his head in his hands and sobs into the stony silence. Unsympathetic faces stare down at him. 'I'm so sorry. It was an accident. I didn't mean—'

I interrupt him. 'This wasn't an accident. This was planned.'

'You don't know that.' Billy jumps, still clinging onto denial.

'Oh, get real, even you can't think loading fire into a pool of petrol is an accident,' King John sneers. 'The girl's right. Two tents. One less than last camp. First ten they said. They planned the whole thing.'

'They didn't say we would die.' Billy's shaking his head so hard it's gonna fall off, finding the lie of Reality way easier to swallow.

Arti puts his hand on his shoulder. 'Dude.'

'How can you all be so calm?' Billy cries.

'No point in panicking, it will only get us hurt,' Arti says.

Demi comes out of one tent and ducks straight into the other.

'Arti's right,' Rhodri says. 'Skye wants us to freak out. She loves the chaos.'

'And it makes for good entertainment, hun,' Lewis says gently. 'Don't give her that.'

Billy turns to Lewis. 'I should have believed you. I wish I...' He buries his face in Lewis' shoulder and sobs.

Faith rolls her eyes. 'Blubbering will only get you—'

'Can't you see he's terrified,' I shout at her stupid face.

'I say the Werewolves fess up.' Rhodri puts his hands on his hips. 'No Werewolves equals no game, end of.'

'Or the Werewolves die, and they make more

Werewolves from the rest of us,' King John says. 'Game's gonna play till the end no matter what.'

Rhodri starts to argue when Demi bursts out of the tent, our attention immediately diverted by the look on his worried face. 'I can't find Mai.'

Demi rushes out of camp and I follow. We don't get far. We find Mai stood in front of the towering gatehouse, her small frame dwarfed by the imposing set of castle doors, barring our way from whatever lies inside.

'Bit of an anti-climax,' I say, needing to ease the adrenaline coursing through my veins.

Her face is tilted upwards, her eyes glued to the top of the castle wall.

'I never knew,' she says quietly. 'Cali.' Old grief comes rushing in like a bullet train. 'I never knew how terrified she must have been.' She grabs my hand. 'You must have all been so scared. I'm so, so sorry.' A sob escapes her mouth.

Demi holds her in his arms.

'We're not all getting out of here,' she says into his shoulder. It's a statement not a question, the same grim realisation that's sweeping through the camp.

Demi's lips turn upwards in a thin smile. I admire their bravery. I wish I felt the same and wasn't shitting my pants every second we're in here. I need to be braver. I need to be less Billy, more Mai.

Mai rubs her eyes, smearing more make-up over her cheeks. She looks like a warrior readying for battle.

'Alri?' Rhodri ambles over, his eyes flicking from Mai to me to Demi. Lewis, Faith and Billy follow with Arti bringing up the rear, limping painfully. King John's stayed in camp with Ravi.

Mai turns her chin upwards and shouts, 'Skye Greenhill, the Host or whatever. I know you're up there, hiding in your castle like some two-bit Disney princess.'

We stare upwards, transfixed on the tower.

'Fuck this.' Rhodri steps forward. 'Come out, Skye. We know you're there; we saw you watching. That wasn't clever game play. That was murder. You'll pay for what you did today, I promise you. You're no genius, just a spineless coward hiding behind your fortress walls.'

We wait. There's no movement on the tower. Rhodri continues. 'Just what I thought, you don't dare face us, just like before when you hid behind Henry.'

'Careful,' Lewis says. 'Not exactly sure what we're doing but it doesn't do well to poke the bear, especially when said bear is in total control of our fate.'

'Stay back then,' Rhodri growls. 'No one asked you to do anything.'

'Why do you always need to play the hero?' Lewis shouts in frustration.

Rhodri turns to him. 'At least I know what a hero is.'

'There's no I in team you know,' Lewis spits.

'There's two in idiot,' Rhodri spits back.

There's an angry gasp from Mai.

'She's got a nerve,' Demi growls.

Skye's on top of the battlements, leaning through the gaps in the stone, the silver wolf mask glistening like a star.

'You sure it's her?' Demi whispers. 'Can't see her face.'

'It's her,' I say. The way she casually leans out, resting on her folded arms, her body relaxed. 'That's Skye.'

'Well, now you have me what are you going to do with me?' she shouts.

She's playing with us. The drones have gone, the recording lights are off, there are no wolf-masked guards in sight. She stands alone on the tower.

Mai's fists are clenched by her sides. 'I will end you.'

Skye's laughter rains down on us like acid. 'Oh, Mai. You're so sweet. Here I am, safe up here while you're down there playing for your inconsequential little life.'

Mai stands her ground.

'So that's really what we're doing? Playing for our lives?' Arti steps forward, limping on his bad leg. 'This whole game is just an excuse for murder?'

Skye waves her hand dismissively. 'No need to be so dramatic. It's just a game, a very, very dangerous game. You knew the risks when you decided to play.'

'No one signed up to die,' Mai says, her small body shaking with anger.

Skye leans further over. 'Poor, Mai. You're just like your sister. Cali was clueless too. She trotted along to her death like a meek little lamb. Do you have sheep in China, or should I go with something more culturally appropriate, maybe a goat? Or a…' Skye trails off mid-sentence.

There's a noise from the top of the tower. Skye's silver wolf mask flashes in the sunlight as her head whips round to a noise behind. Her arms fly up in a protective move. The surprised cry morphs into a scream when she jolts backwards. Another scream and her body flies over the crenulations. My eyes are glued to the almost comical way her hands flap wildly, grasping at the air as she falls. Her body plunges towards us. She hits the ground with a splintering thud, the indescribable sound of her neck breaking on the frozen grass. She lands face down in an unnatural position, like a puppet who's been dropped and left where it fell, tangled and bent and utterly broken.

I search the battlements for any sign of movement. Did she fall or was she pushed and, if so, who pushed her?

'What just happened?' Mai squeaks looking from floor to sky and back again.

Nobody answers. The fall has dislodged the wolf mask exposing her blonde hair. Mai reaches for it.

'Mai, no,' Demi says, disgust layering an air of grim satisfaction. 'She's dead. That's all we need to know.'

'We need to know it's her.' Mai pulls off the remains of the mask.

It's Skye. Blood trickles from her mouth and nose and ears. Her eyes stare vacantly. Even in death she's beautiful.

Staring at her face, my heart leaps in relief-tinged

shock. A painful howl bursts from Demi. He lunges at her body, poised to kick. Rhodri and Arti grab him. He pulls himself out of their grip and walks away. No one follows. We leave him alone with his grief. Hands shield eyes as we all stare upwards, searching for any answers to what the hell just happened.

'What's all the noise? We could hear you in camp...' King John stops, staring down at Skye's dead body. Ravi's two steps behind, his mouth open in shocked surprise.

'Guys?' Lewis says, grinning stupidly. 'Don't you realise what this means?' All the tension spills from his body. 'Skye Greenhill is dead.' He drops to his knees, laughing into the sky. 'It's over.'

27

She's dead. It's over. We can go home.

Skye's dead. My brain keeps repeating the words, forcing my eyes to believe what's right in front of them. Skye. Is. Dead.

Mai's staring down at her body with hate-filled grief. Rhodri's eyes flit from body to wall and back again, confusion suppressing hope. Lewis is happy-sobbing beside me. Billy's laughter's verging on hysterical, like someone who got in way too far over their head and is now beyond relieved it's over.

'Wow.' Arti pulls his hair back from his face, a move I've seen him do whenever he's stressing, all signs of pain gone as the gravity of the situation works better than any medicine.

I don't get Ravi; his emotions don't appear to match Demi's anger or Mai's hatred. I can't see Faith's reaction; her face is buried in Rhodri's chest. The relief in his eyes makes it real.

Skye Greenhill is dead.

There's movement on the battlements.

'Woo hoo!'

The shout gets our attention.

'The wicked witch is D.E.A.D.' Someone's jumping around on the battlements. They stumble. 'Whoopsie.'

'Max.' Lewis points and laughs and cries. 'It's Max.'

'Max.' I laugh into the air.

Max leans over the turret pointing down towards Skye's body. 'I did it. *I* saved us. It's over. We. Are FREEEEEE.'

'Max,' Rhodri screams.

'Rhodri,' Max screams back.

'You bloody legend.' Rhodri laughs.

'I am a bloody legend. Who's the coward now, ehh?' he screams into the sky.

'He must have pushed her; she didn't even see him coming,' Mai says, admiration dripping from her words.

The air is thick with the sounds of celebration. I remember how he was in the tower, half mad with terror. Skye must have broken him to make him do what he just did. I'm glad he came through for us and I'm desperately trying to ignore the questions that nibble at my happiness: where did he disappear to last night? Has he been hiding all this time? How? Where?

'Max, get down here, mun,' Rhodri shouts. Max holds his thumbs up high.

There's a sudden rush of movement as guards swarm across the towers. His celebratory shouts become cries of shock when he's overpowered.

'Max?' Rhodri screams. 'Max!'

All we see from beneath is Max disappearing out of sight.

'What just happened?' Lewis spins around talking randomly to anyone. 'What the hell just happened?'

With an ear-piercing war cry Rhodri slams his shoulder into the gatehouse door. He tries over and over, screaming for Max but the door doesn't budge. Exhausted, he beats his fists against the wooden surface.

'I don't get it,' Lewis says. 'It's over, yes?'

The top of the tower remains empty. We stare from turret to gate waiting for the doors to open and Max to come out, game over.

'Hello?' Mai shouts. My pulse begins to race. Something doesn't feel right.

The wooden doors groan open. A line of guards run through in perfect formation. Their uniformed bodies surround Skye, pushing us back from the gatehouse doors. Lifting her broken body, they carry her into the inner ward. The huge doors close behind them with a definitive crash, leaving us trapped on the outside.

'Hey!' Mai shouts. 'You can't just leave us out here.'

'You have to let us go,' Lewis shouts. 'Don't they?' He looks at Billy, then at me. 'She's dead. It's over. Without Skye there is no game. They have to let us go.'

'She had help.' Everyone turns to me. 'Max told me she was working with—'

I'm interrupted by a noise, a repetitive thudding of boots on stone as an army marches across the battlements, dressed all in black, shiny wolf masks glinting menacingly in the waning winter light. They spread out, turning to face us in one organised movement. In their hands are high-tech bows, the glossy black metal gleaming. The modern take on medieval weaponry serves as a terrifying reminder of where we are. And what we are: powerless and utterly defenceless.

'Holy shit,' Demi whispers as we huddle in a circle below. 'Who called for reinforcements?'

'And what's with those bows?' I say.

'So they won't disturb the locals when they shoot someone,' King John says, his voice grim.

A dragon drone buzzes into sight and meanders towards us.

King John grabs the scroll hanging underneath. He reads, '*Castle Dwellers, you are called to the second meeting of the Castle Council. Follow the dragon immediately. Two of you will be nominated and one of you will run the Gauntlet. Who will face the biggest survival challenge yet? You decide.*'

We all talk over each other, all asking the same uneasy questions: Castle Council? The game's still in play? Where the hell is Max?

My heart thumps a techno beat as I conjure images of the Gauntlet in my head, each more terrifying than the last.

King John lowers the scroll. 'Biggest survival challenge yet?'

The archers raise their bows in a synchronised move designed to intimidate and terrify. And it works.

We huddle closer together, faces haunted, eyes wide, confusion racing over every face. The archers' presence signifies a definitive turning point in the game.

'I think we've just levelled up, guys. And there's a new boss in town,' King John says. His voice may be strong, but he keeps his body pressed into our tight huddle.

'What the hell is going on? Who is this?' Demi's eyes fly around the circle searching for answers.

'Max told me Skye had a backer, a silent investor,' I say. 'I guess they're not so silent anymore?'

'Who?' Rhodri's gaze collides with mine.

'He didn't say, only that he was super rich and powerful,' I say.

'And just as unhinged as Skye apparently,' Mai says.

Rhodri's gaze makes me squirm. 'Why didn't you tell us before?'

'Don't.' I hold his gaze. How dare he? 'I just know they, whoever *they* are, are way more powerful than Skye.'

'Then we're screwed,' Mai says unhelpfully.

Ravi falls to his knees, cupping his hands over his head as he quietly sobs.

King John shakes away any sign of fear and steps out of the circle, turning to face us. 'What did you expect? Just because your nemesis got pancaked doesn't mean the show's over. Get real people.' He waves his arm towards the archers on the battlements. '*They* are not an effect. They're not some glorified set dressing. They're for real. This show is way too big to stop now and you're all idiots if you think otherwise. We've got two choices, play the game and take our chances or become a medieval shooting game of fish-in-the-barrel. The way I see it is there are two ways out of here, in a body bag or super-shitting rich and, I'll tell you now, I ain't dying today.'

The archers raise their bows and aim at our heads. Faith swears, ducking behind her arms. Billy and Lewis press against me. We all hold our breaths.

'King John's wrong,' I whisper, my heart banging against my chest. 'There is another choice. Stand up to this guy and take him out.'

'That's a suicide mission,' Lewis whispers back. 'We need to do better than that.'

'Move.' The shout comes from the battlements, an AI command filled with real power and might, so loud we all jump out of our skins. A single arrow hits the ground in front of Rhodri.

'Holy fuck.' Rhodri's shocked scream flies into the air. Like terrified animals we scatter, breaking from the circle in one panicked move.

'I'm not hanging around to become a pincushion. I'll take my chances on this Gauntlet thing.' King John pulls Ravi up by his elbows and runs towards the waiting dragon drone.

'He's right,' says Faith. 'Whatever it is, it's better than being shot at.' Grabbing Rhodri's arm, she follows behind King John's retreating back.

Rhodri turns to us as he leaves. 'Guys please, we have no choice.'

I can't move; my brief rebellion shattered into tiny pieces. I don't miss the smirk on Faith's face when she marches Rhodri away while I remain a quivering mess behind Lewis. I hate the way she's become me, while I've turned into everything I once hated. Not wanting to give her a win, however small, I force my brain to get a grip. Grabbing Lewis and Billy I push myself forward, following the retreating dragon drone.

Behind us, Mai and Demi stand with Arti, helping him limp away from the gatehouse doors.

Lewis throws me a desperate look. 'I've thought of another option. DC Brown piles in guns-a-blazing and we all get home in time for *The Chase*.' I keep my mouth closed. How would it help to tell him DC Brown is dead? Taking my silence as disagreement he breathes a long painful breath. 'No? Then we are proper screwed.'

28

We spill into the Castle Council clearing like lemmings, all too terrified to give any thought to our surroundings. Only once I'm sat by the fire do I dare to breathe again. Draigodân's waiting for us, perched on his virtual rock. Putting distance between the archers and my body made the paralysing terror fade a little, but staring into the dragon's eyes makes my heart begin its techno beat all over again. Is it my paranoia or has he changed? He seems bigger, the gleam in his eyes more dangerous, his snarling lips even more terrifying than before.

'They don't seriously expect us to carry on playing like nothing's happened?' Billy says.

'Well judging by the welcome I'm guessing a wrap party isn't on the cards.' Faith leans back on her stool.

'How are you not bricking it?' Billy says.

She looks at him with a cynical smirk. 'I—'

Draigodân interrupts. 'Welcome to the second Castle Council. Castle Dwellers, can you identify the murdering monsters sat amongst you? Who has shown their true colours? Who is hiding the beast within them? Will you eliminate an innocent tonight? Choose carefully. Wrong decisions have fatal consequences in this game.'

Draigodân laughs. The sound makes my insides curl.

'Shiiiit, he is seriously pissed.' Lewis' eyes grow wider.

'Who are you?' I shout without thinking. 'What do you want with us?'

'Kass, don't, please.' Lewis' fingers dig into my arm.

Draigodân's eyes land on mine, flashing angrily. He smiles, his lips curling upwards to reveal a row of razor-sharp teeth. *It's just a hologram. He's not real*, my head whispers but my feet still step back in terror.

'I am Contestant Originated Holographic Interactive Narration system 2.0. I am Draigodân.'

Arti's voice is strong. 'This is insane. We're not doing this.'

Draigodân's head snaps around to face him.

Demi jumps up. 'Arti, please. My brother said those words once and was murdered for them. Don't make the same mistake.'

Arti folds his arms and stares straight at the dragon, a perfect Hercules in the firelight. 'This isn't the game I signed up for. I knew I'd be putting myself at risk, that's on me but I'm not sending anyone to the Gauntlet, whatever it is. I won't hurt people.'

Mai stands, her once perfect make-up streaked down her cheeks. 'Arti's speaking the truth. What they gonna do that they haven't done already?'

'Kill us?' Demi whispers.

'Stop it,' Billy says in frantic denial. 'We don't know what this Gauntlet is exactly; ultimate survival doesn't mean anyone will actually die.'

Lewis turns to him, counting on his fingers. 'Um,

hello? What about Sandra? Ophelia? Marcus?' He hesitates. 'That dude with the glasses.'

'Michael,' King John snaps. 'His name was Michael.'

Lewis visibly shrinks. 'Sorry.'

'The only thing you can be sure of is this Gauntlet will be dangerous,' I say.

'I'm not choosing anyone to die,' Mai says. 'They can't make me do that.'

'They can,' Rhodri says, his eyes dark. 'And they will.'

Ravi mumbles something but we all ignore him.

'Rhodri's right. We need to play the game.' I desperately want to fight back but I'm too terrified of the repercussions. It's impossible. Every time I try to channel strong and brave, terror and desperation stomp all over them.

Ravi pushes himself into the firelight to be seen. 'Pick me. Please.'

'No!' The cry is almost unanimous.

'The man's practically begging,' King John argues.

The group erupts into loud denial as we all emphatically reject his offer.

'What about you?' Billy says. 'You put your whole team at risk for an immunity shield.'

King John smirks and pulls a shield from his tunic, letting the small dragon hang around his neck. 'I think you just answered your own question there, boy.'

Angry voices rumble round the fire.

Ravi holds up his hand to silence us. 'I must take responsibility for my actions. I killed them. I didn't mean to. I didn't know. I'll take my chances on the Gauntlet. Let me make this right. Please. I'm the only choice.'

No one speaks. To put Ravi up is to put him in massive danger, but what choice do we have? I just can't bring myself to do it.

'Please,' Ravi says, his eyes searching the circle.

Mai nods, total respect crossing her face. 'I nominate Ravi.'

King John folds his arms across his chest, his face smug. 'Seconded.'

A collective sigh of relief flies around the fire as the impossible decision is made, and Ravi becomes the scapegoat we didn't know we needed.

'Cowards,' King John says. 'Your faces are so easy to read, even in the dark.' He points to Ravi. 'Not one of you feels bad for him. You're all just thanking the gods it wasn't you.'

'Easy to say with an immunity shield hanging around your neck,' Arti says as everyone drops their eyes. 'Don't see you offering.'

'Not about to throw away my dreams on a load of misguided misfits I hardly know,' King John says.

'Nice,' Faith sneers.

Draigodân appears. 'One nomination has been made.'

Ravi steps forward, his head high.

Draigodân speaks again, 'Two nominations are required for each Castle Council. You now have two minutes to nominate again.'

Horrified denial skitters around the fire.

Mai takes a step back. 'I won't do it,' she says.

Demi throws her a desperate look but steps back too, glaring defiantly at the dragon.

'Neither will I.' Arti stands up towering head and shoulders over Mai.

Draigodân drops his head to stare over the fire. 'Are you refusing to play?'

'I won't accuse.' Mai's face is set strong. 'Not again.'

Draigodân's eyes narrow. We all take a step back as he opens his mouth. An explosion of flame spews right at Mai. I cover my face from the heat. Arti reacts quickly pushing Mai out of its path and they both fall on the grass. Arti doubles over in pain as his burnt leg scrapes against the floor. The thick smell of burning wraps around us, the ground around us scorched and blackened.

Draigodân settles, smoke wafting from his nostrils.

'How did he do that?' Billy squeals. 'How did he just do that?'

'I am Draigodân. You will nominate because I command it.' Draigodân lifts his head high and bellows. 'Do I make myself clear?'

Draigodân's giant form bears down on us, terrifyingly real and horrifyingly deadly. My heart is banging so loudly I'm scared he will turn on me.

King John steps forward. 'I nominate Arti.' We all respond with varying degrees of disgust. He points at the dragon. 'That's the rules. Nominate two and he's the weakest link. Someone second me already before we're all toast.'

'Seconded,' Faith says.

'Are you serious?' I shout. 'He's injured.'

'Think.' Faith hisses at me. 'Only one gets sent to the Gauntlet. It's just a paper exercise. Don't piss them off.'

'Why Arti?' Billy asks.

'Would you rather it was you?' Faith says.

Billy pales but stays quiet.

This nomination is making me sick but Faith's right. We only have to vote for one to run the Gauntlet and Ravi has already sacrificed himself. Arti will be safe as long as everyone votes for Ravi.

'It's them or us,' Faith says her voice completely wobble free.

'You think?' I whisper back, shocked by how she's able to compartmentalise potential murder.

'Don't paint me the bad guy,' she says. 'Tactical voting. It is what it is. The way to stay alive is to make sure it isn't you up there.'

She's right. I hate that she's right.

Mai's frowning at Faith.

'It doesn't mean anything. We all vote for Ravi.'

Because that makes it so much easier.

I kept quiet through the discussions, not wanting to accuse or second. I thought by not participating I could somehow excuse myself from what we were about to do, but it hasn't worked. As Arti and Ravi take off their mics and step into the pillories, I realise saying nothing's made me as guilty as everyone else. I'm ashamed by my own cowardice.

Draigodân watches, as impartial as Switzerland and just as cold. When Arti and Ravi are both secured, he speaks.

'Two Castle Dwellers are accused of the murder of Sandra; a crime so heinous the audience have decided to waive the right of reply.'

Wait, what?

Draigodân continues. 'At the last Castle Council both accused walked free. In the name of justice, there will be a double lynching tonight. Both accused have therefore been found guilty. Both will run the Gauntlet.'

'You can't do that.' Rhodri leaps up. 'They have the right to a defence.' Draigodân's head moves towards him, but he doesn't back down. 'The rules say we vote. That we decide who faces the Gauntlet. One per round, that's the rules.'

'The rules have changed.' As Draigodân speaks smoke escapes from his nostrils. 'I am Draigodân. This is my game now.'

A sob catches in my throat at the dragon's words. Whoever is behind Draigodân is running the show, and so far they're making Skye look like a kitten.

'Sit down,' King John hisses at Rhodri. 'Unless you want to be a kebab.'

Rhodri hesitates his face red with rage. I will him to think before he gets himself killed.

'Rhodri, don't,' Arti says from the pillory.

Rhodri sits, turning his face away from the camera to hide the tears I know he's fighting.

Draigodân watches. 'Ravi and Arti, you have both been found guilty of murder. Your true status will be revealed by the Gauntlet.' He turns his head. 'Ravi, you have a popularity percentage of thirty-four. This will be converted into a thirty-four-second head start.'

Ravi whimpers. He's shaking. This is so wrong. I stare into the camera. Why isn't anyone stopping this?

'A head start from what?' Billy cries.

Draigodân turns to Arti. 'You have a popularity percentage of sixty-four. This will be converted into a sixty-four-second head start.'

'Over a minute,' I whisper to Demi. 'That's good, right? He's fit and strong.'

'He's a body builder. He's heavy, not fast. As long as he needs strength not speed, he should do good. As long as he doesn't need to run he…' He stops with a gulp. 'He can still do good even with his bad leg.'

'Yeah.' I try to sound positive. An old man and an injured body builder? Even to the most optimistic, their odds of beating the Gauntlet are not good and in this game failure is not an option.

29

We've been led onto a wooden viewing platform that runs the length of the inner castle wall. From here we can see everything. It's fully dark now and the night sky is blanketed with stars. Floodlights illuminate the Gauntlet. Even my imagination couldn't dream of the horror below me – a terrifying gladiator game of life or death.

By the starting line are three standing beams, high then low then high, designed for the contestant to weave over and under. Underneath each high beam is a bed of spikes – fall backwards or mistime your jump and you could hurt yourself badly on their lethal spears. Next there's a maze. Upright logs stand shoulder to shoulder, their tops carved into more needle-sharp points.

My eyes move to the next challenge, a long glass bridge lined with flagpoles all merrily waving the *Blood Moon* flag in the nighttime breeze. It looks okay, apart from the hundreds of silver spears beneath that wink at us through the transparent floor daring us to shatter the delicate glass above. Next a vertical climbing wall. A small platform on top leads to a rope bridge which leads in turn to a smaller platform with a rope swing. The very last challenge is literally a leap of faith. The Gauntlet sits on a stretch of grass that weaves around the castle and out onto the very far bank. There are no castle walls on the far side.

'Shiiit.' Lewis' eyes rest on the last challenge. 'There's a way out. If you make it to the end you're free.'

I grimace at the cruel irony of the Gauntlet.

Billy pulls his shoulders back. 'They'll get out. They have to.'

Demi catches my eye, his brow raised. 'Who'd have thought our chance of freedom depended on Arti and a forty-something dad from Leicester?'

'He's not from Leicester,' King John corrects him. 'He's from Leeds, he told me. And he has no family, never married.'

'You're wrong,' I say, his words grating against my memories. The trumpets make us jump as they launch into an ear-splitting fanfare.

'Look.' Billy points. Ravi and Arti are on the start line. Their chainmail has been replaced with coloured tunics, red for Ravi and yellow for Arti.

'So the cameras can see them in the dark,' Mai says.

Arti's swept his hair up into a bun. He looks calm. Ravi is hopping from foot to foot.

Draigodân appears on the furthest tower.

'The voting is now closed. It's time for you to face the Gauntlet.'

'Voting?' Lewis fires out questions in one long panic. 'Whose voting? The audience? What are they voting for?'

A drum beats slowly, thudding into the black like a gigantic heartbeat. Two dragon drones enter the space, bright boxes bobbing underneath. They hover above Arti and Ravi.

Draigodân speaks. 'The audience have voted. I can now reveal that each accused has been given an advantage.'

'Thank god,' Demi whispers.

Arti and Ravi grab the boxes and open them.

'Holy shit,' Billy says.

'I can't see.' Lewis leans over the side.

Both Arti and Ravi are holding something.

'Is that a gun?' Lewis squeals. 'It's a gun. Why do they need a piggin' gun?'

Lewis is shushed quickly before the archers lining the walls turn our way.

Draigodân speaks again. 'As legend and folklore document, the only way to kill a werewolf is with a silver bullet. You both have one silver bullet in your pistol. Use it wisely. It might just save your life.'

The drumbeat grows faster and the tension intensifies. Lewis' foot is tapping against the wooden floor, a tic that always drives me mad. Now it only adds to the rising sense of dread. Drones are flying into position. Cameras train down from the turrets, no angle wasted, no potential drama to be missed.

Draigodân speaks again. 'Arti, you will go on the first trumpet.' Arti stares straight ahead. 'Ravi, you will go on the second.' Ravi doesn't react. I'm not sure he even hears.

'Something doesn't feel right,' Rhodri says. 'Like they're not telling us everything.'

'Hundred per cent,' says Mai.

Faith covers her eyes. 'I can't watch.'

'You nominated, Arti. You and him.' Billy nods to King John.

'And I stand by it,' King John says. 'Better him than me.'

'And it's not like we had a choice,' Faith snaps.

'Oh, there's always a choice. We may not like it, but there's always a choice,' King John says.

The shrill sound of a trumpet buries Faith's reply. Arti leaps off the starting line. He throws himself over the first beam, squeezing his huge form under the low one. Somersaulting over the third he lands on the spikes below.

His screams jar against our ears when the spikes penetrate his burnt and blistered skin, gouging out the flesh from his already injured leg. He staggers to standing.

'Shit,' Mai says.

Clutching his leg, he lurches into the maze and disappears.

'Follow the drones,' Demi says pointing as the drones zigzag back and forth across the maze.

The trumpet calls again, its brassy trill signalling Ravi's start. He sprints under and over the beams, diving into the maze with surprising speed.

'Amazing what adrenaline will do,' King John says. 'There's life in the old dog yet.'

'Shit man,' Billy shouts. 'Shut up.'

'You don't like it, yet you're still glued to it. We're not so different from the audience.'

Both men have disappeared inside the maze. It's agonising to watch but even more agonising not to.

A new sound enters the arena. Howls. Loud and wild and dangerous, slicing menacingly through the dark. The air is filled with excited whining, scrambling, barking.

Billy points to the start line. 'Look.'

Nothing could prepare me for the sight of the wolf pack. They're huge, way bigger than any dog, and strong. They sprint forward in a deadly formation, their grey fur rippling in the moonlight. I count six. Jaws gnash and noses sniff as they track their prey, wild and ravenous and out for the kill.

And I'm projected right back to the forest.

One glance at Rhodri's bloodless face tells me he's thinking the same. The hunt we heard in the forest was real. The wolves were real. And now those wolves are in this castle. And they're hunting us.

My heart hammers against my chest as the threat against Arti and Ravi escalates to an unbearable level.

And the drones hover like hunting hawks.

Arti and Ravi emerge from the maze.

Arti's leaning on Ravi who's struggling under his giant weight. Ravi's lips are moving fast but I can only imagine his words of encouragement. He drags him over the glass bridge, David to Goliath.

'Move,' I scream into the Gauntlet, conscious of the wolves closing in. 'Keep moving.'

They stop at the climbing wall.

'No, no, no, don't stop,' I yell.

'Shit,' Demi says. 'He'll never get up there.'

Ravi's up first. He's light but small and struggles to grab onto the climbing holds. Arti leans heavily against the wall.

I keep a frantic watch on the maze. They need to get to higher ground, and they need to be quick.

'Come on, Arti. You got this,' Rhodri shouts and we all join in, shouting encouragement until our voices crack and break.

The first two wolves emerge from the maze. 'Move,' I scream. 'Get higher.'

Arti tries to climb, pulling himself up, his one good foot hopping from coloured hold to hold.

The two wolves are on the bridge, one black, one grey, their feet thundering against the glass. Ravi's lying on the top platform urgently gesturing at Arti.

'Take his arm,' Billy screams.

'He won't do it,' Lewis says. 'He's scared of pulling Ravi down.'

Arti's stuck, unable to move up or down the wall, pain and exhaustion paralysing him.

'Climb,' Lewis screams. 'You have to climb.'

Arti tries to jump to the next climbing hold, fingers outstretched. He misses, his body thudding into the wall. Sliding back to the ground he doubles over in agony.

The two wolves close in. Arti raises his pistol.

'He only has one bullet,' Mai sobs.

'Don't give up, man. Climb,' Rhodri screams.

'What the hell is he doing?' Billy points at Ravi. He's half climbed, half fallen back down the climbing wall. Standing shoulder to shoulder with Arti he points his pistol at the approaching wolves.

The wolves leap into the air.

A gun shot fires across the Gauntlet. The black wolf drops to the floor like a stone. Another shot followed by an agonising yelp as Arti shoots the grey wolf in the head. The wolves lay silenced at their feet, an explosion of blood and brains splattered across the glass floor.

A collective cheer colours the air and our fists pump the sky, more relief than celebration. Ravi waves the pistol at us in victory.

'Guys?' Mai's tone makes us turn.

Another wolf bursts from the maze, bigger than the rest, its fur peppered with silver. It's followed by three more. My heart flies into my mouth and chokes me quiet. I recognise the leader from the woods, the ripped ear and the jagged scar running from eye to mouth visible in the bright floodlights. Arti and Ravi desperately scramble up the wall trying to reach safety. They're too late. The wolf closes the space between them in a heartbeat clamping its teeth around Arti's leg and pulling him down, shaking him in his deadly grip like a giant chew toy. Arti fights but the wolf is too strong.

I clamp my hands over my ears to muffle the unimaginable sound of terror. The other wolves leap at

Ravi, and he falls under a mass of fur. The sound of biting and tearing and ripping fights against agonising, ear-piercing screams as the wolves tear our friends apart.

The drones all rise in a synchronised manoeuvre, retreating from the Gauntlet like a murmuration of starlings.

And the lights on the Gauntlet snap to black.

30

The camp seems smaller when we return. Maybe it's the night dark that's invaded while we were gone. Or maybe it's the sense of dread that's clamped around us like a too-tight coat. This game has ramped into overdrive and the horrific reality of our situation has defeated even the most optimistic.

I sit with Demi and Mai, as close to the fire as I can get. Lewis and Billy have retreated to the tents. Faith's joined them. Hidden in a blanket, she's perched on Billy's bed. I can't find Rhodri; my eyes still default to him every time I need comfort.

I focus on the amber crackle of the burning logs. King John's words roll around my brain as persistent as the cold that gnaws at my bones. He said Ravi told him he was from Leeds, but Amara was from Leicester. And if Ravi had no family, he lied to us, reinvented himself as Amara's dad to gain our trust and win a fortune. I wonder if he realised how high the price would be. Did he confess to King John to ease his guilty conscience? I should feel anger towards him for using her to piggyback on us to get through the game, but I feel nothing.

'He was always gonna die, you know.' King John joins us. It's not his words that get my attention, it's his voice, way softer than his usual snarky tone. 'Ravi was ill, not long left. This was his final joke on life he said. He wanted to go out with a bang.'

I cringe.

He leans in. 'So, you didn't kill him. That ship had already sailed.'

'Why would he confide in you?' Rhodri appears. My heart leaps and my brain commands it to stop.

King John raises his hands. 'Don't kill the messenger. Thought you'd like to know is all. Soothe those guilty consciences.'

'I don't feel guilty,' Mai says. She's lying. She's way too quick to jump in. It's not hard to figure out; we're all on the same page.

'Do you think he was a Werewolf and that's why he put himself up?' Billy asks.

'He put himself up because he killed a bunch of kids on that lake and couldn't live with himself,' King John says. 'Then he tried to save Arti. There's a whole redemption arc happening there.'

Mai throws a stick into the fire. 'We need to find that investor, find him and burn him.'

Demi places a calming hand on Mai. 'Careful.'

Mai glares up at the camera. 'I don't care. Are you watching, you sick bastard? Come down here and face us instead of hiding behind your army of dogs.' Demi places himself between Mai and the drone. 'We've gotta get out of here,' she hisses.

'She's not wrong,' I whisper, my thoughts turning to Thea. 'We have no idea who this investor is or what he wants.'

Faith comes out of the tent, followed by Lewis. 'Nothing's changed. Game's still on. They still have your friend Max.'

'I'm not leaving him behind,' Rhodri says, so tense he's about to snap.

Faith puts her hand on his shoulder. 'So, we play. It's pretty clear we have no choice.'

Mai stands. 'We do have a choice; we can do this madman's bidding, or we can fight.' She holds up her hand for silence. 'The Werewolves stay hidden, but they don't put a name in the fire. No name, no murder.'

'And they will die,' Faith says. 'You heard Draigodân, play the game or be eliminated. Break the rules … same result.'

'We're going to die anyway,' Mai says. 'At least we can go out fighting.'

'I'd rather take my chances in the game,' Faith says.

'I don't like the idea of sacrificing the Werewolves just to save our own skins,' Demi says. 'And even if we do get to the end of the Gauntlet or finish the game, there's no guarantee he'll let us go.'

King John flexes. 'I reckon he will. He's all about following the rules, albeit his rules. Reckon the viewers won't take too kindly to him changing them at this stage or seeing us all fail, where's the fun in that?'

'Fun?' Mai scoffs.

'I admit the odds aren't good,' King John says. 'The game demands a winner so at least one of us will make it out of here. Just make sure it's you.'

'Is it you?' Rhodri lashes out at Billy. 'Are you a Werewolf?'

Billy glares right back. 'I'm a Peasant.'

Lewis steps in. 'Wind your neck in, Welsh. We don't need your big-boy bully tactics in here.'

'Nice,' Rhodri snarls.

'You've been acting weird since we got here, even moodier than usual.' Lewis points to me.

I shake my head. 'Lewis, no…'

The words I was dreading tumble out of Lewis' mouth. 'Hooking up with someone else in front of your girlfriend is an all-time low, even for you.'

Rhodri's face turns the same shade as the fire.

Faith steps up. 'You can talk. Don't think we don't see you skulking into corners with your boyfriend.'

'He's not my boyfriend.' It's Lewis' turn to go red.

'Don't make it personal, guys,' Mai says.

'Way to go with the assumption,' Billy stands.

''Cause you're not doing the exact same,' Faith cries.

'I'm not throwing myself onto someone else's boyfriend to win,' Billy shouts.

'Oh, cause you're not playing a game,' Faith shouts back.

'Guys.' I nod towards the drone. 'Don't give them what they want.'

Faith turns on me. 'Oh, stop with the little Miss Perfect crap. It's bullshit.'

'Really?' I snap back. 'At least I don't go around stealing—'

'Am I interrupting?' a familiar voice shouts over the din. 'Max!'

Rhodri, Lewis and I dive on him, argument forgotten in a heartbeat and I'm smothered by arms and chests. I untangle myself from the tight knot, being that close to Rhodri brings its own pain. Faith's watching me, a weird look plastered on her face. Maybe it's her conscience, if she even has one. I glare back.

'Whoopsie.' Max's trademark saying spills into the air.

Laughing, the boys release him and I get a proper look. He's dressed like us. His face is clean and without the trails of dried blood and mud he looks much better. His eye and cheek are still swollen and dirty blue under his dark skin but he's smiling.

'Thought I'd never see you again,' he says. 'Thought I'd never see *anyone* again. It means so much that you came.'

'Course.' Rhodri nudges him. 'Who else can I annihilate at COD?'

'Haha, keep dreaming, Tom Jones,' Max says.

'Why are you here?' King John cuts through the banter in his usual perfunctory manner.

Max sits at the fire. 'It's a punishment. For killing Skye.' A huge grin crosses his face. 'Can you believe I did that?'

Demi slaps him on the back. 'Great move, bro.'

'Tayo's brother, right?' Max says.

Demi nods and gestures to Mai. 'Mai is Cali's sister.'

Max's eyes rest on King John.

'Oh, I'm here for the win,' King John says.

'Not sure anyone in here is a winner,' Max says, holding King John's gaze. King John looks away.

Max rubs his gloved hands against the flames. He's a very different Max from the one I spent the night with: more relaxed, way less desperate. Is he just hiding the freakage like Lewis?

I shake away the doubt. He's one of us, like Lewis and Rhodri. I watch my best friend and my … ex … boyfriend. Our trust and friendship goes beyond the game. Right?

'I still don't understand why you're here?' Faith says to Max, interrupting my paranoid thoughts. 'Sorry, Faith. Also not related to anyone, just here for the money. Worst decision ever.'

'You seem to be taking it very well,' Max says with a friendly smile.

Faith smiles back. 'Bricking it on the inside, not gonna lie.'

'You know exactly what you're doing.' The words leave my mouth before I can stop them.

'It's one thing to know on paper and another to live it,' Faith says. 'I didn't sign up for all this pain and death.'

'But you did sign up for a game you knew you had a possibility of not surviving. You're either stupid or have a death wish, probably both.' I don't hold back on the sarcasm.

'Uhhh, what am I missing?' Max looks from Faith to me.

'Rhodri can't keep it in his trousers,' Lewis says.

'Leave it, tangerine boy,' Rhodri snaps.

'Okay, we've already done this.' Mai jumps up. 'You're all missing the point. Max is here.' She waits for us to get it. We don't. 'Max is *here*. Why keep playing? We came to get justice and that's been done thanks to Max. I for one don't want to die if I can help it.'

'Then let's get the hell out of here,' Demi says.

'No,' Lewis says, smothering his microphone in his tunic, gesturing for everyone else to do the same. 'Thea's here, in the castle.'

Rhodri covers his microphone and whispers. 'Thea's here?'

'How? When?' Demi stammers.

'I found her, last night, but I couldn't get to her,' I say, my cheeks heating up with guilt.

'And you're telling us this now?' Mai's face clouds with mistrust. 'What else are you originals not telling us?'

'Hey, they didn't tell me either.' Rhodri's face is a mix of hurt and anger.

I open my mouth to tell him exactly what I think; how dare he judge me right now. King John stops me with a clap. 'Nice one,' he says not bothering to cover his microphone. 'Just when we thought it was safe to leave, you spring a plot twist on everyone. Very convenient.'

'Says the guy who wants to win at all costs,' says Billy.

Faith turns to King John. 'You think they're making it up?'

'It's a game, people. Trust no one?' King John says. 'What a perfect way to make us play on. Save the girl we all remember from the first series.'

'I didn't actually like her to be fair,' Billy says. 'Thought she was a bit toxic.' He stops, seeing Lewis and I glaring at him. 'Probably the way she was edited. Doesn't mean we shouldn't save her.'

'It's true,' Max says. 'I heard her at night. It's all a bit hazy but it was her.' Everyone speaks at once. Max raises his palms in the air. 'I've no idea how they got her or how she's doing; I just know she's here.'

'Kass said Skye had a silent partner?' Billy says. 'It's them in charge now, right?'

Max nods. 'They call him the Investor. No one knows his identity. He hides under a mask.'

'And behind Draigodân,' Rhodri says.

Demi folds his arms. 'So, why would this Investor guy care about making Kass play on?'

'Because I'm an investment,' I say. 'I'm his star player.' I look at Rhodri and Lewis. 'Or one of them. He cares about the audience. They've paid to see us play. Thea's his insurance that we do.'

'He's killing us for ratings?' Lewis says.

'I don't think you realise how much money is at stake here,' Max says. 'People have paid a fortune to watch us play. The viewers aren't your ordinary dark web crowd.

We're not talking scumbags and murderers. These people are rich and powerful, hiding in the dark to protect their identities, playing a game outside the law because they can. That in itself is enough to get them off. Anything you do is the icing on the cake. Imagine what they'd do to him if the show was cancelled before they had their showstopper finale.'

'I don't give a bollocks what happens to this Investor or his uber-rich audience,' Mai says.

Max rubs his forehead. 'It's more than that.' He lowers his voice, covering his microphone in both hands, leaning into the crackling fire. 'The twins.'

'Ophelia and Portia?' Demi says.

'They're his kids.' Max lets his words sink in. 'They're *Lie or Die* superfans, desperate to play. They were supposed to play a couple of rounds and go out. They were never meant to get hurt. They had protection, but Skye took her eye off the ball.' Max looks at me. 'Correction, Skye was so obsessed with you that she slipped up.' He looks at Rhodri. 'They were never supposed to be on the losing raft; they were told to get on yours. Ophelia was never supposed to die.'

Mai frowns. 'Not getting it. How were they protected?'

'Marcus and Arti,' Max says. 'Marcus was employed by the Investor and Arti had some deal with Skye. Like bodyguards. Portia wants revenge. So, when you nominated Ravi and Arti, she manipulated the rules for her own purpose.'

'Because Ravi pushed the button?' Mai says. 'She blamed him. And Arti failed to protect them.'

'So, when we put Arti up in the council…'

'They changed it to a double eviction.' Max finishes Demi's sentence. He lifts his chin, all bravado gone. 'This guy is dangerous. He'll finish the show at any cost. And Portia wants revenge. We have to play. Werewolves must keep hunting Peasants and Peasants must keep nominating or we—'

'Die?' Rhodri finishes his sentence.

The camp falls into a horrified silence.

'You think that sob story about his wife was all one big move to get the audience on his side?' King John nudges me, his lips turned into a cynical smear.

'No, I don't.' I glare at him. Even if I did I would never admit it to him. 'Arti was genuine, I'm sure of it, he was a good guy in a terrible position.' I look over at Rhodri. 'He was prepared to do anything for those he loved.'

'Win by any means,' Demi says. 'This game makes monsters of us all.'

'Agreed,' Max says.

'How do you now so much about everything?' King John stares at Max, brows furrowed. Max stares back and shrugs. 'Skye told me. She loved to boast. I think it was her way of getting back at us for the first show. She would laugh at how stupid you all were, how she could manipulate you so easily. And when the guards talked, I listened.' He pats his black eye carefully. 'Helped take my mind off things.'

King John continues to stare at him, his face one big suspicious frown.

'How did you—'

'Leave him alone,' I say stepping in between him and Max, anger rippling up my spine. 'I know he's telling the truth; he said the exact same thing to me last night.' *Besides it's Max, he would never.*

King John's face clouds. 'And you actually trust him?'

Rhodri steps in. 'With my life.' He gets right in King John's face daring him to argue. 'Max is one of us.'

'He's an original,' Mai steps up. 'So back off, mister.'

We all stare angrily at King John, united behind Max.

King John holds up his palms and backs up. 'Then you're all fools.' He shakes his head. 'First rule of the game, remember?'

'Like we need reminding,' Rhodri growls.

Demi uncurls his palms, letting his microphone hang around his neck. 'So, we keep playing until one side is left?' He glances up at the drone. 'Werewolf or Peasant?'

'That moon's almost over the tower.' Mai brushes her hands down her thighs.

'I say we stay up,' King John says.

We all groan, exhaustion etched into everyone's faces.

'We need sleep if we're going to face more trials tomorrow,' Billy says. 'I don't want to be the next one culled.'

'Would you rather be Werewolf supper?' Faith snaps.

Max puts his hand up. 'Okay, don't shoot me but I've been locked up for days. How many Werewolves have you caught?'

'Skye didn't tell you that then?' King John snaps.

'None,' Demi says, ignoring him. 'Unless Ravi and Arti were.'

Max grimaces. 'And they murder by putting names in the fire, right?'

'We heard the wolves howling,' Billy says. 'I'm Billy, by the way – amazing to meet you, total fan. I guess it was a distraction so the Werewolves could murder Sandra.'

'Don't be a silly billy.' Rhodri's smile fades. 'Howling wolves or game-playing Werewolves didn't kill her, Skye did. Sandra's dead because that was Skye's game.'

Mai takes charge. 'We should sleep in shifts, watch the fire. If someone gets up, we'll see them.'

'I'll take first shift,' Rhodri says.

'No,' Max says. 'I'll do it. Obviously I'm a Peasant, not gonna put another Werewolf in here when you're so crap at catching them.'

'Unless that's a clever double bluff,' says Demi with a wary chuckle.

'Hand on heart,' Max says. I believe him. Max has very obvious tics when he's lying, and I'm not seeing them now.

'I'll stay with you,' Mai says.

'Just don't murder me while everyone's sleeping.' Max pulls a dragon shield out from his chainmail. 'Actually, you can't. They gave me a special Werewolf immunity. I can't be murdered, tonight.'

'Nine left,' Demi says. 'If we include Max. And we've no clue how many Werewolves.'

We regard one another with wary eyes, way too terrified to make any kind of rational decision. At least one of us is a Werewolf and lying right to our faces. And if they want any chance of staying alive they've no choice but to put one name in the fire tonight. Peasant or Werewolf. Since when did playing a character in a game show become a death warrant?

Draigodân appears. The lack of light around him and the movement of his wings gives the impression he's hovering in the air. It's terrifyingly beautiful. Rhodri moves to my side of the fire. I hate the way my skin goosebumps every time he's close. My brain may be on my side, but my body betrays me at every turn.

Draigodân speaks, 'The blood moon is rising. Before the wolves claim the night, I can inform you that Arti died...' he pauses for dramatic effect '... a Peasant.'

There's a sharp intake of breath as we wait for Ravi's status.

'And Ravi ... was...' he waits, another unbearable pause for maximum impact '... a Peasant.'

A unified cry of dismay sounds through the night air when we realise that we've yet to catch a Werewolf and there are still two blood moons to survive. My mind's racing. Even if some of the lake victims were Werewolves, probability demands that there must be at least one still left in play, probably more. With the Alpha's ability to create more Werewolves at any time, the Peasant's chances of winning are fading as fast as the winter sun.

31

Can't sleep. Lying on the camp bed listening to the wind buffeting the sides of the tent I stare up at the stars, my brain on mad auto-drive. Lewis is sparko; he can literally sleep through anything. He's always been that way, ever since we were little and slept over at each other's houses. Thea was like me. We'd laugh as Lewis snored, oblivious to our secret whispers over his sleeping face. *Thea.*

My eyes refuse to close despite my exhaustion. He's in the other tent with *her* and I'm trying to make sense of his actions. Maybe Skye threatened him like she did me with Thea and he can't tell me. Maybe he has some plan to get us all out of here. Or maybe he's just over me and I'm fooling myself. Maybe it is what it is and that one time in the car was just that, an opportunity. The *maybes* keep rolling through my mind like a playlist on repeat, refusing to let me be.

It's weird, the ever-present mind-blowing fear is getting easier to stomach. Like an old enemy, its presence has become familiar, and familiarity makes it tolerable. But the hopelessness and the guilt that's clung to me since Rhodri's seismic dumping is eating me alive.

I can't keep saving you.

His words clatter around my head and my brain replays that kiss over and over. Maybe that's it; maybe he likes his girlfriends strong like Faith. Like I was before this game turned me upside down and shook out every bit of brave I had.

Maybe.

And now I'm trapped in here with him and there's nowhere to run unless one of us... Don't even think it. Concentrate on Thea. Concentrate on finding her and getting out.

Out of this game and far away from him.

I wake to shuffling outside. I push the confusion from my fog-filled mind. The moon's moved beyond the tower. It's past midnight. The moon bleeds while the world watches in fascination as our deaths become entertainment, our lives nothing more than a percentage on a viewing-figure poll.

I recognise the quiet hum of voices outside. Rhodri's talking to Max. I watch him through the walls hating the way my heart still flips when I look at him. Faith appears; the excited flip is replaced by a sharp stabbing pain. She takes his hand and they disappear into the night black. I wait for them to return. They don't.

I reach for my microphone hanging on the hook beside my bed. Slipping it back over my head I creep out of the tent.

Max is pushing a stick into the fire, making patterns in the soot. He smiles as I approach then returns to his idle pastime.

'Where's Mai?' I say, trying not to be too obvious while all the time staring into the darkness searching for two shadowed figures.

'Resting, figured I could take one for the team.'

I nod half listening, scanning the dark for any sign of movement.

He points the stick in the direction of the towers. 'He went that way, with that girl. Is it just me or does she look like Lara Croft?' I can't look at him, if I gaze into those sympathetic eyes I'll lose it. 'Kass, what's going on?'

I shrug, grateful that the dark hides my burning cheeks. What do I say?

Max watches me. 'Second thoughts, she's nothing like Lara. Way too obvious with none of her class.'

'Did he say anything to you?' I say, hating myself for asking.

Max's face screws up into one big frown. 'We're literally fighting for our lives and you two are having a lover's tiff? Come on, you're both better than that.'

'Tell that to Fai-dri' I say.

Confusion fills his face.

'Doesn't matter,' I mutter.

He carries on. 'Skye's messing with you. Even dead she's in your head.'

He's right but that doesn't make me feel better.

'Think. If Rhodri's behaving strangely there's a reason for it. You and him are like Geralt and Yennerfer.' It's my turn to be confused. 'You're his Girl Next Door remember?'

My heart flips as he calls me by the trope used to describe me in the first game, his words wrapping around me like a warm hug.

'Lover's tiff?' I say.

'Oh, I get it, Fai- dri, Faith and Rhodri. Cute,' he says.

'Sorry, what?'

'In the original game of Werewolf one player, the Cupid, can choose two other players at random to be the Lovers.'

'Yeah,' Max says. He's a Werewolf mastermind, if anyone knows this it's him. 'From then on, their fates are intertwined. They become one player, like the twins. If one wins so does the other and if one dies, the other dies of a broken heart. You think there's a version of the Lovers card in play?'

'You said Skye was messing with us. What if she's made a Lovers card and Rhodri and Faith are the Lovers?' I bash my palm into my forehead. 'Why didn't I think of this before? He has to make us believe they're together.'

'It's possible,' Max says. 'You know Rhodri better than anyone, maybe you should trust him?'

My hope is quickly drowned by a huge dollopful of fear as my head reminds my heart of the one rule of this game … trust no one. I messed up majorly in the last game by trusting the wrong people at the wrong time. What if I'm wrong again?

Grabbing a torch, I plunge it into the fire in one decisive move. I need to talk to him. Max jumps up.

'Stay,' I say. 'Make sure no names get put in there.'

Max stands anyway, his voice begging. 'Kass, think, you're not being rational.'

The logical part of me knows he's right but my heart has overridden all common sense. I have to know if I'm being played, and all the horror witnessed over the last days has led me down a path of not giving a shit. In a way it's easier to cope with it all if you just accept the inevitable and adopt a *laissez-faire* attitude like King John.

Max tries again. 'Kass please, wandering around on your own is crazy.'

Crazy maybe but I need to know the truth. I take a step into the darkness but a hand clamps round my shoulder and an angry whisper warms my ear.

'What the bollocksy-bollocks are you doing?' I turn to Lewis, his eyes angry in the firelight.

'Nothing.' I shift my feet awkwardly.

'Really? 'Cause it looks like you're about to do something unbelievably self-destructive and go chasing after some boy.' He does an over-theatrical point at himself. 'I'm thinking no way would she be that stupid or bloody shallow to be worrying about her love life when she could actually end up real-life dead.' He does that thing where he reads my thoughts.

Grabbing my elbow he marches me away from the campfire, into the quiet shadows by the castle wall. 'Do I need to point out the archers all over these walls just waiting to pierce you like a pincushion. My god, wake up and smell the stupid.' His hands are planted firmly on his hips. 'What the actual hell, Kass? Did you even think? If something happens to you, I'm dead and so is Thea, and all because of a guy? I mean *really*? I could kill him myself for doing this to you.'

'You've got it all wrong. It's not his fault. I'm pretty sure he's being forced.'

'Oh, I see. Skye or' – he waves his hand around in the air – 'this Investor guy has a gun to his penis and is forcing him to point it at her? The boy's eighteen. He has the emotional stability of a boxing kangaroo and right now the gloves are off. He's freaking out and thinking with his balls not his brain. Listen to yourself, don't be that girl.'

I stare at my feet. There's truth to his words; we both hid behind sex rather than face the horror of the forest. It's not that huge a leap for him to be doing it again. 'I just need to know.'

'Girl, we're playing for our lives and trying to save our best friend. We can't do that if you are thinking with Miss Vajayjay. Get. A. Grip.'

'I *am* thinking about the game. If he's being forced to play a role then he's in trouble. Maybe he's being blackmailed. Maybe he's trying to save us.'

'Or maybe he's a colossal arsehole. Listen to yourself, hun, where's the I-don't-need-a-man-to-save-me girl I call my forever friend?'

'She died.' I sniff. 'In the last game.'

'Did she bollocks.' Lewis prods my chest. 'She's still in there, you just need to find her.'

He goes quiet, like he's having an argument with himself in his head.

'What?' I say.

'Nothing,' he says but guilt flashes across his face like a neon sign.

'Tell me,' I say.

He frowns. 'Look, I wasn't going to—'

'What?' My voice rises with urgency.

'Billy saw them. Last night.' He won't look at me. 'Rhodri and *her*.'

'Okay?' My heart is trying to break through my chest. Lewis never calls him Rhodri, always Welsh.

'They were … y'know.'

'Kissing,' I say. 'I know. I saw them too but it's not what you think.'

'I think it's exactly what I think,' he says. 'But right now I'm more worried about what you think.'

'Don't you see?' My mouth's on autopilot. 'It makes total sense. If they were the Lovers, he'd have to prove it. Y'know, seduce her for the cameras, make us all believe it was for real. Especially me.'

'This wasn't just for the cameras. Billy said it looked pretty steamy.' If possible, Lewis looks even more uncomfortable. 'And they're not the Lovers, million per cent.'

'You don't know that.' My voice is a pathetic whine of denial. 'How could you know that?'

He pulls me further away from the camp. 'Because Billy had the Lovers card,' he whispers smothering his microphone. 'And he picked me.'

The moon goes behind a cloud as if it's hiding from the news and the world goes black.

'What do you mean?' I say, playing for time while my brain catches up.

'Billy picked the Lovers card in the second row of the rock. He got to choose his Lover. He chose me.'

Oh.

'So, you see there's no way Rhodri and Faith are the Lovers, because I am. With Billy.'

Leaning against the wall I shuffle down to a heap on the cold grass. How could I have been so gullible and so damn stupid? He's right. I'm not *that* girl. I refuse to play the snivelling ex-girlfriend trope ruled by rampant teenage hormones. When I think of how I've been making excuses for him my stomach twists into one huge vomit-filled knot. Now I know, I know, I was today-years-old when I realised that even in a game of life and death, boys are cheating pricks.

Except Lewis, Lewis I can trust with my life. Maverick and Goose, his pop-culture reference, not mine. He squeezes my hand in his. 'I hate that he mugged you off. I know how much you liked him.'

He crouches next to me. I'm shivering. Curling his arm gently around my shoulder he pulls me close, resting his chin on the top of my head. 'Sorry, hun, you deserve so much better.'

I nod. I hear him, every word.

And I get it now.

Trust no one, that's the one rule of this game. When will I learn?

Billy is playing the Lovers card. Billy picked Lewis. And Rhodri is a lying cheat.

32

Lewis and I stay huddled in the corner, away from the camp, grateful for the small amount of privacy from the ruined stones, until even the drone hovering above our heads gets bored and moves away to find something or someone more entertaining. Lewis tries to hug away the misery. It doesn't work but knowing he's on my side helps a little.

A wolf howls across the castle grounds.

'It's starting,' he says, his arm stiffening around me.

'What is?' I say, head back in the game.

'Last night, when Sandra was murdered, it began with a wolf howl.' Above us on the battlements shadows move. 'We should get back to the fire. The audience are expecting a murder tonight and I don't doubt they'll deliver, one way or another.'

The wolf howls again, a low warning that sets my teeth on edge and my pulse racing. Small red dots move across the darkness, the drones dancing above us, positioning themselves over the camp.

Bodies are grouped in front of the campfire, nervous energy crackling in the midnight air. Mai's taking charge, her small frame weaving around the bodies, her bright hair electrified by the firelight.

'Stick together,' she says. 'Safety in numbers.'

'And while we're all here no name can be put in the fire,' King John says.

'The Werewolves are really going to do that, even now?' Billy asks.

'What planet were you born on, lad? They have no choice. It's kill or be killed,' King John replies.

'That's exactly how a Werewolf would justify murder,' Mai says.

'Or how a Peasant would explain this game to a total numbnut,' King John retorts.

'Hey,' says Billy.

'Where's Rhodri?' Demi turns to the tents. 'And Faith. Are they still sleeping?'

'They went for a walk,' Max says, his eyes wide.

'Are you kidding me?' Demi says.

'Guess they needed some private time.' King John thrusts his hips in a move that leaves little to the imagination.

'Shut. Up,' Lewis growls.

'What?' King John says. 'You can't blame them. Everyone deals with stress in different ways.'

My cheeks explode as I remember how Rhodri and I dealt with stress in the woods. *Stop it*, my brain screams in misery.

Another wolf howl rips the air. We step closer to the fire and to each other, the threat out there far worse than the threat among us. Drones circle above.

'Shit,' Billy squeaks.

'Chill,' Mai says. 'They're trying to make you panic, stay strong.'

'It's an effect,' Demi says. 'They're playing with us.'

'What if they're not?' Billy says. 'What if they've let the wolves out and they're coming for us? What if they tear us apart like Arti and—'

'Billy, shut up,' Mai snaps.

Howls and barks and growls overlap, growing closer, getting louder, creating a terrifying sound that wraps itself around us so tightly it's suffocating.

A loud scream pierces through the noise. Everyone scatters in panic, staring desperately into the dark.

'That was a girl,' Lewis says, his voice unnaturally high. 'That wasn't an effect. That was real.'

'Rhodri and Faith are out there,' Max says almost crying.

'It's Faith. They've got Faith.' Billy's close to losing it, edging slowly backwards into the dark. Lewis rushes to his side leaving me alone on the opposite side of the fire.

'Help me!' The scream is wild and smothered by a cacophony of barks and growls. 'Somebody, help me.'

Mai dives into the darkness, followed by Demi. Our circle breaks into chaos and bodies run in every direction.

'Help me!' The scream rings out again.

'That's not Faith,' I say. My brain jumps into auto-gear and my legs move of their own accord. Without thinking I run towards the sound, not caring that the dark holds nothing but danger.

'Wait,' someone shouts behind me. I don't care, fuelled by fear-filled adrenaline I run towards the scream, my only thought to get to the girl I know is out there.

The girl who needs my help.

Thea.

33

I run across the grassy bank following the huge stone wall that separates me from the inner ward desperate to find a way to Thea. There's a small door in the wall and I throw my body against it. It's locked. I keep moving, following the wall as it circles around the inner ward. The moon gifts me slivers of light that coat the grey stone like drops of silver. It's quiet: no screams, no howls, just a suffocating silence. I try to steady my nerves.

I need to get in. I need to get back to her. Tears of frustration streak down my cheeks and I wipe them away angrily. Damn, Skye. Damn her rich Investor. Damn him to hell. I swear on my life I will find him and make him pay for all of this.

A sound makes me jump. Demi bursts from the darkness.

'Hey?' He stops, keeping his distance as he watches me suspiciously.

'I'm fine.' A movement on the battlements above makes me realise just how lucky I am not to have been target practice for the archers. 'And I'm not a Werewolf.'

Demi smiles like he wants to believe me but comes no closer. 'Me neither. I lost Mai. Must have got turned around in the dark,' he says. 'We should get back to the fire before…' He starts to back away. I glance up at the castle walls reluctant to leave.

'We'll find her.' Demi's eyes shine with sincerity. 'I promise. Please, we shouldn't be out here.'

I force a smile on my lips, grateful for his show of solidarity and follow him back to camp.

Lewis runs to greet us, wrapping his arms around me and whispering in my ear. 'It wasn't Thea. I'm sure of it. They're messing with our heads.' I hug him tight. 'Please stop with the hero dashes,' he says. 'My big gay heart can't take it.'

Everyone's back at the fire, shaken and wide-eyed. My eyes fall on Rhodri. Faith's clinging onto him in a move I'm sure she's doing more for show than fear.

'Did anyone stay by the fire?' Max says pushing his hand through his messy curls.

'When we got back there was no one here,' Rhodri says.

'I ran.' Billy shrugs. 'Wasn't thinking. I thought Faith needed help.'

'I followed him.' Lewis gestures to Billy.

'I just ran,' Max says. 'Wasn't thinking properly on account of all the bricking it.'

'Me too,' Demi says.

King John points to the fire. 'A name's missing.'

Max plunges a stick into the fire and drags out a smoking wooden tile, black and burnt.

'Is that Mai's?' I say.

Worried faces sweep around the circle.

Mai's not here.

Mai's body is curled up in the bottom of the dragon pit. The front of her tunic's ripped; long straight rips like huge claws run down the front of her chest. Her arms are bare, her gloves removed, and her sleeves torn away exposing her skin below.

She's laying between the dragons, her once beautifully applied make-up smeared down her cheeks: the lightning bolt, worn for Cali, nothing but a dirty yellow smudge.

Demi's grief turns to anger. 'This is all your fault,' he says through a jagged sob.

"Scuse me?' Faith crosses her arms over her chest.

'She was coming to help you. If you hadn't gone off to do whatever then we wouldn't have left camp. She'd be alive.'

'You think I killed her?'

Anger flashes across Demi's face. 'Someone put her name in the fire.'

'I wasn't even here,' Faith says.

'Where were you?' Max looks at Rhodri.

'What's it to you?' Rhodri adopts a fuck-you approach to being questioned; at least he's staying true to character.

'Mai's dead,' Max says. 'That whole stunt was designed to get us out of camp. Someone knew we'd try to help; someone was waiting for us all to leave the fire.'

'It wasn't like that, we were—' Rhodri stops, a red blush fills his cheeks. 'It wasn't me or her.'

'Why should we believe—' Demi is interrupted again.

'Leave them be.' King John jumps down into the dragon pit and crouches next to Mai's body. 'Look.'

He holds her palm up to catch the torch light. Three jagged lines have been cut into her flesh, oozing with fresh red blood – the mark of the Werewolves. Just like Sandra. Lifting her lifeless body, he shines his torch onto her back. An arrow sits lodged between her shoulders.

'We may not have fired the arrow, but we killed her,' he says. 'Sure as shit.'

We all fall quiet as he gently places her back on the ground and closes her eyes.

And another innocent is dead.

34

A dewy fog descends on the castle. The sun's early morning light is stoically battling to break through despite the moon's refusal to leave, reminding us of what has been and threatening us with what's to come.

We're gathered beneath the inner ward towers, right where Skye fell. It looks so normal, yet the image of her broken body is imprinted on my brain. The terror-filled acceptance is the same in everyone's eyes, as we prepare for the third day of this waking nightmare. Cameras train down on us. We're so used to them now even the buzzing drones have become part of the norm. A fanfare sounds. The wooden doors groan and creak and open to reveal the inner ward.

This is it, the last part of the castle.

'Almost there. You got this,' Rhodri whispers in my ear, so close he makes me jump. I push through the gate, not in eagerness to get in but in desperation to put space between me and him.

The inner courtyard is huge, a grassy square surrounded by impenetrable walls way too high to climb. A large building stands to my left with four huge gothic stained-glass windows.

In the middle of the green there's an old well, a stone circle almost flat to the floor covered by an iron grate. Towers sit on each corner with walls and buildings surrounding us on every side in varying states of ruin.

My pulse races. Thea's here, I'm sure of it. If I could only figure out a way to distract the cameras and slip away.

A dragon drone hovers in the middle of the green. As we approach, it moves to the large building with the gothic windows, disappearing into the dark doorway.

'I guess we follow,' King John says, striding after it. Not having a better plan, we all trail after him.

The Great Hall is pretty, well, great. There's a long banqueting table next to a roaring fire in the biggest fireplace I've ever seen. The windows are even grander from the inside, their glassy colours reflecting on the floor like a man-made rainbow. The magnificent ceiling towers overhead, wooden arches meet timber trusses high above. The stone floor's hard and cold, but the straw and flowers strewn all over make it warm and inviting. At one end, butting up against the wooden panelling are proper beds, piled high with blankets and pillows. They remind me of how exhausted I am.

Faith finds a scroll balanced on the mantel, unrolling it she reads: '*Welcome to day three of* Blood Moon, *the ultimate reality-survival show in which the weak die and the strong die trying.*' Her voice grates against my exhaustion, like nails on a blackboard. '*To celebrate this achievement the audience have voted to give you a day of feasting. A hot shower and dry clothes await the* Blood Moon *finalists.*'

No smiles cross our faces. Nothing comes for free in this game. My stomach is full of nervous butterflies, if butterflies had pointy wings and razor-sharp teeth. It was different when Skye was in charge, I knew how she worked.

'Seven.' Lewis nudges me and points to the beds. 'There're only seven.'

It takes me a minute to catch on. When I do my stomach lurches, fiercely evicting all my fatigue in one dry gag. Seven beds but there are eight of us. Someone won't survive till nightfall. I send Lewis a look of love and he answers with a shaky smile. We can both read the subtext: don't let it be one of us.

I'm sat between Demi and Lewis. Billy, Faith and Max sit opposite. King John and Rhodri sit at either end like the lords of the castle. We've had warm showers and put on dry costumes. My body is singing with warmth. After days out in the January cold it feels weird not to see sky above our heads.

The table is crammed with food: roasted meat, potatoes, carrots, cabbage with bacon, parsnips, cauliflower smothered in delicious cheesy sauce and jugs of gravy. The smell is incredible. Hunger overrides all my senses.

Once our bellies are full and our thirst quenched, we laze in our chairs by the crackling fire, content but not happy, sated but not satisfied. The whole Last Supper metaphor's not lost on me. We feast, but no one relaxes, any noise or slight buzz of the cameras makes us tense.

Max's name has been added to the plaques that hang from the fireplace, a clear signal no one is safe. We've no idea what's coming next, but we know it will be worse than what's been before. Suspicion's murdered trust. No one dares say or do too much for fear of being branded a Werewolf.

And there's a fate even worse than death, the Gauntlet showed us that.

I keep my eyes down and my mouth shut. Just being here is exhausting, surviving almost impossible.

Lewis pokes the round of stale bread used as a plate. 'What's with the plates?'

'It was traditional in medieval times to have a bread plate. After the feast they would throw them to the poor,' Billy says. 'Fun fact.'

'History bores me.' King John's face is covered in three-day stubble growth making him slightly less intimidating and a little more human.

Faith turns to me, elbows on the table. 'What do you think, Kass?'

'About history?' I say my lips curling into a sneer.

Faith shrugs. 'About anything. You've been middle of the road the whole game. How's about sticking your neck above the parapet once in a while.'

'What's that supposed to mean?'

She's waving a carrot in the air. It's taking all my strength not to reach over and shove it down her throat.

She smirks. 'Well, if I remember, you were the first to be nominated, then you got free and have gone under the radar ever since. Sooo, you're either a Werewolf or a coward.' Waving carrot again, it's really pissing me off. 'So how will history write you? Murderer or loser?'

The atmosphere around the table is full-on awkward. Is that how they all see me? No one jumps to my defence, even Lewis is staring into his hands.

Faith sits back in her chair, hugging a knee to her chest. I sneak a peek at Rhodri. He catches me looking and I hold his gaze until he looks away.

Demi's watching me and I silently curse Faith for reminding everyone of that first nomination.

Draigodân appears above the fireplace like a phoenix rising from the flames.

'Castle Dwellers.' His wings flap behind him making a low-key swishing noise. 'I hope you've enjoyed your feast and are rested and revived.' We say nothing, ignoring the cameras that have snapped on overhead. 'Now, it is time for you to sing for your supper. Last night, the Werewolves struck again. Mai, sweet Mai, was murdered in the dead of night and heartlessly thrown to the dragons. Justice is a feast best served warm. Tonight, before the candles burn down, two of you will be nominated and one of you will face the Gauntlet.' He stretches, his regal wings spanning the length of the hall and disappears.

King John leans forward on his elbow, waving one hand around the table in a lazy circle. 'Who's a Werewolf, who's a Werewolf? I think…' we all watch as he slowly points to Billy '… you're a Werewolf. The whole rat boy Billy's a mad fan of Lewis doesn't wash with me. Why are you really here and what's your game?'

Panic flashes in Billy's eyes. 'I am a mad fan of Lewis and I'm here for the money like everyone else.'

King John relaxes in his chair. 'I just want to win.'

'Why?' I say. 'Why put yourself through all this for nothing. It's insane. Do you have some kind of death wish?'

'I like to fly close to the sun; it's one hell of a ride,' he says matter-of-factly. 'Once you stop worrying about the hows and the whys and the whens, that's when you really live. I am just in it for the game and if I don't make it, I've made my peace with that.' He leans into the table. 'But if I do? What a rush.' He smacks his palm down hard. 'Now that's worth dying for. The Ultimate Champion. What a hero.'

'A champion's not the same as a hero,' Billy says. 'A champion puts winning above all else, but a hero acts selflessly for the greater good.'

The whole table watches King John's reaction. He leans forward and pops a potato into his mouth. 'Fun fact.'

Watching King John and his not-give-a-shit attitude breaks something within me. Being silent isn't the same as being strong. If Billy is eliminated, so is Lewis, and I won't let that happen. I need to stop hiding in the background and fight.

'I nominate Kass,' Faith speaks slowly and precisely. 'Who's with me?'

'No one, clearly,' Lewis says quickly. 'You need a second and that ain't happening.'

'I nominate Faith,' I say, the force of my words propelling me out of my chair.

'On what grounds?' King John says. 'You can't nominate because she nicked your fella.'

My cheeks heat up. 'Faith's a Werewolf. I'm sure of it. She has been one step ahead of us at every turn. She used the Fai-dri thing as a smoke screen. She knew everyone would think I was jealous and question my motives—'

'Kass.' The sound of Rhodri's voice stops me mid-argument. 'Don't.'

The frantic look in his eyes catches me off guard. I hesitate.

'Seconded,' Lewis shouts.

Rhodri roughly pushes his chair away from the table.

'Woah, mate.' Max jumps up when his bread plate almost falls onto his lap. 'Steady.'

Rhodri doesn't hear. He moves to the window, back to us, shoulders tense. What *is* his problem? Is he *that* into her?

There's a definite challenge in Faith's eyes. 'Bring it on. It's your funeral.'

I don't get what's happening, she's way too calm and Rhodri's way too stressed.

'I nominate Billy,' King John says.

'No,' Lewis cries out.

King John ignores him. 'We need to speed this up before the blood moon rises and we all become wolf food.'

'Seconded,' Demi says. Stony cold and determined he nods to King John.

'Job done.' King John rests his feet on the table. 'May the best person win.'

35

Faith and Billy stand on a raised platform in the middle of the green, facing us. This time there are no pillories to humiliate them. We're all in a line: Max, Lewis, King John, Demi, me and Rhodri. I want to be closer to Lewis, he must be terrified, but I'm too scared to move out of line. Between us is the well. The grate has been removed, and the dark black hole is large enough for a body to fall through, a whole new stomach-churning way to die.

Billy's terrified eyes keep flitting from the drones to the archers. I long to grab their bows and shoot down every single camera that's making entertainment of our fear and pain.

Rhodri's statue still; his sallow cheeks ping against the black of his costume. His jaw's tightly shut, arms straight by his side, fists clenched into tight balls. There's a frantic energy coming off him as he stares straight ahead.

Faith in contrast stands relaxed. I don't get it; why is she so calm?

'I'm waiting for your accusation.'

I jump, realising Draigodân's talking to me. *Shit*. I don't like Faith, but I won't send her to her death. Draigodân's beady eyes stare right at me but I struggle to speak the words that will condemn her.

'I…' There's no way.

There's movement on the top of the walls as the guards aim their bows down at us.

'I can't,' I whisper.

Faith talks directly to me. 'Let me help you out. This isn't about the game, or me being a Werewolf. This is personal. You can't stand the fact he likes me more than you and, the minute you came through the castle gates, he dropped you like a tonne of shit.'

What the?

'Girl, you are de-luded.' Lewis waves his finger at her in angry swirls. 'You are so guilty; you have dog written all over you.'

'Lewis, stop,' I hiss.

'Really?' Faith turns to him. ''Cause you don't have an ulterior motive in trying to save your boyfriend here?'

'He's not my boyfriend,' Lewis shouts. 'Because I have the sense to realise we're in a game and none of this is real, including your petty mean-girl crush.'

'Enough.' Fire shoots from Draigodân's mouth. We all jump back, silenced.

Black swirls rise in the air, twirling to a silent melody. The cloying smell of smoke lingers.

King John steps forward. 'I vote Billy. He's a Werewolf, always sniffing around, listening to chats and watching us. He's guilty, I'd bet my life on it.' He places a black stone at Billy's feet.

No one else moves. No one wants to condemn. A

whizzing hiss fills the silence when a flurry of arrows rain down, missing us by millimetres.

King John shouts. 'Vote, you idiots. You can't save them. If you don't vote they'll kill us all.'

Draigodân opens his mouth like a weapon, smoke curling from his lips.

Rhodri steps forward placing his stone at Billy's feet.

Demi's next. He votes for Faith.

Lewis votes for Faith, his hand shaking as he places his stone. I try to catch his eye but he keeps his head down.

Max steps forward and turns to Draigodân. 'Don't set me on fire but I have no stone.'

Standing in front of the dragon, Max looks so small. Draigodân tilts his head. 'You have just entered the game therefore you have not earned the right to vote.'

Max breathes a huge sigh of relief. Pulling on his top, he shuffles back into line.

Two pebbles each. I have the final vote.

The black stone is smooth in my hand. I hate Faith but I won't kill her. But if I choose Billy, Lewis will share his fate, bound to him by the Lovers card. Faith stands a better chance on the Gauntlet. She's stronger and fitter. I doubt Lewis would make it over the first hurdles let alone shoot a pistol. My mind is making me dizzy trying to find a solution to this impossible dilemma. I have no choice.

I step forward avoiding Faith's eyes and drop the stone at her feet.

She leans into me. 'You've no idea what you've done, you stupid cow.'

My head snaps up to her face. Her voice is filled with anger but the glint in her eyes is full-on delight. She's *happy* I voted for her?

Draigodân speaks. 'Castle Dwellers, you have voted three to two for Faith to be eliminated from the game.'

Billy falls to his knees in relief. Faith remains defiant in the torchlight. Delving inside the neck of her tunic she pulls out a pendant. It's red and shiny and heart shaped. My heart stops in one agonising beat and the whole world turns to slow mo.

'Draigodân,' she speaks confidently, lifting the pendant for him to see.

'What is it?' Demi whispers.

'A heart,' Max says. 'It's the Lovers card. The Lovers are tied together by their love, if one is eliminated the other dies of a broken heart.' He gulps. 'Oh.'

Draigodân appears to be looking at the heart pendant still held high by a triumphant Faith. 'I can confirm that the Lovers card is in play and therefore the two players tied together by this card will face elimination by the Gauntlet. Will the second Lover please reveal themselves.'

'What's going on? What is that?' Lewis is talking to Billy, horror and confusion mixed into one. 'Billy?'

Billy is sobbing, muttering, 'I'm sorry' over and over.

Sounds and vision blur together as the wave of terror crashes over me. Rhodri reaches inside his tunic and raises his hand high. The red heart clutched in his fist sparkles in the torchlight.

Rhodri's voice is clear. 'I'm the Lover.'

I'm aware of screaming but I can't stop.

Panic and confusion reigns over the green. Only Faith remains calm as she steps toward Rhodri.

'Lewis and Billy. Lewis and Billy,' is all I can repeat, pleading with Lewis to tell Draigodân there's been a mistake, that Rhodri is free. But Lewis is as confused as me.

'Oh, you've been played like a guitar, girl.' Faith's words are like weapons, each one stabbing sharper than the last. 'By eliminating me you have killed your Welsh boy.'

My eyes flit from Faith to Billy. He's still on his knees mumbling apologies.

'NO,' I scream. Grabbing him by the shoulders, I yank him to standing. 'You lied?'

Billy staggers backwards. 'I'm so sorry.' He points to Faith. 'I'd no idea she was the Lover for real. I'd no idea that character card would be in play. It was a gamble.'

'Why?' Lewis is as angry as me. 'You've been lying this whole time, making me think we had a bond? Why?'

'I wanted to win,' Billy cries. 'The best way to do that was to ally myself to you. If Kass thought you would be eliminated, she wouldn't put me up and nor would you.' He rushes forward to Rhodri. 'I'm so sorry. I didn't know.' Rhodri says nothing as Billy begs for his forgiveness. 'I'm so sorry… I didn't…'

I don't see the punch as Rhodri's fist meets Billy's face and he drops to the floor.

No one runs to help him; all eyes are on Rhodri.

'Couldn't stand the whining any longer,' he says. Grabbing Faith by the arm, he turns to Draigodân, his face hard. 'Let's do this.'

'NO,' I scream again placing myself between Rhodri and Draigodân. All the bullshit of the past twenty-four hours melts away and all that's left is the truth. I'm damn well going to fight for the boy I love. 'It's my fault. I put her up, take me. I did this.'

'Stop.' Rhodri's voice is calm.

'But you didn't know what she was; she lied to you,' I say clutching at straws. 'You didn't know.'

He takes my hands in his and walks me away from Draigodân. 'I knew what she was and I knew what I was doing.' He drops my hands, his face emotionless, eyes deep dark. 'And I'd do it again in a heartbeat.'

'No,' I cry.

He pulls me into him and whispers in my ear. 'I had no choice. They'll hurt Carys.'

His hands fall from mine, his eyes begging me to keep quiet.

I choke back the tears, his words echoing in my ears, leaving me beaten. Carys, his little sister. I should've known Skye would threaten the person he loves the most.

I nod to show I understand. Relief flashes on his face. Tearing his eyes from mine, Rhodri places himself in front of Draigodân and holds his head high. It's okay. It's good. I keep my glass half full and stubbornly hope for the best. Rhodri can beat the Gauntlet. He's not injured like Arti or old like Ravi. He can conquer the obstacles and out run the wolves. And he'll have Faith to help him.

They can do this. They'll be fine.

Right?

'Wait.' Demi's holding something in his hand. 'I have an action card, and I want to play it.'

'Not another bloody card?' King John says. 'How many of these things are there?'

'Shut up,' I snap.

'I have the Chalice of Resurrection. I've the power to bring someone back.' Demi pushes the card in front of a hovering drone-cam.

Draigodân appears to be thinking. I hold my breath for so long my lungs burn. Finally, he speaks. 'The Chalice of Resurrection cannot save a Lover. Rhodri will be eliminated.'

Max walks in front of Rhodri, strong and brave and quite unlike the Max I know. 'The rules state the Chalice of Resurrection is all powerful and can be played to counter any action card played or save any character, including a Werewolf.'

Draigodân's head glitches. 'Two action cards cannot be played at once.' His voice has become strangely robotic.

Max stays calm. 'There's one action card in play. The Lovers is technically a character card.'

'The player voted out by the Castle Council must be eliminated.' Draigodân glitches again.

'Rhodri wasn't voted out, Faith was,' Max says.

'Rhodri must be eliminated.' Draigodân's neck sways from side to side. 'Rhodri…' He disappears.

The only sound is the painful staccato of our breath.

'Have we broken Draigodân?' Demi whispers.

'Shhh,' Lewis hushes when Draigodân's image reappears in front of us.

'Castle Dwellers, an action card has been played.' He's talking like the last few minutes never happened. 'The Chalice of Resurrection has the ability to save one chosen for elimination.' He turns towards Demi. 'Who do you wish to save?'

'Rhodri,' Demi says. 'I wish to save Rhodri.'

Rhodri laughs bitterly. It takes all my strength not to jump on him. He's safe.

Slow clapping sounds behind us. 'Well played, team.' Faith's voice is honey smooth. 'Didn't see that coming.'

'Why are you doing this?' I turn to Faith.

'One word.' The look she gives me is pure hate-filled anger. 'Henry.'

What?

'Who the hell is Henry?' King John's words shatter the stunned silence. 'The boy from the first game? Skye's little bitch?' His hand hits his head. 'Wow.'

Demi steps towards Faith, his face clouded with shock. 'You know Henry?'

'More than that,' I say as the penny finally drops and my brain catches up with my memory. I knew I recognised her. Now I see it's blatantly obvious: her athletic Lara Croft build, her striking good looks, the way in which her mouth turns upwards into a snide smirk. Exactly like Henry's. I take a punt. 'You're his sister.'

She laughs. 'You think you're the only ones grieving so hard that revenge is the one thing keeping you alive?' She moves around us. 'Do you have any idea what it's like to mourn when the world says your dead brother was a monster? That he had it coming? Any idea what that does to the mother who lives with the pain and guilt every day, hounded so badly she doesn't leave the house for fear of what people might do? And if the son is a monster, then the father must be too, right? Stands to reason that they must all be rotten to the core. They must pay for the deeds of the dead. You destroyed my family. I wanted to hurt you as much as you hurt me. When Skye called, I came running.'

'We've all paid the price for Henry's actions,' I say. 'And it was Skye who pushed the knife in his back.'

'She said you'd say that.' Faith's face is inches from mine. I don't flinch. 'Said you'd deny it because little Girl Next Door didn't have the balls to own her actions. She said you were a cheat and a liar.'

'Faith, I'm telling you the truth. I didn't kill Henry.'

'Liar,' Faith screams into my face.

'I'm not lying.' I stare into her eyes. 'But I'm glad he's

gone. He was a fame whore. He killed my friends for nothing more than a twisted chance at celebrity.'

Draigodân appears again. 'Faith, you have been eliminated. It's time to leave the castle.'

Two guards appear at the edge of the green but make no move to come closer.

'What do you mean leave the castle?' Demi asks.

Ignoring him, Faith looks straight at me. 'No Gauntlet for me. Sorry to disappoint. We have an arrangement, me and the big man. I'm immune. I'm not part of the game for real. I'm just here to stir shit up and boy has it been fun. See, unlike you losers, I have a free pass to freedom.'

No wonder she's so calm. She's been working with them this entire time. She's not in any danger. She never was.

'Oh, and I'm a Werewolf.' She holds her hands up. 'Spoiler. It's about time you caught one of us. You think you have it all figured out, you stupid little band of OGs and revengers.' The drones rise high, turning their cameras away from us. 'You're wrong. You're all clueless. No one in here is who they say. There are others hiding their truths. The one truth in here is that you're all going to die. Do you have any idea who you are playing with?' Draigodân raises his head behind her. 'The big man? The Investor? Skye was an amateur; you're in the major leagues now.' Draigodân leans in closer to her, his eyes gleaming. 'You've no clue what he's planning, no idea what this is all for. It's bigger than Reality, bigger than you can even imagine. He's going to—'

The gust of fire exploding from Draigodân's mouth throws us all back onto the grass. The rush that sounds in my ears is overtaken by an agonising scream as Faith is consumed by flames.

Draigodân lifts his head towards the ramparts. Before we can react, the screaming is cut off by a punctured gasp. Faith stops her desperate dance and drops to the floor like a firestone. Two arrows burn from her back. Up on the ramparts the archers lower their bows.

Guards spill into the area dousing the body with water until the flames sizzle and die. Picking up her blackened body, they exit through the gate.

It took less than two minutes.

We watch in shocked silence, hands clamped over mouths and noses to keep out the overpowering bouquet of smoke and sulphur and burning flesh. Someone's throwing up behind me, the sound of retching the only noise.

Draigodân raises his head and surveys us, running his tongue over his razor-sharp teeth.

My legs have turned to jelly. I crouch, my fists pushing against the cold grass.

An arm folds gently around my shoulders. 'Steady, *cariad*,' a voice whispers in my ear and the tears freefall from my eyes. I sob with heart-wrenching relief and concentrate on not passing out.

36

Max knocks against my bed. 'Whoopsie.' He catches my eye then walks slowly across the hall. He doesn't look back, but his body language screams, *follow me*.

Slipping out of bed, I automatically reach for my microphone. Screw it. I'm so sick of playing by the rules. I jump up, leaving it behind. The camera whirrs around to me. Shit, how can we talk properly when they are watching our every move?

I catch Lewis' eye. He nods, even without words he gets me. He turns and marches up to Billy.

'You owe me an explanation,' he says loudly, flicking his hair dramatically. It works; the cameras all turn towards them. 'I cannot begin to tell you how hurt I am. It's not the game play; it's the straight up lying.' He falls dramatically on the bed and the drones surround him. I can't help the smile that crosses my lips as he launches into an Oscar-worthy performance, allowing me to slip out of the hall undetected.

Max is outside with Rhodri. We squeeze into a dark corner. In the black costumes, the shadows give us some privacy.

'We don't have long.' Max gestures to the space around his neck where the microphone usually hangs, his voice urgent. 'I say we stage a coup.' A patrolling drone passes and we all freeze. It doesn't stop. We're doing a pretty good job of blending. 'Mai was right. We have the choice not to play.'

Rhodri's face bleeds ghost white. Turning away he punches the stone wall in frustration. 'I can't, man. They have Carys. They'll hurt her if I...' He swallows his words in a sob.

'Max is right,' I say. 'If we're going to get out of here we need to stop being scared. They have Thea too. And it sounds like this guy can get to anyone, anytime, if he wants to. We need to stop him. I think Carys would want you to fight.'

I wait. Have I gone too far by mentioning his sister? Rhodri stays silent, his head resting against the cold stone, eyes shut tight. 'I can't risk it,' he whispers.

'How do you even know they have her?' Max speaks quickly as Rhodri's head snaps up. 'Go with me. Skye showed Kass a video of Thea, right?'

'In the status room.' I shudder as Thea's terrified face fills my head. 'I saw her.'

Rhodri's eyes flare angrily. 'She didn't show me nothing.'

'And you believed her?' Max says.

'Course I fucking believed her.' Rhodri's jaw tenses. 'Even if she's not here they can still hurt her. You said this guy was powerful.'

'Even if we do exactly what he wants there's no guarantee he won't still hurt them,' Max says. 'I'm sorry, but it's true. And if you don't make it, what happens to them then? The only way to make it safe is to stop him. And the only way to stop him is to get out of here. Dude, don't let this guy define you. We need the badass boy from Porthcawl right now.' Max steps close to him, squeezing his arm.

'You don't think he's got her?' Rhodri's voice breaks in pain. 'You don't think she's here?'

Max shakes his head slowly. 'Do you trust me?'

Rhodri folds his hand over Max's, his face flooding with emotions. Standing straight he closes his eyes and inhales deeply. 'Fuck it. I am done with this bullshit. I'm sick of being messed with and threatened and held to ransom. I say screw the game and screw the Investor. We need to find out the truth and get the fuck out.'

Lewis' angry voice filters through the air as his argument with Billy gets more heated inside the hall, reminding us we don't have much time.

King John appears from the shadows. 'Well don't you have everything wrapped up and tied in a nice convenient little bow?' He's talking directly to Max. 'How do you know so much about everything?'

'I … don't… I…' Max stumbles over his words.

'That performance by your boy in there may trick the cameras but not me. Figured I was missing something.' King John's voice is heavy with suspicion. 'Like a Werewolf meeting. How long do you think you're gonna get away with no mics on? That's a rule break. You know they can still see you right?'

'What they gonna do?' Rhodri says. 'They've already killed me once.'

We shuffle reluctantly to let King John into the circle.

'How do we know we can trust you?' Rhodri glares at King John.

'You don't.' King John thumps his chest. 'But look, I'm not mic'd up.' He nudges Rhodri. 'Relax, I'm just trying to be a team player.'

'Ha,' I snort.

'We make a truce. No names get put in the fire tonight,' Rhodri says. Everyone looks sceptical. 'You know the Werewolves aren't really killing right? They're forced to give a name and Production does the rest.'

'Says a Werewolf,' King John mutters.

'Whatever,' Rhodri says. 'I'm just saying that they're as much the victims as the Peasants and we shouldn't vilify them. We need to trust each other.'

'So, you a Werewolf or not?' King John stares at Rhodri, his face one big suspicious question.

'Glad to see you're understanding my point,' says Rhodri. 'Stand down soldier and try thinking big picture.' Rhodri's eyes rest on me. 'Could you find your way back to Thea?'

'I think so,' I say. 'I'm pretty sure it's one of these doors off here.'

'What about the cameras?' King John says snarkily. 'I think you're forgetting that we're being watched twenty-four seven.'

'At least I have a plan,' says Rhodri.

'I have a plan too,' King John says. 'To win.'

Rhodri throws his hands up. 'Unbelievable.'

Max puts his hand on Rhodri's shoulder. 'Leave it. You can't reason with a mad man.'

Draigodân appears in a flourish of fire, lighting up our hiding place and bellows. 'All contestants must return to the Great Hall.'

'Told you,' King John says. 'It's mics back round necks like a ball and chain.'

An arrow hits the ground.

'Woah,' King John cries. 'That almost hit me.'

'Go,' Max whispers to me and Rhodri. 'Get Thea. I'll tell the others.'

'I think we'll need a bigger distraction,' King John says.

Draigodân breathes a wall of fire in our direction.

'All right,' King John shouts as we dodge the flames. 'Go,' he mouths to us. Grabbing Max, he heads back into the hall. 'We're being herded like sheep,' he moans. 'Do I look like a bloody sheep?'

'You seriously want me to answer that,' Max says as they disappear around the corner.

Rhodri and I press our bodies against the stone wall. We don't have to wait long. Panicked voices rise into the night, followed by crashing. There's a scream, more crashing and an acrid stench of burning. Cries of 'Fire!' follow, a cacophony of noise designed to cause confusion. And it's working, all the drones are speeding towards the hall.

Scanning the scene, I search for the door the guards took me through that first night.

'Close your eyes, try to remember,' Rhodri whispers in my ear.

I squeeze my eyes shut. I remember the feeling of the bridge, the hollow sound of wood, the cold shade of the inner gatehouse as I was pushed through, the feel of the ground beneath my boots.

'There were cobbles.' I open my eyes. In the far corner a small path of cobbles leads to an open door.

'There,' I say.

Rhodri takes my hand. Keeping to the shadows we duck around the green. From here the full extent of Max's distraction becomes clear. Smoke billows from the door of the Great Hall. Max, Lewis, Billy, Demi and King John are tearing around shouting and screaming and generally causing confusion. Wolf guards are shouting orders as they try to contain them and put out the flames. They must have set fire to the table, which explains the stench of burning wood. So far our absence has gone unnoticed in the chaos.

We climb the steep stairs quickly, careful not to slip on the uneven steps, listening for sounds of footsteps on the stone.

Thea's room is the first door we reach. Stepping onto the small platform, I stop.

It's open.

'You sure this is the room?' Rhodri walks inside, his voice echoing in the emptiness.

Searching the doorway, I pull the small piece of black cloth from the hole in the wall. 'Definitely.'

The room's empty. A fireplace dominates the far wall, clean and empty, no sign of recent use. There's no evidence that someone's been staying here. A single chair sits in the middle of the room, a small black box perched on the seat.

Rhodri picks it up. 'Bluetooth speaker.'

'Why? What's it…' My brain catches up with my mouth but still I don't believe. 'I saw her. She was here, in this room.'

'Did you?' Rhodri says. 'Or did you see what Skye wanted you to see?'

A million thoughts are flooding through my mind. 'Max heard her, I *talked* to her through the door, she was here.'

'But neither of you *saw* her, in real life?' Rhodri asks. He points to the speaker. 'I bet your conversation was pretty generic.'

'Skye had her ring, the one we got made. It had the inscription.'

'I think we've established she's been watching us. You and Lewis were quite vocal about those rings, I remember,' he says. 'You posted about them.'

Shit, he's right. We put them all over our Insta. I kick myself for being so stupid.

In the first game Henry manipulated our images and our voices to create deep fakes of the dead. Skye could totally fake Thea. I almost choke on the realisation.

'She isn't here.' The thought hits me like a wrecking ball. 'She never was.'

37

Thea's not here.

'Looks like Skye fooled both of us,' Rhodi says.

I struggle to breathe, the true extent of Skye's manipulation becoming crystal clear. 'She knew the only way to make me play was to threaten someone I loved. But she couldn't get to Thea, so she faked her.'

Rhodri's eyes flash with rage. 'That's so twisted.'

'Max said she wanted to mess with me, and she has. All I've thought about was getting to Thea.' My stomach rolls. 'And it was all for nothing.'

'No,' Rhodri says. 'You and Lewis came here for Max, remember? Don't let her mind games screw with you.'

'Don't you see? Max was right. It was all a lie; she manipulated us both into playing and, like idiots, we fell for it.' I try to calm my racing breath and push the hopelessness down into my guts. Something's bugging me. 'When we met in the tent you had no clue Max had been taken. And you didn't know about Carys until later. Why did you come?'

'You,' he says quietly. 'I knew if I'd got a message, you would too. When you didn't reply to my texts, I figured that was why. I came for you.'

'I didn't ask you to,' I say. Is all this somehow my fault? 'I wanted you to stay away.'

'Figures.' He smiles. 'But I came anyway. Then she

told me she had Carys, and I lost it. All I could think of was keeping her safe. I'm so sorry.' It's barely a whisper leaving his mouth.

I reach for the back of the chair to steady myself. He steps forward, his arms reaching for me. I breathe in deeply, taking in his familiar scent as my body responds without thought to our surroundings or the situation. Being this close to him is intoxicating.

'It wasn't real.' His lips brush my ear sending shivers down my back. 'You know that right? She said I had to convince you.' His voice cracks. 'I had to make you believe I meant it.'

'But you kissed her more than once,' I say stepping back, putting space between us, hurt closing around my heart like a fist. 'Billy saw you.'

Rhodri swears under his breath. 'Billy lied. He was looking out for himself by screwing the rest of us. I didn't do anything with Faith. I was looking for a way inside. I was trying to find…'

'Carys.' I finish for him.

'I couldn't tell you.' His hand brushes his hair. 'I had to make you believe. I swear. I had no choice.'

The pain and regret in his voice is so strong that I believe him completely.

'I know.' I can't keep the wobble out of my words. 'But the feelings were real. On my part that is. I don't know how much more I can deal with right now.'

He frowns. 'Understood.'

I wait for him to say more, to convince me his feelings are true, but he doesn't. This game has broken us. I can't even trust my own instincts. We stand awkwardly with the chair between us. I don't know what to say to him. I don't have the capacity to deal with us, here, in this place, after everything that's happened.

I speak to break the spell. 'How would they know I'd come up here?'

'The Dungeon card,' Rhodri says. 'Skye choreographed it all perfectly.'

'Marcus put it in my pocket,' I say mentally retracing my steps. 'And he was working for Skye. That got me to Max. When I woke up, Max was gone and the door was open.' I look at Rhodri. 'She staged the whole thing and off I went like a gullible little puppet.'

'Where'd Max go?' Rhodri says.

'No idea,' I say. 'I thought they'd moved him to another room. I went to look for him but then I heard Thea. The next time I saw him he was pushing Skye off the tower.'

'Something doesn't add up,' Rhodri says. 'Why would she put you in a room with Max in the first place? We need to be careful.'

''Cause I was being positively reckless up till now.' A small smile dances on my lips.

Rhodri puts the speaker down. 'We need to be completely sure neither Thea nor Carys are in the castle. Remember the last game, that room with all the monitors?'

'MCR,' I say. 'Main control room.'

'That. We need to check the cameras,' Rhodri says. 'If they're here we'll see them from there.'

'Easy,' I mumble.

Having no idea where to go, we go up, past the room with DC Brown's body and past Max's room. At the top of the spiral staircase is a long corridor. It's dark and claustrophobic. The stone roof kisses Rhodri's head forcing him to duck. There's light from small side windows where the moon is granted meagre visiting rights but there's nothing from the other side of the moat, just a slumbering black.

We hurry towards a light at the end, passing an inner window. Gazing down, the Great Hall is even bigger without the table. Food is strewn over the floor in pools of water, the once yellow straw now black and burnt. Max is below, deep in conversation. I can't see who he's talking to, but his hands gesticulate wildly.

At the end of the corridor, another spiral staircase beckons us downwards. We follow the multi-coloured cables that snake along the walls, different sizes and colours weaved together with cable ties hung loosely onto the walls. We're close.

The steps are narrow and worn with age. We climb down slowly, one hand gripping the inner column, the other pushing against the outside wall. We stop at a small landing and a wooden door, light shining from within.

Rhodri points to the colourful procession of wires all running into it. Putting his ear to the door, he signals a thumbs up. We enter cautiously.

The makeshift MCR's empty. It has the feeling of being occupied only moments before. The steam rising from the coffee cup on the desk suggests that whoever was here has only just left, and the seat turned over in the middle of the room says they went in a hurry.

'We need to be quick,' I say. 'If they've gone to check the fire they won't be long.'

Rhodri nods, letting out an impressed whistle. 'Look at all this.'

In front of us are banks of monitors showing images of the castle grounds and the remaining cast. On the desk sit various machines with hundreds of coloured buttons and levers. The sight's nothing new – we saw it all in the first game – but what's different is the top rows of screens. Mai's there, Sandra and Marcus, and every fallen contestant who became a victim of this evil game, their close-ups all in a line, their faces distorted by the three red lines of the Werewolf mark.

The surviving contestants' profiles are in the middle monitors, all staring out in glorious technicolour. Below them is another screen, our faces stacked on top of each other. Against each face is a coloured horizontal line with a percentage at the end. King John is on the top, followed by Demi, Lewis, Rhodri, me, with Billy at the bottom.

'What's that?' I point to the percentage lines.

'Leaderboard,' Rhodri says. 'It's tallying audience votes.'

I can't help but shudder at the thought of these people watching us for their entertainment.

'They're not here.' Rhodri's studying the monitors.

I agree. One screen is split into two, one half showing Thea's cell, the other Max's. Thea would be here, she'd be monitored. Carys too. It really was all a lie.

Rhodri points to the monitors. 'All this kit has that dragon logo on it not the *Blood Moon* wolf head.'

He's right. Every piece of equipment is marked with the red dragon circle, the exact same logo as the guards.

'I guess that's something to do with the Investor?'

Rhodri nods. 'He has his own army of loyal soldiers. Makes me sick.'

'Why?' I say. 'Why would they willingly be a part of this?'

'Fuck knows,' Rhodri says. 'Who knows why anyone follows nutters without question. This Investor guy is obviously making it worth their while.'

'Worth turning a blind eye to murder?' I say. 'Do you think he has something on them? Like Carys and Thea?'

'No idea,' Rhodri says. 'The weak will always follow the strong. It's been that way since forever. As long as he doesn't show weakness, they'll be his willing disciples. Whatever their reasons, I hope they burn in hell.'

I recognise the vision mixer from the first show, the machine used to cut from camera to camera to create output for the live feed.

In the corner a monitor's scrolling messages. I lean in to read them as they move across the screen.

King John to win
Love the guy from Wales
Why did Faith not run the gauntlet?
Fixed
Productions faking it. Not real. It's all a scam
Can't believe Mai's dead, LOVED her
Kill Kass, she's so meh
Hang on, are there people in there we can't vote for?
We vote but it doesn't count. Not right
I did not see that coming
Demi is HOT
Team Lewis!

As I lean in to read the scrolling messages my hand presses against the mixer.

'Help.' Thea's voice bursts into the room making us both jump.

'Shit,' Rhodri says.

I press the button again, holding it down. 'Kass, help me.' I press again, tapping it quickly. 'He-He-He-lp me-m-m-me.' Anger burns my cheeks as I make rap beats with my best friend's voice.

'It's a recording, probably taken from the last show's footage.' I bang my fist. 'I really, really hate these people.'

'Where's Max?' Rhodri's question pulls me back to

the now. I search for his picture. It's not there. Neither is his name on the leaderboard. He's missing, just like Ophelia and Portia.

'Why would he be missing?' I say.

Rhodri shrugs. 'He was a late arrival. And he was being punished. I don't think they expected him to go into the game.'

'Maybe,' I say, distracted by the scrolling messages. 'Some viewers are angry that their votes aren't counting, and the rules keep changing.'

Rhodri humphs. 'I'm more concerned about that leaderboard. We're not doing well. If there's an audience vote we'll bomb.'

I snort. 'Like I care whether they like me.'

'Bigger picture,' Rhodri says. 'If we're liked, we've more chance of getting out of here; we get bigger time advantages. We need to up our game.'

'How?' I mumble, hating the idea of playing up to the camera.

'You're not gonna like this but I have an idea,' Rhodri says. 'We lean into the love.'

'Lean into the love?' I know exactly what he means but I can't believe he's suggesting it.

'Audiences love a happy ending. We've had the love triangle. If we show them we're the *real* Lovers we could gain votes. It could win us the game.'

'Not interested in winning,' I say but I get his point. Short of making them all turn off, I can't see another way.

'I get how you feel and how this must seem, but we need to play the game to our advantage. Then, when we get out of here we can mend.' He takes my hand in his. 'Survive, then mend.'

The emotion on his face is so raw I almost burst into tears. I take a step closer to him.

'Have you found them yet?' A voice blasts through the speakers. We freeze. 'They went looking for Thea. I told them to. They can't have gone far.' The voice isn't the robotic voice of a wolf mask. It's stern and impatient. 'Hello?'

But that's not the reason we don't speak.

The voice coming through the speaker belongs to Max.

38

'What's going on?' The voice is clearly expecting a response.

Rhodri doesn't move. I put my finger to my lips and press the flashing red button on the desk, speaking gruffly into the microphone. 'No sign of them on the cameras.'

'Keep looking.' The voice sounds impatient.

'Will do,' I say, hoping the trembling in my voice doesn't translate through the mic.

'We need to go,' I say. Rhodri still doesn't move. I'm not sure he can. Is this one betrayal too many? 'Rhodri?'

'Max?' he whispers, hurt exploding in his eyes like shrapnel. Max was his person: the one he nursed back to health; the one he trusted with his life. He clenches and unclenches his fist. I hold my breath.

Striding to the door, he flings it open.

Out on the small stairway a flurry of footsteps echoes from beneath. Someone's running up the stairs.

'Quick,' Rhodri says.

We run along the claustrophobic corridor. I will my feet faster as the shouts behind get louder. I turn to look back and almost plough into Rhodri's static body.

The way forward is blocked by guards.

We're trapped.

Rhodri's body tenses as he prepares to fight.

'Don't,' I say. It's useless; there're too many of them.

The guards march us through the corridors. They

push us through a door and into a room. It's huge, almost the size of the Great Hall and just as grand. A fire rages in the spectacular fireplace warming the room and casting light into its shadowed corners. Brightly coloured tapestries hang from the walls.

They leave us in the middle of the floor. A fancy chair sits at one end raised on a podium, throne-like. A figure walks in, dressed in black, their tailored suit edged in sumptuous crimson fur. Their wolf mask is fashioned differently to all the rest; glossy blood red, it shines like a gemstone in the torch light. The ears stand taller, the features more sharply defined, the jawline exaggerated, a mouth opened enough to show sharp teeth protruding. It oozes strength and wealth and power. The mask of the Alpha.

The Investor.

Crimson gloves cover hands, every inch of skin covered to mask the identity beneath. They sit, leaning an elbow on one side of the chair, observing us with a lazy stare.

I clasp my hands tightly to stop the uncontrollable shake.

Rhodri stands beside me, anger pulsing from him.

The Investor speaks, voice low and lazy through the mask. 'So, the famous Kass and Rhodri. Two of my celebrity players. Are you lost?'

We say nothing.

'Did no one explain the concept of a rule break to you two crazy kids?' He chuckles then turns his head to the side in a dramatic pose. 'There's a certain resemblance to Anubis, don't you think?' The red mask sparkles in the torchlight. 'The Egyptian? Guide to the Underworld? We've a certain symmetry, Anubis and I – me being the guide to the dark web.'

His fingers drum on the arm of the chair.

'My daughter wants you dead.' His voice is completely lacking emotion. 'She holds you' – he points to Rhodri – 'responsible.'

'For what?' I can't help the question slipping from my mouth or it's incredulous tone.

The mask turns to me. 'My girls should have been on your raft. It was the safest place you see, you being our star players. But you' – the mask snaps back to Rhodri – 'refused them, and none too nicely, young man. Then my Ophelia died. I'm aware it's an irrational blame caused by grief, but it helps to put the blame somewhere and if I can give my Portia some comfort…' He waves his hand dismissively. 'Production was also to blame, and they've been dealt with.'

'You forced Max to kill Skye?' Rhodri's voice is dangerously quiet.

'Forced is a strong word,' he says. 'Max wanted to help and was all too happy to oblige when the moment presented itself.'

A small cry leaves Rhodri's lips.

'You mustn't be too hard on your friend. Not everyone's cut out to be a hero. The world would be very boring if it was only filled with good and bad. It needs nuance. It needs those who are happy to traverse both. Max was easy to seduce into the programme, so eager to dance to Skye's tune. The poor boy just wanted to live. And when she was in breach of her contract, Max was happy to help. It's not his fault. It's just who he is.' He leans toward to me. 'I have to admit to being a little disappointed in you, my dear. You were just so eager to trust at every stage. So quick to believe Skye had Thea, so easily convinced that Rhodri would leave you for another, that you just weren't deserving enough. And did you not consider it strange that Skye would put you in a room with Max?' He waves his hand. 'We're not lacking for space. Max played his roles perfectly, from the kidnapped friend to Skye's imprisoned confidant, giving you just the right amount of information. The T-shirt was his idea; a necessary detail he knew you would understand. He was able to give us so much invaluable information to help us persuade you two into the game. That you didn't see him coming is baffling to me.'

His words are buzzing in my ears like wasps; they just keep stinging. I dig my nails into my palms.

He sits back on his throne. 'But Max's guilty conscience might be getting the better of him. Or he's enjoying playing both sides.'

'You'll pay for this,' Rhodri says.

The Investor's fists clench. 'I already have. My daughters were not to be harmed. Skye assured me there were measures in place to keep them out of danger but she took her eye off the ball. So you see, I understand why my daughter wants you dead, because I want that too.'

'You deserve everything you got,' Rhodri growls. 'You put your daughters in the way of danger.'

The Investor bangs his fists on the chair. 'They'd never have been in danger if that incompetent girl had done her job.' He pauses, his chest rising rapidly. 'But you are right, and I must live with that for the rest of my life. I should have said no, but what father wants to deny his children?'

This guy is even crazier than Skye. To put his own kids in a game like this and believe they'd be safe? To be that privileged to believe that you can control everything? It's King Canute levels of disillusionment and the tide's turned just as fiercely on him.

He carries on. 'Skye was a genius; her natural propensity for producing was remarkable. She had an instinct for drama and such an eye for detail. But she wasn't a team player. She didn't have the show's interests at heart, and my beloved Ophelia paid the price.'

This guy is so far from the real world he could be on another planet.

'I digress,' he says. 'As I said, Portia wants you dead. But the show must go on. We must give the audience their big finale. You must be punished. Time may be a great healer, but I find revenge to be a very effective medicine. It was how we were able to get so many of your friends to agree to play after all.' He leans forward in his seat to stare at us both. 'Where are your microphones?'

The question is rhetorical. Like a cat with a mouse, he's enjoying playing with us. With a wave of his gloved hand a guard steps forward and clips new mic packs round our waists looping the cables over our heads like a noose.

'As you are aware, failure to wear your microphone is considered a rule break. In this game, rule breaks will not be tolerated.' He gestures to a guard. 'Find the boy Lewis. He will be the next victim of the Werewolves. Find him and kill him.'

'No,' I scream, falling to my knees. 'Please.'

Rhodri lunges forward but his way is blocked. A guard whispers in the Investor's ear.

'Oh, I see. Good point. Kill another then. I don't care which. Surprise me.'

My fingers grip the cold floor as the room spins.

'Why are you doing this?' Rhodri says.

'To fulfil a need of course,' the Investor says, his voice light. 'You created this, you and all those reality shows that came before. By giving Skye and the boy, what was his name? Harry? Henry? By giving them a platform, you created a need. A gap in the market if you will. You showed that everything is possible with just a little bit of ingenuity and imagination.'

Rhodri's shaking his head. 'We didn't create nothing.'

'You fed the monster and now it's grown greedy. We live in a world of overindulgence and overstimulation.' He stands, waving his arms like an evangelical preacher. 'We

SEE everything. We witness war and disaster and disease. We swipe past a small child dying in their mother's arms to like a cute kitten playing. We watch soldiers in a war we created, then comment and heart our favourite recipe. We buy endless tat, because TikTok made us do it. We watch the world through complacent eyes and bear judgement from our sofas. We've become so dehumanised and desensitised that we don't see the reality playing on our phone screens. To feed such a beast we must create more and more content. We must evolve and adapt to our audience. We must be resourceful and imaginative and daring.'

'By killing people?' I sob.

He waves his hand dismissively. 'My friends are bored. When you can do anything and buy everything the world becomes a tedious place. To do something dangerous is titillating. It makes us *feel* again.' He steps towards me and I'm staring at his shiny shoes. 'Don't worry. This will all be forgotten in an internet second as the next sensation sweeps the world. I'm thinking about diversifying into space travel, maybe Mars.'

Hands grab me and I'm dragged to my feet. I'm staring into the wolf mask. Crystal blue eyes stare back at me, cold and hard.

'You will return to the game, and you'll play to the end, or I will kill everyone you love and make you watch. I may not have them here in the castle, as you two detectives have so cleverly deduced, but I can reach anyone.

Anytime.' With a flourish of his hand, he strides out of the room.

The guards let me go and I stumble. Rhodri's arms wrap around my waist, holding me.

They lead us out of the throne room. As I pass a guard at the door I stop.

'Why?' I say straight into the masked eyes. 'What does he promise you that's so good you would look the other way?'

I don't expect an answer but as we walk out the door the guard speaks.

'There's more to his world than you could ever imagine. That life comes at a price. It's one I'm willing to pay.'

I follow the guards. I've never felt so helpless and so scared as I prepare to return to the game knowing that my friend is a traitor and each and every one of us is going to die.

39

The Great Hall stinks of wet wood and stale smoke. The fire in the fireplace is burning furiously, trying to warm every corner of the damp room. The cameras are still set high on the rig, little lights sparkling from every corner like blood moon stars, unharmed by Max's small fire distraction.

Demi's perched on the end of his bed. Max is pacing. King John's lying on his bed, arms under his head, staring up at the ceiling. They rush to greet us, all except King John.

I'm smothered in a Lewis bear hug. 'I thought you'd found Thea and legged it.' He sobs.

Peeling myself out of his grip I note the haunted look in his red eyes and the way his bottom lip quivers as he chews it.

'No way would I leave you here,' I say frowning as he wipes tears from his cheeks with the back of his hand. He pushes his shoulders back with a resolute smile as though pushing down a bucket-load of pain.

'I wouldn't blame you,' he says, his eyes searching.

'She's not here,' I say. 'I mean literally not here, in this castle. It was Skye and her AI tricks.'

Lewis' face says it all, as shock and disbelief mix into a cocktail of anger. 'Then it was all for nothing.' He crumples to the floor and sobs.

I crouch by him but my comfort's hollow. He's right; Skye's outmanoeuvred us at every step and I can't find a way out of this mess.

'Hey, you saved me,' Max says. 'And I can't tell you how grateful I am.'

I ignore him as my anger rages. He's showing no signs of knowing that we know he's a mole and until the Investor tells him, we have an advantage.

'I made a fire,' he says, grinning at me and Rhodri. 'My mum always told me not to play with fire but, hey, who knew how much fun it could be.' Rhodri turns away without responding.

Keep quiet and watch him, that's our plan. But, now he's here in front of me, it's so much harder to keep my cool.

Oblivious Max carries on. 'Well, looking at the glass half full, at least Thea is safe and at home, just like Carys. We can thank all the gods that they're—'

It all happens so quick. Rhodri lets out a noise like a howling wolf, making my insides curdle. Spinning on his heel he lunges towards Max. Grabbing him, he pushes him across the room and slams his body into the stone wall. Max lets out a shocked cry, his body crunching into the stone. Rhodri holds him upright, his hand wrapped tight around Max's neck.

Demi dives towards them but is held back by King John.

'Why'd you do it?' Rhodri's voice is scary calm, his

face millimetres away from Max's, so close their noses are touching.

Max tries to move his arms up to Rhodri's hands, but Rhodri slams him back against the wall again making him cry out in shock and fear. 'I... I...'

Rhodri's hand squeezes around his neck. Max coughs and chokes as his eyes widen with panic, his fingers clawing at Rhodri.

'Rhodri no, he can't breathe,' Lewis cries, but Rhodri doesn't hear.

'Tell me, or I swear I'll break your neck,' he growls.

Max's mouth opens and closes as if he's trying to speak but the hand at his throat forces him mute.

King John places a hand on Rhodri's shoulder. 'Stand down, soldier,' he says, his voice smooth. 'You're no killer. Let the boy down.'

Rhodri's angry gaze is fixed on Max. With a sudden push, he drops Max and steps back.

Max slides down the wall, his hands cupping his neck, gasping for air. A hand-shaped mark circles his neck.

'What the bloody hell is going on?' Demi says.

Rhodri kicks at Max. 'Why don't you tell them? Tell them how you've been working for them this entire time. Tell them how you betrayed us all.'

Max's head is down, a mop of unruly dark hair hiding his face. His shoulders rise and fall in a disjointed dance while he sobs over and over. 'I'm so sorry... So sorry...'

'Why?' Lewis says.

'I had no choice,' he sobs.

'We all have a choice, brother.' Demi's face creases with disgust.

Max's head flips up, his eyes blazing. 'I'm not like you. I'm not strong, or brave or good in a crisis. After *Lie or Die* I vowed never to be the victim again. Never to be weak. Never again the coward who gets trolled, who gets the hate and the death threats.' His eyes flash with anger. 'When Skye came to me with her plan I said yes. You're right, that was my choice. I wasn't going to be the victim. I refuse to be a victim, not again, not ever.'

'Well congratu-fucking-lations,' says Rhodri. 'You're dead as a dodo now. You think *they're* coming to help you? You're one of us now – a player in the game – and you've betrayed the only people who could've saved you.'

Max shakes his head, his curls bobbing as manically as his denial. 'But I was helping you. I told you about Carys so you would find a way out. I sent you to Thea. I was helping.'

'You were helping yourself,' Rhodri says in disgust. 'You were playing both sides to save your own skin.'

Max cries and splutters his denial. He cowers at Rhodri's feet and my emotions swing to revulsion. Even if he's genuine; he can't be trusted.

'Rhodri please… I can still help… I know things.' Max snivels and whines. 'Please…'

Rhodri stares down at him, his face stone cold.

'I fucking loved you, man,' he sobs and turns on his heel.

One by one we all turn our backs on Max and follow Rhodri out of the hall.

The January sun is rising reluctantly, spreading its miserly light over the castle moat. I shiver with relief. We survived the night and the final blood moon.

I make a mental head count when the boys come out of the hall.

Five? My chest tightens. There're six of us excluding Max, someone else is missing.

'Where's Billy?' I say kicking myself for being so distracted by Max that I didn't notice him missing sooner.

'Billy's gone,' Lewis murmurs. He's turning a name plaque in his hands, charred and half burnt with Billy's name in bold. 'I wasn't watching it, not with all the fire distraction and the running around. We said we weren't playing. I thought we were safe. One minute he was here then… We were going to tell you when you got back but things kicked off… I can't see him, I…' His eyes fill with pain. 'I just can't…'

'I'm so sorry.' I hug him tight, my guilty conscience screaming in my head. This is our fault. Billy's dead because we broke the rules. I catch Demi's eye over his shoulder.

'He's behind the hall,' he says quietly.

'You saw him?' I say.

He nods. 'We went looking, me and King John.'

Hearing his name King John moves closer nodding a grim confirmation. 'Right before you came back. Reckon we don't all need to see him.'

'So much for trusting one another.' Lewis pushes out of my embrace spitting the words at King John. 'We said no killing tonight and now Billy is dead.'

'What are you implying?' King John folds his arms across his chest.

'Nothing,' Lewis says, his gangly frame towering over King John. 'I'm *accusing* you of murdering him. You put his name in the fire when we were creating a diversion. No one was watching. We thought it was safe.'

I step in quickly. 'It wasn't the W—'

'How do we know you didn't do it? Or them?' King John points to me and Rhodri. 'How do we know they really went looking for this Thea, if she was really even missing? We only believed it because he said it.' He nods towards Max. 'And he's been lying all along.'

'You wanna find out?' Rhodri's up in King John's face quicker than a lightning bolt. Demi steps between them.

'Let's try to keep it together,' Demi says, his calm cracking under the mountain of pressure. 'It was obviously Max if the last revelation is true.'

'What d'you mean *if* it's true?' I say, suspicion creeping

up my spine. Could Demi be a mole too? Is he even Tayo's brother or is that a lie like Ravi, designed to make us trust him?

Demi shuffles awkwardly. 'I want to believe you; I really do.'

'Then believe me,' I say.

He stares into my eyes trying to read my thoughts, his expression so like his brother that my heart cries out in pain. Every part of me is saying I can trust him, just like I trusted Tayo.

'The Werewolves didn't kill Billy, the Investor did.' The weight of half a dozen eyes falls on me. I push on. 'We were caught and taken to him. He told the guards to kill someone. We didn't know who it would be or when. We didn't know it was Billy. Billy died because we broke the rules.'

'It could have been any one of us,' Rhodri says standing by my side. 'The game means more to this guy than our lives. Billy died so the game could play on.'

Lewis whimpers and the sound breaks my heart. I squeeze his arm. 'I'm so sorry.'

Lewis pulls away from me. 'I have no idea what to do with that information.'

'Ignore it?' King John says with a sneer. 'Don't you think it's all a little convenient that when she is out of sight things happen. She took the lead in the first game and she's doing it again, running around with the lad and playing hero. Who says we have to believe her? Who says she's not making it all up? Who says she's not the Werewolf we're looking for?'

'You're crazy,' I gasp. 'Why would I lie?'

'Hello, game?' King John says.

Rhodri shouts into his face. 'Production's pissing around with the game and it's messing with our heads.' He backs off, calming slightly. 'We're all spiralling. We need to keep it together.'

'Don't you see, they're trying to divide us?' I can't keep the frantic begging out of my voice. 'Demi, please.'

Demi's eyes are filled with conflict as they move between us.

'She's not lying,' Lewis says. 'Trust me.'

King John's hostile laugh fills the green. 'Now that's the funniest thing I've heard in this game. If we're talking trust, then why don't the Werewolves actually show themselves? They can't divide us if we are all playing on the same team.'

'That's not gonna happen anytime soon,' Rhodri says.

'Why not?' King John asks.

'Because as soon as they do, you'll eliminate them. Why would they trust you?' Rhodri says.

'Chicken and egg innit?' King John says. 'Chicken and egg.'

Rhodri walks away in no particular direction, his hands combing his short hair in frustration.

Tension crackles in the air, charged and dangerous as lightning readying to strike. Mistrust and paranoia have taken over, fuelled by the absolute knowledge that none of us are safe.

Demi speaks first. 'You say it's not you but there must be Werewolves still in the game, right? We know about Faith. There must be more?'

'It doesn't matter who's Werewolf or who's Peasant. Don't you see? *We* are not the enemy.'

'And I get that,' Demi says. 'But you're all OGs. You have history. You're protecting each other which means sacrificing us. How do we know anything you've said is true?'

'Demi's right,' King John says. 'There are four of you original game players left and only two of us,' he gestures to Demi. 'If we believe your little story about the Investor going rogue, then what? We refuse to nominate? I'm not great at maths but even I can see than we have a four to two ratio here and we ain't winning.'

'But Max?' I say.

Demi shrugs. 'Could all be lies, part of some plan that we're not part of.'

'Demi, please,' I say. 'There is no plan. I'm not a Werewolf, I swear.'

Demi turns to Lewis. 'Are you?'

Lewis stares back, unflinching. 'Yes.' My heart stops in a shattering beat. Demi looks like he's been punched in the mouth. 'I'm a Werewolf.'

We all distance ourselves from Lewis like he's radioactive.

'Why didn't you tell me?' I whisper as a familiar sense of *déjà vu* threatens

Lewis' eyes flood with guilt. 'That's the game. Telling you would put you in danger. Skye told me if I didn't play they would hurt you. I was trying to protect you.' He turns back to the group. 'And I know they're telling the truth about how he died because Billy was a Werewolf too and I didn't put his name in the fire. We stayed true. Now he's dead. And I'm next.'

'Hey, come on… I know you were close, but you can't just give up—'

Lewis cuts Rhodri off. 'Yes, but no. We are, were, but that's not it.' He thumps his head with his palm. 'Urghh, I'm not explaining myself.'

'Majority rules,' King John says. 'What he's trying to say is that if we kill him, we win. If we kill him…'

'Stop saying kill,' I shout. 'We don't need to do this.'

'If we don't accuse him then who?' King John says. 'Someone has to run the Gauntlet. The life of one for the good of the group.'

I don't know what to say. I've been here before with Thea and the memory crashes over me like raining rocks. I can't do it. I can't make him run the Gauntlet. I can't send Lewis to his death.

Looking around, I'm not sure they all feel the same.

40

I stand in front of Lewis. 'No one is killing anyone.'

'But … it's the Gauntlet, he … he has a chance,' Demi stutters and I turn on him.

'I can't believe you would agree to this. Tayo would never…'

'I'm not him,' he shouts. 'I am Ademide Asagu. Brother of Tayo Asagu. I'm not *him*. I'm not even half the hero he was. I could never be.'

'Demi I—'

'Do you have any idea how hard it is to live in the shadow of a ghost? It was hard to live up to him when he was alive, but now? Don't you think I see the same look on your faces that I see on my parents. That you all think the wrong brother lives?'

'Demi, no,' I say. 'Please I—'

Demi nods. 'Save it.'

Awkard pause as we all regard each other with suspicious eyes.

'Hate to come back to the elephant in the room or should I say Werewolf?' King John says, and I turn on him, all my pain and anger directed at his stupid smug face.

'Shut your mouth,' I snap.

Rhodri steps in front of King John. 'It makes no difference. The rules say majority wins; therefore the Peasants win five to one. We don't have to kill him to win.'

'We have one Castle Council left, one more accusation,' Demi says.

'I won't survive that Gauntlet,' Lewis says. 'I'm a dead man walking.'

'Shut up, Lewis,' Rhodri growls.

Lewis ignores him. 'I'd rather die by your hand than by theirs.'

'Stop talking,' I shout. The screaming panic in my head is making it too hard to think. 'There must be another way.' The sun is creeping higher into the morning sky. 'Before Draigodân comes for Castle Council.'

'Bite me,' Max says stepping out onto the green.

'So not funny right now,' I say turning my back on him.

'I'm being serious,' Max says, his eyes puffy and red. 'Lewis is the Alpha Werewolf; he has the power to change Peasants into Werewolves.'

'Is this true? You're the Alpha?' Rhodri says. Lewis nods. Rhodri's expression is incredulous. 'Why haven't you done it?'

Lewis throws his hands in the air. 'Uh hello? Least Werewolf-friendly contestant here? You know I hate this game and how crap I am at it. Never expected to play. Never asked to be a Werewolf. I've literally no clue what I'm doing. I'd never heard of the Alpha piggin' Werewolf. Faith and Billy were all about the rules and the tactics. They wanted to wait before turning anyone, to keep the money just for us. I was going with the flow, like you told me. Trying not to get killed and waiting for rescue.'

Demi smothers his mic in his fist and gestures for us all to do the same. 'Do you know how many you can turn?'

'Two,' Lewis whispers. 'I can turn two. I have to scratch my mark onto their skin and then they become like me, only not Alpha.'

'If Lewis turns two of us then we are equal,' I say, hope rising quicker than the sun. 'No side is in the majority. Neither side wins.'

'And there's no losing side to run the Gauntlet,' Demi says slowly. 'It works. If they try to break the rules the audience will see. They have to announce a draw and let us all go, it's the only solution that's fair.'

'You think they care about fair?' King John mutters.

'The Investor cares about the game and the rules,' Max says. 'He can't change the endgame at this late stage without pissing off a load of the audience and I don't think he'll want to do that.'

'You're clutching at straws,' King John says.

'You have a better idea?' Rhodri growls.

'Please tell me you still have the claw,' Max says.

Lewis runs over to the well and pulls out a black pouch. He slips a strange metal gadget over his glove. Three sharp talons protrude from his fingers.

Demi looks up at the camera. 'Won't they see us?'

'We're not breaking any rules,' I say. 'It's part of the game. The Alpha can change two Peasants of their choice, whenever they choose.'

'Who?' King John says. Lewis points to me and Rhodri. 'Of course, turn the OGs so you can stick together and kill us in our sleep.'

'There is no sleep, unless we do this before the sun rises Lewis is going to die. And according to the Investor the rest of us will die soon after.'

'He can't do that,' Max says. 'The audience won't allow it. He needs to play by the rules, or at the very least make it look like he is.'

'We're so far past the rules it's unreal,' says Rhodri. 'Man's not playing with a full deck.'

'Don't underestimate him,' Max speaks softly. 'The guy doesn't abide by laws, he makes them. He makes governments and destroys them. This is a whole other level of power.'

'Like the Illuminati,' Demi says, shivering.

'More like Deep State. All I know is he's more powerful than we can imagine and that makes him beyond dangerous.'

'But you said the audience wouldn't like it,' Demi says. 'If they're not happy, they'll switch off right?'

'That would be a disaster,' Max says. 'He'd lose his revenue streams. It wouldn't destroy him, but it would sting. It's more than that. It would be a huge blow to his gigantic ego. This isn't about money; it's about power. Failure makes him look weak and weakness can destroy him.'

'I don't understand,' Demi says. 'The audience are

seeing and hearing everything, how are they not getting it?'

'Because they're not,' Rhodri says grimly. Max nods. 'They're only seeing what he wants them to see.'

'Exactly,' Max says. 'They're seeing an edited version of our reality. What I've just said, about the sponsors and stuff? That will be edited out.

'Haven't you seen the way the drones move away whenever there's a death?' Rhodri says. 'Skye's the queen of the mis-direct: show the audience just enough violence and death to titillate but not too much to burst the Reality illusion… *Was* the queen.' He looks around for a camera drone. 'Let them edit that out.'

'Then we make them see,' I say, an idea forming in my mind. 'We make them see that this is real, that we are real.'

Lewis nudges me. 'We need to get you bit already. You need to turn into a Werewolf before the dragon wakes.'

Rhodri and I stand in front of Lewis, gloves off.

'Roll up your sleeves,' Lewis says, tugging up his left sleeve to reveal a gash on his arm, red and scabby. 'It's gonna hurt, not gonna lie.'

'Do it.' Rhodri holds out his tattooed arm and Lewis takes hold of his wrist. The sharp talons sink into Rhodri's flesh and with one quick move three gashes appear on his skin, swelling with bright red blood. Rhodri makes no noise as the sharp claw kisses his skin. When it's done, he pulls down his sleeve.

Lewis wipes Rhodri's blood from the claw and turns to me.

'Your turn.'

41

A dragon drone hovers in the middle of the Great Hall. It's funny how its presence doesn't elicit a reaction now. We know why it's here, and we're ready.

Demi pulls the scroll from under its belly and reads. *'You have been invited... Castle Council... Take torch ... yada yada yada.'* He screws it up and throws it on the floor. 'Show time.'

We grab our torches and leave the hall.

'You okay?' Rhodri gestures to my hand wrapped around my arm. Squeezing it helps with the stinging.

'Just a scratch,' I say, the now automatic smile imprinted on my lips.

The dragon drone's joined by three camera drones as we cross the green. They buzz quickly over our heads as we follow through another gatehouse, the opposite direction to the way we came in.

Rhodri hangs back, letting the others go first. 'Do you trust me?' he whispers. I hate myself for hesitating. The hurt flashing across his face tells me he saw it too.

He faces me, one hand reaching out to gently brush the hair from my eyes. He waits for a drone to turn in our direction, its beady eye flashing red. Pulling me into his arms his lips find mine. I'm too shocked to do anything but go with it. Pressing my cold lips to his, I kiss him back. It takes a minute to realise what he's doing – upping our profile, giving the viewers a love story to feast on. My arms automatically curl around his back as I lean into his kiss. I could so easily forget where we are. For a brief instant all I can think of is the here and now and Rhodri.

It ends too soon. Taking my hand, he places it over his heart, pressing his palm gently on my chest. He rests his forehead on mine, peering into my eyes, a smile playing on his lips.

'That should do it.' He kisses me lightly, leaving my heart thumping loudly and my head screaming for more. It may only be Reality real, but there was nothing fake in that for me. Taking my hand in his, he walks me to the gatehouse.

The drone follows our every move. My heart and head are jousting right now as they try to analyse the kiss. I know it was for the cameras – he did the exact same with Faith – but it felt like so much more, like old Rhodri, pre-*Blood Moon*. Was he trying to tell me something or am I reading way too much into a cynical move for votes? As we reach the huge doorway, he stops, his green eyes glowing.

'*Fy merch Saesneg hynod.*' The gentle lilt makes my heart flip but it's the words that make it sing, words he taught me in a car in a forest, words meant just for me. *My extraordinary English girl.*

My hand reaches for his note before I remember it's not there. It doesn't matter. Despite the terror and the panic, that someone believes in me, that *he* believes in me, no matter what, gives me a boost. I can do this. Whatever happens in this Castle Council, I sure as hell won't let them win.

We gather in a new area for the final Castle Council. Another campfire blazes in the centre of a grassy area framed by a curved wall. We place our torches around the fire, each one a single flame burning in the dawning light. This is the final round. The big finale.

Draigodân appears on the east wall of the tower, his red-scaled torso perched on his virtual rock.

'Welcome to the final round of *Blood Moon*. The game show where reality meets actuality, and the truth almost never wins.'

What does that even mean?

'Only six of you remain. Have the Werewolves successfully lied and murdered their way to a treacherous victory? Or have the Peasants done enough to stop them?' He bows his head. 'Please gather around the fire.'

We make a circle. Max is cowering between me and Demi. I focus on Lewis across the fire.

'Three Werewolves were hidden in the game. One was given Alpha status and the ability to recruit a further two Werewolves into their pack. Peasants, to win you must be in the majority. In this group of six, four of you must reveal yourselves as innocents.' He changes position, flexing his wings. 'Werewolves did you use your special powers to your best advantage, or did greed become the majority vote? To win, the Werewolves must reveal a majority of four or more.'

Lewis' foot is drumming on the floor, a tell-tale sign that he's bricking it. Max tugs on his tunic, a move I used to find endearing. Tension pours from Rhodri and Demi. Only King John is relaxed, stroking his goatee casually. Have we done enough to survive this? The suspense is making me sick. I focus on the memory of Rhodri's lips on mine and his hand placed over my heart.

Draigodân pulls himself up to full height. 'Castle Dwellers, will you now reveal your status.'

We remove our gloves and tug up our sleeves. The thick material has stuck to the dried blood beneath making me flinch as I roll it up to reveal the three-clawed mark of the Werewolf.

We all extend our arms out towards the fire. Lewis, Rhodri and I bear the Werewolf mark. No wonder we didn't see it before. We all assumed that, because of the gloves, it would be on the hand not the arm. King John, Demi and Max are mark free, just as planned. Relief rushes through me. I hadn't realised how little I trusted everyone until this moment. How, until the reveal, there was still a seed of doubt that someone could be lying.

The others must feel the same as a collective sigh rolls around the campfire. Grins and cheers erupt as we all reach the same conclusion.

'Checkmate,' Rhodri says.

Draigodân doesn't flinch or glitch as the cameras circle the fire. The hairs on the back of my neck begin to rise.

'Do you think they knew what we were going to do?' I whisper to Rhodri as mistrust sidles up my spine. This was all Max's idea. 'Like before we did?'

We all turn to Max. He throws up his hands, indignation plastered all over his face. 'What did you expect? You didn't even try to hide it. I didn't plan this, I swear. They're recording *everything*. You know when you take your mics off at night they can still hear you? And the whole hiding the mic in your top? Scrunching it up? Guess what? It doesn't work.' He leans in and whispers, 'I told you I was sorry. I would never—'

'Betray us?' growls Rhodri.

Max immediately shuts up. I almost feel sorry for him.

Draigodân speaks. 'We have reached a tie, a most diplomatic solution. But this is not a game of diplomacy. *Blood Moon* demands a winner.' My heart hits the floor. *Shit*. 'Lewis, you are the Alpha Werewolf and have done an outstanding job.'

'Hardly,' Lewis says uncomfortably.

'The audience have been voting for the best way to decide the winners.' Draigodân pauses to let the gasp that echoes round the campfire settle into horrified silence. Production were one step ahead of us all along; they knew we would figure out the whole voting thing and we played right into their hands. 'The winners will be decided on the Gauntlet. Those who complete it successfully will win a share of the ten million prize fund, the title of Ultimate Champion and their freedom.'

'What? Wait.' Max steps forward, his face flushed. 'No. This wasn't part of the plan. I'm not supposed to be here. No one said anything about running the Gauntlet.'

Draigodân turns to Max. 'Castle Dweller, step back.'

Max stands his ground. 'I demand to see Production. There's been a misunderstanding. I was promised my freedom if I played along. I did what you wanted. I got them to play the game. I did my part.'

'Fucking hell,' Rhodri throws his hands in the air. 'How many times are you going to betray us?'

Max turns to Rhodri, flustered. 'No, I didn't mean… I meant all of us… I—'

'Stop,' Rhodri cries. 'Just stop.'

Max hesitates. He looks from Rhodri to Draigodân. Instead of stepping back he takes a step closer to the dragon. 'I demand to speak to the Investor.'

Draigodân leans in close to Max. I brace myself. 'Step. Back.'

Max steps back, his fist tugging on the corner of his tunic. 'This isn't supposed to happen.' He sobs. 'It's not fair.' I wouldn't bet on his chances. I guess karma really is a bitch.

King John is the only one looking smug right now,

and why shouldn't he; he's ex-special forces and, by his own admission, the one most confident at conquering the Gauntlet.

'Lewis, please step up onto the podium.'

Lewis recoils like he's been shot. What now? Stepping in front of Draigodân, he stares at me over the fire, eyes wild.

'Lewis, you have been voted the viewers' favourite and have been granted a reward. As the Alpha you must now make a decision that will determine the fate of your Werewolf pack.'

The Investor's voice is rattling around my head refusing to be silenced. *Portia wants you dead.*

'Max was right,' I whisper to Rhodri. 'He's not going to let us go.'

Rhodri squeezes my hand tightly.

'Lewis please lift the timer over and place it back on its stand.'

Lewis does as he's told and the sand spills through the small hole. 'Please take the object on the stand.' My stomach is churning. Lewis picks up a gold dragon on a red ribbon and holds it up.

Draigodân talks directly to Lewis. 'Lewis, the audience have gifted you a special power. You must now make a choice. You may choose one of your pack to go free. Or … take the reward for yourself and exit the castle.'

Lewis looks like he's about to puke.

'You can only save one.' Draigodân smiles. 'Who shall

it be? Will you save one of your friends, or claim the reward for yourself? You have until the sand runs out to decide. When you have made your choice, place the dragon pendant around the neck of the contestant you wish to save.' He speaks directly into a camera drone. 'Who dies? The Alpha decides.'

Lewis falls to his knees. I long to comfort him, but I daren't. How can I demand that he choose me when saving my life will probably cost him his own?

The sand in the timer falls fast, collecting in a tidy pyramid in the bottom of the glass.

But Lewis doesn't move.

'*Strong like mountains,*' I say. When he doesn't reply to our childhood saying I finish it for him. '*Strong like steel. Always.* I love you, Lewis, no matter what. And I'll be okay.'

His eyes find mine in the morning sun.

I make my voice strong. 'I'll be fine. You need to go. Get help. You can save us all.'

Lewis gasps painfully, his eyes raised to the sky, his whole body shaking. Pulling himself to standing he raises his arms, the pendant dangling from his fingers.

The last grains of sand hit the bottom of the glass.

Never taking his eyes from Draigodân, he places it around his neck.

'I choose to save myself.' His lips wobble as he tries to hold in the pain and the anger. It's taking all my strength to stay standing. Two guards enter the area.

'You have made your choice.' Draigodân sounds matter of fact. 'Please leave the castle.'

The guards place their hands on Lewis' elbows.

'Kass?' he cries. As they push him away he struggles, screaming over his shoulder. 'I love you, Kass Kennedy. I love you.' We hear his cries long after he's disappeared from view.

'Wow.' King John wipes his forehead. 'I thought the boy would sacrifice himself. Guess you weren't as tight as you thought.'

I ignore him. Rhodri's about to blow up and I squeeze his arm gently. What's the point? It really doesn't matter what King John thinks. I focus on the fact that Lewis is free, that he will get out and get help, although I doubt they'll just let him walk into the first police station he sees. And if he does reach help, we'll all be dead by the time they return. I say a silent prayer that he's safe. Knowing one of us will survive gives me comfort.

Draigodân's tails swishes in the air. 'The game is almost done. Soon the winner or winners will be announced, and the Ultimate Champions named.' He flaps his wings. 'I will see you all at the Gauntlet. Bring your very best game, for anything less will be your downfall.'

42

The Gauntlet looks much bigger from the starting line and way more intimidating. Those who've survived the last four days and three nights stand with me. They've removed our chainmail, gloves and microphones and given each of us a coloured tunic to wear. Rhodri's in blue, King John orange, Demi green, Max purple and I'm pink. I briefly consider arguing the toss at the archaic gender stereotype in putting me, the only girl left, in baby pink, but I need to save my energy for what's to come. Let them reduce me to a type, that's fine. The anger blazing in my belly will carry me across this course and to my freedom.

'Stick with me,' Rhodri says. I love him for his loyalty, but I don't need a babysitter.

'Thanks, but I can do this,' I say. 'For everyone who died. The world needs to know what happened here.'

Rhodri reads my mind and chuckles. 'Hey, I'm not being chivalrous. I've learnt to never underestimate the Girl Next Door. Have you ever considered that I might need saving?'

I tear my eyes away from the course long enough to give him a quick smile. 'Never. You are the strongest person I know. A true hero.'

Amusement briefly flashes across his face. 'Yeah, I know. I just wanted you to say it.'

Max is sobbing not so quietly next to Demi.

'Chill.' For all his talk of being the underdog in the family, Demi's pretty calm right now. 'We've got this.'

'It's not fair,' wails Max. 'I've no chance.' He falls to his knees staring up into the sky. 'Please. Let me out of here.'

Rhodri strides over to him. 'Get up.' He half pulls him to his feet. 'Have some pride, mun.'

Max grabs hold of his arm. 'I'm sorry,' he sobs. 'I'm so sorry.'

'We all are.' Rhodri peels him off and returns to his place in the line. He doesn't look at Max again.

King John turns to us. 'Don't expect me to double back to help any of you. When that whistle blows, you're on your own, understood?'

'Loud and clear,' I say.

'What a dick,' Max says so incredulously I have to swallow my laugh.

The drums roll from the top of the towers. I take one last look at the cameras trained down on us. What does it take to be a spectator in these games? What would it take for them to switch off, to reject the monster they created?

Draigodân appears, along with a wall of screens either side of the Gauntlet projected onto the stone walls just like our MIVs. Each screen has a silhouetted head and shoulders in the middle. At first I assume that they're the fallen contestants but as more and more appear across the castle walls I realise that they're spectator avatars. The audience are watching, like a huge virtual concert, each one of their twisted souls hiding in plain sight.

'Welcome, spectators, to the most challenging and deadly reality game ever streamed,' Draigodân says. 'Watch as our final five battle for the title of Ultimate Champion and a share in the biggest game show prize fund of ten million pounds.'

Demi whistles in awe. 'There're hundreds of them.'

'Even bigger than the Eras tour,' Rhodri says. He's exaggerating but not by much. The castle wall is filled with windows, a giant mosaic of anonymous profiles, a virtual crowd gathered to watch our final trial.

'It's like the bloody Colosseum,' Demi says. 'And we're about to be fed to the lions.'

'Wolves,' King John says. There's a pinch of doubt in his usually over-confident voice.

'Nothing's changed people.' Rhodri's voice is strong. 'We've got this. Let's show these fat cats that we're for real and they're all sick bastards.'

We push our shoulders back in a move of solidarity, the Gauntlet looming before us, the ultimate challenge of survival.

A loud cheering sounds out across the castle. We all turn in confusion.

'It's fake,' Demi says. 'They're playing it in through the speakers.'

Draigodân continues. 'Castle Dwellers, to beat the Gauntlet you must be both strong and shrewd. Waiting for you on the bridge is an advantage. Whoever reaches it first may claim the *Blood Moon* pistol. But there's only one silver bullet, so use it wisely. Whoever reaches the end of the Gauntlet will win their freedom and their fortune.'

'That's cheery,' Demi mutters.

'The trumpets will be your signal. Rhodri, you are the audience favourite and will go on the first trumpet. Kass, you will go on my second.'

Rhodri smiles at me. The PDA worked; how fickle this audience is and how predictable. King John is third. He's looking like he's swallowed something sour. I do a little curtsy making sure he sees the *screw you* plastered all over my face.

'Demi you will go on the fourth trumpet. Max on the fifth,' Draigodân says. Max sobs into his hands. 'The drums will signal the release of the *Blood Moon* wolves. Be fast, they're hungry today. Good luck, Castle Dwellers. May the blood of the moon bleed for your safe passage through the Gauntlet.'

'Wait.' Someone is strolling towards us, flanked by an army of guards. The silver mask glitters and gleams in the sunlight and their cloak shimmers like a sea of pearls. 'I wish to congratulate these brave contestants for reaching the final trial.'

What the...? I'm staring at a ghost.

'There's a new Host,' Rhodri whispers.

'Who?' I whisper back.

The new Host talks straight to the drone bobbing in front of them, completely comfortable in their presenting role. 'Your actions have not gone unnoticed and your commitment to the show must be commended.'

'Are they having a laugh?' I mutter. I clasp my hands together tightly, the temptation to lash out too great.

The Host stops in front of Rhodri.

'We've loved watching you play.' They turn to the screens and the profiles, arms in the air. 'May our favourite win.' With a swish of their cloak, they step towards Rhodri, leaning in close. Rhodri is swamped by the voluminous silver cloak as they whisper something in his ear. Rhodri's expression changes, from anger to surprise.

What the hell are they saying to him?

The exchange is quick. The Host walks out of the line and out of view. Rhodri's head is bowed, his shoulders slumped, unnaturally still.

Something's wrong; he's clutching his side.

The trumpet sounds: Rhodri's cue. He doesn't move.

'Rhodri, you're up,' King John says.

The second fanfare sounds, my cue. Still Rhodri doesn't move. His chin's dropped to his chest. A warning prickles over my skin. Something's not right.

The third trumpet sounds. King John sprints off the starting line, leaping over the high beam like a pro-athlete.

'Rhodri?' I whisper. He turns to face me. His hands are clutching his side. No, he's clutching something stuck *in* his side and blood is squeezing through his fingers.

'Don't,' I shout as he starts to pull the dagger hilt out.

'Stay still.' I've seen too many A&E shows to know that pulling out the blade can be fatal.

He looks at me, his eyes glazed. 'Kass?'

As I reach him his legs give way. Demi's there too and together we catch his fall and help him to the ground.

Frantically I examine his side, the blue vest is oozing red around the jewelled handle of a dagger, pushed tightly into his flesh.

The final trumpet sounds. Max hovers by our side. 'I-I'm sorry,' he stammers.

'Go.' I don't even look at him. 'What happened?'

'Portia,' Rhodri gasps.

'The new Host was Portia?' Demi says.

I press my hands around the dagger hilt. The blood is warm as it seeps through my fingers. 'No, no, no.'

'Why you? Why…?' Demi struggles to find the words.

Rhodri's trying to catch his breath as his face contorts from confusion to pain and back again. 'She said she wanted me to suffer like Ophelia.'

A loud drum roll sounds across the arena eclipsed by the sound of frenzied barks.

I catch Demi's eyes over Rhodri's head. 'We need to go,' he mouths.

'Can you stand?'

'Sure.' We get him to his feet. 'I'm fine.' He pushes past us, one hand glued to his side. 'Come on.'

All we can do is follow. I refuse to acknowledge the

sympathy that's plastered over Demi's face or the sorrow in his eyes.

'He's fine,' I mutter. An overwhelming desperation threatens to gobble me up before the *Blood Moon* wolves even reach me.

We're so close to freedom, so impossibly close to getting out of here that the idea of failing now is almost too much to bear. But I won't let them win, not Skye, the Investor or the hundreds of nameless profiles watching from the wall. I breathe in determination and breathe out fear. I need to get Rhodri out of here or bloody well die trying.

Progress is slow. The first obstacle made the wound a hundred times worse. Ignoring our pleas to go round the high beam and take whatever penalty comes, Rhodri threw himself over, using his height and the shit tonne of adrenaline coursing through his veins to twist his body like a high jumper, narrowly missing the spikes below, leaving the white rubber surface smeared red. We get him to the maze where he leans against the walls pretending he's okay. He's lying. The blood dripping through his fingers tells the real truth. Leaning on Demi he manages to stagger through the twisting path. I keep a constant watch over my shoulder, waiting for the wolves to appear. Not looking where I'm going, I almost trip over the body lying on the floor.

My scream echoes through the maze until I remember the wolves and clamp my hand hard against my mouth.

Max, the friend we came here to save, is lying face down in a pool of blood, an arrow sticking out of his neck, face contorted, his springy curls tumbling over dead eyes.

Demi's shoulders shake as he bites back the tears.

'Shit,' Rhodri cries, banging a bloody fist against the wall, his sobs jarring against his ragged breathing.

I turn away, swallowing down the waves of puke threatening to projectile all over the narrow path. Poor Max. Whatever he did, he only did to survive. He didn't deserve this. Max was the reason we came. It really was all for nothing.

Demi leans down and closes Max's eyes. There's a sharp tearing as he rips Max's T right off his back.

'Demi no,' I cry.

'It's for him,' Demi says, handing the purple shirt to Rhodri who wraps it around the dagger hilt.

Rhodri points a bloody finger towards Max. 'It's not just the wolves that are hunting us.'

As if on cue, an arrow hits the ground by my feet. Another narrowly misses Demi.

'We need to keep moving.' Rhodri pushes himself off the wall with a determined burst of energy.

We weave around the maze as quickly as we can, adrenaline and fear surging through our bodies in equal measure, dodging arrows in a morbid dance of death. The wolves behind are getting louder, howling excitedly as they pick up Rhodri's blood trail. We hit a dead end and double back, using Rhodri's bloodied hand marks to map the way we came, trying another route.

Rhodri weakens at every turn. Each dodge and dive fills his face with pain. But he fights on, and the arrows fail to hit their mark. We're practically carrying him, his weight heavy on my shoulders.

And the wolves get closer.

'Leave me.' Rhodri leans on the walls and closes his eyes, sweat beading on his forehead despite the winter cold. 'I'm slowing you down.'

I shake my head so hard it hurts. 'We need to keep going.'

'I can't.' He gasps, his chest rising rapidly as he tries to catch his breath.

'You can,' I demand.

Rhodri grabs my hand. 'Kass,' he whispers my name through trembling lips. 'I'm not going to make it.'

Pain rips through my body, his agony becoming mine. I clutch his hand. 'I'm not doing this without you, so you bloody better keep going.'

'Shhh.' Demi holds up his hand.

I can't hear anything save the whirr of the drones. The wolves have stopped their excited howling.

'The wolves have found Max,' Rhodri says, gritting his teeth as he pushes himself off the wall. 'He's buying us some time.'

43

We fall out of the maze exhausted and terrified. Rhodri's worse; it doesn't take a doctor to know this amount of blood is bad. He knows it too. His cheeks have turned an unnatural shade of grey and he's breathing in agonising fractured gasps. We don't have much time.

'Get up.' I cringe at the harshness in my voice, terror painting me an unsympathetic nurse. 'We need to keep moving.'

The glass bridge lies ahead, running over a deep pit filled with sharp metal spikes. We hold Rhodri between us, dragging him up the ramp and onto the glass. We tread lightly. I pray that our combined weight won't break it. On the other side stands a platform with a podium.

Demi nods towards it. 'The gun.'

The glass is slippery beneath our boots, made worse by Rhodri's blood splattering the glassy surface.

The wolves begin their frenzied song again. Panicking, I look at Demi.

'Let me take him. You go for the gun,' he says.

I start to protest as Rhodri lifts his hand, his voice weak. 'Me and the big man will follow you.'

'We don't even know if it's there,' I sob. 'King John has probably taken it.'

'Nah,' Rhodri says trying to smile. 'A bullet is beneath him. He kills wolves with his bare hands. Go.'

I turn on my heel. My boot slides through a blood splatter, turning my ankle and sending me flying onto the hard surface. I freeze, waiting for any tell-tale sign of splintering glass underneath my body.

'Kass?' I'm not sure if that's Rhodri or Demi. A sharp pain tears through my ankle.

Shit

The howls reach fever pitch. They're close.

Rhodri screams, 'Run.'

Drawing on every inch of strength I have, I haul myself up and limp across the glass, ignoring the hot pain in my ankle. The bridge rises up in front of me. It must be twenty metres long. I force myself on until I reach the podium.

The gun's still there, sat in a small case, one silver bullet next to it. I've never held a gun before let alone a loaded one and I scream in frustration as my fingers shake too much to hold the bullet steady.

Demi's running towards me.

'You left him,' I scream.

'He told me to,' Demi says. 'He's going to hold off the wolves as long as he can.'

'What do you mean hold off… NO.' I start to run back, but Demi grabs me. I struggle but his arms hold me tight.

'We are not leaving him,' I hiss between gritted teeth. Using all my strength I push Demi away and run back over the bridge.

'*Cariad?*' Rhodri smiles as I kneel next to him. The sharp spikes sparkle a warning beneath us.

'We need to go.' I can't pull him to his feet, he's too heavy and the glass too slippery. 'Rhodri please.'

Rhodri lifts his head, his forehead glistening with sweat. 'You're hurt. You need all your strength to get up that wall.'

'I'm fine,' I lie. 'We can do this.'

'Demi can't help both of us…' he says, each word punctuated with pain.

'I can do it,' I say, knowing exactly what he's thinking. 'I … I'm not Arti.'

'I need you to go.' His fingers find my chin and force my face to his. 'Listen to me. One of us needs to make it and I'm nominating you.'

All the strength I've held onto so tightly vanishes as the boy I love begs me to make an impossible choice. I'm vaguely aware of Demi behind us, holding out the gun. Rhodri takes it and drops it in his lap. His eyes never leave mine, his bloodied thumb caressing my cheek, gently wiping away my tears. Pulling me towards him he kisses me.

I've never been kissed like this before. It's warm and tender and filled with a million unspoken words. I melt into his touch, the world and the game forgotten, all the pain and the fear gone in this one moment. It's a kiss that speaks of love and of what could have been. It's a kiss that says goodbye.

He pulls away, resting his forehead to mine, his beautiful green eyes begging.

A wolf leaps out of the maze. It stops and sniffs, the scent of fresh blood thick in the air. My whole body shakes, but I stay with Rhodri, my eyes locked on his.

Three more wolves spill from the maze, their fur stained red.

Rhodri smiles, never taking his eyes from mine. 'I love you, *cariad*, but right now I need you to run. And don't look back. Do it for me. Do it for Carys.'

I won't leave him. I hold his head in my hands, covering his face with kisses, tasting the salty tears that stream down my cheeks and onto his lips. He gently pushes me away, his hands slipping down to his side, his fingers curling around the dagger.

'No!' My hands find his. 'No.'

With one quick movement he pulls the dagger out. The wound responds. Bright red blood gushes from the knife hole. I try to stop the bleeding, pressing my palms to the wound as blood flows over my skin and through my fingers.

'Go,' Rhodri gasps.

'No,' I scream, but Demi pulls me away, dragging me across the bridge.

The pack leader jumps onto the bottom of the bridge, hackles up from head to tail, lips curled into a menacing growl. He moves cautiously, bent low to the ground, taking his time, focused on Rhodri. The others follow.

Rhodri's sitting up, leaning against the side of the bridge, dagger in his hand, gun in his lap.

Demi pulls me across the bridge to the podium. The wolves close around Rhodri. Hunt over, they take their time, howling excitedly, circling their prize.

I'm crying and screaming and fighting but Demi won't let me go.

'Listen to me. He said to let him do this for you. So you could live.'

Rhodri's screaming like a warrior. His dagger flashes through the air, slashing through fur and bone as his screams are swallowed by the excited chorus of wolf song.

'Look at me.' Demi's arms hold me tight.

A wolf falls to the floor with a whimpering yelp. Another attacks, bolstered by a chorus of angry growls. Weakened by his wound and the wolves' relentless onslaught, Rhodri drops the dagger, slumping onto his side.

'Rhodri.' My cries are swallowed by my sobs. The wolves attack efficiently and quickly. With triumphant howls they claim their prize and Rhodri's body disappears under a sea of fur and blood.

I fight wildly but Demi refuses to let me go.

The wolves disperse. The leader drags Rhodri across the bridge, his boot held firm in its deadly jaws. Rhodri doesn't move.

'Leave him alone.' The scream that leaves my lips is brutal and rips me apart. The leader's head snaps up. I recognise the jagged scar and his misshaped ear as his eyes lock onto mine. He snaps and growls, dropping Rhodri, his leg thudding on the glassy floor.

'Leave him alone,' I scream again, waving my arms to get his attention.

'Kass no,' Demi cries.

The wolf leaps forward.

'Run,' Demi cries pulling me towards the climbing wall.

The wolf tears across the bridge straight towards us.

There's a fresh gash in its cheek, raw and bleeding and I take comfort in knowing that Rhodri fought back. Its muzzle drips red. Its amber eyes blaze dangerously wild.

Shit. Fear overrides grief when I turn to the wall and reality sinks in. It's too high. There's no time. Demi is begging me to climb. Laying on the platform above, his outstretched arms gesturing madly. I grab his hand and he pulls me up but my palms are slippery with Rhodri's blood and I lose my grip. I tumble back to the floor, pain searing through my ankle.

The wolf's close. I can hear its rapid panting. I turn to face it, pressing my back into the climbing wall. The smell of blood mixes with saliva as its muzzle sniffs the air in front of me. I close my eyes and brace myself.

An explosive gunshot rings through the air followed by the sound of splintering glass. Opening my eyes it takes my brain a minute to catch up. It's the bridge that's shot, not the wolf. The wolf's back legs fall into nothing when the glass beneath him disappears, it's front paws scrambling for the platform where I'm stood. With a cry I kick out. My boot connects with his muzzle, and he falls with a yelping howl, suddenly silenced, impaled on the sharp spikes below.

The other wolves are stuck on the other side. Too scared to tread on the breaking glass, they pace nervously back and forth.

Rhodri's lying face down on the bridge, arm outstretched, the silver pistol in his hand.

'Rhodri,' I scream. The gaping hole between us widens, making him impossible to reach. 'Rhodri.' All I can do is scream and will him awake but he lies on the glass bleeding and broken.

Splinters meander down the glassy surface towards his lifeless body. The cracks splay out like a giant spider's web underneath him. The wolves pace and panic as the whole surface weakens under their heavy paws. Their weight's too much for the broken glass to bear and it shatters into a thousand shards. The wolves realise their peril too late and plummet to their deaths, speared on the sharp spikes below.

And Rhodri falls with them.

Howls morph into silence.

He used his only bullet to save me. He knew that if he shot the glass the wolves would fall. And he knew he would fall with them.

I can't catch a breath, every intake of air slices into my throat, choking, strangling, suffocating.

Rhodri is gone.

44

The arena is heavy with anticipation as the audience watch and wait. I'm fighting the urge to throw myself down onto the spikes, to be with Rhodri one last time. Nothing is right. Nothing makes sense. There's nothing left to fight for.

My feet edge towards the end of the platform. I close my eyes. Rhodri's in my head; his smiling face and emerald-green eyes comfort me and his arms wrap around me. One more step…

'No.' Demi pulls me back. 'That's not what he wanted.'

What does it matter what he wanted? My thoughts are candyfloss sticky. I can't get my head around it. The thought's too big. It won't fit inside my brain.

'He said to give you this.' Demi's pushing something into my hand.

I stare down at the crumpled note that Rhodri wrote in the car.

'He said you'd know what to do.'

'He was wrong.' The words feel like chalk in my mouth. My hand makes a fist around the wrapper. My body doubles in two and I drop to the floor. Rhodri, Lewis, Thea. They've all left me.

'Kass. Please,' Demi begs.

I'm aware of his fear but I can't help him. I've nothing left. We can't beat this. This game is more than next level.

This is not Skye and her crazy sidekick. This is power personified and I'm way too insignificant to beat its privileged arse.

'We need to go.' Demi is struggling between sympathy and desperation. He hovers by my side stubbornly refusing to leave me. I wish I had the energy to care. Let them win. Thea and Lewis are free, and Rhodri is… I curl into a ball and wait for them to finish what Skye started.

My mind transports me to another place, away from this Gauntlet and away from the pain. All is dark and quiet as I disappear inside my head and wait.

'Get up.' Tayo's voice interrupts the calm. 'Get up, Kass. You have to fight.'

I want to sleep. I'm so tired of fighting.

Mai's here. 'Kass Kennedy, you live the crap out of life. For us.'

'And for me.' Rhodri's in my head, and my heart dances. His eyes sparkle. There's no sign of pain. 'You're so close.'

He turns to leave and I'm suddenly cold. I shout his name, but he can't hear. He's walking away from me, into the misty folds of my mind. I run towards him, but I can't keep up. 'You just need to get up,' he says over his shoulder. 'Get up, Kass.'

'Rhodri,' I shout into the mist, but he's gone, and I'm left alone.

The faces of those I love flicker before my eyes in a cinematic flashback of love.

'You're not alone, hun.' Lewis is inside my head.

My body creases with a pain so intense I struggle to breathe.

'You are strong.' Thea's voice.

I breathe in raw, jagged breaths.

'*Cariad*.' Rhodri's right in my face. He frowns and shouts, 'I fucking died so you could live, so get the hell up, Kass Kennedy, and do something extraordinary.'

I gasp for air like a fish out of water driving the words through my brain, however painful, like a hammer on a nail. He sacrificed himself so I could live. Rhodri is d…

I can't say it.

My head chants to my heart. *I'm strong and I am loved.*

All the anger I've been carrying since *Lie or Die* ignites deep in my belly and obliterates the paralysing pain in one furious blaze.

Rhodri is dead.

How many innocents must die before these people are satisfied?

I know exactly what to do. I'm going to kill the monster.

My eyes fly open.

I'm staring into the face of Draigodân.

45

'Get. Up.' Draigodân's eyes flash.

'Or what?' I say, unafraid of the fire-breathing dragon, unafraid for the first time in this whole horrific game.

'Or I will finish you,' Draigodân snarls.

I pull myself up, never taking my eyes from his. 'On what grounds. I've followed your rules, played your game. It's over.'

'We must have a winner. The audience demands an Ultimate Champion.'

Draigodân's words take me by surprise. 'King John didn't make it? Where is he?'

'Right here,' a voice shouts from behind. King John's swinging back across the bridge like a modern-day Tarzan. 'Check me out. I make it look easy even in reverse.' He jumps down onto the platform.

Demi stares at him open mouthed. 'Are you mad?'

'Probably.' He shrugs. 'I was on the last swing; the end was in sight. There's a monitor at the finish line. I guess it's there for the winners to gloat and boy was I ready to gloat.' His eyes find mine, suddenly serious. 'I saw Rhodri.'

I bite my lip and don't let go until I taste blood.

'What he did so you two could finish?' His face fills with genuine emotion. 'So, I was about to take the win and I couldn't do it. Figured you might not be okay.'

Draigodân flaps his wings impatiently. 'The game requires a winner.'

King John holds his palm in front of the dragon's face. 'Hello? We are talking.'

'King John, you—'

'John,' King John interrupts me. 'Hearing it come out of your mouth has made me realise how wank that sounds. I'm sorry about Rhodri, I really am. There really is a whole world of difference between a hero and a champion.' He leans in and whispers, 'Do you trust me?'

Up until about two minutes ago I'd have laughed at that question. Now the sincerity in his eyes makes me nod.

'Okay,' he says as surprised as me by that answer. 'So, what's the plan?'

I cup my hand in front of my mouth so the drones and static mics won't pick up my words. 'I want to speak to them.' I jerk my head towards the screens. 'But he'll just cut the feed as soon as I start.'

'Not if I get to the control room and stop them,' he says. 'I'll protect the live feed.' He points towards the inner ward. 'It's in that tower yeah?' I nod. 'Sweet. Give me five minutes.'

'How?' Demi says.

John winks. There's a flagpole about two metres from the platform. John makes an impossible leap, grabbing the pole as his body crashes into it. He shimmies down like a city base jumper. As he hits the ground, he rolls. Jumping up, he sprints into the corner and disappears behind the set, dodging the arrows raining down on him.

I stare up to the wall of screens and profiles.

Demi puts his hand on my arm. 'Kass, please, we can't trust the guy. We need to do as Draigodân says. We need to finish—'

'I'm not going anywhere.' There's a camera drone right next to me, hovering expectantly in the air. I lunge and grab it. It whirrs angrily in my hands. 'I have something I want to say.' Lifting the drone to my face I talk directly into the camera speaking quickly before Draigodân cuts me off. 'You've been watching us this whole time, but you can't see us. Are we even real to you? If you turn off, do we disappear?' I take a painful breath. 'Rhodri is d-dead.' The word's like a weapon. Without taking my eyes from the camera, I wipe my hands down my face leaving Rhodri's blood streaked on my cheeks. It's warm against my skin and I fight back the tears. 'This is real.'

The screen wall remains unchanged. The profiles don't flicker or turn to black. These people stick together, an underground society fuelled by money and power. How can I make them listen when my world is so far from theirs and I live in a time where life is nothing more than a fleeting image on a reel, a snap, a story, entertainment for an instant then forgotten?

'It's not working,' I say as doubt takes over. 'They're so desensitised they don't even care.'

'Make them care.' Demi takes the drone from me.

'Make us real.' He runs back to the shattered bridge, pointing the camera into the abyss where the wolves lay quietly with Rhodri.

I try again. 'Rhodri is dead. So is Max. He was just a boy so terrified that he chose to put his friends in danger rather than to face the horrors of this game.' Demi's back by my side, my own personal cameraman and I welcome the lens he's pointing in my face. 'Marcus, Mai, Billy. So many dead for your amusement. Arti, Ravi, victims of the Gauntlet set up for your entertainment. They died for you, because of you. He created the ultimate game, but you *chose* to watch. It may be our blood, but it's covering your hands. I—'

The recording light on the drone snaps off. *Shit*. He's cut the feed. We can only wait for John to reach the MCR and pray he doesn't fail.

'Enough.' Draigodân's fire shoots in our direction, heat burning my face. 'Remaining players will proceed through the Gauntlet. Failure to do so will result in—'

'You can't kill us.' Still holding the drone, Demi stands in front of Draigodân, chest out. 'You promised the audience a champion.'

Draigodân's nostrils flair and smoke, but he does nothing.

'You need us,' I say, and the realisation empowers me. 'If the game stops now there is no grand finale. You fail before your followers. And with failure comes weakness. How can you be all-powerful like Anubis if you are weak?'

Draigodân's eyes narrow, but I'm not talking to him; I'm talking directly to the Investor.

'And how will they react when they discover you couldn't even protect your own daughter?' I say.

Draigodân's head lurches backwards. 'You will not talk of my daughter.'

I push on, pouring acid into the open wound, playing for time. 'Ophelia died because you were showing off, proving that you are stronger, richer, more powerful. But you couldn't keep her safe. You thought you could control Skye, but you were wrong. You failed to see just how dangerous she was. That was your downfall. You were stupid enough to risk your daughter's life in Skye's game of death.' As I speak the recording light blinks on.

'He's bloody done it,' Demi whispers. 'He's found the MCR.'

I pretend not to notice the drone recording everything we say and the wall of audience now watching in real time. Draigodân shows no signs of realising that the feed's back on. I turn my body so that the dragon is facing away from the watching wall.

'How do you think your audience will feel when they find out you lied to them? That you've been manipulating the game all along. That you planted fake contestants in the game so your daughters could play safely and then changed the rules to satisfy Portia's need for revenge? How you allowed her to stage manage the game and injure the most popular contestant, knowing that injury would kill him on the Gauntlet?' Draigodân's head rocks back and forth his eyes gleaming dangerously. I keep pushing. 'I wouldn't want to invest in a liar and a cheat. I could never trust someone who lies right to my face and turns the truth into a commodity to serve his own purpose. Someone whose mental capacity is surely compromised, their decision-making questionable. What will the audience say when they hear that Ophelia burned in that lake and you did nothing…?'

'Shut up,' Draigodân screams. 'You think I care what they think? You think I need them? They're pathetic and stupid and spineless, followers not leaders. They'll do nothing without my say. I manipulate them as easily as I manipulated you all into playing. People are sheep, wealth doesn't change that. Show them strength and they'll follow pathetically behind. They're all expendable. Your threats don't scare me, girl. I can kill you in an instant, just like I killed your friends. I can do anything. I can change the game if I want to because I have all the power. I'm more powerful than Anubis. I'm more powerful than a god.'

'But you can't make me play,' I say. 'You can scare me and threaten me, but if you want this game to end you will have to kill me.'

'Finish the game.' Draigodân growls.

'No.' I don't move.

Draigodân leans in closer. 'Finish. The. Game.'

I raise my head to the dragon. 'Make me.'

'Watch out,' screams Demi.

Flames shoot from Draigodân's mouth. The heat hits us like a solid wall and we fall back onto the platform. But the flames don't find their mark; he's too far away. He can't reach us.

Parts of the Gauntlet sizzle and crackle, a reminder of Draigodân's power.

A whistling cuts past my ear and an arrow thuds to the floor next to my feet. I ignore it.

'Talk to them.' Demi gestures to the wall, dodging the arrows. 'You've got their attention.'

Another whistle, this time a sharp pain as another slices past my shoulder. My hand reaches to the spot and comes away bleeding. I raise my bloody hand to the camera. 'This game is nothing more than murder. He murdered my friends and now he'll murder us, right in front of you.'

'They can't see you. We are not live. They only see what I want them to...' Draigodân glitches. 'How did you?'

I smile up at him. 'I guess you're not as powerful as you thought.'

Draigodân raises his head to the castle walls and screams, 'Stop!' as arrows hail down on us.

Too late. A grunt from Demi makes me turn to see him hit.

'Don't stop,' he says to me through gritted teeth, one hand clutched to his thigh. His eyes grow wide as he looks at me. 'Oh, shit.'

I follow his gaze down my body. There's an arrow sticking out from my flesh, its iron head buried deep in my side. It looks absurd, like some cartoon or joke prop quivering in the breeze. Only the blood pooling at my shirt and the throb radiating from the wound signal it's real. My fingers wrap around the wooden shaft firmly seeded in my flesh and I turn back to the audience.

I pull myself up straight. 'My name is Kass Kennedy. I am seventeen years old. I was tricked into this game to save my friends. I've been blackmailed and threatened and lied to.' Draigodân rages, fire spilling from his mouth, but it can't reach us. Demi holds the drone steady. 'I don't want money. I'm not interested in fame. I'm not asking for your sympathy.' The wobble in my voice seeps through my whole body making my legs weak. 'I want to live.'

There's no pain now, which is weird. The blood seeping through my fingers tells me this is bad. I'm shivering, suddenly cold. My legs disintegrate beneath me and my body crumbles in front of the watching wall.

John was right when he talked about death. When you look it in the eyes it's not so scary anymore.

Draigodân hovers over his imaginary rock.

Demi's collapsed on the platform, breathing in short sharp breaths, the drone by his side. He has the look of a soldier who's given up.

And I'm not okay with that.

I shunt up on my elbows and talk into the camera. 'This was never about extreme Reality and pushing the boundaries. This was about revenge and power. By watching, you are complicit. You've let him take your power. You've given him control. Only you have the power to end it.' It hurts to breathe now. I grit my teeth and push on. 'Everyone has a price. I've heard that said a whole lot in this game. Decide yours. Be strong. Don't let him win.'

I'm so tired. Every small movement's a struggle. But I'm not finished yet. I reach for the drone camera and turn it to face the screens. 'Take a look at yourselves.' I pan the camera across the hundreds of profiles silently watching. My mind is slipping away, and I have to force it back to the present. 'Are you so broken that you can't tell what's real anymore? Make your choice. Embrace the truth. Take back your power.'

The Gauntlet falls silent save for our jagged, punctured breaths.

The wall of screens changes.

It's blinking.

Slowly the windows are turning black.

'It's working,' Demi sobs.

One by one the audience turn off. The blinking accelerates as the avatars disappear and the squares go blank. Like an illegal rave the wall begins a frantic dance. And I stare at it in wonder. One small action sending a gigantic message to the Investor:

We don't want this. We're not with you. You are finished.

Draigodân lifts his head towards the sky and roars a

long flame-filled cry; so angry it makes the air tremble. His wings extend behind his body and he launches into the sky and disappears.

There's movement on the walls. Even if we could move there's nowhere to go. We're trapped on this platform like sitting ducks. I prepare for the arrows, unafraid.

'They're leaving.' Demi gasps.

I struggle to look up. The archers are marching off the wall, their boots thumping against the castle stone in one long continuous beat. Their backs disappear to the rhythmic sound of retreat.

'He's gone.' Demi's struggling. 'Draigodân's gone.'

As the last windows turn to black and the wall returns to castle stone, the anger and hatred fizzles from my veins.

There's no victory dance, no cheer of celebration, just numbing relief.

Demi laughs and cries and bleeds, weeping tears of relief that the game is done.

For three nights the blood moon bled, and we survived.

A new noise fills the arena, a whirring like a giant drone. Its loud pulse pumps into the space where silence lived.

Demi points to the tower. Behind the castle walls a helicopter rises into the air. On its tail is the red dragon logo. 'The bastard's running.'

From the helicopter a glossy wolf mask catches the sun, glinting through the cabin glass. The helicopter turns and speeds away from the castle. Anubis the guardian of the Underworld abandons us on the very edge of hell.

Dizzy squares are filling my view. There's a warmth growing in my gut, flooding my body with a comforting heat. All the pain and fear have gone.

I see Rhodri; he's laughing. His hands held out for mine.

I lie on the platform, my cheek on the hard floor and reach my hand out to his.

And the world fades to black.

46

Some weeks later

My shoes sink into the rain-soaked grass, but I won't move. I can't. I'm still so angry with him for leaving me. The cold is nipping at my skin, seeping into my almost healed wounds making my side throb again. I've no clue how long I've been here. It feels like hours since they lowered his coffin into the muddy ground, but I can't bring myself to leave him.

How do I move on without him?

Demi's waiting patiently by my shoulder. The last few weeks have been hard. His eyes have that haunted post-*Lie or Die* look that's become the new normal.

The rain steps up its efforts, like the sky itself is weeping.

'Man that's brutal. We should find some cover,' he says hunching his shoulders against the Welsh weather. 'You good?'

I nod. We both know I'm not. He gets it. He was there. We both run the Gauntlet every night in our sleep, only in my dreams we all make it to the end and the leap of faith to freedom.

In my dreams no one is left behind.

I feel like I'm unravelling. There's a huge gaping hole where once there was him. It's like he carved himself right through me and left nothing but hollow space behind.

'Will I ever get over it? Him?' I don't expect Demi to answer; it's just good to know he understands.

'I don't think so,' he says after a time. 'But I think that's okay. I think grief is not an emotion we can overcome. It's a feeling, a way of telling us that we've lived something special, that something incredible and beautiful touched our soul.' He smiles a sad smile. 'The pain will get easier, give it time. It won't always feel this way.'

'I miss him,' I whisper.

'I know,' he whispers back.

Thea and Lewis are coming towards us. I rub the back of my hand over my cheeks and attempt a shaky smile.

'We are way too young to be going to this many funerals,' Thea says, wrinkling her nose as she studies my face.

Lewis nods his agreement. 'They need to pull their fingers out and catch the bastard.' His voice is gritty with grief. He nods towards the police presence surrounding the church, a sight we've become used to since our rescue and the disappearance of the Investor.

They have no clues. There was no one left at the castle alive, all wolf-headed guards and crew escaped along with the Investor, their identities as mysterious to the police as they were to us. They left no footprint, real or virtual, disappearing into the Welsh mist as efficiently as Draigodân.

All that remained were the bodies of the fallen. And Rhodri, down to earth, heart of gold, fiercely protective of those he loved Rhodri. My breath shudders.

Lewis hovers next to me. 'Shall I get your mum and dad, hun?'

I find my parents in the funeral crowd, huddled together with Rhodri's mum and sister, united by our shared grief.

My mum's arm is draped protectively around Carys' small shoulders as she talks to her quietly.

I don't need to imagine her words of comfort. I've heard them all over the last few weeks as she's patiently tried to ease my pain and convince me that I'm safe.

Dad's eyes flit fearfully through the mass of suited bodies until he finds me. He smiles a tight smile. I nod in reply. Even from a distance I can see the worry etched into his haggard face and the pain that's left its mark like an ugly scar.

'Kass?' Lewis is still waiting for my reply.

Shaking my head, I turn my attention back to my friends. Lewis' jet-black hair is being bullied by the wind and the rain and he's fighting a losing battle to keep control of it. The heavy weight of guilt is lodged in his eyes. It never leaves him. He's got stuck down the rabbit hole of blame and remorse and we can't find the words to get him out. He saved my life, and Demi's. If he hadn't shown the police how to get to us just in time we would be with Rhodri and the others right now. But he won't accept it, no matter what we say he always counters with his truth. If he'd stayed would things have turned out differently? If he'd gotten there sooner, would Rhodri be alive? What if he'd saved Rhodri instead of himself…?

His eyes lock onto mine reflecting my sadness right back at me. I take his hand in mine and vow never to let it go.

'What you got there?' he says.

I'd forgotten the envelope clutched in my hand. I push the grief aside. 'Some kid gave it to me,' I say, looking for the small, suited boy that ran up after the service and pressed it into my hand. My mind tries to recall the conversation, but my memory's vague.

'You gonna open it?' Thea says, gently encouraging.

The envelope is blank. I turn it over and over in my hand waiting for a spark of interest, a spark of anything other than this all-consuming sorrow that threatens to swallow me whole.

'You sure I can't get someone?' Lewis' brow creases with concern.

I force myself to get a grip. 'It's just a card. Nothing bad has ever come from a card, right?'

I look up to see them staring at me, open mouthed.

'I'm kidding,' I say. 'Jeez, sense of humour.' When did we forget how to laugh?

'We're standing in a graveyard,' Thea says with a humph. 'Just open it already.'

Rhodri would have got it. He'd have found it

inappropriately funny, probably sworn a lot or said something in Welsh. Pain hits my chest as his memory consumes me. I rip open the envelope and take out a piece of card, flipping it over in my hands.

On the card is a code:

AUDIENCE15776480

There's a QR underneath.

I turn it over quickly.

On the other side is a red logo, one we've seen before. It's a dragon in a circle eating its tail…

The symbol of the Investor.

A shock ricochets through my body like lightning. The card falls from my fingers onto the soggy grass. I stare down at the symbol, my whole body trembling. Lewis and Thea lead me away quickly, their arms hung protectively around my shoulders. I'm aware of the looks of concern that pass between them.

Lewis shakes his head like a wet dog, his voice unnaturally bright. 'Look at me. I'm a mess. What was I thinking? Everyone knows it rains in Wales. Should've brought a bloody brolly.'

I pull myself together for their sakes as well as mine. It's over. The Investor can't hurt us now. He's had his fun and moved on; we're way too insignificant to remain on his radar for long. I almost believe my own rhetoric as I smile at my friends, sandwiched between Lewis and Thea – almost.

'Thanks for coming,' I say to Thea.

'Course,' she says. She's not left our side since we've been back. She's become our rock. The old Thea may have gone, swept away by the first show and all that came after, but new Thea has emerged stronger and more resilient than ever before. I always loved her, but I didn't know how much I needed her until now.

'I'm sad that I didn't get to meet John in real life, I thought he would be here,' Thea says and smiles. 'Or should I say the King? He sounds like…'

'Wait.' Demi's shout makes us stop and turn back. He's walking towards us, slowed by his limp, waving the soaked card in the air. 'Kass, come here.'

'No.' My body tenses. I dig my heels in and refuse to move.

He holds out his phone and edges closer. 'It's okay. It's good. I scanned the QR, look.'

It's a website, crypto currency.

Demi's breathing quickly, his eyes dancing. 'It's an account. In your name.'

He's right. I can see my name at the top along with a number – a big number.

'What even is this?' Lewis says taking the card.

'A hell of a lot of Bitcoin.' Demi's voice rises excitedly. 'I'm gonna go out on a limb and guess ten million pounds worth.'

'Holy shit,' Thea squeaks.

'From the Investor?' I say. 'I don't get it.'

Lewis holds up the card. 'No. Look at the code. Audience.'

'You think…' Thea's voice is loud in the graveyard quiet. She whispers, 'You think the audience have honoured the prize fund?'

Demi shrugs. 'Who knows, Bitcoin's pretty untraceable. But I can tell you one thing for sure. You're rich.'

'Why?' I say, taking the card from Lewis. 'Why me? Why not all of us?'

'You were their winner.' Thea links her arm through mine. 'Because you made it real. You opened their eyes.'

'Space rockets.' They look at me like I've lost my mind.

'Hun, did you hear what Demi just said?' Lewis' cheeks have more colour in them than I've seen in weeks. 'You're minted.'

I nod as my head unfuzzes. 'When the boy gave me the envelope he said, "Space rockets. Today the dragon will fly".'

Demi's already on his phone.

'What does it mean?' Thea points to the police car waiting by the trees. 'Should we?'

I shake my head impatiently. If the police know who the Investor is, they're not telling, and our DC Brown replacement has shared little enthusiasm for catching them. It's as though a veil has been pulled over the whole thing and everyone's pretending it never happened.

Demi's flicking through news reels. He holds up his phone to show a video of a space rocket launching today.

'What's this got to do with us?' Lewis says.

Demi zooms into the rocket. On its side is the dragon symbol.

'The dragon flies,' Demi whispers.

There's a collective intake of breath as we all register his words. Is this money from the audience? Did I really get through to them and their collective conscience? Or is it from the Investor, a bribe designed to keep us quiet? My heart thumps in my ears. Anger rolls through my veins like thunder.

This is big, ten million pounds big. The Investor and his audience are way more powerful than I could ever imagine. For the first time since the game, I feel something other than grief. The storm grows inside my soul.

If this money is designed to keep us quiet.

To pretend it never happened, that the game didn't exist.

That Rhodri didn't die.

A seismic thunderclap of anger explodes within me.

Then I am not okay with that.

The Investor's wolf-masked face crashes into my head, mocking me with a glossy sneer.

The overwhelming need for justice holds me upright like a scaffold, building an iron cage around my heart and reinforcing my bones with a steely determination.

I won't stay quiet. I won't forget.

The card crumples as my fingers curl into a tight fist, my mind screaming for revenge. I lift my chin to the sky and make a silent vow.

You will pay for all you've done.

And I am coming for you.

CONTACTS

If you have experienced some of the issues that affect the characters in *Lie or Die: Blood Moon* please know you are not alone and there are people you can talk to (in confidence). Don't be afraid to reach out, it really can help.

For mental health support and practical advice:
Young Minds
youngminds.org.uk

For a digital mental health service:
Kooth
kooth.com

For help with grief and bereavement:
Winston's Wish
winstonswish.org
Support line: 08088 020 021

ACKNOWLEDGEMENTS

First in a long line of thanks most definitely goes to my agent extraordinaire, Saskia Leach. This journey is a rollercoaster of highs and lows, and you single-handedly steer me through. Thank you for always having my back – you really are the best!

Huge thanks to Penny Thomas for her continued belief in my stories and to the Firefly Press team, with a special shout out to my editor, Hayley Fairhead, who gently pushes me out of my comfort zone to make my stories better.

All the book bloggers, reviewers, booksellers, librarians, teachers, schools and pupils, who have championed *Lie or Die* and shouted their enthusiasm loud and far – thank you all.

To my brilliant writer friends: my writing wifey – Jan Dunning, Josie Jaffrey, Annette Casely, Cara Miller, Katja Kayne, Sue Cunningham, Michelle Nangle. To my UV group, the 2022 committee and Sara Grant, GEA and the brilliant YA community. Plus, the incredibly talented '25 debut group – it's a struggle to keep up with you all!

To Sarah – my oldest friend (old as in years known, not years lived!), Mark and Amy. Thank you for all your support and for putting me up on my many trips to Wales, always supplying much-needed coffee or wine, often both!

To Dimitry Davidoff for creating the game that has gone on to have worldwide influence and to Andrew Plotkin for adapting it to Werewolf and giving me the excuse to have so much fun with terrifying beasts and spooky castles.

To Vuk, Luc and Lobo who taught me the language of wolves and how these beautiful and shy creatures will not and do not behave in the manner of the *Blood Moon* wolves unless deeply provoked and threatened – a sad reminder of the majesty of nature and the cruelty of man.

To Caerphilly Castle – yes, yes I know it's a castle not a person, but it has been my very favourite place for most of my life and a huge inspiration. It blows my mind to think of twelve-year-old me walking around the setting for my *second* book – living proof that dreams can come true.

To Helen, we miss you terribly. Give Jim a huge hug from us. x

To the best edit-dogs ever, Luna and Harley, who sit patiently by my side no matter what and love every single word I write.

To Family Clack! Cam for bringing my social media campaigns to life and Finn whose music makes it sing. Ali, you are the biggest champion of my work and a true champion in real life, I can't wait to see what's coming next. And Imi, my second agent and best manager. It's been a wild year, and I have loved having you by my side sharing the adventure and planning plot twists. I love you all. You're my world and my inspiration.

And to Tim, my rock, my best friend, my editor and my guide, who has believed in me, hundred per cent, for more years than I care to count!

Finally, to you the reader. I hope you've enjoyed reading my story as much as I enjoyed writing it. Your support means the world to me, and I thank you from the bottom of my heart. If you haven't tried Mafia yet, grab a group of friends and give it a go. But remember the one rule – **TRUST NO ONE!**

I hope you'll join me on the next adventure – I can promise it will be a wild ride!

Find out how it all began for Kass in *Lie or Die*.

Out now!

When Kass is cast in the reality-TV show
Lie or Die, she must discover who is a murderous
agent and who is innocent before she's eliminated.
But when contestants start to die for real, Kass
realises this isn't a game but a fight for survival.

A dark, reality-TV thriller, for fans of *The Traitors*.